ALL
OUR YESTERDAYS

BY THE SAME AUTHOR

THE SEA AND THE JUNGLE
OLD JUNK
LONDON RIVER
WAITING FOR DAYLIGHT
TIDEMARKS
UNDER THE RED ENSIGN
GIFTS OF FORTUNE
GALLIONS REACH
ILLUSION

H. M. TOMLINSON

ALL
OUR YESTERDAYS

★

" This was my Country, and it may be yet ;
But something flew between me and the sun."
—Edmund Blunden

LONDON
WILLIAM HEINEMANN LTD.

FIRST PUBLISHED 1930

PRINTED IN GREAT BRITAIN AT
THE WINDMILL PRESS, KINGSWOOD
SURREY

To

DOROTHY

MARGERY AND CHARLEY

CONTENTS

PART ONE

THE YEAR
1900

PART ONE

CHAPTER I

THE traffic of Dockland, where my omnibus stopped, loosened into a broadway. There the vans and lorries, released from the congestion of narrow streets, opened out and made speed in an uproar of iron-shod wheels and hooves on granite blocks. I could hear progress. It was on its way. It was pouring about in a triumphant muddle of noise too loud to be doubted. There was no need to repose on faith in the favoured evolution of man. That wonderful conjuration of good things out of this planet by the steam-engine and the cotton-jenny was dominant. There was assurance in the very noise made by the magic while it was at work, for it excluded thought. My bus was at a standstill, but it merely paused for more passengers, and was getting them fast. The topmasts of a few sailing ships overlooked us from an ancient and exclusive wall, but they at least could remind us of the advance in our welfare made in but a few years. There they were. Those clipper ships were still in sight, though they were forever in the past, with the wooden walls and the Elizabethan era,

I

to which they belonged. I looked down and read idly the destinations shown in the port-marks of some bales on a lorry which rolled by us—Basrah, Karachi, and Masulipatam.

Those names and that lorry were not passing us by chance, for the portal to the East India Dock, a substantial symbol left by John Company to distinguish that shipping parish, was just opposite. The lorry with its merchandise for the Orient had come along inevitably in the logic of the years. It met us not haphazardly, but through predestination. That solemn portal to its fleet of Indiamen had been built by the old company of merchant adventurers only a century before. The East India Company had gone, but the lorry with its load of bales was a sign that we were busily involved in the consequences of Clive. Ours was the opulent benefaction, and we could go thankfully forward whither the continuation of the logic of affairs would take us. In its haste the successful tide of life was even clangorous, but there was hardihood in its noise, and while waiting for our omnibus to make the next stage I could read on cargoes for ships the names which showed how wide was our Empire and how fertile was our security.

The bus had halted by a tavern, the " Sir John Franklin." Under the upper windows of the tavern was a portrait, a smeared relic of a famous occasion when the public rejoiced over a long and prosperous reign ; the relic was still recent enough to be in accord with the times. In that picture of Queen Victoria the proud regal regard was the worse for the weather, but there it remained, with a legend beneath weakened by rain into a chromatic illegibility, though I could spell out the words " bless her." A number of seamen, ironworkers, and dockers, idled in groups about the broadwalk beneath. They lounged against walls, or stood on the kerb and stared, their hands in their pockets, unconscious of the significance of the Franklins and Clives, their benefactors, and of the inspiration of the confident Victorian pageant in which even I had my place, though only on a bus seat. The dark postern gate to the dock of the East India Company was open, and the stones of the grim structure framed a bright vista of the basin, as though to the past, a past which was tranquil, for now it was apart from life. The lagoon within was a mirror. Not a breath, not a tremor of the present flawed its polished silver. The policeman at the gate, it seemed to me, was the sentinel who would forbid us to return to what had been. We must keep on. I could see the black length of one clipper, with its white ports, but she was set in another day. Yet that day had only just gone. We could look into yesterday. It was still shining.

We must keep on, and on we went. The hooves of the horses of our bus suddenly exploded into the general clatter. Two workmen had taken the seat in front of me, and they were arguing. It was about a lady. One of the stout fellows was convinced of her virtue. He declared that she was a beauty. His companion, though he praised, did so grudgingly. He was a trifle doubting ; a timid fellow, perhaps, who could not bravely admire because he was not man enough. He hinted that she might not conduct herself as well as some people seemed to think she would. How did they know ? Besides, she was too big. He found some courage in the sound of his own opposition. " Damned great thing," he blurted out. " Nice penny she would cost, too."

" An' she's worth it. Besides, you've had some of it, as far as I know."

" Same as you. I'm not saying anything about that. What I mean is, it's a rotten idea, the bigger the better. Where's it going to stop ? "

" Stop ? " His companion was scornfully silent as he stooped to knock out his pipe deliberately on the deck of the bus. I eyed the vane of a sailing ship over us. " Stop ? What for ? Who wants it to stop ? Where'd we be if it stopped ? "

" 'Ave it your way then. What I say is, every time we build another it's bigger than the last. We're just about overdoin' it, I say. Why, George, look what's happened since you and me went into the yard. One time you could see all round the job, see what you was doing. They looked like ships. Now what is it ? Nothing but bloody great engines.'

" You bet they're engines. What d'yer want, pig-styes ? No satisfying some of you fellers. Every-thing's engines now, ain't it ? They'll get bigger yet, and lots more of 'em, I hope. It's according to nature. Why, I remember my old father used to say he expected some day horses would have clock-work guts and run the Derby on wheels."

" I hope everybody'll enjoy it."

" Of course they will. They'll enjoy it. That's the sort of horse they'll like, because it's the horse they'll know. When you know, you don't know any different."

The other fellow took his cap off, and readjusted it slowly. " Getting old, I suppose," he reflected. " Never get used to it. But when I looked up at 'er the other morning, the morning Bill was carted off to the 'orspital, it seemed to me the great brute had taken charge of us. The more we do for them the more they want. Men won't count soon."

His friend chuckled harshly. " Stands to reason you can't monkey about with them, that size, and the staging high enough for a church steeple. But they'll be bigger yet, mark my words. Bound to get bigger. That's how things go. Before we've done with the yard, Jim, to-day's launch will look like a penny steamer."

The horses of the 'bus slowed as they toiled up the ascent to the bridge which crosses Bow Creek into Canning Town. " Nothing to stop 'em getting more length and beam every time. We shall have the next one soon, too, with any luck. Fact is, you and me are getting old, Jim. But we shall have to keep up with things, while we can check in when the hooter goes. Anyhow, hav'n't we given a good lead to the young 'uns? Look at her! There she is!"

Beyond the mudflats, gasometers, the yards of the barge-builders, and the stretches of gross marsh weeds, I could see the lady. She was a battleship. Her prow, projecting from the web of her staging, was superior to the parish. She could have been a permanent structure there, and the principal feature of the district. She was more conspicuous than even a near church tower.

"Look at her, Jim. Tell me if she ain't a fine job. Ever seen a better?"

Jim said nothing. He, like every other passenger of the 'bus, had his head turned to the wonder of the day, the noblest ship ever built by us; and justly ours, because once we have taken a direction which we know is right, and on which we shall prosper, then whatever belongs to that road is inevitable, for it is just that an ideal should have its rewards. So this was one of our cardinal days. The most powerful battleship we had ever built was to be launched within the hour. The arid streets about us had no colour except what had been bestowed upon them by their myriad chimneys. They looked as though poverty had been born there, and there had grown aged, but would never die. But we were maintaining a great tradition, which was known to all the world. Dingy and barren as our neighbourhood might seem, it was from here the Indiamen came, and here the *Great Eastern* was built, and here we awed covetous enemies with the birth of the world's first ironclad ; and not so long ago, either. Though felicity did not appear to be more than an occasional guest, for our streets were subdued to the sombre cast of woe, yet science, you could see, dwelt with us. It had brusquely intersected our pavements with railway metals, and had built great docks where liners, to justify us, came from China to moor at the ends of London's slums. It had magnified us with chemical factories, flour mills, sugar, soap, and rubber works, so that it was easy, when you were used to it, to endure a smell for which you had no name. It was only a drab smell, the essence of our elements. Here was the England made by coal and iron, the enormous darkness and rumble which had come in a century out of fertile minds and busy hands quickened by discovery and desire ; so not much was likely to be noticeable of that beauty which shines from truth as it unfolds, because we had not yet come to that. A century is not long. It is but fair to remember that men were making flint implements, with little varia-tion, while glacial ages came and went, and the slow sea foundered the land, and then gave it back to the

B

sun.   Plenty of time was ours, therefore, to attain to
what was lovely and of good report.   That day, that
afternoon, we were to add more to the strength of
our State, and the safety of its wealth.   What we had
gained we must secure ; and there she was, a ship
stronger than ever, to counterpoise the weight of our
need.

Because of her, that day was a holiday.   We
thronged the road to the shipyard.   Mothers with
their infants crowded at the street corners to watch
us on our way to honour the work of their husbands
and sons.   And ahead of us, for all to see, was the
occasion, towering higher and mightier as we approached it, a little awe-inspiring in its magnitude, the
chief work of the Thames.   So massively was she
elevated that you could have imagined she had drawn
up the substance of the place, had diminished what
was about her as her belly swelled.   The greater she
grew, then the meaner became the homes beneath
her shadow.   She had taken their virtue, as she had
absorbed from their inhabitants their time, their skill,
and their energy.   The goodness of the parish might
have been drawn up to put upon the sky the form
of a brooding giant.   She lorded it over us, haughty
and terrible, and her gaily fluttering bunting was a
sign of the buoyancy with which she possessed her
threatening strength.   She was called forth by us,
and she was there, ready to be furnished with her
guns.   The timbers in which we had caged her could

no more hold her now than cobwebs. When I stood under her, amid the litter of industry, dust and rust and chips of wood and scraps of metal, and looked up past the projection of her smooth body, it was as though black calamity were impending and might fall upon us through the chance of an unlucky jolt. Yet that was only the doubt of a witness who stood nervously under a shape so dark and vast; his confidence that his fellows knew what they were doing faltered when threatened by so ominous a symbol of their faith. I took my eyes from the giddy height of her, and a group of workmen paused near me; and one, an evident leader, with a mallet in his fist, contemplated Leviathan for some moments, contemplated her calmly, and with fond approbation. One of the men spoke. " Does she want another touch there, Mr. Bolt ? "

Their leader considered this. " No. She'll do. She's all right."

CHAPTER II

THE benches of a temporary gallery, from which the
dainty touch of Lady Carroll would send the warship
about her business, were crowded with guests. Most
of us did not know much about ships; we were
happy, expectant, and ignorant. I do not think any
of us doubted that the launch of so vast a shape of
metal from the earth to the water could be other
than bland and appropriate. We may doubt the
warranty of the priest, but never that of the mathema-
tician. And the successful launch of a ship is the
final solution to a host of converging problems. It
is the visible assurance of a human achievement in
a dramatic instant. In a moment the ship comes to
life. The thoughts and devices of a multitude of
men, not obviously relevant when there is but a
conception to be embodied in ore and timber, slowly
converge and associate materially. A skeleton and a
shape arise. Then a day comes when a crowd of
rusty and grimy midgets stand surveying from the
rubbish of their labours the giant they have evoked.
Above them, the projection of many thoughts, is now
their single desire in being, the colossus on the ways,
the proof in steel, obscuring very Heaven, that

as men wish so is their world. They willed her, and she is there, ready to crush them if they have erred.

The prow of the ship, which almost touched our high gallery, dimmed the light. The hull dilated beyond us in noble curves, daring in their light inclusion of strength and mass, and hid the river; we could not see the water on which that shape would float, if ever it did float. The monster appeared to be set everlastingly on the place where men had built it, as though to mock them with the fate of temerarious ambition. Perhaps this time they had been too clever. Direct daylight was shut out from us above; I could not see to what height that moulded promontory of steel was elevated. If we peered upwards, what we saw was an extension of the outflaring walls of metal and the celebrant garlands and ensigns. Far below us, on the ground, we watched manikins scurrying in and out of a forest of struts and beams on urgent but ambiguous duties. Now and then, daringly, they vanished under the bulging threat of the hull, and then we understood that that huge body was precariously balanced over the earth, and might go too soon or too late, because it was upheld on no more than a bold though careful guess; so that it was forgivable to question whether our neighbours knew enough to control the prodigy they had evoked. Faith wavered in a chill draught of doubt.

Yet about me I could see no signs of misgiving.

My neighbours and their friends, assembled to admire that promise of the future, knew full well that the skilled work of their fellows must go right and do right, and therefore they admired. The thousands of distant witnesses heaped in the stands were restless and obscure strata, pinkish and misty under the eager bunting. It was the flags, banners, and pennants, flamboyantly exultant, which betrayed our flushed enthusiasm.

Our mayor, whose daily task, when not acting as mayor, was to persuade local housewives to purchase pianos for which they had no use, joined us severely, in his robes and insignia. And after him, descending the improvised gallery to the launching table in nervous deliberation, came a large and rosy cleric in the vestments of his sacred office. He approached his place with a heavy but wary tread. He glanced about him bravely but hesitatingly, prepared to face whatever needed his ministration, though I thought the magnitude of this profane scene, and its unfamiliar aspect, a little intimidated him. For the nose of a great ship, where water cannot be seen, projecting among guests gathered in a mid-air staging, doubtless must have appeared extraordinary to one to whom the affairs of men are of profound moral significance. Yet his free and leisurely manner, and the unrestrained sonority of his voice, as he conversed with the manager of the works, confided to us that, after all, the armoured ram of a new warship, though so unusual to him, could be as rightly an object for godly solicitude as a baby at the font.

"Why, yes, just where you are is as good a place for you as any," the manager assured the priest. "She mustn't go without your word. Must have a prayer." The manager's voice rose above the buzzing of voices, and he smiled at the cleric, and then glanced knowingly to the seats behind him, where near me sat members of his staff. He did not wink at us. There was no need.

The clergyman laughed politely at the compliment, though he knew it was true. Then he became grave. "I say," he said, "I'm so very glad to hear, you know, that it is not a custom here to christen ships with wine. Quite right. Very good, very good. A most barbarous practice, and an anachronism, in a civilized country. I've often thought, sir, that if people only knew the ancient meaning behind these surviving pagan superstitions, then they would die a natural death."

The manager screwed his eyes and nodded, but he did not answer. The clergyman continued to speak, but there was some nearer grumbling behind me, subdued but scornful. "Pagan superstition! He doesn't know what he's talking about. She's got to have her drink. Somebody will get hurt if she doesn't. She'll have blood. A lot he knows about launching a ship."

The priest, who was still talking, did not hear that,

It was only a muttering at a distance from his own favoured seat. He remained unaware that in spite of the marvels of modern engineering in that diocese, there yet persisted a few heresies and false lights which were secretly held, and were more ancient than all the articles of his faith, and perhaps were as abiding.

The manager, who was watching everything, rose with sudden alacrity, and his authoritative expression lapsed to a happy guise, benign and expectant. A pretty little woman had appeared with a party of friends at the top of a gangway. The manager hurried past us to greet her. Lady Carroll had arrived. When she stood at the launching table we had something better than the ship to look at. The honour of her position animated the wife of the owner of the Carroll Line of ships, whose house-flag was famous in our parish. The manager explained to her the wonders of the creation to which she was to give life. She made pleasing gestures of astonishment. The expanse of her hat of golden straw, which had a chaplet of red roses, unluckily hid her face unless she turned to survey the gallery; which she did, at times, for she was kind, and knew we were there. And whenever she did that it was easy to forgive her hat, and the ribbons under her chin, because they proved an encouraging ambush for eyes so innocent yet lively with inviting curiosity in us. She even joked with the ecclesiast. He must be careful. Unless he did his part well, then the ship would not obey her command when she told it to go.

"Oh, won't it," muttered a critic behind me. There was some contempt for the fine company in his growls. "I hope her ladyship's next baby will launch as easy, that's all."

The confusion of voices presently was hushed. The ecclesiast's official mumble alone was heard, but he was addressing the ship. He raised a gracious hand over her ram. The manager gave a quick glance below, and nodded to Lady Carroll, who confided a few words cheerfully to the hull before her, though I heard nothing but "and good luck to you."

We stared then in silence at that prow. It was as before. Then I suspected that a splash of paint on the bow, which was obvious because of the accidental oddity of its outline, might be closing with a post of the staging. But perhaps I had moved my head. Did she intend to go?

That cheer started her. But her movement was hardly perceptible. Yes, the splash of paint had almost eclipsed behind the post. She was off. Some beams below splintered and crashed. The uncertain cheering rose to a continuous roar. A space had grown somehow between us and that nose. She was leaving us, slowly and severely, in a steady glide, which had opened a gulf before our high gallery. Her glide increased to a headlong descent in rigid uprightness, which surprised us with a view of her complete form in swiftly diminishing perspective.   We saw the water break white from her stern as she rushed into the river, but could hear nothing but our own applause.   She curtsied to us, and anchored.   She was in being.   Her life had begun.   Yet her going had left a great emptiness, a dizzy expanse of day before and below us.

Lady Carroll stood prominent in that high light with the officials, surveying in happiness the consequence of the mere approval of her touch.   "We hope to begin to fill that vacant place again soon," said the manager to her.

"Well," she confided, "perhaps I ought not to tell you, but I think I've heard that the opportunity won't be long coming to you."   She turned her back on the ship she had launched, making pretty movements with her hands as she said more to the manager, who escorted her.   A man behind me brushed past to look over the rail of the gallery, and the suspicious activity of little figures below in the yard took me with him to see what was happening.   We stared down.

"There it is," said my fellow watcher.   "I knew she would."

A workman was sprawled on his back beneath us, as if he had fallen asleep where the forefoot of the warship had been.   His mates were gathering about him.

"I said so," said the man beside me, nodding at the scene below.   "She was bound to have her rights."

CHAPTER III

A LOST stranger, as at dusk he paused at that corner
to consider how he should turn to find London's
broad stream of life, might have thought he had
wandered to the end of time, that he was at the verge
of recorded things, and that about him was a huddle
of wreckage from the late reign of man abandoned
to night for ever; but it was only a street corner by
the Isle of Dogs a little before its people were sure
it was time to light their lamps. The dusk took the
dinginess of the place for its own. I glanced round
in the hope that Jones was coming—but he was not
—and had the feeling myself, though no lost stranger,
so still was the neighbourhood in its surrender to
night, that perhaps we had come at last to the wan
years. Perhaps it was our destiny to see no more
now than the continuity of the drab and mechanical
in expansion; perhaps not even a Jones would arrive,
though he had promised to meet me. He was
bringing a man with him, he had said, who desired
promotion for a likely lad. To what fair prospect
could be promoted youth and its bright hope, from
that corner?

A figure sauntered by me. I had known him, and had listened to his voice in awe, since I was a child : the night-watchman. He crossed to the opposite corner, paused, and lifted his head to give to the dark his familiar evening chant, with its melancholy falling note, " Par-r-st—nine-o-clock ! " He waited to see whether anyone, perhaps a lighterman for an early tide, would beg his peremptory summons on the knocker of the door to begin work before daybreak, for the life of that parish moved to the pulse of the sea ; but he was ignored. Nobody heard him who wanted him. He went to another corner out of sight, and I could hear him, an admonitory muezzin, warning careless and unrepentant souls who did not know that night was at hand, and his call came fainter from still more distant streets, while no man heeded. " Past nine o'clock ! "

In that place, at that time, blurred and tranced in its half-light, sunk indifferently in its settled monotony, you could have heard in the call of the night-watchman a tender and lamenting appeal. O Jerusalem, Jerusalem ! For men looked another way, and his cry was lost. The May of that year was the first of this new century, but it had come to communities disciplined into ordered ways. There could be no magic of spring-time. Our new century was without a herald ; we merely continued what we were doing, and heard no warning, no sound in the air, from unseen wonders predestined. We were not looking

for portents. Our sky was but murky. Only the
factories would expand. A hundred years before, in
1800, Europe was changing monstrously its shape and
customary ways before men's astonished eyes, as
though it were cloudland to a storm which had
begun. The first flash from the French Revolution
had touched and stirred the dry bones in valleys which
were remote in medieval shades ; the dead then were
rattling to life. One little man was disordering the
thrones of august dynasties as though they were
kitchen chairs ; divine and immemorial rights, which
it had been sacrilege to touch, burned in bonfires with
the surprising ease of trash and chaff. At Marengo
the First Consul of the Grand Nation had just made the
ancient powers of Hapsburg and Romanoff look as
though playful Zeus had awakened at last to confuse
mortal projects with a derisive thunderbolt. By the
light of 1800, when it dawned, men were exultant, or
they were afraid, as they watched the establishment of
their work take other aspects under the compulsion of
new thoughts and new powers.

But our new century was only the same as before to
London. We were safe from change through the
wakening of passion, or from mischance latent in the
order of our life. The surface of our accustomed
ways, hardened by the traffic of a century of engines,
would never again flow molten through the heat of
central fire ; the earth had lost its heart. Lord,
though we had a war, and we had another one then,

for I could see the placards of a newspaper shop, it was a war fabled to us from somewhere far south of the equator, from among South African kopjes and spuits and desert scenes, where soldiers died of errors and of fevers and not by the sword; and its glory was mocked by the ribald, who said it was no more than a trick to expand the claims of usurers, a war devised by money-lenders with dubious names who wanted new ground for the larger growth of gold, and so must use a rich compost of the bones of young men. Mammon himself is without blood, yet must be fed with it. And who cared? The springs of life were stagnant in a desert of factories. Surprise and joy had gone from a drama which could have no curtain, because there could be no triumph in serving truth, nor nobility in defeat before the gates of folly. What could likely lads make of it?

A group of seamen shambled by, idle and incurious. Only a native, who knew the tokens, would have known that these men had but just landed from a voyage round the world, and were not sure what they should do with themselves. They would not disturb that street, which was safe at last from even the way-wardness of hilarious sailors, though it was still their street, for its length continued London's main thoroughfares on the decks of ships to Capo Bon Esperenza, to Canton River, and the Antipodes. Those seamen did not even glance at the pawnshop which was behind me; but I did; there was nothing else to do. This was the corner where Jones should have met me. We both knew this pawnshop, which was one of the best where pawnshops are as necessary as taverns. Displayed in its window was a dish of Nankin ware, which offered an assortment of the teeth of sperm whales, each tooth with a ship etched upon it. I could see one ship plainly, the brig *Lucy*, Captain James Durkie, 1850. It helped to pass the time to recall old Durkie, for he retired to live just round the corner, and had chased us, when we were likely lads, from his garden patch, his white locks that of a charging fury, but one leg of hampering wood. There were ships' chronometers, telescopes, a regiment of silver watches that recorded all the hours, for forgotten reasons, in unknown lost years ; and a family Bible. The Bible was open at a picture of Cain vigorously making the dreadful precedent. Abel had no chance against that athletic attack. Cain in a panther skin was certainly the better man, the admirable hero superior to the gentleness of a pious mind ; though a stern Eye was watching the scene from a lofty cloud, which Cain was too busy to note. Yet in spite of the disapproval of the Eye, Abel was lost, and his altar done for. At the back of the varied array of flotsam, and put there because, very likely, the shrewd pawnbroker knew that eager interest in them was going, or had gone, was a pile of medals for many campaigns, of decorations for valour, as dusty and forlorn as the shells children gathered on a holiday long ago.

No Jones yet. Nothing had happened, except that the fried-fish shop a little down the street warned me of the passage of time with a sizzling in a fiercer note and a more powerful smell; at least, the local suppers were in boiling oil. I opened the evening paper again, but the headlines were the same as before. In truth, they hardly varied from day to day. "British Cavalry Ambushed at Pietersfontein."

Of course. What else could one expect? Those artful enemies of ours, those Boers! They had the gift of invisibility. They were always surprising our generals—who had not yet had time to learn they were not manœuvring at Aldershot—and thus ending the likelihood of our lads. Boers, who were only farmers, behaved as no gentleman trained to arms would ever expect. They dropped out of the clouds, it might be supposed, just to make the British Staff College appear as resourceful as a school for young ladies when a cow ambles on to the croquet lawn. Mafeking, however, had not fallen yet. That was some comfort. I read again, in pained perplexity, a quotation from the French press, "Le sou des Boers," for it seemed as if the good which such great men as Cecil Rhodes and Joseph Chamberlain desired for South Africa was not everywhere understood. The editor of the London evening paper, I could see, was annoyed by this wilful misreading of British aims, for he was well aware that their beneficial intent could be mistaken only through malice; he italicised his

indignation and, to show it was just, translated the
French comment : " We are not biased enemies of
the British nation, but we have a horror of grasping
financiers, the men of prey who have concocted in cold
blood this rascally war.   They have committed the
greatest of crimes, *lèse-humanité*.   To be sure, there is
no longer a Europe, nor yet an America.   Ah, ideal
abode of the human conscience, founded by Socrates,
sanctified by Christ, illuminated in flashes of lightning
by the French Revolution, what has become of thee ?
Our house is divided against itself and is falling
asunder.   Peace reigns everywhere, save on the banks
of the Vaal, but it is an armed peace, a poisoned peace,
which is eating us up, and from which we are all
dying."

The loud sizzling of the fried-fish shop accompanied
my reading of this eloquent passage, as though the
fond hope of an ideal abode for the human conscience
were being steadily hissed ; the cries of delight from
unseen children somewhere near at their larks showed
their unconcern for a poisoned peace from which we
were all dying ; and there came my friend Jones.
But not alone.   He had a large and jocund stranger
with him, and as they stopped I thought I had seen the
man before—yes, once, and he had a mallet in his fist
then, and had announced with a prompt and quiet
confidence which subdued me that a warship about to
be launched down the ways was " all right."

But Jones appeared to be a trifle embarrassed.   A

tall man, and diffident when caught in episodes that were rough and instinctive, his frail length was bent as though overweighted by his black beard, and so his spectacles had slid to the point of his nose.

" Do you know Mr. Bolt ? " he asked me, retreating his spectacles to safety.

" Not him.   You know damwell he don't."   Mr. Bolt struck my shoulder heartily.   " How are you, mister.   It's a fine day.   It's a lovely night . . . what do you want to say ? "   He put that abrupt question to me a little inimically.   " Go on.   Say it, if you want to."

I did not want to say anything.   I had only winced when my shoulder gave way.   So I looked at Jones, but he was looking at his watch.   " I'm afraid," said Jones, " we had better be quick about our little business.   We must be off, Mr. Bolt.   There is a meeting . . ."

" That's right.   It's here.   There ain't a better one.   Whadyer mean by business ?   You come and hear Dolly Mashem sing 'You can't diddle me.'   It'll fix your spectacles to rights, ole Jones. Come on."

Jones smiled tactfully, and began to make excuses. " I'm afraid . . ." he began.

" Afraid ? "   Mr. Bolt thrust his face at Jones to peer at him with fierce and sudden suspicion.   Then he shook his head sadly.   " 'Course you are, with a dial like a pro-Boer.   Jones," he said, " you want to get that face soled and heeled. Your whiskers are falling off the uppers. They'll let in the rain."

My friend explained that the time at his disposal was now less than it had been. " I must go."

" Mean to say you'd argue with a shipwright after he's told you—after he's *told* you—that the Thames Ironworks has got another ruddy warship to build? Eh? Don't you know what that means? Hav'n't you got sense? "

" Well, well. Let's be off home. The district needs work, of course . . ."

" Work? Work be damned. Who wants to work? Ole Jones, it means fifty-two more pay days. That's what it means. Come and feel what it's like to be glad."

" Not to-night."

" No? Not to-night? Why not to-night? " Mr. Bolt spread wide his arms appealingly, and began to sing a popular mission hymn in a strange and shaky falsetto voice which seemed ventriloquial from so broad a beam in a shipwright. " ' Thou—would'st—be—saved. . . . Why—not—to—night? ' . . . There you are. Now you come along. Come and soak that pro-Boer face in a little beer and look at Dolly's legs."

But Jones was merely kindly, and declined. He made a sign to me, which was useless, for there could be no doubt about an iron-worker's quality with so affectionate a grip on my arm. I was learning how strong the hand of a man could be.

Mr. Bolt shook his head despondently as though he were long-suffering. "Right you are, ole Jones. You cut along. Fare thee well, my blue-eyed charmer. I want to talk to this gentleman. I don't want to talk to you. You're not in Christian frame of mind. You ought to get right with God, you ought. I know whad'll happen to you, one of these fine nights. Mark my words, ole Jones, you'll have that shop of yours wrecked by decent people, and serve you jolly well right. If we all had faces like yours . . ."

But Jones was crossing the street. "Hi, you! See what I mean? If we all had faces like yours we'd lose this war." Mr. Bolt's advice grew in volume as the distance increased between us and Jones, whose retreating back was deaf. "You hear me? I say we'd lose this war. We'd lose every dam thing. Take that face home and boil it."

A local interest began to grow in our discussion, and some wayfarers paused in hope, but hope died when it was seen that the tall thin man would accept any reference to his appearance, however insulting.

Mr. Bolt turned slowly to me, his hearty expression beaming with challenging good humour. "Now Mr. Whatsisname, that lively party's gone, but you're here. Ain't you here? Between you and me I want to ask you something . . . what is it? . . . why don't you speak? Lorst your voice?" He put his hand on my shoulder, took off his hat, and gazed at me sorrowfully and affectionately, while he sang a love song in the strange voice he reserved for singing. "We met—'twas in a crowd—and I thought—he would shun me." His falsetto notes ceased on a minor, and then, with the rusty throat of a shipwright, he enquired harshly, "What you wasting my time for? Don't you know we'll be late?"

He forced back his hat over his reluctant hair, offered me a cheroot like a rough black stick, and lit one himself. "Now we'll do," he assured me. "Let's toddle along and see Dolly."

We left the light of that pawnshop, and Mr. Bolt took my arm in affection. He fell silent and moody.

"Was I rude to ole Jones?" he asked me presently.

He appeared to be considering this probability. He sighed deeply. "My God," suddenly exclaimed Mr. Bolt, "y'know, sometimes I feel I'd like to make this dead and alive hole jump by starting a pneumatic chisel on it. Bur-r-r-r. Like that. See what I mean? If I was only young enough, same as you are, I'd be off to the war. You ought to go. It'ud cheer you up. 'Member the old song? 'If I was only long enough a soldier I would be.' That's me. Now, ole Jones, he's sensible. He's got too much brains. They keep him at home attending to his business. They make him unhappy. Never give him a day off. That's the worst of brains. If you've got 'em, there are, you're bound to use 'em.

An' whad good they do yer? No good, only show you other people are wrong, which is quite right. Look at me!"

Mr. Bolt stopped for a moment and tapped his chest, to indicate himself. "Look at me, Mr. Whatsisname. What with steam hammers and pneumatic chisels and boilerplate I can't hear I got any brains. No brains. No dam fear. Thas what steam hammers do for you. Punch 'em out."

Then we walked on. He shook his head dolefully. "Thas it. Punch 'em out. When I get home, though," he continued, "and look at the kids, and wonder who'd be a shipwright out of work, some of my brains come back to me, and so I hurry up. Mus' get round to 'Spotted Dog' before closing time, before it's too late. . . . Oh, yes. That reminds me . . . wait a minute . . . I want to ask you something."

A thought for the career of his likely lad checked him, I guessed, and Mr. Bolt gazed round him to collect his thoughts. Then he saw the brightly lighted entrance to the Theatre of Varieties. "Here we are," he remarked with relief. "Come on, or we shan't see Dolly."

In we went. Mr. Bolt was notably wide and bulky across the shoulders. His brooding grey eyes, I could see now, were humane as well as truculent, and his clean-shaven face was massive and candid, and had a leathery texture which gave confidence in his lasting power.   There was sardonic tenacity in his mouth and chin, but beer had pouted his lips that night into a little petulance.   One could be sure he was a cunning craftsman, and could handle refractory steel with casual firmness.   We found the hall was full, and that we must watch from the promenade.   Mr. Bolt took his hat off, glanced round as though to be sure trouble was absent, ran a hand over his turbulent sandy hair, which suggested romantic generosity as well as promptitude to heat, and then signed to me with a twist of his mouth and a thumb which pointed backwards to the bar.   We had one, and then another, and then went to lean on the bulwarks of the promenade.

" The house is full," I said.

" Of course," replied Mr. Bolt quickly and respectfully.   " Dolly's on to-night."

There was something in the air of that music-hall, its depth murky with the incense of tobacco smoke, which had a soothing effect on my companion. Perhaps it was because he was within the influence of art.   He became peaceful with devotion in this temple.   A wizard was before us, dressed as a Chinese mandarin, who juggled with silver balls, keeping a hypnotising stream of them weaving through the air with but slight movements of his hands.   We watched him, and were as still as the buxom statues of the Muses that posed by the proscenium, on whose seminudity the plaster drapery was set at a moment of danger.   There was not a stir in the spread of heads

between us and the performer.   That the balls should
continue in unbroken circuit was of grave concern to
us all.   The Chinaman brought them deftly to a halt,
and our feet thundered.   The heads before us were
released on their necks.   A man below me stooped to
fumble under his seat, hauled out a demijohn, and
raised it above his lips.   Then he rubbed his cuff over
the mouth of the jar, and handed it to the lady sitting
beside him, and she tilted it above her face, while the
bangles of her bonnet danced to the happy rhythm of
her refreshment.

We waited, though not for long, for soon an
expansive lady in a corsage at high tension tripped
saucily before us on high-heeled shoes.   Her lusty
thighs, and the immediate uproar, told me who she
was.   Dolly was an endearing name for one with a
wink intimate with full liberty.   Mr. Bolt nudged me,
but there was no need for it.   For some moments
Dolly was permitted only to nod brightly to us like a
sister and distribute favours with her eyes.   Then she
sang that song, a little hoarsely, which Mr. Bolt had
promised, and the jovial house helped with the chorus.
Dolly retired ; and the jaunty poise of elderly curves so
ample on feet so diminutive was sensational.   But
soon the singer came back bringing with her a soldier
of the line in the uniform of South African work.
He smartly raised his hand to his solar helmet when we
cheered him.   Dolly flourished a Union Jack in each
hand, and this was almost too much for us.   It

released the emotions with which the news of the day had filled us. She sang "Soldiers of the Queen" while the man in khaki stood to stern and unblinking attention even when the flags were waved in his face.

It must have been during the last verse, which we sang with her, that a surly fellow near me made a comment. Perhaps it was merely to himself; he may have supposed it would have been drowned unnoted in the noise of our common enthusiasm. He grumbled, I thought, that we were likely to be rewarded in a way which would be unenjoyable, though we had asked for it. The lady with the bangles in her bonnet must have heard him, for she bounced round menacingly. " 'Ere," she cried, "yore name Kruger?" Her companion turned also, though more carefully, for he was nursing his amphora of beer. " What's more," he added slowly, " you can get what trouble you want by asking for it, and 'ave it now." But the critic, who was a young man, already was disappearing. Mr. Bolt, I noticed, eyed the vanishing interrupter with louring disfavour.

" It'd do me good," he muttered darkly.

" What's that ? " I asked.

" Dot him one. I haven't hit a man because he wanted it for years and years."

The approach of a lank and lugubrious apparition to the footlights, whose nose was remarkable in a chalky face, composed the interlude. He was a comedian. He wore a tiny hat with difficulty. He gulped a song abruptly, in but one note, and occasionally interrupted it with an anecdote. He told us that once he had an African parrot. Its name was Kruger, for its origin was low, and the audience laughed derisively. It was always fooling the dog with false calls, a bright little terrier named Joe. "Good ole Joe," we cried. "That's right," agreed the comedian; "he had such a sharp nose for rats that I named him Joe," and we applauded so good a reason for a Christian name. But one day, he told us, the artful African bird called mockingly to Joe once too often. It was therefore found under the table, disfeathered and repentant, saying to itself, "I know what's the matter with me. I know what's the matter with me. I talk too damn much."

The comedian maintained his calm pause beyond our merriment. He was sure of us. He was leisurely giving his hat the right groggy tilt, before telling us another story, when a discordant cry shocked us.

"To hell with Chamberlain!"

The comedian only stared, in an attitude of sincere woe, with his hand on his hat. He had no wit ready for this. The blasphemy stilled us. Then the pit and stalls began to move confusedly. Unhappy howls arose in the remote gallery, where it was known the next performance might be out of its view. The heads below me, which had been expressionless, were now reversed, for the entertainment was in the opposite direction. I was looking at angry faces swarming. They were mounting the back of the seats and were coming towards me. I dodged a missile in flight. The man with the demijohn was peering about eagerly for someone to whom he could give it. We were all looking for whoever deserved to have it, when another voice cut the confusion clearly and with sombre warning : " Make your peace with God."

I could see that fellow, an elderly crank who paraded our streets whenever the Sunday was fine and he was persuaded that his neighbours might be enjoying themselves, and who then bore sandwich boards advertising wrath and the latter end of people such as we were.

Mr. Bolt marked the last interrupter. " Silly old fool," he breathed aloud, in wonder at such courage in the aged. But the grey-haired prophet was already submerged. There was no need to do more to him. He foundered in a surging current of heads ; though certainly he was not the offender, for the first voice bawled provocatively again, " It's a mugs' war ! "

There he was ; there he was for but a brief glimpse. But he did not completely founder, like the elderly peace-maker. He came to the surface again and disturbed it vehemently. Eager advice was cried from those who were too distant to aid to those who were near enough. " Wring his neck." We were told where we ought to kick him. The offender was propelled through the riot. A woman's market basket, which rose and fell with regularity about the place where probably he was, marked his progress. He came clear of the press, disarranged but active, still gasping taunts.   Many were trying to grapple him.

" Hand him over," shouted Mr. Bolt.   But nobody showed readiness to surrender a gratification so unusual.   Mr. Bolt therefore took the young man, and lightly whirled him free from his other assailants. The response of the rebel in his gyration was so agile and unexpected that the shipwright's face was jarred and his hat took flight.   A hurtling bottle brought down the plate-glass of the bar in a shocking avalanche.

Now I had lost Mr. Bolt.   A woman stood near me clasping her child rigidly and with her frightened face bleeding.   I could see only that woman, and the storm raised by an unlucky word cast into the peace of our hearts.   I was part of it, crunching over broken glass in a weight of straining bodies.   " You one of the swine ? " demanded a whoop near me.   I saw the fellow and wondered if I were his target, for his malignant squint misdirected his cry, and then he vanished as he slipped on glass.   The torrent brawled down a corridor and shot me outside into the night.

FOR a moment that London street changed its wont as I plunged into it ; its levels revolved and its lamps were rockets. I got up from the road. Somebody's walking stick must have had a hard knob, but my hat had saved me from the worst of its public spirit. I looked round to make sure I was there. The street resumed its still and familiar aspect. There was mockery in the quiet and impassive shadow of that background. It had only pretended to move ; it was then as it had been always, the establishment of the safe and accustomed. Scattered about the road were groups of its people in savage argument. The heat of their words was the only proof that for an instant, through the old brick and macadam of fatherland, the glow of transforming fire had reddened. But the place instantly had blackened again. I may have been mistaken. The threat of no primary furnace had opened and shut. It was only my head in a tavern brawl.

The night was large and calm. It was surely unaware of any different news. The streets were deserted beyond the scene of that outbreak of wildfire, and the farther I got from it the more settled did the

security of the familiar appear to be. Confidence
returned. Bow Bridge, over which kings with gay
retinues once went to hunt the deer at Hainhault, was
as though change had crossed it for the last time.
And Stratford-atte-Bow, where grisly walls enclosed
backwaters of the industrial Lea as inky as creeks of
Lethe, smelling of the dregs of time, had evidently
worked through all its elegant deer. No more would
its serfs and villeins, when they were overpressed by
hard taskmasters, dive for defiant billhooks and fare
forth; they had lost that impulse. And the last
highwayman had passed through it; and no more
outside its parish church would it shirt the martyrs in
fire. Its life in the green was done. Nevertheless,
possibly it was only waiting in the pause at midnight,
for nobody knew what. It surrendered no secret.
The shadowy masses of its factories stood dark and
spectral over the sleepers of another age, who made no
sign, for they had submitted, perhaps, to the incubus.
But if ever those sleepers awakened, and girded
themselves, and went hunting again . . . there were
many of them now. Had they better not sleep on, as
things were?

I reached my own room among the railway-sidings
and the workshops, and tried to escape into a book,
but the wag with the red nose, who forgot how to
give his hat a laughable tilt when Chamberlain was
ordered to hell, stood before the print; and the
ferocity of the matron whose passion infected even her

potato basket; and the shipwright's cheerless smile when his hand clamped the rebel's neck. . . .

It must have been about three in the morning. The candle was out. The only sign of the hour was Arcturus, which appeared at a parting of the window curtains, and stared and winked down at me before eclipsing behind the other curtain. The earth was shouldering into the east. I could watch the sky and its starry host move past us. The unseen leisurely old clock, a monument of antiquity itself, had me in arrest, now I was awake again, and was marching me solemnly, one predestined step after another, towards eternity. But I wanted a shorter sleep before that. To count those deliberate steps measuring me into the future was not helpful; they were too slow; I had to wait for the next tick. They were too slow, when my thoughts were following the quick change in the horoscope of a riot. It was unpleasant, the way a rending plunge of shattered glass kept raw in the memory. That crash is raucous with its emphasis on ruin.

There was nothing for it but to light the candle again. Hullo, Jones had been in! There was his pipe. Didn't notice it when I came in. Glad I missed him. A philosopher is welcome when all you want is to have hope confirmed, but when he only mildly quizzes the facts to tell you they indicate, most probably, what you fear, then he is no better than a house without a fire when the wind is north. To the devil with old Jones, too !   Glad I missed his judicious voice, and his sociable guesses at what was in store for everybody if we allowed the rods of our own fashion-ing to pickle to ripeness.   He wasn't human, with that chuckle, as he concluded an unfortunate estimate. Chuckles over the discomfiture of rascals is one thing, but they are unsuited to poor mankind's biological destiny.   Well, Jones was something of a mystic, too, one of those people who find it easy to explain intuitively what nobody can know.   He had the silly idea that our simplest acts and thoughts have inevitable consequences, undesigned by us, and, of course, usually most unpleasant.   Nothing is wasted, not even the indifference of fools to the signs of the times.   You cast your ridiculous thought into the air, and it falls on you—or on someone else, maybe— as a brick, after many days.   Jones was not the man to charm the affairs of my night out with Mr. Bolt ; they would but confirm his notion that civilisation is only the shadow of the commonest desires of all of us, and, he would have said, you see what we desire.   A city can be built or lost in a night, according to him, if we all dream the same dream.   And we have such dreams!

Anyhow, it was queer that a comic song should have led to such a chorus.   There is no end to the wonders of biology, for who could have guessed that our sheeplike neighbours would have gone bloody-minded at a shout ?

There was a long shadow on the wall of my room, and it became alive if the candle-flame flickered ; the result of the careless disposal of my hat and coat, so it seemed, for I sought the cause of it. The shadow stood up the wall, bent across the ceiling, and ended over my bed in what had the shape of a cowl. It reminded me of something—something in Whitman. What was it ? " Yet behind all lowering stealing, lo, a shape, Vague as the night, draped interminably, head, front, and form . . . whose face none may see." I reached over and pushed my hat and coat on the floor.

So much for a shadow, Mr. Jones. It went. And while I was stretched across, I fumbled for a book on the table, and found Sir Thomas Browne, by happy chance.

Browne was better. Now I could wait for morning. I knew the friendly touch of those worn covers. They put me out of the loud confusion of the night, remote in the morning sun of earlier dreams at leisure. I met Browne first, long ago, by a window which over-looked a Devon estuary, a quay, and a shipyard. The tide of that day of the past, full and green, had not ebbed. It still was full. The light of that window had not faded. A schooner was on the stocks. I could see a workman with an adze deftly cheesing flakes from her timbers, and then a companion behind me, leaning against his bookshelves, said, " Don't know *Hydrio-taphia* ? Listen to this."

D

I listened. My friend's voice, back in years, was reassuring, and the smell of the clean oak and tar of the shipyard was the healing reek of the earth. And yet there was nothing much in the passage he read, I understood now, but music. Those words would not submit to analysis and comparison. They were not reasonable, so by what power did they take the date out of the calendar ? As if it were not by chance they survived, like the dead bones which outlived the drums and tramplings of three conquests, but were kept by a virtue without even a name though more enduring than empires. The rhapsodist, then, has something to go upon, when he is sure his fair surmise will outlast the show and the tushes of power. I opened the book, and idled with its pages, seeing beyond them that Devon window and its outlook to a fairway brimming with beryl in a morning light, which to hopeful youth had been a prospect of the future, the inevitable brightness of the rise of the tide and sun. Happy youth, with the future confident in the tranquil light of morning !

Then my vagary, afloat in the unsubstantial past, came aground on these cold and stony words : " In brief," Sir Thomas told me, in a changed voice, " I am averse from nothing : my conscience would give me the lye if I should say I absolutely detest or hate any essence but the Devil ; or so at least abhor anything but that we might come to composition. If there be any among those common objects of hatred I do contemn and laugh at, it is that great enemy of Reason, Virtue and Religion, the Multitude : that numerous piece of Monstrosity which, taken asunder, seem man, and the reasonable creatures of God ; but, confused together, make but one great beast, a monstrosity more prodigious than Hydra. It is no breach of charity to call these Fools."

Browne must have been waiting for me, like Jones's pipe. I dropped him on the floor. And now the only light left to me was that of my own candle, a small glim, and I lay considering whether I should move to put that out, too, and trust to the dark, when I noticed my schooner was really a liner. A great liner. The Devon estuary was full and bright. It was morning.

She was off. It was a fine day for the beginning of a long voyage. Her decks were crowded with happy passengers, and her rigging lively with bunting. Perhaps she was only just launched. Yes, there was Bolt. He was leaving her. He had done his job. But he did not speak to me as I passed him on the gangway. He gave me a sly smile. He twisted his mouth in a leery way as he went by, and cocked his thumb back to the ship, as if he knew something about her, but could not tell me then. No time. So I went aboard. I should be late. Mustn't be left behind. It was the most important ship I had ever seen. She was a beauty. Lady Carroll was there, delighted with something ahead I could not see, and a parson in a surplice was nodding solemnly to what she said. The deck lengthened to infinity, and was full of people, all of them glad they were going. They were walking up and down in couples, and pausing at the bulwark to gaze seawards. A few of them were pointing. There was the land. Dolly was waving a handkerchief at a coast I knew was England, though nobody told me so. Nobody spoke. Where were we going ?

I wanted to know. The land was disappearing, and I felt uneasy. It would be out of sight soon. I looked at the faces of the people about me, and they were very gay ; they knew where they were going but they did not see me. I might not have been there. They were staring in admiration at the upperworks of our ship, which was too quiet for a vast affair under weigh. I tried to ask a man where we were going, but he was talking to a lady, and he passed without a glance. Perhaps I should not have spoken to him when he was with a lady. Silly question to ask. Everybody knew where she was going. But where was it ? A loose object was flapping on the deck and I stooped to pick it up. It was a strip of cardboard. As I lifted it I tore the deck. It was part of the deck. I tried to repair the disfigurement, but the paper was wet, and the hole widened. The deck was soft.

I left that enlarging horror in the deck because I could not bear to look at it. I thought I could feel the structure give under my tread. I walked carefully. I

was afraid it would part under me. You can't repair a
deck of soddened cardboard. I went anxiously to the
bulwarks to look for land. There was no land,
there was only the wide sea getting up and rolling
down on us. The bulwarks already were dog-eared.
The ship was wearing.

Nobody who passed it gave more than a careless
glance at that gape in her deck. A man stepped over
it, as though a stone were missing from a footpath. It
was growing worse, that ragged hole. When I
looked down I could see at the bottom of it the black
water pouring along without making a sound.

I wanted to stand there and warn people. Go
round! I wanted to wave them aside, but it was
hopeless, and tried to get them to know they were
walking on rubbish and had better be careful, but they
paid no attention, for somehow I could not reach
them. They did not pause. They only dodged that
black hole while chattering. Two children stopped
to stare curiously into the bottom of the ship. I
wanted to pull them away from the danger but they
laughed silently and ran across the deck, tumbling
against the bulwarks. The bulwarks bulged under
their weight. They would break through and fall
overboard. The children got up and began to
mischief with the dangerous ship, tearing away strips
of it where it was tattered, and looking round artfully
to see if they were observed.

Then everybody was dancing. There was a fiddler

sitting cross-legged on the roof of a deck house. I
did not like that man, for he could see that cavity
beneath him, where the dancers were. He was
fiddling hard to keep their eyes from it. He knew
what it meant. He knew it was a paper ship. He
didn't want them to know. The man was mad.

"Look out," I shouted, "this ship's only cardboard." But I could not hear my own cry. Nobody
heard me, nobody guessed what was under their feet.
They danced and the great ship held on her course.
My God, they'd find out if the weather changed.
There she was, the rotten thing, and what she was
made of giving under them, and they dancing happily
round the gaping warning in her, and that was all.
Wake them up, wake them up !

I looked ahead in alarm and saw a cloud rising out of
the sea, growing blacker and greater and coming our
way fast. Bolt was calmly watching it too. " She's
all right," he said. I tried to grasp him. Shake him.
Make him see. "Here it comes—look out—she'll
never stand it ! " The sky was the colour of hell. I
could hardly see the dancers. There was only the
angry tops of the oncoming waters. " Bolt, she
can't . . ."

But he had gone, and in my desperation to find him
at once in the dark I sat up, to see my candle was
guttering, and its glim burning blue.

The shop where Jones sold tobacco and newspapers, and kept a lot of second-hand books, was opposite All Saints' Church. It was as reasonable to expect to find the parish priest in the back-parlour of that shop, if you knew where to look for him, as at the vicarage, but most of his parishioners did not know that, and they were not told. That room was sanctuary for a few neighbours whose opinions elsewhere were discordant, for husbands who sought a brief exile from domesticity, for visitors from a distance who had heard of it, and in odd hours for shy and likely youngsters of near streets who were wistful for a word of horizons out of sight of their own chimney pots. There were parishioners of probity who complained that the spirit of that back-parlour was more destructive of the virtues which have made our country what it is than the most potent to be experienced in the local gin-palace; but those critics were afraid to buy even a newspaper at Jones' shop; they did not know his smoking mixture; they had never viewed their own virtues and good works through its blue mist.

No attractively advertised packets of tobacco, designed to enslave credulous men who are the

victims allotted to eloquence, could be bought at that
shop.   You could get there no popular and vociferated
label.   You might not have guessed that Jones sold
tobacco, or had an opinion about pipes or anything
else.   He kept the right stuff out of sight in a row of
the traditional earthenware vases, behind the locked
mahogany doors of an old cabinet which had come
from the West Indian brig *Creole Girl*.   It was
easy to guess that cupboard harboured rum long ago.
In those umber jars was alleviation which only the
bookseller knew how to compose and dispense.   He
did not want you to buy it unless you were sure you
could not do without it.   Each jar was named in gilt
and black letters, but because of the age of the jars, and
years of fondling, and because of the esoteric nature of
their lettering, the names were part of the mystery of
the jars.   But what name could you give to the smell
which spread when Jones opened his cupboard, and
the evening was beginning ?

I had gone to the shop with an empty pouch.   The
muslin curtain of its interior door hid the shopkeeper,
thus fulfilling its purpose, but I could hear his voice.
He had visitors, and so was neglecting his business.
Now and then they laughed.   Waiting there was
merely an opportunity to look round.   If you could
not amuse yourself for five minutes in that shop
without attention then you could go out.   A boy came
in, sure of what he wanted, took *Ally Sloper's Half
Holiday*, and left his penny on the counter.   The

periodicals, neatly arranged in ranks to show their titles, were scattered with coins. Jones had been absent for as long as eighteen pence. The shop-keeper had abandoned his shop to its resources ; but his regular customers would know where to look for what they wanted. There was the *Family Herald*, and *Bow Bells*, and *Jack Harkaway*, and the *Boys' Own Paper*, and a pile of Mr. Stead's *Penny Poets*—Jones pretended he knew the way to bestow accurately the *Ingoldsby Legends* on this poetless boy, and Shelley on that, and Whitman on such a young man, and Tom Hood on that hungry girl, but at least his pretences could be amusing—and the last issue of Cassell's *Popular Educator*, and some subversive prints to be obtained only at that shop, such as the *Freethinker*, *Justice* and the *Clarion*. There was also a choice of cheap booklets on divination and fortune-telling. The bookseller could explain that most of the women of the district trusted more, through bitter experience, to the pattern of the dregs at the bottom of a teacup, or to the howling of dogs at night, than to the Four Gospels, because they spent their lives in patient endurance on the verge of a declivity, which kept them fearful of a landslide on the morrow ; and so they observed carefully the way the cat behaved, in case the Almighty would relent with a timely hint to the sinner who humbly confessed His power and watched His ways in misgiving. At the back of Jones's shop were shelves disorderly with old books, but nobody knew whether they were part of the unsaleable stock, or whether they were the shop-keeper's personal library. *Aurora Leigh* was always there, next to Young's *Night Thoughts*, but there was no need to buy either of them, because Jones had marked all the warrantable passages, and he had a soft and confiding voice in the reading of verse.

The vicar looked in at the door, saw only me, and departed before I could recall myself from the pages of Humboldt to hail him. He thought I was a stranger. He had called for the *Review of Mycology*, a quarterly which evidently was waiting on the counter for him and for no one else in the East End of London. An observant shepherd was Talbot, who doubted that much could be done for sheep, which are feckless creatures, who will look up in expectation, yet never know when they have been fed, and so he left us to group and ramble as sheepish impulses and bot flies moved us. He secluded himself with Dante, and brooded with a microscope over diatoms and minute fungi, adding thus to his wonder over the strangeness of life, yet losing, in the miracle of toadstools, some of his faith in his ability to save sheep.

The vicar vanished, and I returned to the Orinoco with the German baron, whose four volumes were new to the shelves. The tobacconist, who had seen nothing of the outer world except the country between Paternoster Row of St. Paul's and Booksellers Row in the Strand, had a weakness for old travel; and he would argue that Mandeville's was a happier book than *Through Darkest Africa*, and got closer to the truth, for its author was an honest liar and not a commercial traveller like Stanley. Jones and his visitors were still rumbling a conversation within, which was clearly a good and lasting one. Still, if one had to wait in his shop for a week there would be old journeys to make, north, south, east, and west. But I wanted a smoke.

The curtains moved and an eye appeared at a corner. The door opened. "Why wait there?" Talbot was behind me again, pushing Mycology into his pocket. "Do you know Langham?" asked Jones, as I fronted one of his visitors.

I did not, and I observed the slightly condescending smile of that frolicsome young Radical member of Parliament with interest. We had heard much of him of late. The mention of his name could make true patriots inarticulate through a sudden pressure of words. Besides, his younger brother was one of our curates, though not a man to be met in that particular concealment.

Talbot's pale bushy eyebrows went up in affected surprise. "Why, Langham! What have we to do with you?"

The visitor with the decorative hair laughed and brushed one of its dark points back from his forehead with a plump hand. For so dumpy a hand it was too white. His laugh showed the quick lines of his bright lips to be more desultory than was needed by the gift for emotional eloquence. His long and slender body was disposed lazily. There was a gold cross on his watch chain, and it may have hinted that there had been a time when he was almost persuaded to give his vivid persuasiveness to the church.

" I've run down to see, among other things, what you were doing with my strict and faithful brother."

" Oh ! Word of a bishopric for him, or something ? But he was born for gaiters, from what I've seen of him. Though this is not the room in which shovel hats are fitted to the just, is it, Jones ? "

" No. I'm told young Langham calls it an anarchists' kitchen."

" Well, it is, isn't it ? " asked Langham genially.

One of the brown jars was on the table with its lid off, and a pull of its contents hung loosely about it like a shaggy mane. The vicar stood filling his pipe at it. Langham, in the pause, eyed with amused curiosity a large oleograph in a recess of the wall. It was now brightly illuminated because the bookseller had moved the lamp to a higher vantage. I was so used to that picture that now, for the first time, I inspected it to learn its story. The lamp might have been placed so that the treasure could be displayed. A number of warriors in white uniform were regarding haughtily an opposite group of soldiers in red and blue, whose expression was downcast, and one of the dejected heroes, a very little one, was offering his sword, hilt foremost, to a big opponent with side-whiskers. Below was a legend: " The Surrender of Napoleon III to King William of Prussia at Sedan, 1870."

" That's a gaudy decoration, Jones," commented Langham. " What's its merit, beyond its beauty ? Is the subject still a painful memory with your neighbours—they know all about it ? "

The bookseller pondered his decoration. " No, I don't say they do. If it were that picture on the other wall, of the Israelites crossing the Red Sea on foot, you'd know how true it was, and wouldn't ask. That picture just happens to be here, like the tobacco jar. You see, I was a youngster when my father brought it home and hung it up where it is now. He stood where you are with his hammer, after he had done it, telling me all about it. I remember he told me he didn't expect to live to see its companion picture beside it, showing the sword turned the other way, thank God, but I should, with luck, mark his words. And there you are. Do you want to know anything of that picture showing the sea obliging your friends the Israelites ? "

Langham's easy and mellow laugh was a pleasant habit of his. It made him a comfortable companion, in spite of his sharp nose and bantering eyes. " No. Not now. But I hope you'll be able to make yourself happy without the companion to that lovely thing. They'll have to grow a bigger Napoleon than that, for

the right picture.   That one looks as if he were not
even sure of keeping his trousers up, poor devil—too
big for him.   So your father felt that way about it, did
he ? "

Then the vicar was reminiscent.   He told us, while
dabbing his pipe with the dangerous flame of a large
spill of paper, that once such memorials of the tragedy
were popular about there.   " I remember them, even
in homes which used to send to the ' Anti-Gallican '
tavern for the supper beer—a public house named out
of an earlier public hatred for that Napoleon's uncle.
You'd see such pictures everywhere.   We felt sorry
for France when she tumbled, though more important
people were secretly glad to see our old enemy offset
by a new power.   Their idea was it made us safer . . .
but, Langham, you surprise me, as a young statesman,
with all the power and the glory waiting for you to
take it, when you say we must wait for Napoleons.
They depend on us, don't they ?   They get the
chance to grow big when we've left sufficient lunacy
lying about for them to work upon ?   I've always
supposed it was possible to judge the silliness of a
nation of dear stupids by the size of their Napoleon.
As a coming statesman you ought to know the
conditions for your success."

" Oh, come, that's below the belt.   It's not fair to
hit a chap that way, when he risks disfigurement
every time he appears in public to say what he thinks of
killing Boers.   The ' Absent Minded Beggar ' isn't my

favourite hymn, Talbot, but I understand your
congregation prefers the worst thing Kipling ever
wrote to the ' Church's One Foundation,' these days.
Isn't that so ? "

Talbot smiled sadly.

" Well," said the bookseller, " the picture is there
only because it was never taken down."

" As for our good friends the French," Langham
went on, " from all I hear they'd rejoice if Mr. Kruger
didn't leave enough of our dear flag to wipe an
orphan's nose. That picture would puzzle Paris
more than it does me. We are not very popular on
the Continent."

The vicar admitted it. " Yes, even the Russians, so
I read in to-day's paper, pause while hanging Finns to
rebuke us for bullying small nations. By the look of
things you'd think this planet was entering a dark patch
in the sky—the dust of a dead star was infecting us.
I don't know how else to account for these feverish
cycles in humanity. We get stung by a celestial bug,
maybe."

" No chance for us ? I say, but this won't do.
What about Jesus ? "

The priest was stoppering his pipe, and paused,
eyeing the bowl.

" Go on. Your resignation depends on your
answer."

Talbot sighed. " I suppose it does. The objective
and fatal bug must be a figment. No, I can't mount

him. Perhaps the truth is the trouble is in our system, and there has been insufficient time yet to get it all out. It comes out badly now and then just as some rare toadstools do at times. That may be it. I was looking up a fungus just before I came out. Nobody remembers having seen it before, but there it is all of a sudden—thousands of it. Presently it will disappear for years and years, and we'll forget it. The blessed spores wait in the soil, though you don't know it. They make a display whenever the temperature and moisture are precisely right together, I suppose, and that doesn't often happen."

" And so now you think some leprous spores in us have got the happy conjunction all right ? "

The bookseller was cheerfully attentive, maybe heartened by the thought that evil was but a germ of human origin, which might perish without a helpful conjunction of events. " Well, Mr. Talbot, as you've mentioned trouble, our young friend Charley Holt in the corner there tells me the Thames have got some more of it to build. Langham, I guess that's the friendly work of your pal Lady Carroll—something to feed to the mob, eh ? Something to keep us quiet and occupied ? " He turned again to a man recessed in a place missed by the lamplight. " They've begun on it, haven't they ? "

A young man leaned into the light and nodded diffidently. " So father says. They're laying the keel now."

" Fifty-two more pay days eh ? That's what your dad told me it meant. We may have more pay days than that, if this is the Sabbatical time for the bugs or toadstools or whatever it is. Your dad's quite bonny about it, of course."

Young Bolt grinned, and shifted in his seat. He had his father's shoulders and much more than his father's height. His good-natured gaze had moved in interest to each of the speakers in turn, but he had kept in his shadow, where only his eyes were alert and bright.

" Bolt here," the bookseller explained to me, " is the young man you ought to have heard about on the night of the rumpus at the music hall, but didn't. It doesn't matter now. He is chucking his job as a school teacher. He wants to be a pressman, and with the pressmen stand, a frown upon his forehead, and a pen in his right hand. Don't you, Bolt ? And Langham is seeing to it. It's the *Morning News*."

" Why, what's the matter with that new warship, Jones," chaffed Langham, " why get stuffy about it ? It was supposed you'd like to have it. You've surely thought of what it means—beer for the shipwrights, some of the back rent for the landlords, you selling the starting prices and racing news like hot cakes every afternoon, and Talbot here with a full offertory every Sunday. Isn't that so ? You ask Bolt whether his dad hasn't got a bit on the Derby already, on the strength of armour-plate."

E

"You're corrupt. It's not right this young man should hear a Radical idealist talk like that. It's not right. You should try to remember that some day he may have to choose between right and wrong for a leading article, and here you are, confusing him before he starts."

"No fear. He won't find much confusion in a newspaper office about right and wrong—not enough to worry him. One or two expressions of heartfelt grief from the powers behind the scenes, after he has trespassed innocently where there was nothing to warn him off, will soon teach him what's what. I'm like the vicar here." Langham waved a hand in comic eloquence. "I'm the sworn enemy of the devil, but I know he lives in the basement among the cooking pots, and that the angels are out of sight of the roofs. You ask your parish priest. He'll tell you. That's right, Talbot, isn't it?"

"Well, I won't deny it, if you're talking now of the place we live in, and not of another city which was of more interest to Augustine."

Our distinguished visitor lost something of his languor and ironic playfulness, and sat up. "I like that. That's pretty cool. And now tell me when last a layman was reminded of the Holy City by an official remembrancer? We always thought it was one of the lost cities, gone to brickbats like Memphis. Every pulpit in this country would come down if the servants of God made reckless comparisons between

Birmingham and Zion, and you know it. Your friends would rather attack the whole hierarchy of angels than Joseph Chamberlain. They don't doubt the sacred nature of the business when the bishops bless the flags to lead the bayonets into Naboth's vineyard. That's so, isn't it? It's a beautiful example to the Christian child, coming in lawn sleeves to chuck dynamite into the devil's broth with a benediction." Langham shook a finger at the priest. "Chamberlain and Rhodes have started the dogs barking, and you can hear the scabbards rattling all over Europe now. Any protests? The church doing anything about it? No, if there's anybody fool enough to face the mob and take the chance of getting out of the back door of a protest meeting, it's a layman. You go to Trafalgar Square and try it. It really isn't popular, and it just happens that some of us are risking it. We should love to get an archbishop to approve our preference for the City of God over Johannesburg." Langham recrossed his legs. "Now Talbot, what are our chances?"

The vicar was unmoved. "Peccavi," he said, and mused. "It was only last Sunday, after I had hinted to my flock, only hinted, that the bell wether they were following down a slippery slope had all the signs of being a sinful goat, that your own brother protested warmly in the vestry afterwards, as one good Englishman to another. I don't know. This difference of ours cuts clean across family and church, and it is bound to leave most of us, and most of the church, on the side of—well, Birmingham.   Everybody is sure about that prosperous city.   I'm told it's only two hours run out of Euston.   But the city not made with hands . . . I find it not easy to point it out. Its towers are faint and far, even from a pulpit—I'm seldom sure about them myself throughout the round week—they're not easy to make out, even when we feel that without their promise we couldn't stand Babylon for another day.   So I've ceased to expect them to be more than empty air to those whose trust is in Baal and the familiar solid walls."

" So you're letting it go ? "

" I didn't say so.   I didn't say so.   I can't help Babylon, I can't do anything for it, that's all, and I don't live in Zion.   I don't see what there is for me to do, beyond trying to keep the lamp alight, in case there should be anyone who expects to see it, on a dark night."

There was Langham's mellow laugh, and his hand went out to give some reassuring pats to Talbot's back.   " Don't feel old yet.   There's lot of time yet before you should get tired of watching.   Here I am, just down for a look at the lamp."   He sat smiling and making some idle designs on the table with a paper knife, and we said no more for a time.

" That brother of mine—where in these streets am I likely to find him ?   Shall I have to leave without seeing him ? "

" I've no idea. He's so energetic and serious. He might be anywhere. A little too serious and handsome for an assistant priest, maybe, so wherever he is you'll find the ladies will be ministering to him. Do you know, he has already a cupboard full of new slippers and gifts—you haven't seen it ?—all worked over with devoted designs, and they never make him laugh, never."

"I know. He wouldn't laugh. An admiring crowd of tremulous nymphs would only convince him of his goodness. He'll be surer than ever of his virtue when the ladies admit it."

" Well, between ourselves, I'm not. Of course, I don't know how such a fellow looks at it, but a mere mortal man might feel that if he deserves a reward he ought to take it, out of justice to himself, especially when it is offered so nicely."

Langham was amused. " Half his jolly luck ! Why didn't I enter the church. A good-looking revivalist ought to be as happy in life as a long-haired fellow with a fiddle."

" Yes. More. That's it. What with his evangelical fervour, his patriotism, and his lovely eyes, he gets all the attention there is to offer. No good sitting down by the waters of Babylon and weeping with the remembrance of Zion while he's about. For all the good it does I might as well preach on diatoms."

" Then for goodness sake preach on then, Mr.

Talbot," exclaimed Jones. " Let's have something reasonable. I'm sick of candles and tears. I was dipping yesterday into your scientific journal, and your diatoms were a great comfort. They took me out of myself. Let's have some more along that line. We've got the idea that we're the only things alive that count. Look at Langham there—what with elections, jobs, the important people he meets the same as we meet the postman and the dustman, and the way he gets into the papers, he's bound to suppose the sun has got only one good reason for rising. But he may be wrong. It's a frightful thought. Perhaps I didn't get your meaning right, but from your article in that journal the idea came to me that if some blight killed off the tiny vegetable atoms in the sea and turned all the grass and trees black, then we'd simply melt away, Buckingham Palace, the Admiralty, All Saints, the Workhouse, the Bank of England, and the cat on the hearthrug, and we'd go nearly as quick as snow in June. It gave me a queer sensation to learn that our whole box of tricks depends on a speck of jelly behaving itself properly."

The vicar seemed pleased. His candid grey eyes with their whitish lashes, which made you feel, when he regarded you, that pure cunning was considering whatever you had carefully omitted to say, now rested on the bookseller. He turned to Langham. " That man Jones has got an ideal job, better than yours, better than mine. Books and tobacco. I envy him.

If a boy comes in for a penny blood-and-thunder, it's here for him, and more, for Jones sits on his counter and asks the kid if he has ever read *Treasure Island*, and it's a lucky child who can tell Jones he hasn't. I could almost forgive him the racing editions of the Radical press and the Sunday newspapers."

" That ought to get him past Peter, unless the last issue of the *Freethinker* is sticking out of his coat-tails. You seem more comfortable in this squalid hole than others are at the other end of the town. But listen—I think I ought to be going. I want to ask this. If I take the Town Hall down here for a protest meeting against this damned war, what are all you nice, good, peace-loving Christian freethinkers going to do about it ? "

Talbot shut his eyes. " Nothing."

" Eh ? " Langham, standing up, paused in the buttoning of his overcoat. " Nothing ? But I thought most of you were intelligent working people who were not spoofed by the flag-wagging and the oratory. This is an enlightened industrial community, isn't it ? Two confirmed men of peace like you, too, to lead it. What's the matter ? Are you going to leave the protests and the half-bricks to a few pariahs who are not afraid of Birmingham ? "

" No, no. You can't have our Town Hall. It's the only one we've got. I'm afraid you don't under-stand. It's all too late now, Langham. Here's the usual trouble with peace. We want to begin it after

the guns have gone off. We've got this uproar
because most of us asked for it—I don't say we asked
for it in this form and at this time, but all we were
doing was certain to bring it about. It's useless now
for you to blame us, or the good folk down here who
are cheering the troops and throwing bricks at you
because you won't join the chorus with Kipling.
That's no good. Look to yourself and your political
friends. I know them. Most of them are all in a
muddle about honour, prestige, and rights. They
trust in God, like Cromwell, but only when their
powder is dry. And that is wise, for if you've got the
powder it's because you need it, so it ought to be dry.
What we have we hold, and that always means taking a
bit more when we can get it, to round off the property
and make the rest safe, doesn't it ? You must have
some powder, Langham, in consequence. It's easier to
trust in God when you feel pretty sure you can get
what you want. And there you have it. Most of
your political friends are just like the other good
Romans, determined on their Rome and their Empire.
. . . No, hear me out. I know you Liberals temper
your speech with the catchwords of Jerusalem at your
tea-parties and Nonconformist conferences. You use
the words of peace, but like the rest of us you are the
sons of Adam, and war is in your hearts. Your
political friends think they are against war, quite
honestly, but you try them. Give them a bump on a
tender spot. You'd see their old Adam glare with

righteous indignation.   They're not against war, that
outrage on the intelligence, but only a particular war
the reason for which they don't like.   Your friends,
Langham, when they've been in office, have always
made as much gunpowder as the other side, built as
many ships, and laid as many trains to the magazines
for somebody to start with an idiot match, without
meaning, of course, that anything should blow up.
It's no use, you can't have our Town Hall.   You
won't get me to ask for it.   We want to keep the roof
on it.   The honest people down here have taken you
fine fellows at your word—naturally they've supposed
that the ships and the men and the money you've
supplied were all to the good—bound to be useful—
and they've no objection when the war-engine gets
going.   They want to see the wheels go round.
What are guns for, if they never pop off?   And now
the noise has started, it makes an exciting break in
their lives.   They like it.   You'd waste your time
telling them they don't like it.   They know they do.
Everything has come about just as they've always been
told it would, so it must be right.   They trust in
God for luck, too—your God, my God, the Boers'
God . . ."

Talbot paused, for some noisy scuffling had begun
outside the shop.   There were voices, harsh and
challenging I thought—no, revellers were there.
They were lushy.   The scuffling continued.   It was a
slow dance, and the carousers now were singing, " A

little bit off the top will do for me, for me, a little bit off the top will do for me . . . and all I want is a little bit off the top."

"And their God," added Jones. "Poor old God seems to have his work cut out."

YOUNG BOLT, on his way back to Madras Street school for the afternoon, paused by a post-box, weighed the letter again in his mind, then let go his resignation. That settled it. But because he was afflicted at times by the blight of doubt, he saw the fun of this gamble with fortune, and smiled at his sense of release. Settled it? Well, either that or started it. Still, the knowledge of risk, of having the world bare all round you, and a long drop to the bottom if you became playful on a slippery bit, was freshening.

He looked up at the steeple of All Saints. Half-past one! A bit too soon; but there was a chance of meeting Betty Whittaker. She would be going to that affair at the mission hall about then. She had become very interested in the strange activities there, for some reason. What was her reason? She was not warmly religious. No; her smile was hardly of pious resignation. Young Bolt, as he thought it over, could not but admit that. She was not of the sort who had submitted with meek pallor to the smell of incense, and the tinkling of ritual bells, and the other novelties, so satisfying to nature's hunger for rapture, which had made the church mission a little

65

various since Langham's advent—that solemn ninny, with his heavy shoes under his silly black skirt—any more than was a sensible person like himself.   Women were queer.   Bolt was humbly aware that he knew precious little about them.   Langham's was a piffling invasion.   It was a wonder Talbot put up with it, but perhaps he thought it did not count more than a little damp weather occasionally.   Very likely Betty was going to help in the packing of those books and magazines for the soldiers.   Something reasonable, to be sure.   That would be it.   He wanted to tell her that at last a door had opened into Fleet Street for him.   He had no doubt she would be glad to hear it, because his impulse to tell her was so natural.

Now he must face Wylie.   He admired the headmaster;   a quiet, wise old bird, a good counsellor. But Wylie would not understand the reason for this change;   nor was he the man to overlook defection; to him the teaching of the young was as good a job as a fellow could find.   Wylie had ideas about it; he was ahead of his time.   It amused Charley Bolt to remember how the headmaster kept him and Pettifer in his study after school one evening last week, all worked up and calmly glowing over the mystery of the appeal in English prose, plainly able to go on for hours, and reading, in illustration, passages from Donne, Swift, Defoe, and the Bible, reading them well, too, while Pettifer worried, because his landlady's daughter was waiting outside the school gates for him. Pettifer preferred girls to prose, any evening. It was hard to go back on Wylie, who had encouraged him to be a teacher, and persuaded his father to the cost of it, when money was scarce; and Wylie, careless of the consequences, was the first to give him an inkling of what the English language could do. What would happen was certain. The headmaster would pause in patrolling his study, hook thumbs in his trousers' pockets—too much of a barrel round the waistband to push his hands easily into the tight pockets—and eye him squarely for some difficult seconds. Sure then to be called a fool. Deuced unpleasant to be called a fool by Wylie, especially when you were in doubt about your wisdom. The headmaster had a peculiar way of saying fool. He made it a quiet word of great depth. He could make you believe it of yourself. It was easy to persuade his father that school-teaching led nowhere, but that could not be done with Wylie. "Besides, you know something of this work, nothing of that. Here it's a reality, there it's a lottery. All moonshine. You must be a fool."

Young Bolt spied two of his boys stalking a cat. The creature was lazy in the sun, and innocent of prowling evil. The accurate potato exploded it into such panic divergence of legs and tail that the helpless mirth of the lads almost allowed their teacher to catch hold of their collars. Then they flew after the cat, and nearly as fast. As he watched them go, and chuckled, he had just time to see Miss Whittaker briskly seeking the seclusion of the mission hall. She had gone.

Too bad, that. But she must have known he was coming up the street ? Why that evident haste, and at that time of the day ?

Bolt's class was a docile one. There were several young roughs in it, whose boots were shod with iron, but they had learned it was easier to be good. Mr. Bolt could take a fellow, if you refused to come quietly, and lift you with one hand clean over the desk. It bumped the knees. He did it easily too. He never lost his paddy. He was a decent sort of beast, but he was quick, when he started. You ought to have seen Fatty Bensted that day when he kicked Mr. Bolt ! Crikey, we did laugh. He thought Mr. Bolt was going to hit him hard. So did we. Mr. Bolt picked him up.

The boys took their seats, and sat with folded arms. The class in the next room was doing science, and Mr. Tatham in there was bellowing at it. Then, prompted by his shouts, Mr. Tatham's class began to sing-song axioms. " Matter cannot be annihilated—reduced—nothing—destroyed in one form—exists—another form." The apathy which comes from a dreary repetition of truth began to descend on the school. Young Bolt was contemplating Mercator's Projection of the world, which was hanging on a wall in front of him, with the British Empire so magnified upon it in shining scarlet that the rest of the pale and insignificant land and sea was hardly noticeable. He considered that map—geography this afternoon—and wondered whether Betty had seen him coming . . . had she ? . . . of course not . . . but that was strange . . . nobody else was in the street.

The boys who had worried the cat thought they might be dealt with before the work began, and were trying to read their teacher's countenance. They had had experience of him ; his view of a natural performance could be strange. He was thinking of something now. His absent gaze fell on them, and they fidgeted guiltily. " Betty must have seen him, but she was in a hurry."

The little rascals, they were watching him. Pull yourself together. He rapped his desk with a stick, and his class became rigid and waited. He looked big and formidable to the youngsters, with a taut little moustache under a nose slightly bent by a smash at football. His mouth and nose subdued them, but not his eyes, for they were often friendly when sympathy was a surprise. He did funny things. Sometimes, when a boy quickly answered a question, he would order him out to the front of the class, look him up and down, as though he had never seen him before, and then gave him a penny.

Bolt forced himself to his duty. Get this afternoon

over. Two hours to go. There was just a chance
that he could be outside the mission hall, on his way
home, before the sorting and packing of that stuff
for the troops was done. " Now then, Williams, get
out the geography books."

" Please, sir, Williams's asleep."

He was. The teacher looked at the boy, whose
head was askew, and his mouth open, and remembered
the lad was on a round of the streets with milk before
six in the morning. " All right. You do it."

" Keep the books shut. We'll see what you
remember of Asia. What are you doing, Davis ? "

Davis furtively ran his tongue over his thumb nail,
dissolving thereon a lewd device, which he had been
displaying to a grinning neighbour. " Nothink, sir."

" Come here . . . show me your hand."

Davis, with an air of innocence unjustly assailed,
exhibited both hands, turning them about to establish
their purity. Mr. Bolt frowned at the lad, whose
blue eyes, upturned in the confidence which blame-
lessness confers, met his own in wonder at this
unworthy suspicion.

Now what was he to do with the imp ? The young
devil was at some low game, and the rest of them
knew it, if he did not ; but you might as easily pick
up a shadow as the reason for whatever caper only
a child was playing. " Go back to your place,
Davis." Not fair to ask the class what the young
rascal had been doing ; better to be put up with

being fooled again. The teacher turned over some notes about Asia on his desk. He glanced at his boys, and guessed they were secretly amused. He felt some amusement himself. Sin in its artfulness could make you look as silly as a proud virgin in a naughty house. Those tousled heads and vacant faces were a little sample from the world outside, a little bit which often proved more than he could fathom. Not a promising augury for Fleet Street.

The class turned to Asia as though drudgery never changed, yet a boy would become spuriously mettlesome when addressed by name. They wanted to please, though the going was hard.

" Who knows another name for India ? "

Apparently another name for India did not exist for the class. It waited in silence.

" Now, Jenkins, your father is a quartermaster of the *Koh-i-noor*, surely you know ? "

Jenkins, challenged as an expert, cast a considering eye sideways, but nothing came of it.

" Never heard of the Brightest Jewel in the British Crown ? "

" No, sir."

Nobody there knew of such a jewel. Jenkins, pursued to his discomfort with what his father had told him about India, volunteered that his father had said that anybody could have the trip for him.

" What, hasn't he even told you about Bombay ? "

The son of a sailor was troubled. " No, sir. We

F

don't ask him." Then as if he thought his father needed an excuse, he mumbled : " 'E ain't 'ome long enough."

There was something in what Wylie was always telling his staff. No man was wise enough to measure the elements of only one child—and even if he were he ought to have the parents and grand-parents there for walloping, when necessary. A long job, to overtake the consequences of breed and surroundings !

The rivers of China, the names of which the teacher was aware he could not be pronouncing correctly ; the Indus and the Euphrates ; Benares and Hong-Kong ; Mount Everest and the Desert of Gobi ; Canton and Lhassa ; there it all was. The shiny map hung over a blackboard on an easel, the continent of Marco Polo's wanderings, where Nebuchadnezzar and Alexander and Kublai Khan once reigned, and Buddha and Confucius taught. The teacher, pointer in hand, was warming to the implications of the map, and only glanced at the clock when another thought intruded. Then Wylie came in, listened, stroked his grizzled beard, and hooked his thumbs in his pockets. He evidently approved. He smiled.

" You haven't told them where ran the sacred river Alph amid caverns measureless to man."

" No, sir. Not that."

" Why not, Mr. Bolt, why not ? "

" A little bit far, that river, Mr. Wylie ? "

" Not at all, sir. Not at all. If there be one that believeth . . ." and old Wylie thrust out his hand magisterially to the swing doors, and went into the class beyond.

THE headmaster's room, Bolt recognised with a twinge as he went in, was the same as on the day when he entered it first. Then he was a child. The clutter of models, mostly white geometrical solids, was still on the roof of the cupboard of yellow pine. And the shelves of books in brown buckram were still disorderly. The loose volumes were leaning against each other as if they had never been straightened; but he had read all of them, though none with the wonder evoked by the first loan from those shelves, which was Hans Andersen's stories. He would always think of Andersen when he remembered that room. The plaster Nikké was central on the mantelpiece, and on the walls were the sere photographs of the antiquities of Athens and Rome. Those photographs had nothing to do with the curriculum of that elementary school, but were relics of Wylie's honeymoon, so Bolt had heard. He had lost his awe of it, but he felt a touch of the melancholy which comes of a break with the past; and there was Wylie, sitting reading at his table, as he was at the beginning.

The headmaster was reading a report, his head

propped on one hand, when his assistant began to explain. He but glanced up, and then appeared to continue his reading. He was always bickering with the authorities; trying to let in daylight, he called it, and he had been doing that, with no result except that the authorities knew him as a good but cantankerous servant, since the passing of the Education Act. He did not look at his visitor, but bent his gaze on the document before him. Then he rose from his chair, fingered his beard, sighed in mock tragedy, and smiled as though at the caricature of a pleasantry. " Thus it goes. I want you, Bolt, but you must have something else. Very well."

Young Bolt, fumbling at it, put the blame on his chief. " You see, sir, you have brought it about yourself. I might not have thought of this if you hadn't given me more than the work needed. There were the books—you know what I mean—and the ideas. I'm trying to write, too."

" So. I've known for long that we've little control over things, once we've started them. They go their own way. Um ! We do our best, and then we don't recognize it." He shuffled his papers about. " But why a man who wants to write should go to Fleet Street to do it—I don't see it. Isn't that the last place for the pearl ? "

This was a new idea for the junior, and Bolt forgot, for a moment, that he hoped Wylie would not keep him too long.

" And you can write—there are signs, I mean, that you may, in time. I'll confess that your style jars on me a little. You've been reading too much Macaulay, and he's a mastodon. But smashing through a subject is spectacular—a sign of power most readers understand. Um . . . so God forbid, if you're going to Fleet Street, that I should weaken you."

His assistant was troubled. He suppressed a desire to argue. He had been reading Macaulay, but if he began to discuss it there was no telling when it would end.

" You're rather hard on Fleet Street, aren't you, sir ? "

" Hard ? " Wylie made sardonic sounds in his beard. " What does that matter ? That place will survive an old man's laugh in the East End. Take a look at these." The headmaster rummaged in a drawer, and handed to his junior some newspaper cuttings, cheerful and confident contemporary references to science and letters. " Look there."

Bolt smiled as he inspected them. They certainly were funny.

" If you think you can improve that sort of thing, perhaps you'd better go and do it."

Wylie abruptly sat down, propped his head on his hand again, and brought the report under his eyes. Bolt moved to the door. This was quickly over. He paused there and peered round at his chief ; and

Wylie, to his surprise, was leaning back in his chair, sleepily watching him go. Bolt had an impulse to return and offer his hand to his master, but hesitated on the threshold, and went awkwardly out.

He crossed the playground with a sense of lightness. He had got that over; but he was pensive about it, for a reason that was not quite plain because he preferred to hurry on and not to look at it steadily. He had something else to think about. He made his way quickly to the mission hall.

He was not too late, for he could hear from its inner door the sounds which accompany work that is happy and voluntary. Too many women were in there, it was plain. He became conscious, as he waited and listened, that he was really an outsider, and that it was hard to determine to enter a building from which he was averse, and to intrude on people whose mirthful enthusiasm did not concern him. He summoned the courage to give the door a slant. He could see the company at the other end of the hall. It was so occupied that it was unlikely to notice him, and, anyhow, it would fail to see him if he remained in the shadow.

When he was inside he wished, almost at once, that he was out. There was Betty, in a crowd of girls—all girls, except Langham, unless the curate could be called another. That tall and handsome fellow, so like his brother, but refined to a sombre grace and wistful earnestness which gave him, in his black frock, the appeal of a virgin ascetic, was at once an extraneous and picturesque figure to Bolt, who watched him in bemused antipathy. Bolt found himself thinking rapidly, but without a recognizable clue to the cause of his acute interest. While he stood there he learned that in one way of the first importance he could never get into that hall. Yet Betty appeared to be easily at home ; she moved happily at her task, as though she had no thought beyond it. The hall had a smell which closed his soul against further enquiry into it. It was colder in there than in the street. And that curate ! Bolt was convinced the fellow was as much a foreigner to him as any dubious ministrant to what was exotic and meaningless. Yet it was plain to the watcher in the shadow that the Rev. Francis Langham, whose manliness was hardly valid, for it bore the sign of the opposite attributes, was regarded by the ladies as male and most worthy.

But Betty had seen him standing there. That was why Bolt was sure she had not, for it caused her to act as though she was unaware of a doorway. Bolt, who was patient, retired more into the shadow, and she thought he had gone, which was a relief to her. She was wondering whether Francis would remember that for part of the path homeward her way could be his, as sometimes he did. In the allusive and intimate dialogues she held with him, in her fancy, he was Francis, but when addressing him she called him Mr. Langham.

Bolt waited. A light from the western window fell upon Betty, and he determined when he saw it to wait till it was time for her to go; he could easily wait. And she, thinking he had gone, was buoyant in that light. The glow did not give her the aura of a Christian saint. She was a few years older than Bolt. Her corn-coloured hair was ordered into a large coil at the back of her head, and with that and her buxomness, in plain daylight, she had the figure and carriage of a lively and well-favoured young matron; so in a tempered religious glow, which gilded the misty strands of her diffuse hair, and illuminated the full profile and easy poise of her body, she did not belong to late ascetic rites, but to the freedom of the sunny legends in which there was no rule but happiness.

Langham called to her, to ask Miss Whittaker whether she would be so very good as to spare him some copies of *Punch*, and for an instant the curate was confused, as he saw the chance light on her, by a pagan thought; as though she were a surprising visitant from a time not this, and so not subject to our morality. Then, instead of waiting for the papers to be brought to him, promptly he went over to get them, and touched Betty's hand as he received them. There was no hurry about it. Langham's lean and grave face was philanthropic, as he accepted the humorous numbers, and Betty looked up at him as though she were as bounteous as Ceres.

Bolt, who was still waiting for her to come his way, turned about for the door, hooked his fingers in serious thought over his twisted nose, and made no sound, nor looked back, as he went out.

CHAPTER VIII

At a back window of her home Mrs. Bolt paused
to see what sort of a morning it was outside. She
had finished upstairs. That was something done.
Another day was on its way towards the next. Her
family was scattered about its business. Charley had
left his watch on his pillow. Not like him to do
that. Was that lucky?

Her house was in Bateson Street, which is lost in
the midst of the random perspectives of flagstones
and ridges of porous and smoking brick, where live
those outer Londoners who know of Westminster
Abbey because they have heard of it. That street
is but another dry gulley in a desert. It has distinc-
tion, for it has a name. In Bateson Street, too, the
muslin curtains of the parlour windows are discreetly
parted to display pots of geraniums and alabaster
ornaments on small stands just within. A perennial
interest is shown in the street by the midwife, the
dustman, the insurance agent, the tally man, the
vendor of cats' meat, and the undertaker, though a
tough explorer would give it up through tedium at
the heart long before he reached it. But the explorer
has never heard of it. He will never seek it. It is

unchronicled, for it is one of the menial places attendant on the wealth of a city, and so is of no importance, except to us. And Mrs. Bolt, who lived there, without her name would have been lost among its other women, for she so resembled the rest of them that in no picturesque particular could her place be justified in a serious account of that period of her country's history. Her anxieties were so like those of her neighbours that they understood each other well enough. She was nobody, but she was like her neighbours. There were so many of them that unless the Recording Angel has it all down then their lives have been as the shadows which follow the sun, leaving no mark. Mrs. Bolt knew very few of them. She would tell you so. She kept herself to herself.

She stared absently from her upstairs window at the chicken-runs and clothes-lines in the May morning beyond. Bolt's shirts, she mused, were falling to pieces already, the way his big body sweated it would rot anything, never go to that shop again, only fit for dusters. That was young Jack whistling in the kitchen. Forgotten about him. Home from school to-day, of course. Well, she and Bolt must be getting on, they must be getting on, when it was time for that baby to be thinking of looking round for work. Only seemed yesterday, that old tartan frock of his was still in the cupboard, she was looking at it only last week. Time was a robber, taking life away from you while you were doing floors trying to keep things just so and it was nothing if you felt anyhow to-day because soon things would be easier when the boys could help a bit. Then you were beginning to go grey. She was going grey, she was sure of that, just beginning to show plain enough. Well, let it show, she looked as young as some of them, whether or no. That fellow next door was repairing his pigeon-loft, ugly old thing, only fit for the wind to blow down, those birds were a perfect nuisance, the mess they made. Dirt! No good trying to keep the place clean, time that dustbin was emptied; but that would be done as usual just when everybody was going to sit down to eat. That fellow must be out of work again, home at that time of the morning; well, his beastly pigeons wouldn't keep him. There was that pretty white fantail, what a darling; Charley found it in the scullery gobbling rice last Saturday afternoon like billy-ho. Swore we'd trapped it, that fellow there, but went inside when Bolt looked over the fence at him. Charley! Something else now to worry about. The dear boy was a worry, big enough to look after himself, thank God, but giving up the school; it was a mistake to give up anything you'd got after all that trouble and expense. She hoped it was all right. More brains than she had. It was those books again, glad he read books, it kept him from worse things, but where did books lead to, leaving a respectable job better than ever his father had in the shipyard?

Now nothing would suit him but something else, scribbling, if ever you heard of such a thing, newspapers, and what was there in that, nobody wanted to read that stuff when there was work to do. Wasn't safe, changing about, when you are all right. Leave things alone, when you are all right. No need to make trouble for yourself when there it generally is and nobody knows how it gets there.

Mrs. Bolt was holding a bunch of wallflowers in her hand; she put the thick bunch of green and brown to her face and drew in the warm and appeasing scent. What was she carrying those gilliflowers about the house for, might just as well have them left downstairs when she bought them at the door, ought to be in water. No wonder she was worrying about Charley, with that smell under her nose. That was a funny thing. Not many months before that boy came, couldn't help thinking of him when she smelt gilliflowers. Bolt, he'd laugh at her if he knew. He'd never know. He knew nothing about it, the way he went off that morning, the pet he was in. He never knew to this day. Years ago now. What a quick-tempered man Tom Bolt always had been, and never noticed things about the house, never, only if his slippers weren't handy when he came in. Two rooms then. If you could only have your time over again. Thirty-eight shillings a week, and Bolt's job nearly finished. She was properly sick of it that morning, and no wonder, the dark house it was,

damp inside and the rain outside, it was like waiting
with the blessed blinds down for the mutes to carry
you out feet first. Couldn't stand it. Wasn't going
to wait for that. Tom ought to have known, but
he didn't care—he had enough to worry him with
his job very likely, but how was she to know when
he kept his troubles to himself. He'd never tell you
if he was dying. Out he went without saying good-
bye, the pet he was in, and didn't come back again
as usual pretending he'd forgotten something, not
that morning, which would have given any girl the
grizzles, stuck there all day in a place she didn't know
and the first coming. Smashed two cups washing up
when he'd gone. Two out of six. His mother's
old cups. That did it. What with him and the
cups. If he'd come back then she'd have hit him.
Sat down and had a good cry. No good crying, there
was the slop running over the kitchen table, and the
broken crocks on the floor, and that silly patch of
damp on the wall the shape of a black dog. She'd
go. Let Tom come home and find out. Find her
missing. Pick his crocks up himself. He'd know
what it was then. That's what she'd do, go, and
leave him to it. How it was she never knew. She
hadn't moved. She was going to get up and go,
really clear out of it, then the place got lighter, and
she sat there feeling done, and noticed the pattern
of the wallpaper. Never noticed it had any before,
the room was that dark, those underground kitchens

are like being buried alive, and there was enough to think about besides. A bit of sun came down, and the pattern stood out bright, the way the sun got it, and there was a knock at the door. A fellow there selling gilliflowers. You could smell them as soon as the door opened. Well, Tom never knew how a bunch of wallflowers saved him that morning.

Mrs. Bolt began to run a duster over the banisters, and to sing to herself. " You are going far away— far away from your Jeanette."

" Mother ! "

" You call, son ? "

" Hadn't I better go ? I've got to be at that place in Westminster at two o'clock."

" Oh, of course you have."

" What a lark if I get the job."

" I hope you do, if it's all right. A long way to go though. Spend all you earn on getting there and back. That collar of yours clean ? You just go and put on another. You're not going to school now, you should have remembered that."

Mrs. Bolt continued along the banisters with her duster and a little song to herself : " With your gun upon your shoulder—and your bayonet by your side— you'll be winning some fair lady—and be making her your bride."

" Here, haven't you got that collar on yet ? Look at those boots. Don't tell me they were cleaned this morning."

" Yes, I did. They got dusty going to the grocer's.
The butter's on the table. I say, I heard you singing.
You often sing that. I never hear anybody else
sing it."

" I don't suppose you do. My mother used to
sing it. It's an old one."

" I wish I knew where that fellow was going. I
reckon it was to a battle. Why don't you finish it ? "

" I never think about it, you young worry. I don't
know it all."

" Not another verse ? "

" My mother used to sing it, and her mother I
expect, yes, my grandmother used to sing it. Put
that clean collar on at once."

Her son turned to obey. His mother's grandmother ! He could not imagine anything so far off.
No wonder the song was silly, though his mother's.
He was still curious to know where that fellow went ;
but in Bateson Street, though the air and some words
of the song still survived in one of its houses while
a housewife dusted a handrail, nearly a century after
Jeanette sorrowed because a soldier must march
away, that he was going to Waterloo with his bayonet
by his side after an Upstart Corsican was forgotten.

" Mums, may I go now ? "

" Perhaps you better. Now mind how you cross
the streets and be sure to be home as soon as ever
you can. Let me look at you. Did Charley tell you
how to find the place ? "

G

" Yes."

She surveyed her son severely for defects, from a few steps above him, but approved. Wanted a new jacket, that boy. Just like his brother, quiet and plenty of sense, but a little pale and peeky. He'd never be Charley's build, he wanted care. The boy saw his mother's inspection soften, and grinned up at her. You could get anything out of mother. She was easy. Saucy young imp! Two lines came at the corners of her mouth, and leisurely she stepped to the bottom of the stairs. She pinched his chin.

" Got what money you want ? "

" Charley gave me a bob."

" He did, did he. Then you don't want any from me. Now straight there and back and let's know what happened. Sharp's the word and quick's the motion. Off you go."

She opened the door and watched him away ; and Mrs. Whittaker, who was going by on the other side, came over genially, and the door could not be shut. Mrs. Bolt did not ask her in. There was too much to do, and it took some time to exhaust Mrs. Whittaker's knowledge of the parish, because one thing led to another. Mrs. Bolt, indulgent but nervous, therefore said what a fine day it was, and Mrs. Whittaker, gazing down the street after young Jack, said how that boy of yours grows, and she hadn't seen anything of Charley lately, no, not for weeks, it seemed. Mrs. Bolt was polite, and did not ask what Charley was to do with her, but nursed two loaves she took from the baker. She also declined, while continuing her neighbourly conversation, to buy a sewing machine from an eloquent agent who was passing from door to door, and thus she missed a word which concerned Mrs. Whittaker's Betty.

"Ah, these girls of to-day, they'll never be told anything. No. They go their own way, and mother is nobody."

"Different times different manners, Mrs. Whittaker, I expect."

"Manners? That's a new-fangled way of putting it. Manners! I never heard the like. But don't forget your own gals are still at school, Mrs. Bolt, and I'd give 'em manners, at that age, believe me."

Without knowing what this was all about, Mrs. Bolt nodded wisely in agreement, which was the best thing to do, the morning getting on as it was. But she did not like the idea of going inside at once, for after all Mrs. Whittaker was a widow, poor soul, though large enough to look after herself, and with a grown-up daughter, and a pension from the Navy, which was more than she'd ever have.

"Manners!" Mrs. Whittaker was evidently grieved by an inadequate expression of sympathy, to Mrs. Bolt's simple bewilderment. "What next will be called manners? Almost anything, I shouldn't be surprised. Well, I may not know much, but I'm sure you wouldn't call it manners when the travelling draper goes into Mrs. Brown's every Monday he calls, as I've watched him myself, instead of taking her money at the door, same as he would from you and me, though I'll not say there isn't more'n one way of paying what you owe, if you can look at it like that."

"That man never comes to this door, Mrs. Whittaker. I'll watch it."

"I don't say as he does, or needs, with a husband in regular work and the money coming in to get what you want as you want it."

Mrs. Bolt, her thoughts innocently preoccupied with household duties still to be performed, and sure of nothing while standing there gossiping but the endless drift of the talk when the caller was Mrs. Whittaker, stepped back to her doormat.

"Well, I've left a pie in the oven and the children will be in to dinner very soon, so I'll say good-day to you. It's lovely weather, isn't it?"

And Mrs. Whittaker, with surprise and annoyance on her plump and good-natured face, agreed without conviction.

Mrs. Bolt, soothed by the silence of her house, straightened a picture in the passage, and began again. The morning passed, the girls had been sent back to school, and it was getting near time for them all to be home again, and there was the tea to get. Was that Bolt? No, the footsteps passed. She looked out from that window again—whence began

most of her excursions into the outer world—to the
empty distance beyond the chicken-runs of her neighbours, to that dire and fantastic region in which the
branchings of the River Lea were working a tortuous
drainage to the Thames through an ashy chaos of
embankments, mud-flats, and railway-sidings. There
was little to see but nameless gloomy shapes, and no
light from the waters, which were invisible beneath
their long slants of ooze. A group of men was in
the foreground of that nondescript region, playing
pitch-and-toss safe from the notice of the police, who
never ventured into the marshes. She had a fear of
that sinister vacancy of factory and marsh, and had
forbidden her children ever to go that way, and so
what they knew of it, and they knew much, had been
learned in lawless and surreptitious ventures. Those
marshes, canal banks, and wharves, were dismal with
tales of what had happened to the disobedient children
of near streets, and the characters who haunted the
forbidden land were darker by all accounts than the
treacherous mud of its channels.

It would be a good thing when they moved out of
that place, she thought. Look at it ! Dark. Ugly.
Nobody knew what was there. Time they had a
change. One never saw anybody there but those
men ; it was always the same. Always gloomy,
always empty. Now the boys were coming on they
ought to be in a better place. And the girls, what
good was it seeing nothing but those smoky factories

and Bateson Street ?   And the smells !   It wasn't
right.   Not giving them a fair start.   Time they
had a change.   She didn't want them to go through
what she'd gone through.   A brighter chance than
that. Mrs. Bolt brooded on the country beyond
the backyards of Bateson Street as though trying
to divine the future.   A transient evening light came
to transmute the marshes and the vague buildings.
Far away she saw the obscure limit of her survey
of the world.   The obscurity developed an outline,
to her surprise.   The constant settlement of murk
carried a suggestion on its upper ridge of a remote
city, in that light, and a tiny dome was there, above
all the rest.   Of course !   She'd lived there for years,
and never noticed it till that minute.   St. Paul's !
Why, young Jack was up there somewhere.   What
a long way !   She didn't know when she was near
St. Paul's last.   Quite cheered her up, to see that,
just when she was feeling mopey.   Ah ! there was
Tom's latch-key !   He was home.

Mr. Bolt was in his chair, his feet stretched out
in an attitude of release, when she entered the room.
Always felt easier in her mind when he was safe
back from the yard.

" Hullo, old girl, all right ? "

" Well, any fresh news to-day ? "   She stood at
his shoulder, and rested a hand on it.

Her husband thought she meant whether any news
was in the paper, but she was merely solicitous.

" No. Nothing fresh from South Africa. It's my opinion we're having things kept back from us, and that means they're rotten."

His wife said nothing. She was not interested in the war, though she was kindly and patient when Bolt talked about it, which he did too often. Bother the old war !

She was not listening to him then with careful attention to news of the war, but was thinking instead of Charley. She meant to ask Bolt about that.

" I've been thinking a lot about the children to-day, being quiet I suppose, especially about Charley."

" Why, what's the matter with him ? He's all right, isn't he ? " Mr. Bolt sat up to listen.

" Is he ? You think he ought to leave his school ? "

Mr. Bolt grunted, and took his ease again.

" Thought there was something wrong. He knows what he's about, don't you fret."

" I hope he does."

" What do you think ! All the same, I can't help wishing he was doing his bit like some of the other young 'uns. They're off with the volunteers. Show a better spirit, for a lad of his stamp."

" Do you mean to the war ? "

" That's what I said, isn't it ? They want men, don't they ? He's a good 'un."

Mrs. Bolt took her hand from her husband's shoulder, and looked down at him.

" Tom, you don't mean that."

" Then you don't know me. You know the way Charley talks. You've heard him. Running down the whole show. You've heard him. Blaming his own country. It's not right. I don't like it."

" But perhaps we're wrong."

" Now look here, old girl, don't you start, or you'll go and spoil my tea. Where's Jack ? "

" He's gone after that job he was talking about."

" What, that kid ? I'd forgotten about him. That's another on the move." Mr. Bolt was happy about it. " Why, I believe you and me are getting on." His gaze wandered hopefully to the familiar china dogs on the mantelpiece, to the token of a sailor brother at sea, which hung above on a wall like a rolling-pin of blue glass (there was a ship painted on it) to the oleograph of Disraeli beneath it, to the burnish of the brass knobs of the fireplace. " Well, that's news. Hi, if the war lasts long enough Jack may be in time for it, too."

" Tom, don't make such jokes."

Mr. Bolt gathered in his two young daughters noisily, as they came in, and was joyously offensive about their appearance. He regarded them.

" All I can say is, mother, this house is getting too small for us. Won't be room for the canary soon. What a few more years will do for us I don't know."

CHAPTER IX

THE walls of the Office for Foreign Affairs that night
were as mute as sleeping wisdom. They always are.
You could not doubt that its front masked nothing
but the records of what did not concern us. It was
the token of abstractions so vague that no Londoner
who chanced to be passing it could have guessed it
meant anything for him. It was the first time I had
ever paused to observe the building; it happened
that then I was waiting outside it for one of its staff,
who had something to tell me.

As I waited there, listless and free, Whitehall became
more than a principal thoroughfare of the capital.
Any stranger who paused in awe to admire, even any
Londoner, would have seen, that night in May, 1900,
that Whitehall was as much beyond him as the sky.
Its lofty calm was subduing. The night was overcast, and the buildings of our Government were as
dim as the heavens. There stood the home of
Parliament, just as if the lower darkness of earth was
mounting in spires. Perhaps the aspirations of our
elders and counsellors were actually visible after
nightfall, and had the shape of flames straightly
tapering to Heaven but the hue of the dubious. The

grave eloquence of our legislators rose in black peaks,
enduring and memorable, and though they themselves
returned to the place whence they came, the earth
could not forget what they had done. That must
stand. Those great shadows, vague but imminent,
were as impersonal as the sounding word itself:
London. They were nothing to do with me; they
were the past. They were, that night—just as we
should see them on any night of this present year—
merely the suggestion of antiquity, the sombre presentiment of our inscrutable heritage, the abiding
witness of bygone fame. The sounds of the living
city were then, as they always are, but a murmuring
out of a hollow vast of forgotten ages; and the gloom
was the tradition and spell of tales that are told, and
the walls the memorials of deeds that were famous,
though we seldom remember why, merged by night
into a common dedication.

I saw the shadows, while waiting, but as the
ambiguity of our destiny, the omen of a thraldom
which we cannot read, so we need not bother about
it. The loiterer and stranger, even the Londoner,
could gaze in his innocent awe of it, because plainly
he had no part in it. It could touch his life no more
than the secrets of Paris and Berlin and St. Petersburg.
The shadow of a great city is impersonal, like its glory.
It does not fall across the life of one of the Nobodies.
The ordination given to it by its kings and famous
statesmen weaves no spell about the chance path of a

Nobody ; he may stop to admire the show. For the Nobodies, that large family, though they replenish the earth, do not share in the splendour of the past, in which only by inference do we know that they lived. The Nobodies are not seen in the pomp and majesty of history. They are free and unconcerned. The ambiguity of destiny is not for their unravelling.

Even the policeman outside the Foreign Office took no notice of me ; he merely glanced indifferently at the pair of us when I was met by one of its principal clerks. And that young man was so good and confident a talker that I forgot the abstractions about us. He had written a novel which was part of the lively news of the day, and hardly a critic had forgotten to call it brilliant. It had been done at an age when most of us feel that it may be some years yet before we gain the confidence to explain life's oddities to simple people who still continue to wonder why things happen to come about as they do. That young man was my reason for being in Whitehall. My editor had thought that our readers would be amused to learn a secret or two about the fun of the fair from one who was so well qualified to tell us. Though I was curious, and would have valued a few hints, yet I had been doubtful about wasting the time of a writer who could otherwise use it so profitably ; but here was the novelist, even eager to favour us. He had consented to leave urgent work in his office

to perambulate Whitehall with me after dark, while
telling me what one ought to do, to make life real
in a book. He was shrewd on the knotty subject
of construction and plot. He dwelt on that at length,
and quoted many instances from the classics. He
mentioned, naturally, the famous " *Poetics*." A
novel, he explained, should be a little history of
humanity, cunningly selected to betray our essential
attributes, and a plot is its vitality. For what is life,
he asked, without conscious form, and a motive
breathed into it by its creator ? It is chaos. " He
must never let his characters get out of hand, nor
allow irrelevant things to divert for a moment . . ."

I think he stopped then ; anyhow, I heard no more.
The horse of an approaching van did not fall so much
as suddenly decide that he had had enough of it.
He plumped down near us in the way of the traffic.
My instructor told me no more of the poet's part in
revealing the hidden motives of our drama ; he wanted
to see what the driver would do. So did I. The
police came. A score or so of us interrupted the
ordered courses of our lives to watch an irrelevant
episode. It was not art, but Londoners are the heirs
of eternity, and can always spend some of it on a fallen
horse. This one was a reposeful creature, and ignored
even the police. I turned to make an amusing comment to my novelist, but he was not beside me, and
so I had the chance to see an insignificant figure pass
behind the little audience that was watching a fallen

dobbin. It wore a grey frockcoat which was deco-
rated with a single dainty flower, though an
orchid did not accord with a face so rigid and
sharp and an expression that was harsh and narrow.
It took no notice of us. Great God! There went
the man who had given us war! But I doubt that
anyone else there noticed Joseph Chamberlain, for
the horse had not then decided to rise.

When it did get up—it just stood up and rattled
its gear—my opportunity to learn more of the way
by which coarse life may be given an artistic form
was gone. The young poet could not be seen. The
full tide of London resumed its stream, under whatever
inspiration originally had set it going. I sought in
the shadows for my man, but he was lost in them,
somewhere. Again Whitehall began to look as
though men and women, and even statesmen chosen
to be great, were as incidental to it as ownerless and
wandering dogs which drift where they list, unaware
of any compelling plot. I had lost my thread, too;
the line of my purpose was broken. And if the
pallor of Chamberlain's narrow mask had not drifted
by in the gloom I might never have known Whitehall
was haunted by even one potent ghost. My editor
was waiting for my return with some entertaining
comments on the truth about life, by a young satirist
who knew how to make our incoherence artistic and
significant; but I was certain, without thinking it
over, that my editor would never accept, in place of the

sparkling wit of a popular novelist glinting on our
social doings, my meaningless encounters with
Chamberlain's face, the shadows of all the yesterdays,
and a rebel carthorse.

Yet it was sadly evident then that I might as well
hunt there for William the Norman as my modern
author. Both had gone. I could not expect to
learn in that obscurity what I wanted to know. All
that was real was the policeman, who showed me that I
was merely at a loss by calmly patrolling the ambiguity
of our destiny, perhaps watchful that the dark omen
of our thraldom remained undisturbed by the curious,
and to move them on if they made any effort to read it.

I gave a last glance round and left it. Nobody was
about, except the constable, and a boy who stood near
me, with his back turned to the august Foreign Office,
admiring, I thought, the houses of Parliament. He
had the look of Bolt's young brother, but all the
children of his kind are much the same, and Westminster was unlikely for an East End boy, at that hour.

As I had obtained scarcely enough to satisfy my editorial room, it was wiser to dodge it, for the hour was late, and my chief could be depended on to know of a useless task for me, to compensate for ill-spent time.

Fleet Street was waking up to its usual crisis. Midnight was coming. It was growing tense with the pressure of the knowledge of important things which twenty four hours had engendered. The *Daily Telegraph* clock, which after dark takes over the influential duty of the cross of St. Paul's—the cross stands over The Street by day—projected its round pale warning among us. Each narrow side turning of the street was filled with ranks of newspaper carts, waiting for the hour. Their horses, hysterical through a life of rush and excitement, snatched savagely at the elbows of wayfarers, but these were compositors, machine-men, and journalists, sauntering to the Quill Club, or the "Black Dog" or the "Green Dragon" or the "Clachan," and they knew what to expect of professional vice. From basements and walls came the rumble of machinery, already beginning, with the first revolutions of its heavy load of rumours and alarums, to communicate a tremor to the earth.

Wine Office Court is but a hole in the wall, a foot-path out of Fleet Street, and then its narrow passage was unlighted at night except for the bright dabs of the Quill Club windows. It was a modest boast of the club that Goldsmith once wrote in its building, a fact which was never more curious than when you were in the rooms late at night. How did he manage it? Perhaps he had something to write about, and the distraction of good-fellowship could not thwart him.

The bar of the club was immediately within the door. The door mat led to the bar. Bentley, the club familiar, who had seen too much to be surprised by anything that could happen, presided in a white jacket behind the counter with his company of shining pewter pots and chromatic array of bottles. When a member crossed the mat and paused before him no word was passed. Bentley knew. He had been in the club longer than any of us. He understood. He never spoke except when, deferential though with a suggestion of malice, he whispered, " You are wanted at the telephone, sir " ; as though he were aware of the decrees of fate and but waited the predestined signal, of which we could know nothing, to strike a doomed member down. He had a bony aspect, sunken expressionless eyes, and polished his tumblers in ironic deliberation, as though sure of the appropriate hour when that club and its careless frequenters would receive the award of their merit. Then, for the first time, he might laugh.

Potter entered, our chairman, a stiff little man, Quakerish and stern. He paused for a moment, and through his spectacles, with a slight squint, he observed us in cold tolerance. His expression of tired severity, with its trace of disdain for us which he was too indifferent to express, was occasioned by his hard lot. As a busy assistant editor he had no use for literature, though some for golf, and his contempt for the art of writing extended even to those who practised it for his paper; his admiration was not for us, but for such haughty giants of earth as Cecil Rhodes, who take what they want, and receive as though deaf the outbursts of astonishment and indignation about them. It would have cheered Potter to have ridden rough-shod freely over intellectual questioners and the contemptible protests of their knowledge; yet, worse luck, it was his paid duty to maintain the right jeering accent in the news and headlines of a little Radical daily paper, a gamin of a David slinging cheeky stones at the aureate mail of Imperial Mars.

Behind Potter there dawdled in two young members who were communing in secret joy over another strange tale of their office. But they began to share their pleasure at once with anyone on the club mat. Their office was a fount of refreshing surprises to Fleet Street.

" Oh, Potter, do join the *Mail*. You ought to come over to us. That's where all the fun is."

H

Our chairman remained severe before his merry juniors, and waited judicially.

" Do you ever read our society column ? No ? Now don't say you're not anxious to know the colour of the duchess's garters. Anyhow, it's all true, whatever you've heard about Harmsworth's uncanny insight. You have heard of that, haven't you ? Our great man saw at once it would never do for a footman or a parlourmaid to edit the whispers of Park Lane, so a few weeks ago he imported, at a great price, a Johnny straight from the spot, attired like a morning bridegroom. His cambric spats, Potter, white as your shirt ! The chief wants all the best people to know that Carmelite House was built for them, and not for ostlers and knife-boys, of course . . ."

I didn't hear the rest, but there was a gay pantomime, which I supposed pertained to an accidental interview on the office stairs between the great but unpredictable Harmsworth and the young gentleman from Park Lane. Potter was stiff but polite, though not amused.

" And now I hear," said the story-teller aloud, " that Langham is going to write for us."

" Who is ? " asked Potter, disguising an interest suddenly alert.

" Oh, you know. Langham. The rising hope of your party. The chief seems to think he has found another brilliant genius. Our office is giddy with rising and falling stars."

Potter made no reply. Langham wrote leaders for

his own paper, but that was not to be talked about. In his office, Langham's gift for easy invective and stinging mockery was valued, for their newspaper was working against public favour, which was with the war. Once, when opened pen-knives were hurled at the speakers at a meeting for the making of peace, in Trafalgar Square, and Mr. Balfour had pleaded afterwards for the throwers of knives that they had been asked to bear what human nature had found intolerable, Langham's column had been balm.

Potter lit a cigarette. " Has he joined you yet ? "

" Joined us ? Is it likely. How coarse you are. He will use his great talent for the public good, and hide his light in the pay envelope. You don't suppose—there's old Sprig. We must tell him about our bridegroom."

That was what it was always like, that club. You rarely heard the end of a story. You never went into it, after an absence, without feeling that you would find in it a reassuring word about events which, from the open air, had been as noteworthy as a gathering of little clouds, each already rather larger than a man's hand. You would receive a confidence—with nobody but Bentley to overhear it—that what had taken your doubting eye was, after all, only an arrangement of artful smoke designed for the edification of the general reader, and you were a fool to notice it. The blare of the news of the morning, clarion-like but fatuous, might have been as deplorable as an unholy reveille ;

but what of it ?   You trusted that in your club-house
there would be a confiding nudge, and thus the day
cleared of gathering dubiety.   Nothing there.   Why,
every great city of the world was at the far end of the
wires in our many offices, intelligently observed by a
man we knew.   And then our members, in whatever
quaint form they had published the last words heard in
the night hours, would know what was undivulged
and would be reserving a pleasing wink for a friend.
Those great statesmen who made the speeches which,
according to need, steadied or warned an attentive
nation that knew nothing but what it was told,
understood how to qualify the matter behind closed
doors in Fleet Street, or else their opponents did,
which was just as good.   Yet no ; you never left that
club without wondering whether the story you had
heard was not a serial, to be continued, as though you
had been assured that the children were thoroughly
contented and playful below with their experimental
matches and the gas connections. You left the
place, passing through rooms and along corridors
adorned with humorous cartoons of fellow members,
and those pictures suggested that we valued our daily
part in showing light for the community chiefly for its
drollery, a satisfaction to which we were certainly
entitled, as there was not much else in it for us.

We had a lounge at the back of the premises, an
inner sanctuary, named in honour of Goldsmith.   It
was a chamber for repose. It could have been

thought, of some of us, whose labours were doubtful, or whose writings were still to be, or had ceased, that we were exiled from home, and needed no sleep except what was stolen in the chairs of the club. There then were some of those members grouped round a dying fire, which they contemplated as though they could wait till daybreak if no active person came to replenish it before. There were others who were earnestly explaining, beneath the rose, how all would have been well if unluckily it had not gone ill; and, on a couch, an aged man, with white hair long and pure, was sleeping on his back, composed yet sorrowful as a saint witnessing in a trance the just woes of sinners. He was drunk. By the fireplace a lank young member stood idly reminiscent with an arm resting on the mantelpiece. He was addressing his tumbler, which he held before him while slanting its contents this way and that in languid curiosity at its inconstant behaviour. He gave his monologue to his glass. The men in chairs below him betrayed no sign of attention. They were waiting for someone to put more coal on a dying fire.

"What a game ours is," said the young man contemplatively. "Mixing food for chickens—that's all we do. Mixing food for the silly hens. Do 'em good to put a snake in the mixture now and then. That'd shock the birds. Don't you think so, Beadles?"

The man he named merely pulled at a cascade of

grey moustache, and stirred as though he would get up, but relapsed wearily.

"Of course, it's frightfully amusing at first. I admit I liked it. Sort of learning a new game. Forfeits if you make the right move. The wrong move is the right one. Takes a bit of doing, to get the hang of it. You're sure to slip up sometimes, and do what's right. When I first came into the street, the way the fellas who were used to it did the silly thing as naturally as a kid takes toffee, and scored over me, was awfully worrying. Thought I'd never learn it, never. But after a time you get to know how to use the facts without any rotten sense hanging about them. That's it." He considered this with more exactitude. "Why, there's journalists so jolly good they'd show you Jesus grinning through a horse-collar at the cheerful public."

The aged man snored in his sleep on the couch. Nobody answered the member, aggrieved so early in his career. They had heard something like this before, and not seldom. Members who were young and undisciplined would speak in this strain. For a time the rebel at the mantelshelf continued to slant the liquor in his tumbler, still in distant contemplation of it; then swallowed it, as if to put an end to its nonsense, and waved the empty glass at the man with the grey moustache. Suddenly he became a little gay.

"I say, Beedles, I've got an idea. Jolly good. Why not have a public procession of editors and

proprietors and leader writers every year? What do
you think? Rather like the Lord Mayor's Show.
In tableaux. Arranged high on lorries. Scene
one . . ."

"Don't go into details. We know them."

"Oh, all right. But it's a rattlin' good idea.
Then the jolly old public could see why it gets what it's
supposed to want. Old Perkins of the *Sun*, ferinstans,
with his gooseberry eyes directing the course of
Empire in his shirt-sleeves. Ever seen him after
supper? Beedles, would you trust old Perkins to
choose a white rabbit for the kid's birthday? How'd
he know it was a rabbit? Yet look at my paper any
old day. 'We think the true interests of this great
nation would best be served by the imprisonment of
every traitor who says bo to a goose.' That sort of
thing. Or look at it this morning. 'In our opinion
it would prove disastrous to the Empire, and a
calamity to all friends of the best principles of
democratic government, if the greatest war minister of
our long history were forced to resign because our
cavalry has no horses.'"

"Give it a rest," pleaded Beedles. "What does it
matter?"

"I'm going to give it a rest all right." The
young man grinned.

"Well, you're not the first to get the sack. I'm
sacked twice a year. Whoever pays the piper calls the
tune."

"But O damn," exclaimed the youth in testy vivacity, "how was I to know the news about another British general being ambushed was to be held back? They're always being ambushed, aren't they? Sort of wandering round the African landscape asking for it, killing more of their own men than they do Boers. How's a fella to know we didn't expect 'em to?"

"I don't know. I don't know. I didn't see what you wrote. What was it?"

"Nothing much. I was only a little cheery, that's all. Said no officer and gentleman would expect his enemy to hide behind rocks, waiting to bag a legitimate British battery which was going to give him hell. No fella can tell when his proprietor has a lady friend who knows somebody at the War Office, can he? So I've been encouraging the enemy, and I've been undermining the confidence which is essential to the success of our army in the field. That's me, looking for another job."

Beedles rose sadly, intent upon brushing tobacco crumbs out of the creases in his waistcoat into the fireplace. Then he moved towards the door, and on his way paused with bent grey head, as though a thought had stopped him. He published it over his shoulder. "Serves you right for being so clever. That'll teach you. Leave things alone." He shuffled on round the chairs to the exit, but paused again, looking back. "You can't alter things. There they are.   Leave them alone."

The young member sought our eyes for sympathetic understanding, but most of us were men of experience who confessed the powers and took things as we found them.   We ignored his silent appeal for fellowship. One of us scraped out a pipe.   Others still considered the ashes on the hearth.   He put down his empty glass gently and humbly, and declined into a chair, covering his eyes with one hand, perhaps the better to memorise in silence another hard lesson of his craft.

In the wake of Beedles, I was leaving a room in which the luck of the journalist in the chaos of chance had been too starkly revealed.   No repose there.   It was unmannerly, for another member, so late in the evening too, to show us that what we had mistaken for the chairs of our professional ease were really adrift in the dark, and nobody cared tuppence whither.   One might just as well be in the heedless confusion of the office, at its midnight crisis.   But I was beckoned to from a corner of the room.   That hand so cheerfully waved stayed me.   It motioned the confusion of night firmly to a settlement.   I did not know Maynard was in town.   In that moment, as I saw who was there in the corner, I remembered that the Plutonian shore is itself but a relative bogy of the soul.   The chance of chaos, whether fortunate or not, depends a good deal on companionship.   One could push off with Charon, if Jim Maynard were coming along.

"I thought you were in Paris or Tunis or somewhere, trying to learn why the French are so French ? ''

He showed no interest in his recent travel.   He was looking at a man with him, and slowly squeezed my arm to impress me with what he had to say.   Another of those hopeful fellows without experience he was always fostering, no doubt.

" Here is someone you will have to know.   This is Charley Bolt.''

I apologised.   Because of Maynard I had not been observant.   Bolt was pleased to be with us, in the centre of it at last, but embarrassed, as if he thought it was too soon to show himself in that privileged house.

" So you know him ?   That's all right.   I warned him what our street is like, but he would come.   You must keep an eye on him.''

Bolt whispered to us that, after what he had heard, he felt like a child who had eavesdropped on high freemasonry.

We gave him some advice.   " High nothing. Don't take any notice of them.''

We explained that we were really a simple-minded crowd, who knew little except the rules of our own game.   " Sometimes,'' said Maynard, " we'll make you think that commonsense is silly.   But keep straight on.''   The sanctities were profaned for Bolt's benefit.   " Never shock an editor by letting him see you've noticed he is standing on his head.   He knows he is, but it worries him when he is sure that somebody has spotted that though solemn he is upside down.''

Maynard, whenever he joined us in the field, late but elusive, not in need of our advice, but presently to be observed by his sophisticated rivals, in Paris, or on a Welsh coalfield, or when there was trouble in Dublin—or wherever a storm petrel presaged the usual likelihood—was a sign of danger to us, though it would have surprised him had he known it. What had been learned or was guessed, we wondered then, that our eyes had missed? We imagined a fact was there undiscovered by us, and of more than common significance. As a rule, however, it was but Maynard himself. His physical evasiveness, for in threatening circumstances he appeared effeminate and likely to be whisked away by the rude elements, did not deceive us now; though there had been a time when his apparent fragility, and the nervous reticence we mistook for indecision, appeared somewhat comic when seen beside our robust appreciation of life's hard realities. His lasting delicacy still surprised, but was no longer amusing. We had learned that even energy and sound experience may be overtaken and passed, as it were in the flicker of a thought, by a quality in Maynard which some of us were reluctant to define. I suppose it distressed us to confess the superiority of cool discernment over worldly cunning when most industrious; and even when he wrote little, though the spectacle we had witnessed had compelled us to columnar eloquence, yet we were never sure that we had beaten him; it was possible that he had seen through it, and was unmoved by what had caused rapture in us. And that, I think, was a more severe remonstrance, when we thought it over, than his manifest successes. But to his friends, who were mostly younger men uncertain of their bearings, his presence was refuge and an assurance of sympathy at need, though he was as unconscious of it as was that rock of the shadow it afforded in a weary land. His demeanour and complexion were the same, whether the day were wild, or had the tranquil light of holiday upon it. The trace of a smile at his lady-like lips was constant, and some of us thought it was the permanent cast of his good nature, and the foolish were wary of it, in spite of his friendly way, because it could have been of ironic understanding, which chose not to speak.

My conscience began to be more insistent about a return to my editorial room. I made to go, but stayed to tell Maynard that we had been wondering why his journal had not sent him to South Africa. That was the place for him. The bright morning-paper stars were rising thickly there, and they sang together of war, in music, with everybody's approval, that was known as prose-poetry.

" Well, the chief has broached it. I wasn't expecting it, for I'm not a senior. But I'm afraid I couldn't do it. I'm not sure that he would want the stuff when he got it, though he thinks he would, and the generals might not let him have it, in any case."

" They might not."

" I should like to go, but it looks as though one could see the business better from a Boer commando, and that cannot be done."

" Not by no means."

" Not at all. Can't do anything now, as far as I know, but stand by and see whether the fire will burn out, or burn on."

" Burn how ? " I sat down again. " Maynard, when I saw you in the corner just now it cheered me up. Now you're spoiling your pretty face. And you just back from a holiday on the sunny continent and all, while I've been doing murders and politics. It isn't fair. Burn on ? "

" I know. But on the sunny continent they're rather jealous of their sun. Though they can be affable, even in Paris, when our troops are out of luck. They're sure to tell you that, very brightly, in case you may have missed it. Perfect strangers will be ever so friendly then."

Bolt suggested that that was only part of the game.

" I suppose it is."

" And we oughtn't to be surprised by what is perfectly human."

" No, we oughtn't, but we often are, though we shouldn't lose ourselves in sentiment over the Parisians. I was in Paris only this morning. Somehow I've come away with the feeling that they're pretty hard and sharp—as much as a clever lady who has had her day yet missed a lot. I'm afraid they understand other people no better than she does. They're as likely to be as kind. That's what gives the edge to their wit, their Latin wit."

Bolt actually flushed. "Here, I say, that's too bad. Whatever becomes of your little tribute—you gave it to me yourself—to what the French artists are doing? It's right out of tune."

" I'm afraid it does sound rather like it, doesn't it? It isn't very gracious. But we go on learning after we've been cocksure."

" What a holiday! Rained all the time."

" No it didn't. Nothing so conclusive. It was only draughty. The wind was on the chilly side—not only in Paris, either. Vienna and Berlin weren't what you could call warm. But Paris—no doubt about it there—a nasty blast that shot round and got your back as soon as you thought you were sheltered and sat down anywhere. The French certainly have that to their credit. They're more candid, and don't care how you feel."

" That's a touch of winter sunshine, anyhow— something to their credit."

" Quite bright, as far as it goes, isn't it? " Maynard's cheerfulness was an imitation of a wintry gleam. " I know how you want to feel. So do I. We can be as much at home in Chartres and Amiens as anywhere. It's our place. But few Frenchmen would believe that, unless they wanted to, for a reason they were keeping back. Their own point of view exists, but no other is valid. Any suspicion they have about you becomes a fact rather soon, and their famous logic does the rest."

Our pretence to dismay stopped him, and he gave us a chance to hit back, but we were not ready for him. " . . . so you can guess," he assured us, with real geniality, " what is likely to happen when their argument begins at touchiness and fear."

Bolt and I thumped on the table, and a brass ash-tray danced noisily to drown the chance of a logical inference which nobody would wish to hear just before bed-time. The last expression of Latin culture was not to be dismissed thus summarily in a London club after supper. I rang the bell for a waiter. What had become of Maynard's liberal sympathy ?

" It looks as though you were sickening for something, old lad."

" It's only nerves, very likely. Not a good time to be across the Channel. I shall be all right in a minute. This morning they were discussing . . . but you haven't heard of the Jackson case ? "

" No, not that one."

" It goes like this. Jackson is a British naval officer. He fishes. He was on a holiday on the coast of Brittany. One morning he was caught digging in the sands for bait. Would a naval officer dig for worms ? Impossible. Undermining a forti-fication, or trying to make a Channel tunnel on the quiet, as likely as not. So they put him in prison, with the worms in evidence. This morning they were wagging fingers at each other's noses in the cafés, looking very artful, and there's despatches passing solemnly between Whitehall and Paris on what lessons are to be drawn from a can of naval fish-bait."

A friendly member, who was reading near our table, raised his head and spoke over the back of his chair with some chuckling enjoyment.

" You think that bait infectious ? I shouldn't worry over a pot of worms. Worms can't cause international complications, that I know of."

Maynard did not like it. He even dismissed the waiter. He and Bolt left the place with me. " I don't know," he said, going out. " It's only a silly joke, of course. It's nothing. No need to bother about it, and we won't. But that's it. When people are looking for trouble, and I thought across the water they were looking for not much else, perhaps it's because they're afraid of trouble, and want to get it off their minds by starting it."

THE occasion at Lady Carroll's place must have been a few nights later. I had to meet Langham at the House, and went on with him. His company was sheltering. He knew these people. I imagined he was on easy terms with them. As for me, I remember that night well enough because I first saw then some men whose names were so notable and whose opinions were such valued currency, that to me they had been as the shadows of an Olympian drama working to an unknown crisis far removed from the life most of us know; yet all they did beyond the clouds and in the heights was of immediate concern to the lower slopes and the plains. If those men were as mythical as the powers which irradiate and gloom the legends, god-like presences which never appear except to the favoured, yet they had to be assumed by the lowly, just as superstitiously we never dare to deny the destiny which shapes our ends, high destiny that is deaf and blind to all our desires and propitiations. That night I saw some of them.

We were late. There were exterior indications of exclusiveness, of an event of hidden consequence, and then we found ourselves just within a spacious apartment where crystal candelabra were remarkable amid sombre walls of mellowed oak.   It was a sedative chamber.   To me it appeared to be immune from the changes of time.   There was a Rembrandt portrait, on the opposite wall, and that may have caused the illusion.   It suggested a face dimly peering from a time beyond the room, overlooking the assembly through a gilded port in the dark panelling.   That distinguished   stranger   watched   us.   We   were transient; and a morning, when we should not be there, would follow our great day.   That would not matter, for he would see others of a like kind at home in that chamber, and maintaining the right tradition, which was continuous from age to age.

I left our movements to Langham.   Where we then stood sufficed me.   I could see and hear all I wanted to know.   Langham was used to these people, and yet I thought he hesitated so long, content with the show of the animated company, that maybe his occasional dry aside was a measure of defence against the influence of the room, which opposed him. These people were not friendly to his politics.   The conversation was the undertone of a tide lightly confident with its usual control, for now and then a laugh broke in it. He may have felt excluded, as I did myself, although we were suffered to observe thus closely.   I had not sufficient assurance to make my way to our hostess through the groups, which had become established and intimate.

I drew Langham's attention—it passed the time—to the nearest candelabrum, a limpid shower of water drops falling from the ceiling but congealed and suspended; light was caught in it.

He was briefly attentive. "That's something new. Good, isn't it? Diana's choice, of course. Where did she get that? She knows what's good."

His interest left it, and he glanced round in easy cynicism. What did I suppose, he could have been saying, that money could not buy? Look at it. Furniture as ripe as old wine, tapestries, pictures—his inspection checked at Lady Carroll, though delight was there which hinted at something beyond the power even of money. She had not observed us. She was engaged, the delicate heart of a group of eager men; a seductive young matron, her understanding eyes as gracious as her smile, which could have been guarding, perhaps, the remembrance of past fun, for naturally she would wish the right people to know she was a kindred spirit.

"Just look at old Bucktrout with Diana. You've heard of him. Great name in the Zulu War, wasn't it? The old general feels no more than thirty to-night. Quite freshened up. And young Bingley —no, not that one, the next fellow, with the hair arranged like a neat sunset—that's Bingley the poet. He says he's one. Even Bingley knows, without being told, that Diana doesn't class poets with Carroll. They're different. And Harmsworth, too. But I'd

like to know what he's doing here. Thought he
didn't visit. Trust his hostess, though. She knows
who is likely to count."

Sir William came to us. This was the eminent
Carroll, owner of the line of ships with a name as
familiar as Leadenhall Street. This was the man who
kept so many of the chimneys smoking continuously
in Dockland. He came up to us, pert and quick, and
the tails of his coat flicked with a sparrow's jauntiness.
A little man, his long visage as rigid and inscrutable as
a carving in grey wood; you might notice him if he
brought round the plate in church. His blue eyes
were cold enough to survive the warmth of any sun,
and never melt in it. They were as shiny as ice when
he greeted Langham—he nodded to me to acknowledge
I was seen—but their lids became sleepy to Langham's
carefully comic relation of the night's business in the
House, and screwed a little whimsically, his face
averted, to show Langham that the humour of some of
his better points was appreciated. Then his look was
direct and frozen again.

" Diana is over there." He nodded to a far corner.
" She was asking if you were here."

He was quickly away, his coat tails ridiculously like
jauntiness.

The tall figure beside me, with its pale brow on
which curved the light romance of a careless lock,
muttered something. Repelling Carroll in his mind,
very likely, mocking the coat-tails to disenchant the

known power of the ship owner and the glint of his hard and silent mind. Surrender to these people, I had no doubt, was easy, unless you used incantations. Langham knew I had caught him in a loose moment.

" The mistake you journalists make is in seeing things so simply. They're not so simple as you'd think. Look at this room. And there's Carroll. Even his ships don't have to work to make money. It's just as good if the Admiralty forgets a fleet of your transports and leaves it in dock. But don't tell Carroll I said so. He's not supposed to know it himself."

That was better. Langham had disparaged the qualities for the making of the means to power and a place like that. We were encouraged, as we waited there. Perhaps these people were not so formidable. " He's not supposed to know it himself." It was as easy as that.

Lady Carroll saw us. Her invitation reduced the intervening guests to shadows. With sweet malice, or childish innocence—it was not easy to tell which— she broke the news to the old general that this was Langham. The soldier glared. What, what, said his raised eyebrows. But it was not hard for her thus to admit her friendship with the clever young Radical, for he had the danger signals of intelligence, and his protective wit could move with surprising speed, if he knew of the approval of the proper observers. Her gentle malice amused him now. That would prick old

Bucktrout.   It had, too.   The sudden congestion of
the soldier's rosy complexion made his eyebrows and
moustache quite creamy.   The general had been
talkative, leaning forward with clasped hands.   Now
he sat up, crossed his legs, and was noticeably a
personage.   His eyebrows had become fierce, and
were warily at manœuvres.   He spoke with deliberate
enunciation, as if calmly considering the field.

" Were you at the Tournament to-day ? "

Lady Carroll shook her head apologetically.   The
soldier could see she meant she ought to have been at
the military display.

" I fancied the Prince looked rather worn," the
veteran told us, with solemnity.   " It was noticeable
that he had difficulty in getting his breath, when he
rose to speak."

Someone made a suggestion.   Uniform too tight ?
Too many cigars and a heart past its best ?

" Eh, what's that ?   What's that ? " demanded
Bucktrout.   An enemy's trick ?   But he was not sure
of the questioning young man.   Perhaps he was a
doctor.

" Yet his mother is still with us.   Wonderful
woman, wonderful woman," the old soldier went
on.   " Wonderful.   We adored her at the Great
Exhibition, every soldier in the company.   All
that time ago.   And we still have her with us.
It's a great privilege.   I have always said we
should have got this war over years ago.

Scandalous to have to do it in her old age."

" It is," agreed Lady Carroll, kindly, " isn't it ? "

We waited for him to continue. Harmsworth sat in thought, sideways, his head tilted back with the support of a bent arm, a hand to his brow. He looked solid, a little arrogantly apart, and so obviously a caricature of Napoleon that his pose would have been amusing except that its force was not an imitation.

" Ah, forgive me, dear lady," pleaded the general. " I see your husband is free at last. I have something to tell him. I really must go."

Her ladyship was gentle, the next moment, with Harmsworth.

" There ! You see ? That's the kind of man your projects of conquest depend on. Do you feel so certain ? "

Harmsworth showed no anxiety. He regarded with a bull stare and a contemptuous under lip the aged soldier, whose legs could not forget jack boots, stiffly stumping away. He dismissed him. The general ceased to exist. I felt then some contrition for my light regard of that haughty old figure, unaware that it was obsolete.

" They can be made and broken as required," he said indifferently.

" Ah, you have yet to know our War Office," she warned him.

He made a careless gesture with his hand to remove

any slight difficulty there might be in the abolition of great but useless generals.

" Oh, do, please, let us talk of things that are lovely and of nice report," pleaded Bingley. " It's all bandages now. And remounts. Whatever are re- mounts ? And shrapnel. Shrapnel is such a very horrid word, dear lady, don't you think so ? Say yes. Let our talk be without any shrapnel."

" I thought I saw you at Ysaye's recital," said his hostess.

" Now that is so good of you," said Bingley. " How I should like to say you did ! I can only say I was going, though that isn't true, but fell to temptation. I must tell you. I went to the Moore and Burgese fun instead. The clinking of spurs has made me very very depressed." Then he looked up and groaned. " And here they are to clink some more. There's no escape. Here is Maslin—the very War Office itself."

Maslin stood over him and patted his shoulder consolingly. It was surprising to see a monocle remain as firmly as though it were born in his eye, for his face was smooth and acute.

" I heard you "—he was still patting Bingley's shoulder—" asking a poet whether he had been listening to another artist. As if he would give away his admiration to somebody else ! And what are you doing here, Langham ? You should be at your duty. The House is still sitting."

" Let it sit." Langham was reclining gracefully,

with a slight emphasis on being at his ease. He tried
to provoke the newcomer.

"When I left it," Langham added, "your great
leader Balfour was up, but I waited long enough to
hear all I needed of his idea—a Cecil's idea—of the
way the working-classes should be housed. I came
away when I remembered he wouldn't know what a
cradle was, unless he were told."

Langham made little rhetorical movements with a
soft white hand, very effectively. Ideas and words
came freely to him, and he was not too scrupulous of
the use he made of them, for he was a good con-
versationalist. Now he was off. He had the audience
which would listen to him, and he was enjoying the
fun of it.

"Come along, Maslin. Own up. Don't you
think, when the subject is the slums—which you
know so well—that Balfour would learn something of
the foundations of belief if he had to eat his breakfast
kippers in his bedroom? Yes, I know, I know.
I'm in love with Balfour, too. He's a fascinating
improvisor—so gentlemanly and persuasive that his
poor but honest audience never knows his contempt for
it. But of course he can't help it. We must give him his
due. As a Cecil, he naturally would regard the mob as
an insanitary nuisance to be carefully supervised as one
of the penalties of a gentleman's existence. Amicably,
of course. With charm and tact. The beastly mob
is so large and uncertain, don't you think so?"

Langham retained his smile while waiting for an answer, and swept the vagrant lock off his forehead.

Maslin dropped his eye-glass. "Certainly I do. So do you. It's not an easy job either, to keep the mob from destroying itself. If you don't think so, ask the director of the *Daily Mail*. We have to do the multitude good by stealth. As it was from the beginning, beer and circuses. They've got a fascinating circus now, and if you suppose it has lowered the circulation of popular print, here is someone you can ask about it, to make sure. It's no good talking to me, Langham. What we have to do is to give everybody something to think about, something that excites but won't hurt. Then the best people can keep the best positions, and that's the right place for them."

"Suppose that some of us blow the gaff?"

"What frightful taste. How vulgar," exclaimed Bingley. "That's like kicking over the strawberries and cream. And on the lawn. And all the ladies present. It's simply too ghastly to think of. You couldn't do it."

"What's worse, Hoxton doesn't buy poetry," added Maslin, "and never will."

Harmsworth showed signs of tedium. He was curt with Maslin. "Any word through about Mafeking?"

"Not yet."

"Do you think there's a chance our generals by now have tumbled to the fact that the Boer lout can ride and shoot?" asked Langham.

" They're no worse than the statesmen in that, I can promise you." Maslin fixed his eye-glass firmly. " Not a member of the cabinet knew what a remount was till the Boers were riding round and round our cavalry."

" How very queer," said Bingley.   " Are remounts faster than horses ? "

" I suppose we're free to hope that the War Office has been cured of its pride by bullets and typhoid ? " questioned Lady Carroll.   " I have two brothers out there, and I really should like to be sure of it."

" Heaven protect them," said Langham.   " Every war is different from the one for which the experts prepare.   The war the generals always get ready for is the previous war."

At that Harmsworth swerved round to face him. " What do you mean ? " he asked, as though it were an idea strangely new and attractive to him.

Langham outlined a few elementary lessons from history, while the great journalist was in the attitude of alert attention which an energetic man rightly gives to a novel opinion.   Even Langham could not altogether disguise, on the instant, the shock of his surprise that copy-book notions should require an explanation.

Harmsworth listened, but made no comment. Perhaps he was secretly reserving these useful hints for later use.   He continued to be silent and stern.

" I think it's a pity the men have to die while

their generals are learning their business," sighed Lady Carroll.

Maslin and Langham engaged playfully over that. Maslin would have assured her that soldiering is a science, subject, like astronomy, to the compensations of new discoveries, but Langham was gay about the science of it. Sir William joined us, and listened to the evidence of the high cost which youth must pay in war for the practical schooling of its leaders, and the proofs of the inevitable necessity for this, as though it concerned the problem of the rate of exchange, a mystery only the elect may understand. Harmsworth fidgeted with impatience.

" All this is softening rubbish," he snapped. " We must go on with it. We're talking too much. There is work to be done. The worst effect of war," he said, with grim wisdom, " is to reduce the surplus population."

Nobody answered him. Langham gleamed wickedly, but he, too, was dumb ; he even forgot not to seem happy, though his amusement had faded to a fixed and silly grin. We made weak efforts to come nearer to midnight in a light humour; there was gossip of likely though comic preferments and promotions, and frivolity over a contract scandal that was blatant in its design, yet was so easily a successful stratagem combined of sex, greed, and the military art. But all was useless before the seriousness of Harmsworth, who had the future to think about and the good of the commonwealth. A pause was lengthening upon us again, and a word was needed to shorten it, however trivial. Sir William cleared his throat.

"I have been told," he murmured casually, "that Germany has decided to increase its home fleet."

He excited no curiosity. My attention was entangled in the prisms of a chandelier. Langham made a futile effort to quicken a dying conversation.

"Has she?" he said. "That ought to help our Admiralty. A little fast bowling from the Kaiser will keep the game alive."

At Maynard's rooms in Clifford's Inn I was told he was absent on an unknown mission. His rooms indeed were twilight with a long absence. It occurred to me, on the landing of his place, that I had taken nothing out of Jones's tobacco jars, nor had seen Talbot, for some time. Our various occasions were separating us beyond hail. Langham, in the wide sweep of the world's affairs, now rarely and inconspicuously disturbed the distant horizon with his subversive political activities ; yet sometimes there could be no doubt about his light but anonymous touch, soothing to sensitive national honour, in the *Mail*.

What can be made of those flat periods in history in which nothing happened ? Nothing. Who but Harmsworth and a few others would look even for news of the brilliant Langham in the *Mail* ? So history must be unlike life, because men and women continue to live through dull periods though apparently nothing comes of all they do. The empty spread of many days, in which nothing moves and nothing happens, while meanwhile we scheme in secret our own welfare and do what we can to provide surprises for our enemies, is a sterile prospect for the historian. He cannot see anything there. For that matter, nobody knows what begins an earthquake. There immediately it is. One minute you are still satisfied with the comfortable establishment of your foothold, and the next you see the familiar landmarks are off for a run. You have not time even to ponder whether things can ever be the same again.

In the Strand, by Wellington Street, compelled by that foolish habit of a townsman who is always hopeful of entertaining events and anticipates the next good thing, I paused to get the latest evening paper. But the disconsolate vendor had nothing but a placard, which he was still displaying, freely publishing all he knew to anyone that passed. The placard announced " LATEST CRICKET SCORES."

That was all. News of cricket, if the truth could be bought at that late hour of the evening, was the last and best word to be got in London ; but just then I was not waiting for glad tidings from Kennington Oval. Anyhow, whatever were the cricket scores, such news was comforting, and much to be preferred to the tension of nothing. Humanity had its thoughts on play and was innocently occupied.

Uncertain what to do next I looked towards the Lyceum Theatre. Eleanora Duse was there that evening, and " La Princesse Georges," but then it was too late to go in. The familiar colonnade was filled with light, but it was deserted, for the performance could hardly have reached its climax.

Better go home ?   London is one of earth's most desolate wildernesses, where one may wander for days and not meet a fellow creature.   While I was considering a way of escape from solitude, two elderly gentlemen approached each other within the glamour of the theatre's classical portico, stopped and heartily shook hands—I happened to be looking that way—then flourished exultingly their silk hats while they showed their joy, and fell into each other's arms lusciously.

Was this true ?   I woke up and watched, to be sure of it.   On the broad back turned towards me a chimney-pot hat rose and fell with gentle regularity, tapping the back in leisurely affection.

Unusual.   I had a suspicion that the people about me were suddenly quicker.   There were more people. There was a stir in the street.   There was shouting in the distance, but nothing I could see to cause it ; and while I was still looking for whatever was the matter an impulsive lady took me by the arm, shook me fervidly, with an invitation to come and enjoy myself. " Now we shan't be long," she cried.   But I could not respond until I knew more.

A voice began chattering near excitedly.   " A cab —Reggie—a cab—where is one ?   Isn't there one ? Oh, how perfectly lovely it was.   Aren't you glad you came ?   Did you hear what Signora Duse said just before—when she was telling that fellow to look for his wife's lover ? ' Cerca,' she said. Then Comyns Carr walked on. I was sure something good had happened, weren't you ? ' Mafeking,' he said. I can't stand here. Where is a cab ? I shall go mad if I stand still. I must dance."

There were many cabs, but they were full. A hansom idled by then. A sailor reclined on its roof, singing, while within it a soldier and his lass leaned against each other, and sang. There was a fleet of cabs and omnibuses, but they all appeared to be fixed as islands in a slow stream. Somehow, from somewhere, the Strand had filled with a tide of Londoners, a tide conjured to the full by a word.

Mafeking ! But where was the place ? I tried in vain to recall where in South Africa that village was ; though it is not much good seeking the cause of a flood when the dam has burst ; it might have begun, unobserved, at a rat-hole. And as to Mafeking, its intrinsic importance was of no account. Nobody cared where and what it was. My very ignorance gave me my rightful place with the populace that was filling the capital with a pæan of triumph.

Victory ! Rockets curved in the darkness south of the river, and hung in clusters of falling stars. The very sky had caught fire. It was alight and falling. It was joining in.

We all went westward at the pace of the Bacchantes, who are never in much of a hurry to get anywhere, for

K

there they are. What more could a man want?
Some of them, a row of them laughing on a balcony
above us, cheered us on by waving towels over us, by
waving table-cloths, by waving anything, by flaunting
garments never seen except on clothes-lines. The
happy procession in the street shouted its sympathy.
There flew the signals of complete and unquestionable
fellowship. We were one body this night, with no
reserves. *Te Deum* has many voices.

A thin and venerable man shuffled beside me, his
eyes on futurity, and blattered ecstatic fanfares on a
penny trumpet. Perhaps he was Silenus himself,
impoverished under an orderly government which had
been orderly too long. But he had rebelled at last,
and the derisive abandon of his challenge woke in us
the old animation of the groves. And we had to make
up, too, for what we had lost in several thousand
years of polish. Human nature is friendly at bottom,
and responds without formality to what in secret it has
always known to be right, however dutiful it may be,
as a rule, to properly constituted authority. Embraces
were freely given. The ridiculous evasions were
forgotten. We flowed together as naturally as if Pan
had never died. What need have the instincts for
school? They know what to do when, in an expansion
of intuition, the bounds set by politeness are passed and
we are at large. A bare word had released us, and at
once we had abilities we did not know were ours.

Just ahead was an omnibus. It rose above a

confused sea of heads, because men had borrowed for
Carnival millinery from the women, and the women
were otherwise in the bowler hats of hard re-
spectability worn askew. The abandoned noise of
the flood of them mocked ancient landmarks. The
upper deck of the bus was brisk with a crew of girls—
they had boarded it in an assault of piracy bearing
Union Jacks—and their extravagant antics would
have made us on a day of plain duty wonder whether
their freedom would carry them overboard. We did
not worry. Nothing could hurt us any more. The
lesser gods were piping us, and they are more liberal
than God, for instinct tells us that the jolly immortals
give their cherubs charge over care-free limbs which
fling beyond the niggardness of steps that are
measured.

Piccadilly Circus was the volcanic crater of London.
The converging channels poured suppressed fire from
the subterranean city to its crater, and you could
seethe there in the exultant outpouring of a capital's
joy ; though, once the vortex had got you, there was
no escape. There were no citizens. There was a
flux of elemental stuff, roaring and molten, of a weight
and heat to consume a reluctant thought in a spark,
and to burn and bury, if it overflowed, what the
labour of centuries had built. Round the multitude
stood the walls of the crater, echoing the roaring,
lurid with reflections and shifting lights.

I turned aside and struggled east. I had a sudden

desire for an East End bookseller and whatever little company was certain to have gone to him in escape from the eruption. His serenity and his tobacco might do something to reduce the full glare of triumph, and cold daylight, later, would put out the night fires.

It was long after midnight when I neared his place, but the streets were still lively. Under a lamp, as I turned for his shop, a gang of urchins had their heads bent eagerly over a matter of interest in the midst of them. They looked up at my footsteps, and one of them tucked under his arm a bulging object which might have been one of the ancient jars of Jones's unique solace, but such unlikely coincidences are rarely worthy of attention in the street.

The bookseller's shop was open, yet it was in darkness. I tripped over one of its shutters, which was lying on the pavement. The shop had no windows. It was cavernous. The windows had gone. I went in and lit a match, but hesitated at a litter of broken glass, periodicals, and books scattered at my feet. There was only silence beyond.

" Now, anything you want ? " The demand was behind me.

I turned. A policeman was there, and the light of his lantern struck my waistcoat.

" Jones," I said. " I want Jones."

" Not here," he said.

" What's all this—what's happened ? "

" Dunno," said the policeman. " All over in no

time. They took him for a pro-Boer, I suppose, and there you are. Friend of his ? "

We went in, wading through the wreckage. The policeman's bull's-eye traversed the room beyond, and its round of light paused on a tobacco jar broken on the floor, but empty.

" There you are," said the constable. " Nothing here. They've made a proper job of it."

At the vicarage across the road the housekeeper let me in. Mrs. Brown wiped her mouth nervously on the corner of her apron. She showed some haste to shut the door.

Mr. Talbot was away. No, she wasn't sure when he would be back. She thought it was him when I knocked. Expecting him any time. To-morrow perhaps, or Sunday ; sure to be there for Sunday.

Well, it was to-morrow already. Mrs. Brown kept the corner of her apron ready at her mouth, but gave no other sign that the evening had been other than calm ; for she had buried two husbands—as she always said in apology for her indifference to unhappy events—and was stout, placid and slow. " I've had my time," she would explain.

" I'm surprised to find you up, Mrs. Brown."

" No good goin' to bed sir, not knowin' what'd happen next. And I bin waitin' for Mr. Talbot. I thought these goin's on would bring 'im sooner."

" What happened across the way ? "

" A nice thing. Parcel of louts, the brutes. They've smashed up poor old Jones's place."

" So I see, but where is he ? "

" ' E's gone, sir. Went away with Mr. Bolt. Lucky thing for him Mr. Bolt was passin'. But they'd done their worst. 'E come up when the crowd was at it. Took orf to 'orspital, one of 'em. That Mr. Bolt, 'e's strong. I could 'ear the wallops from this very 'ouse. Turned me cold. 'E got poor old Jones out of it. 'E didn't want to go, I must say. Mr. Bolt 'ad to bustle 'im orf. No 'at, no coat."

" I shouldn't have thought young Bolt could have managed it."

" Oh no, sir. It was his father."

So that was it. The experienced shipwright would have managed it with pleasure, quite well.

" Well, Mrs. Brown, if you don't object, I'll rest in the vicar's study till daylight doth appear."

" Do, sir. I'm sure he won't mind."

Not a bit. Talbot, when I could tell him of the celebration, listened as though he had heard something like it before. With his hands behind him, he inspected the backs of his books, here and there idly touching their ranks into uniformity ; or he turned to me in abstraction, while weighing a volume in his hand, and fixed me with a glance under his whitish eyelashes—which made you think they steadied his inspection into instant comprehension—as though politely he were not altogether withholding his attention from my tale.

He turned again to his shelves, fiddling with a

volume. When he spoke I could have supposed he was reading something inscribed on the back of it.

"Did you notice what the *Times* told us this morning? It judged that whatever the reason for last night's pandemonium may have been, we haven't come to the last of it. I don't know quite what we may have to look forward to, and the *Times* didn't say. Didn't know, very likely. But there may be something in it, one way and another."

He sat down at his table and took up an ivory paper knife.

"There's a woman been to see me, for one thing— did you hear her in the next room? You couldn't help it. Well, there's a girl she calls 'her Betty.' I don't know her. Her name is Whittaker. One of my curates knows her, though. Have you met young Langham? He kept Betty out all night. He has confessed as much to me, in great distress. Quite sure his soul is ruined. And what shall he do without one?"

It was useless to ask a layman what a priest could do when so deprived. Why, I hardly dared to look, when I left Talbot, at the gap and ruin of Jones's sanctuary opposite, which was my own loss. And that Sunday, because Jim Maynard wished to learn with what wisdom Scott Holland, the Socialist canon, would enlighten us, the two of us went to St. Paul's. Maynard's attention, I thought, wandered from the eloquence of the sermon. Then, under the dome of London's cathedral, we both stood respectfully, unable to leave till the end of the service, for the cathedral was full. We were both fixed by the solemnity of the heart-felt praise of our massed fellow citizens, who sang, " Now thank we all our God."

PART TWO

THE YEAR
1908

PART TWO

CHAPTER I

THE Chinese boy came into the ship's cabin, no more than a wraith. He slid a tray which in his hands was without substance upon the clothes chest beside the bunk. Maynard was asleep. The steamer was at anchor; she was as silent as the dawn.

The boy regarded the sleeping passenger gravely, and made to leave, but hesitated. The order had been to wake him, but that was dangerous; for his spirit was absent and might be caught inattentive at a distance and have no time to return to the body. Yet these white men were easily angered and were fools. The boy gently tinkled a glass beside the bunk. Maynard sat up abruptly to answer the familiar banal summons to the office. He frowned at the Chinaman as at something puzzling and unexpected. It was not easy to accept that foreign mask at once in substitute for the telephone one heard in a dream. Then he sank back at ease. It was all right. Finished with London!

But had he? No mistake about it? Maynard smiled at the absurdity of it—for an instant he had

147

lived in two places far apart. He did not know for
certain when first awake that there the Chinese face
was, and that the London telephone bell never
rang.

That was going to be the trouble. He was not
sufficiently lost to London yet. Not far enough away;
no more than on the boundary where the things of
two worlds could be confused. You want more than
time and distance to make some things sure. To be
sure of some things you have to be where a telephone
bell cannot ring, even in a dream. That was still a
long way to go.

His eyes roved the cabin approvingly. They
assured him, now he was wide awake, that solidly he
was in another sphere. That tea was in a queer pot,
but it smelt good. He thought about that smell.
His nose was definitely in a new world, and was
curious all the time, even when his thoughts were as
far away as All Saints' Vicarage with Talbot. His
nose presently would bring back his thoughts. Then
his eyes would begin to see where he was. Europe
went below the horizon. It was put out of sight
and out of hearing, and became of no consequence.
It was not his place any more. He had done well to
end it.

Europe, the way it was going, would hardly bear
thinking about. There had been nights at home when
the thought of the huge slow drift of the mindless
crowd the wrong way was horrifying. You wanted

to go out and stop it.   No good.   Nothing could be
done for it.   It was an irresistible drift.   If the
Twelve Apostles had come down in a hurry to head
it another way the police would have run them in.
Christ Himself would have been forced to walk all
the way to Siberia to dig salt for the Czar.   There
was nothing to be done but to edge out of it all.
That serene and happy confidence of everybody in
steel and force !   And nowadays you could not escape
from the general confusion into a shrine, and shut
out telegrams and success with Ave Marias.   It was
too late for that.   And it was no good Buddha trying
to make out you could put your mind clear through
banking houses and editorial rooms because they were
only shadows after all.   He ought to have tried it.
Buddha had never slept on the Thames Embankment
on a cold night with nothing much between his belly
and the east wind but an old newspaper.   London
veritably was there.   Its bleak face was still as
palæolithic as a flint axe.   When its flowing electric
trams chanted the brilliant progress of science to a
homeless man on a wet night, science was merely
bluffing.   Better coconuts and plain savages than
Gothic cathedrals in the midst of iron foundries and
artillery barracks.   Better to start again !

Still, Talbot was over there.   Yes. Talbot was a
doubt.   That man wouldn't leave it.   He had said,
that last night in his study, fidgeting with his old
paper knife, that there could be no escape, that

the weird must be dreed.

Must? Well, he for one wasn't going to dree it. It was not his weird.

The portlight beside Maynard, a round of neutral light, slowly lifted a foot. It brought into view a low coast he had not known was there. In the indifference of dawn that coast seemed not only uninhabited but in an age before the advent of man, hardly created yet out of original night. There was a straight line of gloom where the burnish of the smooth sea ended, and beyond the gloom soared a high mass of coloured vapours, lilac and rose. Those summits of cloudland were looking straight at the coming sun. They knew where the sun was. They could see it. It was going to be a clean sun, too, not smothered by smoke and the reek of ancient errors. Here it had not lost heart. It was still at the task of the first days. Very likely this was no more than the seventh day. All was very early. Perhaps those summits were not clouds. Perhaps they were mountains, and not yet in their final form, but illuminated from within by the glow which was shaping them. Maynard gazed at the tinted heights. Clouds or mountains? It was not easy to declare which was dream and which reality. But the dream was first. It shaped the reality. Its colours were celestial, and the mountains were put in their places as you watched.

The round of the port sank to neutrality again.

Maynard allowed the slow roll of the steamer to have
its way with him. He saw it was useless to try to
confirm whatever a magic casement disclosed. If
you were favoured with a peep, that was enough.
You couldn't prove it. One thing at a time; and
even then only very clever people could be sure they
knew all about it. No need to be curious over what
is good, anyhow. The good could take care of itself.

The grey portlight changed to turquoise. A black
frigate bird drifted across the bright round beside
him, without a movement of its prodigious pinions,
effortless as a shape fixed by the tension of the sunrise.
Life was in that world outside, a new life. The men
began to sluice the deck. That sounded slow and cool.

This might be another beginning. How are you
to know when you are born again? At least, here
was another door, a fair entrance, and to another
order of things. It was certain that not a jolt from
Europe could interrupt the rhythm which poised that
sea-bird aloft as a shape of effortless peace. Perhaps
one sign that life was well-ordered was when you
found yourself free to notice the little things, and to
see that they were good. The little good things
might be the right clues. In the cities there was no
time to see them. Only what was big was important
there, and usually it was so ominously large and out
of control that the man who stopped to think about
it was fixed by fear. Instinct warned you to stand
from under, and yet you couldn't do it. You might

know it was the very shadow of death, but if the mob saw nothing wrong with it, but thought it was a nice shady place, then you could only smoke your pipe and wait for what had to come.   That cockroach waving his feelers in meditation on a bulkhead was better off than most of the industrious and eager muddlers back in London.   He was free to be a cockroach all complete in his own little day.   But the muddlers had contrived civilization into an elaborately unhappy prison from which they could not escape, but only hammer desperately, when they could stand it no longer, on prison gates which they had made not to open.

Reflections from the sea began to waver and dance on the white bulkhead.   The day and the heat had come.   The cabin door opened, and a ship's officer looked in.   " Morning, Maynard ! We're there. Just heard from the shore.   There will be a boat for you after breakfast.   All ready for it ? "   The young man grinned.

CHAPTER II

ALL ready for it? Rather! He took his place in the saloon with the officers at breakfast. In their white uniforms, and in that light, they could have been shy and youthful initiates set apart for service in a happier clime. Maynard blithely greeted the captain, and twirled into position his swivel seat at the table. As he did so he glanced cheerfully through a portlight to a parade of palms along the shore off which they were at anchor. Mountains were in the sky, but far away. So then they really were mountains; made in less than an hour.

The ship's master looked up at him. "Here we are, Mr. Maynard. Sorry to lose you, but have something to eat first."

One of his juniors laughed, but stifled it.

"Why do you laugh?" demanded the captain of his junior. "What do you know that's funny?"

The young officer made no confession. He merely flushed, and straightened the cutlery by his plate.

The captain watched Maynard with cunning drollery. "We ought not to ask you what you are going to do in Novobambia, now you're here. Quinn's Landing isn't a port anybody goes to for fun." He was polite, but solicitous.

Maynard merely attended to his coffee. It might be better to say nothing of his venture. Not sure about it. There was no harm in telling them, that he could see, but it wasn't exactly his business, and it wasn't theirs, and it wouldn't interest them. His orders were to hurry inland, to the head waters of the Mungubeira, with some stores for a friend who was in need of help in his work of medical research. Not so very jolly to discuss hook-worms at breakfast.

The captain kept a humorous eye on Maynard. " Quite right," he said. " I know. Keep it dark."

" It's only science," pleaded Maynard.

" You bet it is." The captain ran a knowing glance round the company at the table. " Funny thing, it always is science, so far as we can tell." He waved his arm to the saloon portlights. " If you look outside you'd think you could see all that was there. Plain as a ship's funnel. But you're not going to fool us. There's a lot there, a whole lot, sir, that's worth knowing. But it's in the dark. I'd give something to hear who is going tc run up a flag over it. England is so slow. I'd put a year's pay on it myself if I knew which way it was going."

" Don't you know ? "

" Everything but the facts. We never know what our passengers are going to do here, especially if they tell us." The captain shook his head at Maynard.

" Anyhow," the chief officer admitted, " Mr. Maynard is English all right."

" Time someone here was." The master frowned at his thoughts. " Our country is so damned slow. All the same, I expect Mr. Maynard knows a thing or two, only he won't tell us. Quite right."

" Men just land here," mused the chief officer, " and now and then we'll pick one up again, more dead than alive, but usually we don't see 'em any more. Can't make out which way they go. They can't very well walk across to the other side. As for me, I wouldn't stay ashore at this hole for a fat pension."

" Nobody will ask you," growled the captain. " We're only sailors. You can see for yourself Mr. Maynard wouldn't trust us. He just sits and smiles at us. But something's going on here. You can't tell me it isn't. Funny thing it's such a great land all of a sudden for—what you call 'em—entomologists, bug-hunters. Things like that. Two Germans and a Frenchman last trip. Quite a run on the bugs here, nowadays. I shouldn't wonder if our own Foreign Office wants a collection of local cockroaches now." The captain smiled at his chief officer with provoking wisdom.

" You make me think this country must be full of artful activity." Maynard was amused. " At home nobody seemed to know its name."

" Activity ? " The captain grunted scornfully.

"You never see a thing move. Just a few dagoes loafing about, and some naked savages in the background, and a thunderstorm to wash out the tracks. You could say it hasn't got a name, not yet."

"There's talk of an oil concession," added the surgeon.

"Not much activity in all that talk. We shan't see any activity till the claim is jumped. Then there'll be a rumpus all right. We want a gunboat here to liven things up."

"By the way, sir," one of the officers called over to the captain, "Mr. Broderic has sent a message to say he can't come aboard. He's sick."

"I have to meet that man," said Maynard.

"Don't worry. You don't need to meet him. He'll meet you. If he doesn't, you won't get far."

"Oh come, sir," protested the surgeon. "That's too bad. I know how natural it is to think evil where all seems so peaceful. Where we can't hear a sound we're suspicious. But what's the matter with Broderic?"

"Nothing, that I know of. Did you hear me say there was, doctor? All I say is, that you won't get far in this country if he doesn't like the cut of your jib. Isn't that right?"

The surgeon was scarcely mollified. "He's the only man I've met on this condemned coast who knows things to talk about beyond gold and concessions."

"Ah, get away with it. It's likely he'd talk about them, isn't it? He knows too much about them."

"I thought perhaps he remembered they weren't everything."

The elderly captain rose, and put on his cap with an aggressive gesture of finality. "I don't know what he remembers, but I know those things are all that matter here, and I'm not the only one, either."

The surgeon eyed his plate sadly. Maynard enjoyed these mealtime disputes. He had got used to them and this happy family in a month's voyage, and here was the last of it.

MAYNARD tallied his stuff ashore, and there he was, forsaken. Now he was free to begin again, in that new way. He looked about him. This place, Quinn's Landing, had a pleasing name, but it showed no curiosity in its visitors.

Nobody was in sight. No Quinn there—who was Quinn?—and no particular significance in making a landing there, so far as he could see, which was not far. He sat down on one of his boxes and waited. He had plenty of time; time might be one there with the silence, and that was fixed. Quinn's Landing was silent, and time had not touched it. It had only the sun blazing newly arrived at the beginning of things. Nothing had begun to move there yet.

Strange trees hung excessive foliage waiting for the first word to stir it. Two canoes were tied to a little jetty close by. How had they got there, with nobody yet to use them? At the upper end of the rough track by which he was sitting was a large shack. Its dry palm thatch shone in the sun like brass, but it appeared to shelter beneath it only a square of residual night. A ladder went up from the track into the interior darkness of the shack. Beyond and above that thatch was the palisade of the forest, which came down to the creek on both sides of him.

If that little bay of cleared and sunlit earth was the threshold to another period for him, how was he going to get beyond its door? Hello! A brown figure—he hadn't noticed it before—stood beside the shack, watching him. Was it alive? It regarded him for a moment, but before he could rise and call out it had gone. No good, perhaps, trying to break original silence with a voice, but he had almost attempted to do it.

Maynard thought he had better start something. If he did not, then there was neither wind nor other life there to originate a movement. He went up and climbed the ladder to a verandah, and entered the cool shadow. The daylight pressed ardently into the roomy apartment through chinks in the walls of dry leaves, brilliant sparks and bright filigree of gold, and showed a central bare rough table and the wrecks of a few cane chairs about. An energetic alarm clock was on a long shelf, loudly measuring solitude. With it was a bottle of Epsom salts, another of carbolic acid, a human skull, a biscuit tin, some specimens of ore, and a framed photograph so yellow that it was hard to say what it had been, but the ghost of a dog was in it. The cheerful heedlessness of the new metal clock had encouraged Maynard to

stroll over the loose and uneven boughs which made
the floor, though they creaked about him as grievously
as a pack of terriers. From that apartment there was
another portal leading deeper into the shack, but it
was screened with a piece of bunting, which was a
Union Jack as far as its folds disclosed.

The curtain was ripped aside, and a gaunt figure
stood there, its hands still holding the divided screen
as though halted by the presence of a stranger, and
resentment for an intrusion were gathering. To
Maynard the flimsy dwelling, with that figure in its
midst, at once changed its character. It was important. He saw he would have to justify himself.
The tall and bony man in a dressing gown stood
inspecting him for some seconds, then shambled
across, barefooted, his mouth a little open through
illness or weariness, but with an easy grip he flung
a lounge chair into place as though it were of straw.

"Mr. Maynard?"

"Yes, Mr. Broderic."

It must be Broderic. The man did not deny it.
They took their ease. Broderic did not look at his
visitor again, and was silent for so long, reclining
languidly with his eyes shut, that Maynard began to
be nervous with a suspicion that presently he would
be faced with a repetition of the surprise and resentment. He was forgotten.

Then the man opened his eyes and began to talk,
while regarding his noisy little clock. He mumbled

to that, dragging his reluctant speech from a dis-
illusionment so profound that useless words, which
had sunk to the bottom of it, were hard to find ; or
else he was very ill.   Maynard was impressed by the
long figure beside him, and sat up in obedience, when
it spoke ; at first he hardly heard what it was saying.
There were not many heads in the world like that.
Its plentiful black hair was dank and untidy.   The
brow was magisterial with its high composure, and
the sharp bony angles at the temples might mean a
freakish use of power, or emaciation, yet the forehead
could wrinkle into tired but sympathetic consideration.
The hollows of the long cheeks were filled with a
chestnut beard.   The thin white nose hooked over
the moustache, and the eyes were in dark pits under
the ridges of the eyebrows.   This was how genius
ought to look ; or maybe Broderic was inhuman.
It would be easy to take his advice and his orders.
He would look at you without humour as though
you were a blackbeetle, if you disputed anything he
said, and then turn away.   A fellow with such a head
might be wrong, but he would put other people
wrong.   What was he doing here ?

Broderic turned suddenly his haggard look on
Maynard.   His accusative movement was confusing ;
perhaps he had noticed that his visitor was not very
attentive.   Those steady eyes were suddenly direct,
condescending, and intimate.   Maynard was partly
reassured by that glance of tepid benevolence from

this strange fellow. But almost as he returned the unhostile greeting, Broderic's faint benevolence faded, and one eye roved a little from its focus—it saw something over Maynard's shoulder? Or perhaps it was concerned with reservations not to be divulged. That eye seemed to leave to its fellow the simple task of taking in a guest. Very queer. It was Broderic whose attention was not fixed.

Nor did it appear that Broderic had more than a detached interest in Maynard's journey. He was casual about it. Why make it? But his tired mumbling hinted that he was past wondering over the activities of other people, which usually were needless and even foolish. Who was this friend of Maynard's, what was he doing on the Mungubeira? " Buckle? Buckle! Oh, yes. I've heard of him. I think I've heard of him. Yes, I remember something about it. He is supposed to be a great authority on insect pests. Well, I hope you get through to him without much trouble. But you won't save the people here. I shouldn't worry about the flies and the trypanosomes. Better leave them alone. They are filthy little beasts, but they reduce our pride. They keep us in place. Besides, they help to kill off outsiders who want to meddle. Confound the meddlers. We have too many of them."

Maynard surmised that Broderic had a better opinion of science than that. This was but a sick man's cynicism. He idly considered a foot of rope which was dangling from a rafter almost over his head. He saw, not quite believing it, that the rope receded gradually. It was alive. It was a snake. There was a cheerless call, perhaps of a bird, in the forest outside.

Broderic began to speak again. Was there any talk in London of Nobobambia? He seldom saw the newspapers. Not much talk? Strange. That was strange. Rather bad, that, too. Something must be going on, eh?

There came a sharp rustling in the shadows of the roof, and a rat dropped to the floor and lay stunned for a moment at Maynard's feet, then scuttled away. Just able to dodge that snake, very likely. Broderic took no notice of the interlude.

Had Mr. Maynard ever met Grey? Maynard hesitated and wondered who Grey was. Who? What, the Foreign Minister? Of course not. That man was a swell—almost a myth. Was it possible for anyone to see him? Grey was rather like God— you only knew of him because of what he let you in for.

Broderic was not amused. He stroked his beard. " Perhaps you are one of those who admire him. I see nothing in him, nothing. If he were not so silent and stately people would laugh. He is silent because if he spoke you would know him. You call him a strong man at home. It's quite natural, for he ignores you and prefers fishing for trout. That's the way of a democracy. It respects the aristocrat who treats it with cool contempt."

"I don't know him, and very little about him. I thought he had a definite opinion about Novobambia."

"Has he? Then what is it?"

"I shouldn't like to say. An English opinion, I suppose. What the value of this land can be in the diplomatic moves is something I couldn't guess. As it is a cause of jealousy, perhaps diplomatists politely look another way, to save offence."

Broderic inclined his head to inspect his young visitor, who at that moment imagined the hidden snake was stealthy again—either that or a draught was agitating the loose fingers of a dry frond overhead. The movement ceased. He turned to his host to smile his cheerful indifference to international politics.

His host then was leaning back and frowning as though asleep and troubled by a dream. "No," he whispered. "No. They do not look another way. You know they do not. Eyes. There they are. The eyes, I tell you. Everywhere." Broderic was quiet for a time, but presently sat up abruptly, and stared over to a corner of the room. "I'd put them out," he said vehemently. "Can't we ever be alone? What do they want here? They see all we do. They never leave us. I'd put them out, I'd blind them."

He turned on Maynard. "Hateful. They're

always watching. I know it. Night does not hide us, no, not even night. They come closer at night. They won't stay in their own place. And there are names, names that are lies—a masquerade—lies in a masquerade, and nobody knows what it is about. Played in the dark. We hear names that mean something, but we don't know what it is, and they come out of the night. You've just come from there. You have, haven't you? They come like the sickness in daylight, like death to people who sleep. Why don't they laugh at us? If they laughed we'd know where they were. But we never know, we never see them, we only hear them at night, in the woods, a long way off, when they've seen all they wanted, creeping away."

Broderic panted after that, and made nervous movements with a yellow hand which rested on the arm of his chair. Maynard sought unhappily for a reassuring word, but could only plead that things were not so bad as that.

" Maybe, maybe." Broderic clapped his hands peremptorily. A woman came and stood beside him, her brown face demure and sullen, the folds of her beggarly white cotton doing their best for a young body so limber and shapely. Her master talked to her, his face haughtily averted, in a language Maynard did not know, so was free to admire the proud submission of the woman. She was like one of the palms, with its crown bent over slightly. Then an old man, obsequious and fearful, who was ignored, brought in refreshment.

" I can find you six men and a guide, Mr. Maynard, but it is hard to get labour here. You haven't much of a cargo, have you? The boys will get you up to the junction of the rivers, then you must look after yourself. I'll give you a chit to the chief there. Now listen to me. It won't do for you to trust anybody, especially if they're sympathetic. I never know from one day to the next what is going on around me. Don't you interfere. Every man is playing his own game, and you can only guess what that is. You would guess wrong. Remember that he isn't what he pretends to be, and you get clear as soon as you can. If you should run up against an American whose name, so he says, is Hoyt, be on your guard. I should push off at daylight to-morrow, if I were you. Get it over. Your guide, Manoel, is a good boy. I must ask you to excuse me now. This fever—I am going to try to shake it off. Make yourself at home."

THEIR dug-out canoe was daft. It was a heavy log when it floated away from Quinn's Landing, but round the first bend of the river, out of sight of home, it went off with the whoop of an idiot. Then for a dreamy period it declined into a silent glide which beguiled Maynard into supposing it had come to reason. Unexpectedly it shivered again, and went up in the air. In a frenzy of corybantic turns once more he waited to be drowned. At first Maynard watched its capers acutely. But watching did not help. That fixed intentness in the torrid heat gave him a stiff neck. He noticed as consolation that usually the trees were near; the distance was brief though the current was unpromising. They would go bottom up in a minute—the next instant. This could not last.

Though their charge had but an inch of freeboard his men showed it no care. They checked its frivolities indifferently, as though it were a tiresome business for them. Manoel with a bamboo pole crouched in the bows, or balanced erect on prehensile toes, regarding the convulsive river with a sneer. That man's sole expression was a sneer. That was what he thought of everything. In spite of its occa-

167   M

sional bouts of lunatic energy the canoe appeared to make no progress against the stream, but now and then they did round another bend, they opened the vista of another reach, which was the same as the last, a blinding mirror sunk deeply beneath the dark walls of the forest.

A tree-trunk shot out of the river just ahead, and it crooked over at them as though it were the confident arm of a monster under water which knew it had got them now. Manoel unfolded himself and fended the threat off with his pole. He spat at the river as he did it. The paddlers ceased work to watch the black talons claw past their heads. Maynard breathed again ; and the canoe then slipped into a polished hollow of the waters which was spinning like a wheel. They revolved fixed in a taut swirl which was boring to the bottom of the river. He saw above him for a moment the dancing rim of the whirlpool. It collapsed, and their canoe bounded on the released wave which swept them under the trees. He ducked from a cluster of pods like cannon-balls hanging there. The foliage lashed and crashed as the men grasped at it to check their runaway, and then the shade stood motionless over them, and the smooth torrent was pouring past his hands which still gripped too hard the sides of the moored canoe. Manoel rolled a cigarette. Buckle's precious cargo of boxes were still luckily above the water.

Maynard laughed to himself. He peered under the fringe of leaves to where the river was in the sun, and the opposite shore. He saw in that pause the shine of the earth in repose with a new and grateful attention, for the old scythe had just made three vicious swipes at them—it meant to get them that time—but it had missed. It was good fun when the show of things came close enough to prove to be not only real but dangerous. It was just as well to know it was solid.

A dread was in it, nevertheless; that cargo of theirs was all the help coming to a man who could not do without it, and if this went on it might not reach him. He could float for a time, but the cargo would find the bottom at once. Then his crew would swim ashore glad their job was over so soon. His men did not change their sulky expressions. They were taking a rest. They talked to each other and looked past him as if he were not there. It was a doubtful bunch, that lot.

They got under way again. For another hour he sat without moving. The sun remained in a lane of blue, and if for a moment he felt he must ease away from the heat which fixed him to his seat, then he looked at the glaring river or his men, and changed his mind. It was like a vivid dream, though it came true if it were disturbed. It was better to keep still and not to interrupt it. That was an old feeling of his, that he was never part of the show, and that the show was the beguiling apparition of a mockery. An obstructing whirlpool or a snag, now and then, was a necessary reminder that he was of the dream, with the water under him and unknown country around. It was so easy for a man to dwindle into a sort of disembodied watchfulness, which saw the world going by as a curious phantasm which reason could not disperse. It was so easy to be merely an impersonal eye, till he happened to notice the inscription on a box at his feet : Maynard, Mungubeira.

Strange ! That was himself.

There, anyhow, was a fact. You have to be positive about your box, when you cannot be sure of yourself. That package nudged him about his charge and its direction. That box had to get to Buckle, and he must take it, or answer for it. But for such a fact a fellow would continue to float through space idly observing that the planets ahead were very like the planets behind, and that they were all going anywhere in meaningless night. When you did not know your whereabouts you had to sit on one of Saturn's rings as you passed, parcel under your arm, and sing out to him, " Hullo, can you tell me the way to Mungubeira ?—got to get this blessed parcel there before daybreak, when the shadows flee away."

Bound to make an effort to get the thing through. God knows what would happen to your parcel if you let it drop into space, with your name on it.

The canoe had been tame for a long spell. They had got through to the level of peace. The only movement was his sweating men and their paddles. The river had slowed. Its current was imperceptible and could have been going either way. Their boat was the head of a wedge of ripples spreading the first flaws in the crystal of an original expansion of light. He saw no land. There were steep precipices of forest and the lustre of a sleeping lagoon. They were the awakeners. Once they passed a chasm in those walls which rose sheer from the water; he peered into Novobambia, into hollow twilight vaults where dim columns upheld a roof of midnight, and the floor was water.

The forest was silent. It was opulent and majestic, the free gesture of a magnanimous earth. This region was still in the dawn of geology; it had not come to Cain yet. So far it had no complications, not even dragons; none that could be seen. It was merely waiting for the advent of good or evil, whichever came first. His errand there was fairly simple, if not easy. There was nothing in it to argue about. It could be shown openly to the angel with the flaming sword standing at the gate, if it happened to be that garden they were likely to pass. It was certain that this time another man really depended on the way he lived. There was no fog of metaphysical doubts about it; there was only a forest of the prime to argue with. His errand was a lucky simplification of the confusion of the world. It was quite a holiday, for a journalist, to have a good hold of one small but dominating fact, and to be carrying it to where it was wanted. All the muddled news of the morning was plain to read now; it was as plain as the scarlet dragon-fly hovering over Manoel's black mop. If he had only a week to live he knew how the seven days ought to go. Maynard's heart rose to the thought of his release, to the prospect of his freedom in which he had one thing to do, and that not for himself. Let men in the sour and soiled places of the world glower at each other from their cities and make their troubles, and let the learned prove that wrong is the natural growth of history and evil as right as roses, if not so sweet : he was out of it.

Manoel shouted and thrust vigorously with his pole. Maynard heard a hissing, the canoe gained a yard, and a shoal of fish, he thought, leaped about them. The paddler in front of him stopped work. A long splinter was stuck in the man's bronze shoulder and his face was turned to it in surprise. Another dart stood upright for a second on the thwart before Maynard, then fell over. The man pulled out the arrow, scrutinized it, and threw it away. He went on paddling with greater energy. Maynard saw the forest with a new interest ; but it was as before, silent and unconcerned. Manoel was urging the men to hurry away from that bit. That bit might have been a little mad, like Broderic, but it was also just as reposeful and noble. Perhaps occasionally it was touched off from within by whatever possessed it and made queer signs, then relapsed into silent nobility again. It talked in arrows unexpectedly and you never knew why. That patch of forest was indistinguishable from the rest of the still green cloud which was Novobambia. Maynard called out in fun to Manoel, but the guide did not hear him, or did not understand. Manoel made no response of fellowship.

At sunrise on the fifth morning, after a scrappy refreshment, Maynard strolled down to the canoe. It was time for them to push off.

The men were not there. Not one of them was in sight. As he looked round that soundless and empty sunrise, in which he forgot to hear the familiar river that was stretched in glassy sheets over beds of white sand, or drew through smooth channels of granite in crystal flexures, he had the idea that like children at play his party had wandered outside reality, were in the region where desire may place the suitable sun, moon and stars to its liking. Their sun, their private day-maker, was drawing the mists out of a tangle of immediate yet inaccessible hills. He could watch a floating hilltop come down from the sky to attach itself accurately to a truncated cone of forest beneath. There formed and stood, as he looked on, a completed peak in the blue. Only the mists were moving, and they could not be seen to go. In that narrow valley the water was the only road through the forest. On the opposite shore the forest was particularized in a line of pale monolithic supports which upheld green cupolas and domes and a cornice with suspended lianes and corbels of flowers. The intervals of the colonnade were cavernous with shadows. He half expected to see elfish figures emerge thence, though whether to laugh or to hoot at him he did not know. The river was between. It was probably safe to stare over. If he had heard unearthly piping in those woods, if a goatish creature had half-shown itself to leer at him, or if a winged white horse had floated down like a meteor from the hills over the trees to drink at the river, that would hardly have been strange then. He himself was the stranger, come back from a later and darker day.

The sun was hot already. Those blessed loafers! Not a sound anywhere. Where were they? He turned for the camp to find them, and in gathering annoyance shot with a tremor of alarm. The unreality of it all made him a little anxious, on a sudden, for dependable companionship. It would want a lot of conscious rectitude in a man to face alone the casual advent of Pegasus in an enchanted land. Where the devil had those fellows got to? They wanted watching. Sometimes he wondered whether they were human, for they rarely spoke, except in asides to each other. They omitted him. They had nothing for his ear. Poor beggars, no doubt too much sun and fever had made them taciturn, and they had no strength to waste. They had no more than enough energy to get them slowly through from morning to night. Well, there loafed Manoel.

To Maynard's mild rebuke, and his order for immediate departure, the guide returned the usual sardonic grimace. Latin and native blood made a thin and bitter mixture. The guide moved to go on, but paused and half-turned with a deepened sneer as though to speak, yet changed his mind when Maynard eyed him. Maynard was left with a suspicion of hostility which was foolish, because groundless. One had to make allowances.

They loaded up and pushed away for the next stage of the river. The rigidity of Novobambia's enchantment began slowly to pass them again, a similar unfolding of the unauthentic panorama, with no sign of a weakening of its sleep. Maynard wished he could be sure they were on the right river. There were many of these waterways and the forest was universal. That country was a maze of channels, and his map was bewildering with names which stood for nothing that was visible when you reached the spot. The map had lines which dotted a confession of uncertainty, and some ignorant blank spaces of complete surrender. He would have to leave it to Manoel. It had to be Manoel, or nothing. If the guide really knew where he was going that was only part of the rum nature of the journey. Faith, Maynard, faith! But faith is wind unless you have something solid to stand upon.

They put ashore at midday for a rest, and the men rested again too long. Or was he impatient? He appeared to feel the heat less than these weaklings.

The place was a bay in the woods, an old clearing, he guessed, now largely overgrown. Maynard explored it while the men were still undecided, and chanced upon a dilapidated hut foundering in rank scrub, but nothing was within it for a sign, nothing but dank gloom, spiders' webs, and the dung of bats.

When he returned the men had not moved. Manoel was in the pose of virtuous rest, and Maynard's patience broke. He shouted at the group. One of the prone figures glanced up at him, but lost his sleepy interest at once. Maynard stood over Manoel, took hold, and gave that contemptuous fellow a hoist. The man turned unexpectedly light; he was on his feet in vicious alacrity, and crouched for a jump with something bright in his hand. Maynard wore stout boots, and Manoel was so shocked by the check to his leap that Maynard had only to pick up the dropped knife.

The other fellows were disappearing in the bush. Maynard noticed that as he assisted Manoel to his feet. The guide's eyes returned no thanks for this attention as he broke to follow the others, and glanced back to see that nothing worse was coming. Maynard helplessly watched the fools vanish. It was lucky they thought he was armed. Well, they would have to return. They could get nowhere, that way.

He remembered his old solution for a quandary : when in doubt about what you ought to do, go to bed.

There he stood for a minute, musing in comic complaint over a foolish predicament. He couldn't run after those fellows. And it was too early for bed : besides, to rest carefree might be a mistake, with those fellows in hiding. Even an aphorism becomes inapplicable when you want to use it. In their alarm or whatever was the matter with them, they had cleared out. They had allowed him all the elbow room and the boat, which would have been more comforting if he had known just when they would be back again.

They would get over this, but a day was being wasted. His own fault, he thought. He ought not to have acted as though Novobambia would be in a grateful hurry to rid itself of trypanosomes. It did not know it had them. Besides, the wilderness could not spot the difference between even John the Baptist and a regular slave-dealer. It had nothing to go upon. It knew only slave-dealers. For that matter, without reflection which it never gave to the subject, not even

178

London knew the difference.   John would get a hell
of a reception in Hyde Park.

He smoked, and contemplated the surrounding
trees. The trees gave away no secret—at most they
might be said to confirm his opinion of the utter
inconsequence of John in the wilderness, whatever
his mission.   In that case, what about himself?   He
did not count.   He must put up with it.   He could
run and play with any patience he could find ; and
he refused to consider, when the jeering doubt
entered, what would happen if he waited in vain.
He had not come to that yet.

Yet waiting was not easy, though he was only
beginning to wait.   Towards dayfall the shadows
drained into the deep clearing, as into a well.   The
cataleptic fringe of the treetops over him might have
been daubed in black on the sunset colours.   He
hummed a tune, to make a noise—he did not sing
aloud ; that might rouse echoes better left alone—
and went down to assure himself of the safety of the
canoe.   Not a leaf stirred, and the day went.

He entered the hut, thought it over, and shaped a
dummy to represent himself asleep near the rotting
door, which was half-open and could not be closed.
The mutineers might return when he was not expecting
them.   He settled himself in a far corner, where at
least the rough ground would help to keep him
wakeful.   He then noticed that while he was awake
the smells had to be breathed in definite quantities.

Sour stuff, owlish and batlike. Thunder began to play remotely a ponderous game among the hills with iron bowls. Between the rumblings he listened for the friendly undertone of the river, but no friendly voice of any sort could be heard.

The hut was that dark he could not see his fingers held up before his eyes. Then something plushy stroked his forehead, and he recoiled against the trash of the wall with a noise which sounded like a forcible entrance. In the hush which followed he strained his ears for a sequel, but only his face was brushed lightly again. It was the wing of a bat, maybe. He was not alone in the hut.

Time does not always fly. He estimated where it stood then, and knew there were at least three hours to midnight and another three to daybreak. That made six. In case he had erred he considered it again, but six was the least he could make it. If he could see the door, if he could see anything, the silence would not be so much like something observant.

There the door was—the bluish ghost of it. A light flickered and vanished. He noticed that the door was still open, but he had no time to see if anyone came in because the night fell on it instantly. The iron bowls bumped and rumbled down a nearer valley. Framed in blue fire for an instant the door stood open again; it jumped in and out of night. A vehement glare burst through all the holes of the shack, and one of the iron bowls shook the floor.

That was a near one—off the pitch he hoped—a careless lob?

No. They were playing his way. They were bowling at him. The fiery ribs of the hut began an incessant jig into nothing and back again. They weren't built for that sort of thing ; they'd fall apart. Sometimes the door stood open long enough for him to watch it. When it was so plain its emptiness was a lie.

When next he saw that door it was paltry and natural. The happy sunlight was pretending there had been no night. His dummy slept where he had put it. Why had he made it ? As usual, the morning earth was as if it were brightly unaware of any black thought left over from yesterday. Now they could get going again. He went down to the river.

The canoe had gone. There had been a hasty unlading. Some of his boxes had been thrown ashore, and some into the river.

He had a panic impulse to run along the shore. After what ? So he did not move. It was all plain enough —he could see for nearly a glassy mile each way on the river. Not a crinkle was on it. The canoe had left no mark. Each end of the beach, too, was stopped by watery forest as high as a cliff. He could take a run as far as that. That settled it. He waded instead to salvage his sunken cargo. He counted the consignment, and found he had the lot, except some food. Not a tin of it, and not a match.

And this meant that now the lethal bugs of Novo-bambia were all reprieved, while he was properly cornered. The mosquitoes and the other little vampires were dancing on their tails about this. There was no grub, nowhere to go, and no way of getting there if a thereabouts existed. And there was something else. According to the gay stories he now began to recall this was the country of a tribe rather attentive to intruders. What were they called ? He could not remember their name, but most likely they would have jolly good reason for their cunning. They had learned all about intruders, and he could not expect exemption because he deserved it. They had to be fair to themselves. Men, even savages, have a perfect right to ignore all just answers to their reasons for doing what they want to do, because if they did not successful careers would end, and goodwill would have a chance.

He surveyed the bay in the forest behind him. Those savages might be watching him at that moment. The leaves were asleep, but he knew the forest did not open its eyes when it was drawing back arrows for visitors. It would be foolish to try to hide from it; if it really were watching him then he would offer a fair mark. A marooned and hungry man who tried to hide on a foreign beach would be a fool.

He examined his cargo. By some lucky chance Buckle's boxes might survive to serve their purpose after all; and it was not his business if they did not. They could be stowed in the hut now—all he could do for them—while he was waiting for whatever was to turn up next. He stacked them there, and sat on one of them to cast his horoscope, for now he had done that job he must leave the hut, turn round three times, and see what luck would send him. He whistled the *Cock o' the North* to set his fix to a lively measure, and got up to go.

He rose at the right moment. The doorway darkened, and he turned to face it. Whatever it was melted as he looked; he thought a small and dark image had looked at him, but it had gone before he could breathe. He jumped to catch that fellow; he

N

must not let this chance slip.   But he was too late.
He stood scanning the prospect of the Mungubeira,
and fancied that the leaves of a bush stirred, and that
he saw a face lurking, yet the clearing was so quiet
and still that as he waited, and nothing more happened,
he began to doubt his experience.   Was he mistaken ?
He would have to be careful ; perhaps his nerves were
up to tricks with him.

This was a consequence of loneliness, and of an
enigma which was shaken only at midnight, and then
by lightning.   Those trees standing haughtily round
certainly had the intentness of guards, and to be secret
with whatever they knew.   He would either have to
risk what they might be hiding, or else stay there and
perish.   He made his way over to the cliff of green
on the far side, the up-river side.   He thought that
if he tried to get out of it he had better head in the
general direction of his journey.   It was the only
thing to do.   It might not be much use doing
anything, but he would have the satisfaction of
annoying the fates by going on till he was knocked
out.   If they were after him, then let them finish
their job.

It was not easy to get near the trees.   A tangle of
vines and spinous stuff was as prohibitive as a barrier
of flames.   The heat and the silence shrilled in his
ears.   If he could only work through to the shade
of the forest he would not feel so light in the head,
either.   The beggars might have left him a meal.

The sun made you feel it was easier to give in. The very foliage was weighed down by the heat. Only the great wasps and butterflies were spry, as if all the quick fierceness of the tropics were in their wings. They annoyed him. He thought their movements insulting.

He stopped to disengage his shirt from more talons in the bushes, and shook his head to get the sweat out of his eyes ; he could not even see what desperately had clutched him. The cursed thorns knew they could stop him. That was why they caught him after he had slipped by.

Could he have seen anyone at that hut door ? Of course not. Nobody could have got out of this place. Only reptiles. They could crawl.

He returned to his shelter for shade, and to steady his limbs, shaking through an energy made anxious with failure. Let the place do its worst . . . would Broderic act when he knew ? He would never know. His men would not tell him. Not likely.

It was daybreak again when he woke finally, sure he heard a voice. He sat up. He felt dull. He accepted it as but one more of the silly episodes of Novobambia that just then he was the occasion for mild amusement to another white man, who stood in the doorway, nursing a rifle. Behind his visitor Maynard saw a group of naked savages, bearing lances, but retired to a polite distance.

" Hullo, Maynard. Thought you were dead."

His visitor maintained a whimsical grin, but did not advance. He was relishing this encounter, but possibly he had a doubt about his reception.

Maynard rose, but he did not answer. He was too surprised. This hut lost in a forest without a name might have been his postal address.

" Sorry to disturb you, but don't you worry. You're not for the casserole. My name is Hoyt. Shall we step outside, or do you prefer the spiders for company ? I'm never sure which an Englishman prefers." Mr. Hoyt hesitated, and then concluded he was welcome. He ran a sharp glance over the medical stores. " You can leave this truck. It'll do fine here."

Hoyt's face was still mocking, but Maynard liked his quick grey eyes. They were sharp and hard, though Hoyt's movements were indolent. Maynard let his visitor see that this interruption was as lucky as he could have wished. But why, he asked, was his name so familiar in Novobambia ?

Hoyt grimaced with an indication that the heavenly knowledge when only a sparrow fell to earth was rather like the whisperings which circulated of doings in that country. " You're in the limelight, young feller. Don't forget it. There are dossiers about you in Berlin and Paris and what not. You've got them guessing." He nodded to the sulky natives waiting outside. " It's a wonder they didn't skewer you at once. They're in it too. They might have thought you were one of Broderic's pals. You were with his men, weren't you?"

Maynard briefly explained the course of his journey.

"Why, that's it, is it? Then these boys are brighter than I thought. It's a wonder they didn't wipe up the lot of you. They'd roast Broderic, and I don't say but what I'd look the other way till it was too late."

"That's fairly strong. What's the matter with him?"

"Now you've got down to it. What is it? I'd ask that. Is he English or French or German or only plain swine?"

"Don't ask me. What's he doing here? I thought he was a trader."

Hoyt chuckled. "We're wasting time. What's anyone doing here? Notice the way the garden lots are staked out by alligators on the river front? This is a lovely country, and because some people badly want it funerals are the cheapest things you know. That reminds me." Hoyt thereupon began a careful scrutiny of the hut. "Haven't been here since old man Sorensen disappeared. Where did he go? I can't see anything, can you? You didn't happen to notice him around in the night?—but not likely— not if he was in Broderic's way."

"The old fellow you are talking about?" Maynard showed his surprise that in so great a solitude it was possible to get in the way of other people. "I should have thought there was plenty of room for lots more here."

"You would, and you ought not to be shot for it, but let me tell you there's no room for anyone we don't want. We clutter up each other's doings pretty bad. I'd like to know who pays Broderic, now. You haven't heard, by any chance?" Hoyt rubbed his scrubby chin reflectively. "It won't be the place where my money comes from—and yet I don't know, because often the strangest thing about money is the reason back of the cashier."

"Good God!" exclaimed Maynard. "I'm not in it. What's it all about? Broderic knows why I'm here."

"Is that so? You told him, naturally. He'd thank you for being so nice about it, and he'd wonder why. But he'd miss your curls and blue eyes."

"You yourself had my name pat enough, I thought."

"Sure. The news gets around. Notice those trees—they hear everything."

Maynard smiled. "They fired at us once."

"Yeh, and missed. They were bad shots."

"What, hear everything and then talk about it?" This American's flitting fancies had a quick habit of settling on realities.

"That's right. We've got no use for telephones. Don't think anything you don't want the exchange to know. But I'll tell you. That pal of yours,

Buckle, that doctor—I happen to know him. I suppose you know there's nothing wrong with him. He's a child, and won't ever learn what's the matter with this world, except bugs are bad for it. He's hideous death on bugs. He'd love Broderic, and you, and me, and everybody, when his eye comes off his microscope, if I'd let him. The child babbled to me about you, and I thought there was an odd chance you were all right, though British. That's why these natives asked me first, before doing what they ought to have done. Step along, and talk as we go. Come and eat."

MAYNARD tripped over a root, was slow in straightening, and was suspiciously alone when he rose. He hurried forward to reassure himself with a sight of Hoyt. He wondered when they would emerge into daylight again, and see reasonable shapes. But Hoyt —there he was, not far ahead—could not be asked. There was no time for anything but marching, and no desire except for food and rest. This was what exhaustion meant. It was many days—it was many camps, anyhow—since he had followed Hoyt out of the clearing into this forest. They went down into Pluto's great abode, and there they were still. Tartarus was To Let. It was empty. They crawled on past its endless dim pillars, through its silent and abandoned halls, and its half-seen recesses that were backwaters of Lethe. Maynard fell into a kind of lucid stupor. He was not even surprised that his body faithfully followed his eyes, for he had forgotten it. He remembered he had a body only when, too indifferent to save himself as he slipped once more, he surrendered limply to the mud. Hoyt came back and stood over him, grinning. " Too soon yet, Maynard. You can't curl up there. Some way to go yet. Be there about night."

Night! Then what was this? They must have descended deeply out of sight of the sky, and day did not know where they were. They were lost where time was dead. Time had stopped, and everlasting murk was unholy with the shadows of things forgotten in a vast crypt that was closed till the last trump; tumbled memorials, elephantine tombs, brooding gargoyles, scarecrows, figures turned to stone, all without a name, all waiting for what would never happen, amid the black bastions and columns which keep oblivion. But that was the real Hoyt ahead of him, and now and then, beyond again, he glimpsed the figures of the natives just before they faded into the silence. He was a spectre himself. He was not quite sure he was there. He was only a vagrant thought in a dream, a lost memory drifting with no chance of finding its intelligible place between a past and a future. Novobambia was part of the dream, if it were there at all. Those shapes about him might be real, but he did not know, for he could not test them. His eyes clung for safety to the long loose figure of Hoyt, striding ahead very materially. Hoyt stopped again, and turned, perhaps to see if he had vanished. Hoyt was right. Shadows thin out, sometimes, and then where are they? There was more stuff in Hoyt's companionable and indulgent grimace than in all the philosophies. When they stopped for a rest, a small patch of forest took on

solidity about them, an area of damp rubbish, a deep
litter of leaves and husks, the detritus of a past life.
About them were the coiled roots of what, by the
look of it, were the foundations of a tree.   Maynard
leaned against an exposed root, or a ridge of lava,
or whatever it was, and in the pause of rest he was
content with the thought that he was nowhere, that
he was out of it.   He was all right with Hoyt.   He
said so.

Hoyt, with his bald head, thin sallow face and
hooked nose, was saturnine.   He smoked his pipe,
and did not reply.   He removed his pipe, looked into
its crater, and said that the whole darned country,
whatever fancy you had of it, was only a cockpit for
big grafters elsewhere.   The grafters would never
see it.   It was no good to them, and none of them
would want it if they could be sure the others didn't.
But the rest would raise hell, in the name of God, if
one of them tried to rush its mineral rights.   "And
look at it," Hoyt invited.   "Look at it.   Did you
ever see anything like this forsaken midnight of
mud ? "

Maynard looked.   He had not seen anything like
it before.   But he did not disapprove.   Utterly
fatigued and at ease, he enjoyed the appearance of a
region of uncontaminated earth.   He did not have
to think.   There was nothing to think about.   He
did not believe Hoyt.   He accepted in lazy gratitude
a harsh but original land.   Europe could not reach as

far as this place. He could see that. It was plainly
outside the rumours and the lies. None of the lies
were here ; only mud and tigers and savages. He
could stand it all, if the savages could. That notion
eased his mind though his body was tired.

All he said was that he saw no signs whatever of
Whitehall.

" What are they like ? Don't know them. But
if you mean London, you'll get the once over from
one of its policemen unless you are quick with the
right grip. And didn't you get it ? How did I find
you ? Yet I don't know . . . Here, time's up !
Come along. Step lively. Eight kilometres to go."

They emerged at last into a large clearing by the
side of a sluggish river, on the opposite shore of
which the forest overhung. The open space was
dotted with huts and the stumps of trees, but it
appeared to be abandoned. Night was at hand.
The place where man had been, but which he had
forsaken, was more forlorn than the forest. Hoyt
crossed briskly to one of the huts, lit a hurricane lamp
within, looked round to see if the interior had been
disturbed, and stood his rifle in a corner.

" Well," he said, rubbing his hands cheerfully,
" here you are, and if you ever see a better home
again you'll be lucky. Wait here long enough, and
I reckon Buckle is sure to come along, if he's still
alive."

Maynard took his ease, too lax with relief to remove

his wet and muddy clothes at first.   He looked round thankfully.   Blue prints were on the walls, diagrams drawn by engineers.   The table was covered with wreckage, empty biscuit tins and bottles, candle-grease flattened into irregular pancakes, and dusty papers. Hoyt busied over coffee.   An astonished bat hung head downwards from a rafter and stared at their lamp.   A lean hound came in, and went to put its sorrowful head against Hoyt's legs.   "Hullo, Bill, you still around ?   Pleased to meet you.   Been having a great time ?   Meet Maynard.   There he is.   He likes this place.   Go and tell him all about it."   The dog looked up at Hoyt gravely, who took its head between his hands and rubbed it with enthusiasm. "Good old Bill," he said, thrusting down his face to rub it on the dog's.

"Look at him, Maynard.   Nice dog, don't you think ?   He can stand up, if the wind's not too strong. Look at him.   Bill's the last of the Novobambia Exploration Company.   That's him.   A large staff once, now there's only poor old Bill.   Come and kiss him for his mother."

"What was the matter ?   No gold here ?   Went bankrupt ? "

"Oh, no.   Not on your life.   Its young men died here a plenty, but they got gold all right.   Its dividends weren't as large as its cemetery, not quite, but they could be seen.   No.   The company got too big for the liking of some people.   That's how it was.

It might have run Novobambia at last, so something happened. What was it? It's you that ought to know. You've just come from Europe."

" Don't ask me."

" Then who in hell am I to ask? What did I bring you here for?"

Maynard smiled wearily, but confidently. If all Novobambia was inimical, this man was safe.

Hoyt swept the rubbish from a corner of the table to the floor, just missing the dog. " Mind your toes, Bill!" He went about producing cups and plates and tinned goods. He pulled an empty box up to the table and indicated another for Maynard with a fork. " Come and quarrel over here."

Maynard was left in the morning, to do what he chose with the day, when Hoyt departed on a journey about which he said nothing. " Have a look round while I'm gone. When you've seen this place, if you know of a way of raising the dead, tell me when I get back."

The clearing was large enough for a township, but its inhabitants were only a few listless half-breeds, who appeared to be there because they had not the spirit to believe they were no longer wanted. They did not even look at him. The hound followed Maynard about, a faithful shadow, and ignored the mongrels of the native huts and their owners. He upheld lugubriously the aristocratic tradition, when there was nothing more to uphold. In the area of the works there was no activity about the entrances to the old galleries of the mine except the continuous briskness of wasps and beetles in the heaps of dry grit and sand. Maynard sat in the sun to watch that life. There was no other life to watch, and the beetles were scurrying emeralds and rubies. They at least were untroubled by the doubts and the interruptions of purposes which crossed. They had received from somewhere a sure direction, and were resolutely intent on keeping it. They did not interfere with each other. Each bright wasp and beetle went sharply about its own affair, which the others ignored. The galleries of the mind beyond, where men had striven for what wealth they knew, were black and cavernous, and Maynard did no more than peer in, for the caverns had the smell of lairage. Just within the forest, and close at hand, beside a trail, and almost foundered in weeds, was a scatter of machinery which had got within sight of its destination, at what cost of labour and ingenuity its bulk unaffectedly hinted under the trees in that solitude remote from the sea; then the human will was broken which was moving it to its place in a profitable conception, and it was dropped and abandoned. Beyond the derelict engines and boilers which had been new, but had never worked, was another little clearing, a surprise to Maynard, who could not guess the purpose of that isolation of sunshine within the woods. He approached it, and saw, from between the trees, a gathering of wooden crosses standing awry; a flock of parrots screamed overhead. He did not give that place a closer inspection; he turned away.

He idled back towards the hut, when the sun was nearing the roof of the western forest, and the obstructions and tree stumps of the clearing began to sink below the incoming tide of shadows. The sky was lustrous, but it dimmed the floor of earth, which was heavy with the burden of its implications and reserve. He saw two men nearing him, and one was Hoyt, by the grace of the figure and the disdain of its stride. The other he did not know till they were facing each other in unspoken appreciation. Hoyt, with a twist of his head and making a wry face, indicated Buckle, as though it were his ill-luck to have to bring together any lonely Englishmen he found at large. He watched them in pretended curiosity to see what creatures so helpless would do when surprisingly confronted. They were amused, and each took an arm of his and marched him between them to the hut.

More of the rubbish on the table was swept to the floor. " No good clearing it all—there's nobody else to come." Hoyt folded his bare lean arms on the board, and the bristles on his hands shone like brass in the lamplight. His face was a little above the narrow spread of light; his amiable but rigid mask was vague. The rafters of the barn were a pale hatchwork in umber; only one wall of the hut was bright.

The domain of their light was brief, and barely upheld the struts and walls of their shelter in the darkness of a continent. Hoyt nodded in brusque joviality to the other two men. " We'll have to make a noise about this. This is going to be a night. I wouldn't swop it for little old Broadway—only don't let the Slave of the Lamp ask me if I want to, or I might weaken on it. The last bottle of whisky goes now. But we can't have the last tin of sausages. It's blown."

Still in a little suspense over what meaning this meeting could have in his affairs, Buckle sat regarding the American in unenlightened approval. His boyish and freckled face, fair hair standing straight up in fixed interest at life's vagaries, and lips a little parted in simple anticipation of the next thing, kept Maynard silently enjoying him. Buckle flattered the faith of his friend with the apparent confirmation that an exemplary but unworldly man will survive the trials of alienating time. But you had to keep close watch on the apparition to maintain it. That expression of Buckle's was familiar, but an effort was demanded to accept it on the upper Mungubeira, for it belonged to the past in a tenement off the Tottenham Court Road when youth was positive and hopeful and never suspected that the world would give no welcome to what was good for it. Buckle turned to Maynard and understood the fun of this unnatural coincidence ; he laughed.

" Hear him laugh," said Hoyt. " Do it again, Buckle. It must make Novobambia so tearing wild."

Buckle was able to do that easily enough. Simple laughter was proper to him. The dog rested its lean head on his knee, and he was thoughtfully puckering one of its velvety ears. He peered from one man to the other, and back again, in a candid pleasure

o

infected by a lurking doubt that gave his cheerfulness a little interrogatory frown. He hardly knew why he was there ; still, he was sanguine of the outcome.

" Say, Maynard," cried Hoyt, " you wouldn't think that man's life work had all been balled up by sons of bitches, would you ? But that's so. Only look at him. You'd guess his rich old aunt had just died and her favourite nephew had her will in his pocket."

The burlesque violence of this comment was amusing, so Buckle's enquiring expression remained buoyant. Hoyt was considering Maynard, who had coiled his small body in a broken cane chair, and was absorbed by the pleasing evidence, which had to be watched, in case it vanished with another laugh, that in circumstances improbable he had found an old friend unchanged by accidents and the years. Maynard guessed, in fact, who was largely responsible for this, and met Hoyt's gaze. His wink told their benefactor that he was known.

" That's right," continued Hoyt. " All balled up. He came out here to keep the flies and bugs off us. You know what they're like ? Yes, you're learning. They make a man rot away, and he never can see why. And what did we do ? Did we make a fuss of him ? If you look in the index you won't find it. Now I'll tell you what it is—there's some of your great magnificos, hidalgos, caciques, and all that, back in Europe. None of us ever meets them, but there they are, and every now and then they give the progress of civilisation their solemn and diplomatic notice, strictly on the quiet, like hell, and then everything has to go the way they want it. They're the boys to show you how Creation ought to have been done. The snag in it is each wants all Creation under his own flag, just to show that trade and true morality go together. So they can't ever agree. When they differ badly about what's good for us, look out, because if we get in the way we'll be pulped between, and won't know what got us, either. Some of those clever God-damned swine thought they'd put a spoke in our wheel here, in case it happened to go round for people whose names they didn't like. You see what I mean? It was against some interest or another that we should go on. And here we are. Your supplies are with the spiders down river. Buckle's test-tubes smash with the whole outfit . . . how's that? Which gang did it? I'd like to hear, but in the cause of civilisation we're bust. The betting is now on the hookworms, and Buckle walks home without a car-fare. That's so, Buckle, isn't it?"

"I suppose so—in a way—but they must have been misinformed," Buckle protested mildly.

"Oh, misinhell!" Hoyt nearly exploded, but relapsed with a sigh. "Yeh, that's what they were. You've said it. Misinformed. I know it, but I wouldn't like to say it myself. That's why they subsidized Broderic. That's why they'd give their money to any pirate who'd sail under false colours for them. They were misinformed. I'd tell the world. You can hear the worm saying that in the belly of the early bird."

A great white moth sailed in, floated slowly round them, circled their lamp majestically, shot in and twanged the hot glass, and dropped convulsive among the litter on the table. Buckle instantly forgot what he had been told. He rose sharply, and bent over the creature ; he touched it with his fingers. It stilled its wings, made ready with an attitude of tremulous attention, and shot off into the night.

" I thought it was," said the naturalist seriously. " That is the second specimen I've seen since I've been here." He returned to his chair and lit his pipe. " That was good. We were lucky to have met that fellow. We may never see anything like it again."

" Don't you think so ? " asked Hoyt quietly.

" No." Buckle was earnest in his doubt. " No. It's one of the loveliest of the rarities. It's worth going a long way to see that."

" You don't think we could have a bit more ? " he was asked.

" More ? What do you mean ? They're hardly ever seen. More ? No, you couldn't."

" Perhaps you're right." Hoyt shook his head mournfully. " Well, I've seen it, if you say so, so now I can go home."

Maynard chuckled. Hoyt turned to him with a gesture to indicate the riddle called Buckle. "What would you do with a man like that? I can't find it in any book. He loses his job, his desk is kicked over and his papers go to make nests for mice, and he forgets it all when he sees a moth."

Buckle protested. "I don't. They can't lose my job. They can only interrupt it. They did it—you know I'm sorry they did, too—just when I was at an interesting point with one of the ticks." He rubbed his nose and made signs with his pipe. "I'd always suspected that fellow. There is not much of him, and he isn't often noticed, though he is always about. No doubt he infests this shack. I think he causes a lot of trouble which is charged to other things. What I wanted was Maynard's supplies, that and a little more time. I might have run him down. But the usual thing happened—I do not expect busy people to know the importance of obscure experiments. Few of us know it. I'll have to leave it for a time. It cannot be helped. My laboratory was closed, of course, when the main job stopped. That was only incidental. We must not blame ignorance for not knowing."

"Huh, you bet we mustn't. Your bugs and experiments, they get no show in a diplomatic riot. Not a comma. They're only something to the good of everybody, and that's no darned good at all to some people. When France and Germany play their great crap game, we don't matter, though we can't live here over four pay-days without getting our bones red-hot . . . I'll tell you what, Buckle. On the last day, when there's the big show-down, and we have to take what we ought to get, you'll feel sorry for poor Mr. Bluebeard. Of course, says you, nobody knows what trouble he had with those women."

Buckle looked sheepish. "I know it's too bad when we can't go on, though we're doing no harm. But we mustn't blame ignorance any more than blindness. It doesn't know it is ignorant. It is part of the conditions of our work, like time and supplies. We always have it about us, but one hardly notices it, except when it jogs one's elbow. Very annoying then, I admit. But a man like me has to remember that if there were no ignorance he wouldn't be wanted. What could I do if there was no ignorance in the world? It would be foolish to expect the interest of anyone in what he did not know was there. It would be silly to worry when he blunders into a job he cannot see."

Hoyt did not reply. He leisurely filled the tin mugs in an ironic silence. The dog strolled to the open door and stood there staring out to learn what that noise was in the night.

Maynard sat up, his hatchet face wedged in his palms. "Hoyt is about right," he confessed. "It isn't ignorance all the time, Buckle, which stops you. Those swells Hoyt told you about, they're not ignorant of work such as yours. They know about it, but it isn't in their line, and it doesn't interest them much. Your job brings light to ignorance. Put it like that. But as for theirs, usually it is better for them to keep their doings dark. They don't want to be seen while they are busy. They're not like you. They hate light. They cannot work safely in it. They put it out, sometimes, when it gets too bright; and they have an apology for causing darkness. Not in the public interest; that's what they say, when they turn out the light. I've learned a little about them. Although I don't know that that is what has happened here, this time."

The scientist was uncomfortable. Who would believe that any man preferred darkness to light, when the difference was known, and light could be got? This did not accord with the men of his experience.

"But I happen to know," cried Hoyt, waving the bottle in his fist, "that that is just what did happen here this time."

"I don't understand." Buckle was feeble, but would not surrender. "You cannot persuade me they intend to do us harm."

"Well," Maynard told him, "I don't suppose they do. What they want is to do good to one crowd of us by doing harm to another crowd."

"But it isn't possible—everybody knows you can't get good that way."

"You're wrong. Everybody does not. It may be your idea, but it isn't everybody's. Most of us see only what is good for number one."

"Then it comes to what I said at first. They're ignorant, merely ignorant. They didn't know what they were doing. So I don't see now how we can blame them."

"Can't we?" asked the American slowly. "Then you listen while I try. Blame them? Not for long. I don't want to waste time. But it would be useful for all of us, it would save a lot of grief, if we shot the damned lot. We ought to do it before they try to do us any more good. This sort of thing can't go on all over the map and only cause a little annoyance now and then. Am I annoyed? Like hell. Would I do anything about it if I could? Look at that gun, Buckle. What's it for?"

Buckle did not look at it. He shook his head sadly, obstinately. "It's no good. It's no good. You can't do anything with that, except make more trouble. Those men can't put out the light. I'm not afraid of that. I say they cannot put it out. I won't believe it. Not all the winds of the world can blow it out. If others do not know it is there, because it is hidden, we do. Don't we? We've got to stand by. It will be wanted, some day."

"All right. Well, you can't stand by it here. You'll have to get it down to the coast. To-morrow we start, and if your light isn't gotten by alligators, or rapids, or fever, or by people on the watch to blow it out, you'll get it down to a steamer, maybe, some day . . . I wish I could see it. That light of yours— I wish I could see it. How do I keep a light I can't see? That's my ignorance. I guess we'll have to try and keep you instead, and risk it."

CHAPTER X

A SMALL steamer was anchored off the mangroves of
the creek. Beyond her the sea and the sky were one
blue depth of subduing heat and light. The huts of
that coastal station, which were crowded down to the
marginal ooze by the forest of the mainland, were
hopelessly discovered by the eye of the day, were too
slight and exposed for that weight of heat. A thin
scarf of smoke from the steamer's funnel, slowly
uncoiling, though no air stirred, was the only movement of noon. The ship was languidly alive, but
of the settlement only its name might have survived,
except that two men in white ducks stood conversing
on the verandah of the largest of the dwellings, their
arms on its rail, looking to the steamer.

They turned to watch a line of men falter down
the track from the forest to the jetty. They could see
white men were with it, and that natives bore a litter
in its midst. The procession stopped under the
verandah. The litter was lowered. The white men,
above and below, scrutinized each other without a
word, for a few moments. The group below was
haggard, bleached and in rags. One had a gun.
That object was conspicuously neat and bright.

"Well, Mr. British Consul, won't you say you know me?"

"I will, Mr. Hoyt, but as you are supposed to be dead I thought I'd like to hear you speak first. Who are your friends? Please bring them up."

Buckle was aided up the steps, fumbling for a foothold, by Hoyt and Maynard.

Hoyt regarded the consul waggishly. "These are countrymen of yours, Mr. Dickson, so they say. They've come through, though everything tried to stop them, even if officially you mustn't believe that." He named his companions.

The consul stared at them, and then put his hand on Hoyt's shoulder. "From all I've heard, everything must have tried, but I see there was an exception. Now I understand—this gentleman is the master of the steamer at the anchorage; speak up, make yourselves easy; we'll have some food at once—ah, now I see, I see. Good for you, Mr. Hoyt. Everything tried to stop you, did it? No names, no names. Don't breathe a word here. That's very funny, but some people didn't remember you well enough, it occurs to me."

"Not so well as I'll remember them."

"No doubt. The same here . . . Well, here's to more good luck. Glad you've come, very glad. How is it now, Dr. Buckle? Is it plain fever? That's all it looks like, so I'm free to tell you that I sent your letters back home last mail. We assumed

—well, what would anyone assume ? "

That pleased Buckle. The ship's master turned to Maynard. "I have letters for you in my ship. They were offered to Quinn's Landing last voyage, but I was told there that you had disappeared, and no word had come down."

"We kept well away from the route to Quinn's Landing."

"Yes, that's plain. You came here. I don't remember that traverse was ever made before. No wonder they thought you were finished."

The consul was evidently gratified by good news he had not expected. "It's lucky the steamer arrived this morning," he said. "As it is, if you had come in three hours later, you would have been too late. She's off at once. You will all leave in her, I suppose ? . . . No, not you, Mr. Hoyt ? Why, won't you get right out of it, now there's a chance ? "

"No, I'm going to disappear again. They don't drive me away. Sorry if it annoys you."

The consul, putting his hand to his mouth, considered Hoyt. "That's it, is it ? . . . I can't stop you, or I would. You know I'll do all I can to help you, and you know how far that will go, don't you ? Hadn't you better think again ? "

"I've done most of the thinking. The fact is, Mr. Consul, I owe something to one or two people around here. I wouldn't like to run away without paying them. We ought to square up, don't you think ? "

The consul tapped his foot. " No. Of course, you wouldn't run away. There are those debts. But wait. You and I will talk later on . . . not now . . . if I may say so, I don't think any of you know what has been going on. I've been more than a little anxious about it. It might have been war. It was really ugly, more than once. The biggest sort of upset was close upon us. To be candid, I got a bit scared. Now we're quiet again—only some distant rumblings. But once or twice I thought we'd have quite a phenomenal storm. Not my fault, you know. You must bear in mind—it's not easy, I'll admit—but, well, you must remember that we unimportant people were merely incidental in the affair. Nothing against Mr. Hoyt. When these international compli-cations begin, men like ourselves can only come in out of the wet, if it happens to be possible. As it was, we were caught in it."

Hoyt nodded, but his face was not promising. " That's all right. Don't worry about little me. I can stand it, if they can. I've got something big back of me, too. Just like George Washington, I'm not French or German, Mr. Consul."

" It doesn't sound like it . . . we wouldn't be talking like this, either, if you were . . . and it is all so impossibly silly, this sort of dispute, imbecile, especially when it's most solemn. There's no sense in it. Take my case. If I may be allowed to say so, I'm doing a dictionary of the principal language here,

and by the time this country is civilized there won't
be anybody to use it. An interesting study, our
language here, with some surprising roots, but when
a civilizing power, whichever it may happen to be,
at last grabs this land, and there are rows of rubber
trees or mining concessions all the way up to where
you've just come from—and it's all coming, you
know, it's coming—then every native will be dead
of measles or syphilis or gin or bullets. Mr. Hoyt,
you're not the only sufferer. Don't you think so.
And that's the sort of man," said Mr. Dickson,
genially, pointing to Dr. Buckle, " there he is, who
makes the happy transformation possible. Without
science it could not be done. There is hardly a
discovery of science but what is at once put to a
barbaric use, for the profit of the energetic barbarians.
It's only more power to the elbows of that sort of
people. We notice, too, what the learned Dr. Buckle
himself gets out of it, eh? No, Mr. Hoyt, you're
not the only sufferer."

" Right. Then I'll be the only sufferer who kicks.
Watch me ! "

Buckle was troubled. " I say, don't do it. Don't
be a fool, Hoyt. There's nothing for us to do here
now, but go. Leave it to them. You come with us."

" I'm afraid it is no good." The consul himself
sadly answered for Hoyt. " It is useless to talk to
him. I know him, and I'll tell you what will happen
to him, if he goes on . . . no, I won't, because as I

am so certain about it you might tell me later on it was my fault.   There is no cure for human folly, that I know of; if you check it in one particular it breaks out in another place.   I'll see if I can make him drunk to-night and get some sense into him. He's much too sober and logical now.   You'll have to leave him to me."

Maynard leaned limply at the door of his cabin on the bridge-deck of the coaster, watching the land. The ship's anchor was home. They were free. He saw two figures returning along the jetty to the house, their backs to the ship; he kept his eye on them. The consul was holding Hoyt by the arm, and they were talking together. They did not look towards him again.

That was over. The black ooze was disturbed and writhing alongside the ship. Novobambia, which for long had been static and without end, was diminishing now and revolving, light and ephemeral, the earth visibly spinning on its eternal pivot. The transition from one thing to another, usually unnoted, was plain, and was rapid—the jetty went, Hoyt and his friend went out of the picture just as Hoyt unexpectedly turned to face seawards, the house followed them, the hill behind it went astern, as though the dissolving views of life had become so swift that for once he could see a period running out. The last dark tongue of the mangroves slipped out of sight. There was the sea, open and empty.

He went inside his cabin. Buckle was asleep in

the lower berth; or else the fellow was comatose, for he was startlingly like a waxen image. Maynard leaned over him to listen to his breathing. No. Buckle was all right. He was sweating hard. That was a bit of good luck. Maynard looked round the cabin, and saw his letters tucked in the rack of the washstand. He took the first; he was quick to get a message in Charley Bolt's handwriting. It was from London, dated August, 1909.

" . . . you knew something, to clear out of England when you did. I happened to become a journalist, so old-timers mournfully explain to me at the Quill Club, just at the time when our placid old planet, always so nicely behaved, and kind to journalists, took to drink, as it were. Is there some maddening celestial nectar in the patch of the Galaxy where in these years our system happens to be, and sun, moon, and stars, kings and crossing-sweepers, are all squiffy together? Even the bright sun has a spotty face, so the observatory says, and we have to suffer for it. Anyhow, once upon a time, the old-timers explain, you could sit in the Club while day passed and most of the night, and you might not be wanted, except for a horse-show or a foundation stone. To-day, something exciting is happening every hour, right round the horizon. Each bonnet has its bee. There's a fellow called Lloyd George, for one thing— you may remember him faintly, from the days of the South African War when we sang *Soldiers of the*

P

Queen together, and he would not join in. He's
coming on, now. He is Chancellor of the Exchequer.
He made a speech at Limehouse over the Budget
which made the bees fairly lift all the bonnets. A
loud and angry buzzing fills the country. His Budget
is called revolutionary. It would amuse you. He is
raising Cain for the good of the common people, so
I gather, and the dukes are weeping into their coronets
about it when they are not begging to be shown his
mutilated corpse. My own view is that he means
nothing by it except at the moment he says it. He
means it then emotionally, but forgets it afterwards.
He enjoys the jolly excitement, and so do we. It
makes you feel as if something great were about to
begin. The dukes and earls, and their bosom friends
in the suburbs where the virginia creepers grow, are
quite tragic about it, and you would think aristocratic
strawberry leaves littered the pavements in this saddest
of all years for what is noble and good, even in
Brixton. But don't worry.

" Though you won't, and I know it. Out in your
tropical grove, untouched since Adam and Eve left
it, you will not understand what I'm talking about.
No stir of this commotion over the birth-throes of
democracy will agitate a single fern of your grot.
What do you care ? Cunning that you are, you got
away from us before our condition was plainly
noticeable. I said you knew what you were doing.
Though why didn't you give me the tip ? Here we

have to work, for things are happening. Yet our country might be going to rack and ruin, and there you still recline, the admiring brown nymphs about you, bringing you cool fruit, kneeling to fan your face, while you idly plait garlands of orchids for their enchanting bosoms. You ought to blush for yourself. When are you going to abjure the dear enticements and the primitive peace, and come back to where real men are stoutly fulfilling God's purpose? Try to make up your mind, if it has not already gone too soft in balm. Do you even remember that you have not sent me a greeting in six months? Though perhaps, worse than all, you have discovered a gold mine, and have turned atheist.

" And what are we doing at home? Pay attention, to get it on your conscience. To show you that this is not intended to be a funny letter, I'll give you an example or two of a week's work. And each week is like the others. It was but recently that the Thames was filled with warships. I suppose to acquaint Londoners with the fact that we have a Navy. Now they know it. I never learned the reason for this terrifying object lesson, but there the ships were, a most dubious but impressive spectacle, stretching from below the Nore to above Westminster Bridge. It has never happened before. Why has it been done now? It is lucky that we have a peaceful Liberal Government, or I'd have been nervous about it, and have wondered what was going on behind the scenes.

" The squadrons of big battleships, including the
Dreadnought herself, were down at Southend, and there
I had to go and live, for I'm supposed by the editor
to be a naval expert; I've lived in Poplar, as you
know.   But I could barely live in Southend; I nearly
died there, in fact, of ptomaines, suffocation, and
worry.   The shore was black with sightseers by day,
and improper by night.   The multitude of holiday-
makers, thoroughly happy playing with their very
own battleships by the beach, ate through Southend
to the last bun and saveloy.   There, all the same, I
had to remain—till a doctor sent me home—for our
loving Radical newspaper had to be satisfied daily with
columns of fun about guns, armour, man-power,
torpedoes, and Happy Jack's comic, because maritime,
encounters with admiring and affectionate little girls
on holiday. Sailors never can do harm.   Their
rollicking bawdiness is only laughable.   It was all a
great lark, with acres of sandwich papers and orange
peel floating out each tide, as though we were trying
to poison the very sea itself.   The tide recovered, I
suppose, but I did not, and went home sick.

" And had barely got over it when I was bundled
off in a hurry to Dover.   The worse our luck, there
is another anxiety added to the life of a journalist:
you may not properly appreciate the fact that men
can fly now. They're always trying, and dying.
Well, there was a rumour that a Frenchman named
Blèriot was to attempt to fly over the channel.

Nobody believed he could. Very few of us thought anything at all about it. But in case he did——! You know our editor, you remember Paddock, who looks more like a poet than any poet ever did, yet has never read a poem in his life. ' I think you had better go,' he said. ' He won't get over, but the other papers are sure to be on the spot.'

" I need not remind you that Paddock used to turn all the experimental attempts at flying into a regular comic feature of his paper. Men would never fly ; they never had. He sent our funny man, as a rule, to cover the hilarious efforts of men to get off the earth, but that day our funny man was doing a murder, so he was not free to make a humorous column out of the drowning of this lunatic French-man.

" Only the journalists were at Dover keeping watch. Nobody doubted that the sea was the sea and that we were still on an island. And nothing happened. The next morning was misty, with no earthly chance of a miracle, and we were all at breakfast, and I was wondering how the trains returned to London. A waiter put my ham and eggs before me, and said ' Blèriot is on the cliffs, sir ! ' Just like that. He was, too, and he hadn't come by boat. Nobody but the coastguard and the birds saw him alight on English grass. There his machine was, a monstrous dragon-fly which misliked me, for it looked sinister sitting there with its queer nose in the air. The chagrin of the journalists—me, too, sir !—was pathetic. We felt as if we had been swindled by this Frenchman. The worst of it is that in the future I suppose we shall have a new form of sport, with irrepressible imbeciles imitating Blèriot, trying to hop from one side to the other, and they will keep us in Dover watching them shower from the sky to drown. Anyhow, one man has flown across the sea—a cripple, too, for Blèriot had hardly recovered from an accident ; a good man, that !

" Talbot asks after you affectionately whenever I drop in at All Saints—the vicarage, not the church —but you have not given me much to tell him, have you ? I have to go and see him, dear Maynard, though my family has moved away from that grey and grim parish of his. He is the only man I know —except one other, who never writes to me, bless him—who does not appear to be disturbed much by the increasing uproar of progress. When I told him the story of our strange adventure at Dover, he only listened, and then turned to stare out of the window. You would have thought the old innocent expected to see Blèriot above the chimney-pots. He is the sole bit of London which is not rapidly changing. He belongs to another order of things, though whether that order is of the good old days, or is far in the future, I will not guess. Why have you not written to him ? If you knew what he thinks of you—it makes me jealous, it do—you would have given him a word to show you had not forgotten him. Write to him at once, you idle man, because he wants to hear something better than the noise made by a journalist who whirls along from one excitement to the next. Come, my lad, drop that lotus bud . . ."

PART THREE

THE YEAR
1914

PART THREE

CHAPTER I

At one end of a great oak table, a piece of editorial furniture on which a scatter of portable telephones projected like miniature black gallows above a wreckage of newspapers, Charley Bolt lolled with his head turned in boredom to gaze out of the window at his elbow. The pages of a manuscript were open before him. Outside, in the half-light of a winter afternoon, he saw a row of pigeons humped on the pantiles of a near roof of Fleet Street. They were always there. There was no other news. There was a lull. Bolt yawned and looked at the clock, and then round the room. Jim Maynard was reading at the other end of the table.

" We're gone a week into this happy new year," commented Bolt, " and nobody has taken down that 1913 calendar yet. That's enough to show you what it is like." He picked up a heavy Government report on the Present State of the Coal Mining Industry, and weighed it. " Let's do something to knock last year off its perch. It hasn't any right there." He flung the report at the calendar.

Fenton, the literary editor, was opposite Bolt, absorbed in the correction of proofs. The abrupt noise made him wince.

"Sorry, Fenton. It was only my foolishness. Tired of waiting for something to happen. Though I don't want anything to happen now before five o'clock, as it hasn't happened yet. I say, Fenton, you've read this novel of mine, I suppose, seeing as how you've handed the stuff back to me; but you haven't said what you think of it." Bolt gave the manuscript in front of him a push, as though in dislike of it. "Don't be afraid to strike. Something is wrong with it, and I can't see what. Tell me what it is. Is it too bad?"

The literary editor leaned back in his chair. He was friendly but judicious. "Not at all. No, it is not at all bad. I think it is good. You ought to go on. I was going to write to you. But if you don't mind my saying so, good writing isn't quite enough for a book. Your stuff is so metaphysical. That's its trouble, to my mind. Abstract. And, er, haven't you noticed that you haven't got a woman in it?"

Bolt sat up, suddenly alert. That was important and true, and he had not thought of it. "Why, no, there isn't—not yet." He paused in concentration, as though he must choose a woman instantly. "But anyway," he murmured, after reflection, " there is a child in it. It's about a child. One must assume . . ."

" Oh, no. I don't think one should. Readers should not be expected to assume. It is hardly right to dump a child like a foundling on a reader's door-step. If you expect him to keep it, it ought to be made attractive—he ought to know where it came from—all about it."

" All about it." Bolt muttered the phrase in the irony of disappointment. " I'd like to meet the man who does know all about it. I say, an author isn't an angel, taking the first and last words out of the book of doom, is he? How on earth is he to know all about it? You surely don't expect . . ."

" Yes, we do. We have a right to expect. We expect a novelist to tell us all about it and to com-pletely surprise us with the common facts. But you've omitted Eve. That's a nice thing. I can see what's the matter with you, Charley, you're afraid of women. But when you write you mustn't be afraid of anything, not even of the ladies. Fancy leaving a baby in a book, and pretending not to know how it got there. We shouldn't mystify life worse than it is. I'm uneasy when it is metaphysical. Try not to be too shy. Dare to look the lady in the eye till she blushes. You needn't worry about her tender feelings. She won't mind."

Mr. Fenton stood his blue pencil on the table and

eyed it exactingly. Then he continued. " The reader doesn't care for metaphysics. He doesn't recognise life born in the air out of an idea—it's as much as he can do to pass an immaculate conception. You see, most likely he is afraid of women. He is glad to meet someone who pretends to know them. As for the ladies, it will amuse them, anything you say. There you are. I think you ought to have something which at least can be said to resemble a love interest, to account for the child."

Charley smiled. " I should have thought—it seems to me that if there's a baby everyone would assume there was a lady in the background somewhere."

" Where ? The background ? That's no place for a lady. We want to see her. Your diffidence is unnatural. Bring her forward. Let her have her due."

Fenton switched on his light. The room was getting dark and he could hardly see Charley. " I recognised and I admired your infant's Wordsworthian clouds of glory, but they're not evidence, except that you can write. It is all very fine to trail those clouds, and I must say it wants considerable skill. But that is all bravura work. The public wants something more earthy—not clouds of glory, Charley, something it knows, napkins, anything it has seen. Leave what the eye hath not seen to the poets."

Maynard was hidden behind his own light, his head in one hand, reading. He closed his book and rose.

"Charley, we shan't be wanted now," he said, "if we make outselves scarce at once. I'm ready when you are."

They left the office together, and took a bus for London Bridge. They passed the classic mass of St. Paul's in its immemorial soot, with its facings of rain-washed stone, as if the chief temple of London was itself a permanent tribute to darkness, and was on the point of being absorbed into the power to which it was dedicated.

"They'll be glad to see you at home again, Jim. When were you there last? Wasn't it when you got back from the tropics?"

"That was when. By the way, that was interesting, your talk with Fenton. You're doing a novel, are you? and you never told me."

"Not likely. It's no more than an experiment, I wouldn't dare show you yet—not till I'm more certain about it. Fenton would examine the fragment as though it were out of a heap of specimens. He's a hard case, and he is used to it, and doesn't care tuppence for me. You wait till it is finished. If I can bring it off, I'll do you proud."

They sat silent for a spell, each secure in comfortable companionship. Their problems lost acuteness when they were together, and without speech. They had learned that fellowship could mitigate life. They turned to look over the side of the bus into the gulf of the Pool of London, a bottomless gloom in which floated wan and irrelevant gleams. That was an old place of theirs for a long pause, to peer into it before parting, at midnight, with hopeful guesses into their future. But the years were hurrying. They were fairly caught in the run of affairs, though somehow they had missed what they wanted. They were beginning to see, in fond retrospection, that the past was growing deep, even deeper than those lights and shapes of the Thames. The romance of the Pool for them was personal to-day, though once it had been outward, with the bright Indies beyond the murk.

" I don't think Fleet Street is good enough for a lifetime," said Bolt. " Its excitement is like child's play, and always with the same toys. But what can we do ? I thought I would try to open the door out of it with a book."

" That might do it. It might. I haven't tried that. The book I should like to write can't be done by me. But I've tried other things."

" You have, and come back."

" And come back. You go out through a door to something different, and after a time somehow you are back in the same place again, you hardly know why. Because the earth is round, I suppose."

They learned at the station that they must wait. A fog somewhere had dislocated the service. They loafed about. " You sent some amusing yarns from St. Moritz," Bolt assured his companion. " Those about the winter sports. Was it really as good as that ? It ought to be tiresome, that deliberate sort of fun, but your stuff read as though you were frisky."

"Well, I felt pretty good. I took Betty Whittaker's boy with me. Talbot asked me to give him some fun. He's a delicate lad. The nipper thoroughly enjoyed it. You should have seen his face when I opened the bedroom shutters the first morning—it was dark when we got there—and he saw his first pink glacier high up in the sunrise. That was worth the journey. He won't forget that. And then the mixture of all sorts of Europeans dancing together at night, as though they'd forgotten everything against each other, that was amusing. Three German girls took Betty's boy off my hands, as much as I'd let them. Sisters, and lovely creatures they were, too— Heine would have made a chapter out of them. Do you ever see Betty now ? "

"Me ? No. Nobody does. I'd like to. You didn't know her, but she—she's all right. I've heard Langham still wants to marry her, out of remorse, to get right with God, or something. But she won't look at him, so I'm told. She's in with the suffra- gettes now, and a bonny fighter she makes, you can bet. Perhaps she's in gaol—window-smashing or some- thing—I don't know. Think of it ! Such a woman and Langham, that doleful ass."

"Don't be hard on him. It's long ago, and he couldn't help it."

" I should say he couldn't. I knew her then. The blessed girls, it's funny, but they make a gift to a fellow like that of what we wouldn't dream of begging for. I'm afraid Fenton is right about me."

" Of course he is, but don't grieve. You can manage without that gift. I don't know Miss Whittaker, but I'd guess there's more of the mother in her boy than the curate. He's a quick and wistful little kid. He wanted to know all about everything, and it woke me up. There was a lark in the train coming home—I don't think I told you. I was trying to explain to the nipper a bit about the way the lakes and mountains were made. Two other men were in the compartment, talking politics in German, rather fiercely. One of them was a big fellow. His overcoat was lined with astrakhan, which always looks immoral and unclean to me. He had pulpy pale hands, with rings sunk in his fat fingers. He appeared so important that I supposed he didn't know I was there. But presently I told the nipper something that was wrong, and that big fellow put me right. He had a proud but kindly smile. He talked English like one of us, only more exact. He assumed I knew no German, and lectured me on English laziness, heaven knows why. ' You English are not what you were,' he said. ' You have got all you want, but excuse me, sir, you will lose it. India you will lose, and Egypt. I have been there, and so it is.' It was curious, but he seemed to know more about our Irish troubles than most of the people here. He even had the inside facts of the Dublin strike—I was at that show myself, and I know that hardly a newspaper allowed the facts to show through its prejudices. But that German, he knew them. He'd got them. He had his conclusions about them, and Carson and the Ulster rebellion, and everything else, all cut and dried. I don't know how he managed it, but whatever he knew he could fit into a cockeyed plan, and that settled it. He wasn't arguing ; he was telling me. His information, I must say, was shockingly various, and exact, as near as I knew. And everything that was going to happen was going to benefit Germany. I think he must have got it out of the book of Daniel. It was useless to argue with him. I'd never met one of his sort before, and it was funny, at first.

" Towards dinner time we stopped in the middle of a big junction. The boy was hungry, and so was I. I could see a buffet in the distance, across the metals, and got up to make a rash break for grub. That German put a kindly hand on my arm. ' Excuse me,' he said, ' there is a buffet on this train. It is also forbidden to cross the lines.'

" I hadn't time to tell him what I knew about the diner of the train, but hopped it quick, and got back only just on the tick. The poor kid was in a state of alarm. The train was moving. He thought he had lost me. When we began to eat, that reminded the German. It made his mouth water, I expect.

He said he was going to the dining-car, and would I
look after his bag? But in a minute he was back
again, very sad. I knew he would be. There was
a diner on the train right enough, but our carriage
was not connected with it. I'd noticed that long
before, but I couldn't let on to him, then, that I knew,
could I? It was too late.

" Perhaps because the chap was hungry, but had no
hope, presently he began the usual revelations about
a coming war. I wasn't very interested. But you
ought to have heard him. It was like an eclipse, to
him, down in the calendar. No doubt about it. He
had that war taped and sealed, too. He asked me if
I'd noticed his artful military railways on the Belgian
frontier. 'We shall be in France in thirty hours,'
he explained airily.

" At last I got tired of it. 'Where do we come
in?' I asked him. He smiled sadly, and he was
awfully polite. 'Excuse me, sir, but we shall see.'
I felt I couldn't stand it any longer. 'You won't
see,' I told him, 'because if you start this foolery
you'll get a brick in the belly so sudden you won't
know where it came from. What do you think
our navy is for?'

" Do you know, that big fellow crumpled up. I felt
sorry I'd spoken. I was a bit ashamed of myself. But
he had been an ass. We got on all right after that.
He was much milder. Not a bad chap at all, apart
from his long-eared confidence."

A porter began to chalk a notice on a board, and the two strolled over to see whether it concerned their train. They saw there were ten more minutes to wait.

Maynard's story, which helped to fill up the blank space of a local fog, gave his friend a vague but profound uneasiness. Charley turned to Jim. " What's wrong with a lot of them ? They talk like that. They've got war on the brain. It might be gin, they're so excited and sure. You call it tedious. It gives me the horrors. My dad talks just that way. Don't for goodness' sake tell him that story of the German. It would start him off for the evening. It would prove right all the feelings he'd ever felt about it. I can't stand it. Tell the mater about Betty's boy and the dancing instead. She'd love to hear it. That's more in her line."

THE home of the Bolts, in that mellowed and worthy southern suburb of London where of a dark evening you might think you were in the open country but for the regularity of the streets, the frequency of the lamps, and the distant jangling of trams, withdrew itself at that hour entirely from public notice. It did not display a light. Its friends would know where it was and nobody else mattered. It had a right. Its people had concluded their daily service to the community, and now they were retired, isolated and content. They had earned peace. Their house no longer existed for outsiders; only its shrubs and outer fence were there, to mark a starting-place for the work next morning. When Charley Bolt turned in at his gate, his friend looked up to see whether this entry was not a mistake. They found a sad porch, in the neglected stucco of semi-detached Victorian sepulture. Then in an instant the interior heat of the house manifested itself; a fanlight came into existence as an illuminated arc above them, and the door opened. What had seemed so dark and unpromising showed a warm and lighted heart. Maynard smelled newly baked cakes. Annie Bolt stood within, to his momentary surprise, though he knew her again. The girl had become a woman, and the cool welcome of such a little woman was, for an instant, disconcerting, as well as pleasurable. Maynard, getting his coat off while resolving his surprise, awkwardly rattled the sticks and umbrellas in the stand. Annie thought Maynard was tired and sad, and she would have liked to put a hand to his coat, but she refrained, for that very reason. He was so much smaller and frailer than that great fellow Charley, and had the appeal of a lost child; a fond imagining that would have tickled her brother, who knew the deceptive metal of which his fragile friend was made.

Mrs. Bolt met them by the stairs, making a play of resisting the exaggerated greeting of her boisterous son. She was in a grey dress, slight and neat, with an old-fashioned cairngorm brooch at her throat. Her hair, silver now, was more decorative than when it was brown. She was brisk in her welcome Maynard, and solicitous for his comfort. " Come along in by the fire." She made a pretence of rebuking her son for being late. " We've been waiting for you—spoiling the tea. There wasn't enough fog to stop you. Don't tell me that."

" Not to stop us, mother, but the trains. You don't know our local service because you won't use it. I don't believe you know the name of your own street yet."

It was a grateful fire she had kept for them.   Mrs.
Bolt was an artist in fires.   She was unaware of gas-
stoves because they were unknown in her young days,
and she was innocently deaf to the treasonable suggestion for installing one.   But in the right deep
good hearth, with coal and blocks of wood, she could
awaken in a guest, and set it glowing, that primitive
instinct which once was fully satisfied when there was
food enough and a lasting blaze in the midst of the
glacial dark and the beasts of the night.

Mr. Bolt was nursing the cat by that fire.   He
abruptly spilled it on the floor as he got up.   Solid
and spruce, he was in his shirt-sleeves.   His coat was
found for him, and his wide shoulders were helped
into it, while he grumbled.   Not all the persuasion
of his daughters, with the tart reminder that he was
not in the shipyard now, would get him into the
custom of wearing a coat in the house.   " Putting
me in irons."

" Think yourself lucky it isn't a strait-waistcoat."

" That's how I get talked to.   How are you, Mr.
Maynard ?   Don't you have any daughters, or you'll
get the life of a dog."

" Why, Tom, Mr. Maynard isn't married," explained
Mrs. Bolt, doubtfully.

" Isn't he ?   Well, he ought to be.   Why should
some of us get all the knocks ? "

Mr. Bolt snuggled his bulk into the curves of a
high-backed chair of Yorkshire yew, which was so

seasoned to his shape, and to that of his father and grandfather before him, that it gleamed in gold and bronze. Maynard, glancing at him, thought the head of that shipwright was admirable; the grizzled hair, plentiful and turbulent, and the massive face with its light eyes and haughty mouth, were rightly framed by the shining semi-circle of the back of the chair. It would still go ill with any stranger who provoked him. His tawny hands rested on the arms of his chair; he lifted his chin and began a jocular crimination of his children. Their mother had ruined their characters with too much ease. It was the same everywhere. You didn't know what a job was like till you had to take your coat off to it, and then after overtime leave it till next morning. There it was, looking at you again. So far as he could see, all that suburb knew was golf and bridge.

Young Jack Bolt spoke up. " Dad, a bit of fun doesn't do us any harm. What's the matter with a little golf, when the office is shut? Surely the ships can look after themselves for an hour or two? "

" Ships? Because you do freight accounts in Carroll's office, and swindle the Government with demurrage, do you think you know anything about ships? Why, you never see them."

" Neither does Carroll himself, yet Lady Carroll can run a theatre for fun on the strength of what he doesn't know about the ships he never sees."

The father shook his head, and his thoughts

resorted sadly to the heart of the fire before him. Down by the side of that fire Annie had sunk, her dress spread in gratifying lines about her. She was attending to a dish of muffins. Maynard noted the complacency of her bent head, with the firelight in the looseness of her fair hair, her cheeks a little scorched, and one trifling foot just showing by the cat, which was a black image of luxurious ease in full possession. Mrs. Bolt was concentrated upon a silver teapot. Polly Bolt, very like her sister except that she was pale and dark, was busy with her mother at the table. Her sweetheart, Mr. Drake, whose work was in the office of the Carroll Line with young Jack, timidly essayed to correct his elder on what young men know of ships. He twiddled a masonic sign on his watch-guard as he spoke. Mr. Bolt glanced sideways quickly at Mr. Drake, as though he had just become aware of that young man's presence.

"What do you know about a job you never see? If you can't touch it you don't know it. Everything nowadays is done happy-go-lucky by those who can't see what they are doing. It's all got too big. Young man, you can't see what you are doing, and you go to play golf hoping it will be all right. That's about the size of it."

"That man," said Mr. Bolt, pointing largely to an old portrait in oils which hung above the blue glass lustres and the spotted china dogs of the mantelpiece, "that man could plan a ship, build her, load her, sail her, and make money out of her. He knew his job. Where's his like to-day ? " Annie briefly glanced up at the portrait of the grandfather she had never seen, but had heard about often enough.

" He didn't make much, Dad," suggested the younger son. " After all, Carroll couldn't build a ship and couldn't navigate one, but he's grown to be a peer and a millionaire out of ships."

" Out of what lots of other people do with his ships," softly hinted Annie, who well knew the uncertainty of her father's temper. " They don't make a living now out of things, but fortunes out of people."

" Here, my girl, what do you know about it ? " Mr. Bolt lifted his eyebrows at Annie, not altogether in disapproval.

" She talks like Lloyd George does about the peers," said Mr. Drake brightly and tactlessly.

It needed all the prompt wiles of Charley and Annie to manœuvre the party away from the loom of that storm. The evening paper, which Mr. Bolt had been reading, was on the floor, and its headlines, even at a distance, proclaimed the public debate, with its open threat of civil war, which then made England anxious through the avowed intent of the Commons of England, now they had taken from the Peers of the Realm their ancient power, to give Ireland the right to govern herself as she pleased. Old Mr. Bolt kept Disraeli and Chamberlain in tender recollection, and was a stout royalist ; he subsided again, still snorting, into his chair.

" All his life," explained Charley cheerfully to Maynard, " father has been giving the best he knows to add to another man's riches. His integrity has been pathetic. Now he can't make out why he is poor himself. Can you, dad ? "

" Oh, you get away. I know you. I don't want your blarney." But he was distinctly mollified.

Mrs. Bolt waited patiently, desiring the talk to slacken, too gentle to interrupt the pleasure it afforded them, though her muffins grew less hot. Her brown eyes roved benevolently from one speaker to another. She rarely gave close attention to the conversation there, unless it concerned the immediate welfare of a member of the family, for her thoughts were on what next to do for them so that they should find anything desired and necessary without knowing how it got there. Lloyd George and his campaigns, Carson and all Ireland, were much less to her than the regularity of the milkman. She assembled her people at the table. Mr. Bolt reversed his large chair at her command. She got them going. She kept them going. She knew food was good for people, that it gave them more cheerful hearts, and she took care to have the best of it, and to supply it generously. That they should enjoy it was the only compliment she desired.

Jim Maynard and Mr. Bolt were easily in accord.

The father approved this young man, who knew even the words of the songs that once were popular but had gone the way of the beautiful ships of an earlier Thames side. If he could not remember the second verse, when the first and the chorus had partly recalled the jovial past, Charley's friend knew a word or two of the way it went. That was something like a sound intelligence. Mr. Bolt became expansive, for Jim showed his good taste, much to Mrs. Bolt's dubiety, in prompting more of those animating stories of younger days in the neighbourhood of Limehouse. What the ship's master said to the owner when told to accept more cargo than she was built to carry, though moderated to the delicacy of the best old tea-service then displayed before them, was still good enough for Jim to encourage, and Mr. Bolt always warmed to good company. Jim surprised Charley, who had never seen his friend so unreserved. He might have known Wapping, from the way he talked of the " Old Mahogany Bar," and " Paddy's Goose." Ratcliffe Highway ? Those places ? Mr. Bolt knew their insides. He described them ; and he remembered one night——

And this also, Charley thought, when the tale was done of one hospitable occasion long ago, is also one of the nights. He would remember it well. Jim, at his ease, his hands clasped behind his head, was watching in delight the vivacity of the shipwright, who, late that evening, glowing face to the fire, sang them a song about a " Pretty Polly Perkins of Padding-ton Green," which nobody there but Mrs. Bolt had ever heard before. Polly's wilful adventures were in many verses, but Mr. Bolt pursued her in frivolous determination. And then Mrs. Bolt, hitherto of almost silent service, moved by the urgent and humorous prompting of her mate, and perhaps because she felt she was in safe and thankful hands, began seriously to acquaint them, in a small and quavering voice, with a correct rendering of a song which was called " Champagne Charley " when the world was young. This was how it went. She ignored the surprise and loud mirth of her children, which they did not control, but went on, giving them as much as she knew of what she could see they relished.

" Come again soon, Mr. Maynard ; come and have a pipe any time you like." Mr. Bolt's invitation was hearty, as though the evening had been altogether to his mind, and he wanted more like it. " Now don't go and forget it, chasing suffragettes, running after bosh. I can tell you something better than that."

Jim was wishing Annie good-night. He promised not to forget.

On my way from Victoria Street to Charing Cross I tried, as one does who is suspicious of a matter through fear, to guess a reason sufficiently bad for Maynard's hasty departure for the Balkans. That is a noisy bit of Europe, with abrupt and unseemly manners—they can be very playful, the active gentlemen of the Balkans; but I could only recall that *The Times* had been pointing out to us, in case we were too busy with domestic affairs to notice it, that spring was coming to the Balkans. " The Turks . . . the Serbs . . . the Bulgarians . . . with the melting of the snows . . ." Now it was March.

But the short cut I was making to Charing Cross through St. James's Park was not so short as I had expected to find it that morning. There was an intermission in the park, an interval which I was unaware had been added to London. The doubt about the Balkans left me. A lawn which sloped up from the lake was alight, yet nobody appeared to have noticed it except a mandarin duck and myself. This wintry earth suspired in little flames of lilac, white and gold. She had remembered the crocuses.

It was a triviality which surprised me. I had

forgotten, in my preoccupation with more important things, that it was possible. That very morning, before entering the park, I had happened to notice the famous leader—though he never was exactly auroral—of those stalwart rebels who in Ulster and at home, had vehemently sworn to give us this evil and that, whatever might be the consequences. There he was. Sir Edward Carson moved unseeing and unseen through the multitude of innocent folk. They obviously did not detect any cause near them to turn bitter their bread, though Sir Edward's face had the imperious inclemency of one who knows his cause is righteous. Not a daffodil was there. His cause not only was righteous, but his men had guns.

The mandarin duck and his wife eyed me enquiringly as I stopped. Perhaps they were curious to see whether one of the human mob would now come to his senses, as he had the chance. I could not fail to notice their idle confidence that all was well. The grass burned in coloured flames. I frowned with a new surmise. So it is possible, I thought, that a life exists which can fulfil its cheerful destiny whatever men may choose to do with theirs. That other life may go on in light and colour when our divergent, strenuous and treasonable energies have spent themselves. Too bad! It displayed itself, that life not ours, and made its jocund but mocking signal to us; mocking to me; for though my mission on that spring day does not matter now, and may not have mattered then, it happened to concern the increasing zest for intolerance in my fellow citizens. Why, the conclusion already was hanging over us, that desolation which is inevitable for turbulent brothers who hate each other because of their devotion to noble principles. We were facing heroically the result of the honesty of our hearts ; yet we did not relent, for we had come to where pride could give sweet reasonableness the look of shameful surrender. No surrender, we cried ! If our British house could not be run as each desired, then we would set fire to it, and thus should it acquire purity. And, for the first time since an English king was challenged in Parliament, to lose his head by the axe through an ineffectual answer, it was being whispered that our Government could not depend on its army as an instrument for the enforcement of its decrees. We were in for trouble ; because what is a Government when its soldiers begin to doubt their special privilege to kill, or would prefer to kill to their own liking ?

So the spring of 1914 was irrelevant to the pavements of London, which normally can be but wet or dry. My surprise, in that pause in the park, was natural. I had forgotten that the earth could incline to the sun, and come in due season to brighter things. Apart from the affairs of men it was developing well, this new year. We were insensibly drawing towards the summer, whatever we should choose to do with it.

R

Summer was coming to our aid. We need only turn from darkness to see that light was come. There before me was the sign. It was remarkable that a Chinese duck should know it and accept it as proper, while I had to stop to ponder in which of the two worlds I stood. Was this spring for us? I could not help thinking it existed apart. It was there, but only for those who desired it. Perhaps one could enter it if one learned the way. The inviting lawn was prismatic, the trees had changed faintly through the beginning of South in the air, an intimation which so stilled them that they could have been expectant in another region, a region near me, lucid and calm, with no visible barrier, but inaccessible. From its boundary I could see, beyond the flawless mirror of the lake and the tinctured exhalations of spring, the Foreign Office, the Admiralty, and Whitehall Gate, and they were white palaces faint in the remoteness of a time that did not exist for men whose hearts were dark and desperate.

I had to leave it. I could not enter it then, had I known the way, because there was another thing to do. We always have another thing in hand, which we dare not forego, even though we fancy we hear a still small voice warning us, and thus the world is able to get on with its lustier improvements. At Whitehall Gate I paused again, for beyond it was the material and busy London, which I must enter; yet it was very uninviting.

Something was up. Mounted constables rode briskly to and fro in a heavy press of people. There were occasional fluxes in the crowd, rushes, and derisive yells. As I sought for a way across the road, keeping as well to the loose margin of the mob as I could, I saw, still as unbelieving as when I noticed the signs of a better life, a group of fellow citizens quick and gay in their intent to tear the clothes from a girl. She faced them frightened but resolute. She sank out of sight by a wall. " Give her a vote," shouted a laughing man, " she'll want it now." A policeman roughly shouldered through that group.

Out in the road was a clear space, and a woman central there with a suffragette banner. Policemen cantered towards her. She advanced to meet them, with the measured stride and port of Juno herself, and I had just time to recognise Betty Whittaker, whose high look was that of yet another righteous cause, before the mob congested about her and the police. She lost her banner, in any case. Somebody plucked at me, and then began to swear. I turned and there was Charley Bolt. It was not easy for me to keep him out of it. " Here, you can't do anything. She doesn't want your help. The police will take care of her."

" The swine ! " he cried. " By God, it's the hue and cry. The dirty hunting dogs ! "

I edged him out of it, and presently we found ourselves in an underground train. Charley was silent. He sat staring before him, seeing nothing, though there in front of him was a man gleefully exhibiting a long rag, the truth of which he was explaining to his eager friends, whose interest and amusement were unusual. They, anyhow, were perfectly happy; but what I required was a brief space of quiet in which I could settle the discordances of my thoughts.

"What is he saying?" Charley at last asked me impetuously. But I had not been listening.

"What are you saying? What's that?" Charley addressed himself directly to the group.

"If you want to know, it's a bit of a girl's drawers —it's a little souvenir . . ."

Charley hooked a finger over his twisted nose, as if trying to understand; then he swiftly rose and leaned over the fellow, some of whose teeth he loosened. He bunched the rag leisurely into a ball, and dropped it out of a window. The group started, made as though to act, but relapsed and merely stared up at him. Charley certainly was large, and looked calmly murderous, though pale.

"Brutal thing——! What's that for?"

"Don't know. Shut up, or I'll do it again."

It occurred to me that it would be better for us to get out at the next station, and so we did. There we saw a flower-seller at the exit. She spoke to us earnestly, and held up for our interest a basket of violets. We had passed her; then Charley stopped

and turned about. " There they are," he remarked,
" the flowers that bloom in the spring." He paid more
than the necessary silver for two bunches, one of
which he gave to me. " I think we had better pro-
pitiate the gods," he mused ; " we've been forgetting
them." As I took his gift I noticed that his knuckles
were grazed, and that his hand trembled a little.

" And that reminds me," he went on, " that I've
got two tickets for some music to-night—Beethoven—
there's a quartette. I think it is time we had some.
Let us go and forget this."

While yet it was the evening of that day I was
waiting for him at the great editorial table, waiting
for him and Beethoven, and was alone in the room.
It was necessary to answer the telephone.

" Mr. Bolt, please ? "

" I'll tell him—I think he's somewhere in the office
—what name ? "

" Tell him Miss Whittaker—he'll know."

Our editorial chief was humming a tune as he came
slowly up a flight of stairs, down which I was hurrying,
trusting to find better fortune in another room.

" Who, Bolt ? Oh, he's gone. I had to send him
to Dublin. He went more than an hour ago. Straight
off ! He told me to tell you, and now you know."

IT began to appear, in the early summer, as though the horizon, the place to which we look for what is to come next, had worked loose. But however it may be explained, it was beyond the wit of man to adjust his reason to the eccentricity of such a year. The prospect could change for the worse if you withdrew your eyes to examine your breakfast egg.

There is but one thing to do when the ordering of the planets cannot be amended ; the heavenly augury had better be allowed to have its way. I permitted myself to go with the ordained but whimsical movement of our celestial body, trusting to be carried in safety, though the mass and speed of everything did seem to be vertiginous and our direction unknown. For that reason, when a ship's steward presently woke me, and said we were getting into Belfast, I wondered, not altogether present, who he was and what he meant. Then through the port window I could see moving past us the half-tide alluvium of a great seaport. A warped black pile went by, solitary in the pallid vacancy of dawn. I had not wanted to go to Belfast, but hurrying events had carried me thither. Into the light framed by the round of the port came

a mudbank with a population of immaculate gulls.
That bank heightened and enlarged ; it mounted soon
into a gloom of scaffolding which enclosed the unborn
body of a great ship.   A wharf wall slowly approached
till I could see its beard of wet algæ.   Above it was
a deserted quay with its sheds and a clock tower.
The face of the clock was still illuminated, though
day had come.   The yellow dial of the night, past its
time, was watchful among the silent and sleeping
buildings which day had discovered.   A far church
bell chimed, a little warning which came easily a long
way in that pellucid silence ; and then, somewhere
to the back of the shed, a cabman started his horse
with a clatter on the cobbles, the first inconsequential
noise of a city getting to its business.   And what a
business was said to be there !

I did not know Belfast, but soon little was visibly
odd about it except the street names, the jaunting cars,
the directions on the electric trams, and the shape of
the police helmet.   I found a blue midsummer
morning, and the semblance of a prosperous city.   I
could see nothing wrong with it ; yet its shipbuilders
and the weavers of its famous linen were ardently
preparing for an anniversary which Belfast had always
celebrated with bonfires and songs.   This summer the
glad day would have a dangerous significance.   The
celebration was over an ancient triumph ; two kings
and their hosts had been warring, and one army was
properly whipped, though long before our day.   In

its pride, the city would not allow this glory to fade. You would have supposed that whatever the battle of long ago meant to the men who fought it, to modern Belfast its importance was that of any arrow-head turned up by a ploughman intent on another kind of harvest; but you would have been wrong.

Upon the walls of the city were scrawled that day the battlecries and the provocations of men who were bones. The men were dust, but their curses lived on, and this was because the dispute arose over the correct way to honour God. It was even possible that this year the celebrant bonfires would involve the city. German war correspondents paid a friendly visit to see it burn, but the flames were too slow in rising for their patience, and they went home again. It may have been that privately its citizens were not inclined to destroy what they owned, however much they prized their invisible past. It was states-men, strategists, and law-givers, men who did not live there, who were most resolute for the noble sacrifice.

But nothing was happening then. Belfast's pave-ments along the crystal fronts of its fine shops were impeded by leisurely and well-dressed women. Its business men were intent and hurried. Its newsboys ran and shouted—though I did not understand them —barefooted imps of panic. The city displayed its imposing municipal buildings, Greek in that classical manner of recent wealth embarrassed by unaccustomed style and raiment. It had numerous factories of red brick, and many new churches, and factories and houses of God together over-topped regions of old slums ; out of the congestion of sad grey homes rose the factories, new, huge and inflamed, as though they were nourished richly by the civic body on which they grew. I was easily at home. Belfast was an excessive tribute to the spontaneity and benefit of our compulsion by machinery.

A newsboy padded swiftly past, crying " Wolf " or " Fire," and as he fled with his cry I had time to see only the word Assassination on his rumpled bill. Of whom ? Was this the beginning ? I was too slow to note all his warning, but they who could see it were undisturbed. The ladies remained leisurely contemplative before the latest fashions, the men of business did not pause. I turned up a side-street, where there was a little shop with a window full of painted images, devotional books, and religious symbols. A virgin within, in blue and white, stood as though gazing down benevolently to a placard on a board outside the shop, a board which announced the assassination of an archduke and his archduchess.

So that was it. That would be far enough away. That murder did not concern our present anxiety. I discovered indeed that the victims were Austrian, and as distant as Serajevo. It was bad, but it was not our trouble. I went on.

I remember of that day a narrow street after dark, and a flaming tar-barrel on its stones. Within the wavering cavern which the flames held open in the night was a ragged and barefooted girl, who danced to the thudding of a drum. Her youth, I thought, had been absorbed by the thirsty factory bricks to make them red and robust, and that had left her own body little better than a bony and barren spool; yet her eyes and copious ruddy hair showed what she might have been. Beating her monotonous tom-tom, she danced with the leaping reflections of the flames, chanting defiant ribaldry.

Before daybreak I left the city, and went out towards the hills, and there, with the smell of the warm moist earth and its lush things of developed summer, and in the broadening and tranquil light, that child of the slums dancing in rags round a tar barrel at night, chanting war songs, went like a dream of far-off days and mischance. The clouds were aground on the hills and I went up to them. As I mounted, the dark earth lightened and broadened below. The sheer limestone turrets of a summit shook in the flood of a great wind; and from that aloof, ancient, and enduring place I could see that the prosperous city below was temporal. It was already illegible. It quivered. The elements were solving it. The morning clouds travelling with the driving flood of light closed over the valley where the city was, and the diminished buildings shimmered, grew thin, and faded, a wraith overtaken by the dawn. Light shone through the city; it disappeared in an empty brightness; and below me where it had been was a plain of silver where better men, should they will it, could write the name of another city, that could loyally meet the dawn, and stand fast.

No light of such a kind, however, was shining through Belfast when I was in its streets again. Light did not manifest itself there, nor anywhere else in Europe, that one could see, to reveal to men the rifts in the structures of their societies. Men supposed, doubtless, that they would have time enough in which to build anew. Just then they had other things to do, and these they performed in a mind that was rigid in its persuasion of virtue and honour. Not next morning, nor in the weeks which followed, did men relent with the conjecture that their cities are but transient, and that they may, because of errors embodied, tumble when stressed by verity, and unexpectedly leave us with sites of virgin mud for our wiser architecture, should we have the heart for it.

As things were, it was hard for us to talk of the present because events moved too fast, and the future we preferred not to think about, for we guessed what it might have in store for us. It was the past which controlled us, and there was no escape from its endowment. What men had predestined must come. Jehovah, that god of wrath and battles, must have known that he was called to his kingdom again. The traditional signs of his favour were besought ; he was reminded of that old controversy with Baal. Wherever in the sands of the Syrian desert the ancient fetish was lost, that mystery of the sacred tabernacle and the symbol of the power of the priests, wherever then it was hidden, the bones of its sacrificial victims must have stirred about it with a memory of old terror, at the echoes of invocations, harsh with renewed hate, crying from the ultimate groves of our own islands. Presbyterian divines, without a thought of the Irish tailor in whose trousers and black frock-coat they stood, named the Amalekites with anger, and called for the sword of the Lord and of Gideon. In the temples of the opposition, with rites modified by the newer and gentler influences of the mother and the babe, the aid of the same god was invoked, but for another cause. The ghosts were stirring ; and though statesmen and lawmakers grew more solemn in their guise of leading the humble, the captains who drew men on to the steep place in a twilight were the spectres of the dead. Old weapons buried where the cattle were grazing in that year's summer were thrusting up bright points through the mould, evil perennial from aboriginal seed, the harvest for our gathering of error which had not perished. Immortal man ! His mere transgressions, buried in antiquity, like the dust of toadstools, will come to life again whenever the heat and darkness are right.

The common rooms of the Belfast hotels were filled

with meddlers, journalists, and politicians. We circulated opinions, rumours, whisky, legends, and lies. We waited in impatience and hope for what we could hardly define, but were sure all the world would desire to know. I met there in beguiling relief, as though he were the sign of more pleasant and stable days that were gone, Charley Bolt, in my hotel one morning. He, though, was not hopeful. He was fretful. He had abandoned Dublin because he did not know what to do there. He had come to me for advice. He was perplexed, I gathered, by impersonal threats and perils, evils in the air, yet in Dublin he could not find one reasonable man to whom he could turn for an interpretation. He said it was not easy to write in a lucid way of preposterous bogies and of a universal, furious, but invisible maggot.

That was it. A necessity nobody understood had merged us all into a headless power. We were a common flood of mankind hurrying on. The waters were rising. Where, Charley asked, had he better wait?

He could not be advised. The confused currents were not of nameable men and women. They were the uprising from sunless springs of ancestral emotions, and already were at the bounds of reason and control. Destruction might overpour anywhere, at any hour. Charley disappeared the same day. One place, he could see, was as good as another. When Charley had gone, Maynard was stranded by an eddy from

London, in our hotel lobby. Our office, evidently, was nervous. But he was indifferent and melancholy. He was even lazy. He said there was nothing now for anyone to do but to wait for it.

But he was wrong. It may not be possible to lessen the danger of crisis, when passions are loose, yet it is easy to increase it. Not a few men saw that. One stout little Napoleon had bustled into Ireland, who knew what use to make of primitive fears and transports ; Lord Northcliffe surveyed, for the good of his printing machines, the scene and its promise. He was pouting and autocratic, and Pandora's box, he left us in no doubt, was his familiar personal trunk ; he did not want it to disappoint him, when the lid was up. He took charge of it. With the stern countenance of authority summoning the spirits of the tempest, he ordered his young writers to their inaugural duties as storm petrels ; they flew about ; their forbidding plumage rebuked the laggard lightnings.

It was, in truth, necessary to supply our own ominous petrels. We were not warned by anything in the sky. That gave us no sign. The sky might have been serenely unaware of our terrestrial scuttlings to and fro with guns, plots, pale earnestness, and secret stores of bullets. The blue of the sky was luminous joy. Not that we paid much attention to the calm canopy for our drama, except to be grateful that a review of Ulster's armed men should have an

appropriate sun. I became embedded, with other
visitors from London, in the good-humoured crowd
which filled the city's chief thoroughfare. On such a
fine afternoon, and as relaxation after a week of toil,
everybody wanted to see the actual weapons.

We heard distant cheering—there they were!
No; here were but His Majesty's red-coats. We
saw them in surprise, and with a presentiment of
alarm, but recovered, and gave them an embarrassed
cheer.

The chattering and expectancy began anew. The
smell of road dust was mingled with that of oranges
and massed humanity. Then in the distance the
encouraging handkerchiefs of the ladies began to
flutter, and a roar increased on its way down to us.
Here came the stalwarts! These men were not
afraid of making civil war. They were in khaki, they
bore Mauser rifles, and marched defiantly to in-
spiriting brass and the exultant drubbing of sheepskins.
The children were held high to see them. Several
jaunting cars followed the Orange rebels, carrying
machine guns. Those unfamiliar engines pointed
back at the holiday makers from their superior seats,
and swayed in such drunken pantomime of insolence
that the crowd could not help its happy laughter going
after them.

Yet rifles have a poor sense of equity. They do
not always discriminate. The next day, Sunday, we
heard it rumoured that they had gone off in Dublin;

men had died there for doing what in Belfast the day before was but an entertainment for applause. The first shots ! We waited in the ensuing quiet, in which men felt their minds rapidly cooling, for our immediate streets to break into flames, because we knew what inflammables were stored there. It is long immunity from an explosion which makes its peril worse. We began to see that then. Few of us have been blown up and buried alive ; so we forget, while gossiping life cheerfully circulates about the cannon silently waiting, that they are cannon.

So intent were we in watching for the first red glare in the sky immediately overhead, that nobody noticed the sign of what could have been a fire beginning far eastward somewhere near the country of the Danube. Its reflection was much too low to be noteworthy in the northern heaven of our brooding night. Yet Maynard, who had some knowledge of the secret trains laid to the powder magazines of the Continent passed the news across to us at breakfast. Austria and Serbia were mobilising.

Most of us regarded the brief message indifferently. What was it to mobilise ? This scientific genesis of calamity was an abstraction to us. One sage and elderly colleague glared at the annoying paragraph through his spectacles, though he did not put his hand to the newspaper ; he was otherwise occupied ; he glanced away to the more interesting platter of grilled breakfast bacon.

S

" To hell with Serbia," he remarked.

There came a night that week, after rain, when Jim and I strolled through the deserted streets of Belfast to the chief telegraph office.   I had no business of my own to do there, so I was free to note that the telegraph clerks, usually so affable, were too engrossed, though there were no signs of more work than usual, to exchange the usual friendly raillery with meddling strangers from another city.

Maynard left the office.   The two of us paused. The little man essayed to light his pipe, under the frigid glare of a street lamp.   The silver rods of a desultory rain were falling through the light of that lamp ; and while I can remember the things that have happened they will continue to fall through it.   Maynard frowned over some difficulty with his pipe ; it was no good ; he put it back in his pocket.   He stood as though considering whatever he may have seen in the empty night behind me.   I could hear a drunken reveller in the next street.   The gutters were running an undertone to the dark.

" Did you catch what that fellow inside told me ? "

" No.   I don't know that he spoke."

" He only whispered it.   They've been all day calling up the fleet reserves."

I felt on the instant a little tight about the throat. This was a fact I would have preferred not to understand too well.   The meaning of so urgent a summons by the State was certain, though it was but a legend to both of us.

"That means . . ." I began, yet left the word unsaid. It was a grisly word to say aloud.

"War. It looks like it, doesn't it? Ireland will look after itself now. We must go home."

Midnight had struck. The drums of Europe were beating to quarters.

The railway terminus at Holyhead next morning was dingy and sullen, for the hour was early. It surprised Bolt to see so many people there, at that hour. He had been recalled from Dublin to London by a mysterious but alarming telegram. Did these people know its meaning? He hoped it meant no more than the anxiety of the timid, yet he had been too intently watching Dublin to look to the rest of the world to see what it was doing.

He recalled his old disputes with his father about war. Now what would Dad say to him? Charley could hear his father saying it. What did I tell you !

Whether all these people were holiday makers, or whether they were moved by the same news, the news he had in his pocket . . . where were those infernal newspapers?

Too early yet? There was no news. Not a sign. The morning was bleak and overcast. The busy and inscrutable crowd, the waiting coaches, the dingy girders of the station, the forlorn squalling of locomotives, and the driver of the London train, who stood in his cab leisurely rubbing his hands with a pull of cotton waste, contemplating the people gravely, as though he knew of a destination not in their ken, had that ironic appearance of the indifferent things of the day, the common day when we fear that life for us has changed.

There in the distance came the news of the morning. The papers were dumped on the platform just before the train was due to depart. A clerk and two boys fell upon the parcels with the indifference of custom to get them unpacked in time. A few passengers, but only a few, waited unconcerned for something to read. But Bolt had never more impatiently held out his penny for news he hoped he would not get. The clerk himself did not even glance at what he was selling. He was not interested. Whether you were tipped the black spot or got an invitation from the Hesperides was all one to him.

The opening of that paper was as startling to Charley as the loosing of a maniacal yell at his ear. The morning broke into a senseless clangour, as with the cries of lunatics in multitudes terrified and contentious, and the beating of brass and iron. The magnified headlines bawled the excitement of the gathering of millions of armed men, with the alarms of Paris, Berlin, London, Brussels, and St. Petersburg. He could hear under it all, in paragraphs more obscure, the protesting cries of the workers in the capitals; though the alarm of Berlin was cut short in its record, as though stifled. It was consternation smothered before it was articulate. And, he then noticed, as though it were a symbolic act, the forewarning of what now would be done in darkness, that the benign and enlightening mind of Jean Jaurès had been put out. Peace, sitting at its dinner in its accustomed seat, had been shot through the head by a madman. Peace was dead.

In London, that first Sunday morning in August, 1914, had the enlarged bright calm of a summer's day of rest. Charley could hear the bells of St. Bride's. The Temple pigeons were preening themselves in the sun. The office of his newspaper was hushed. Many of the staff had been distributed over the Continent, and he sat there, in charge of the day's happenings, waiting for news from absent colleagues. But the world across the channel was dumb.

There was no more news. The array of tape-machines, which till then had never ceased to chatter divorce, cricket, horse-racing, the police courts, and the lives of the great people who dignify the pageant of life, were either asleep or were severed from the world without. Europe, the last they heard of it, was at strife, but it was more silent now than the composed Sabbath. The pigeons made love on the pantiles; and Howard, one of the writers of the articles which lead public opinion, strolled in, because he had nothing else to do, and sat on a corner of Charley's table. He was young, plump, bland, and rational. He belonged to the high caste of scholastic prizemen from Oxford, and his cultured amusement before delusive appearances, and dexterity in showing how to compose awkward junctures in human events with erudition, made him an engaging conjuror in those tricks known as foreign affairs. Charley merely listened to him, and admired. He knew he could never unravel a tangled skein so easily.

"They have been asking for this," explained Howard, "and now here it is. It is not our show. Looking on won't be easy, but it is the only thing for England to do."

They turned sharply to watch a telegraph instrument. They thought it showed signs of waking up. No, nothing there.

Howard swung a plump leg, and resumed. He was a philosophic Socialist, and he was not a little gratified that this crisis demonstrated precisely what he had always said would be the outcome of the intrigues of the Powers to secure control of coal and iron and populations. Yet it would not last long, this war.

"The fighting can't be done without money and supplies. Now just think of it. Here they're emptying the factories of workmen to make soldiers of them; from production to destruction, Bolt. Well, then. How's the wealth to be made? They'll soon exhaust what they've got. Besides, finance and banking, at bottom, rest on nothing but a faith that workers everywhere, grumble as they may, will always obey the factory hooter. But suppose they don't?

Anyhow, the worker cannot follow the drum and attend to the factory hooter at the same time, can he ? I give this war six months. You see what's going on here already. The best people are in a bit of a panic. Their motor cars are loading up at the provision shops while food is cheap. The chap on his way to work notices it. He knows what it means, or he soon will. You can see the fear of the working man already worrying the best people. They are telling the worker what a stout fellow he is, buttering him up, saying the country can rely on his patriotism. Rather ! A nice thing, if he turned round, and found we were all riding on his back ! War always ends in revolutions, and everyone on top here doesn't want one. No fear. We shall keep out of it."

The sun of the day of rest was bright on Howard's gracious and intelligent face. While Charley was admiring it, and trusting that its word was as good, a tape machine came to life. That stopped the swinging of Howard's idle leg, and the flow of his gentle wisdom. The machine hesitated, as though uncertain of its message. It went on again, in rapid and staccato certainty, yet before the two of them could get to it it was still. They reached together for the length of tape, and spelled it out. " German troops entered Luxemburg this afternoon." That was all.

The leader-writer stood looking at the ribbon of paper extended between his hands for fully a minute, as if considering an item of foreign news that was unusual to him. His voice had changed when he spoke to Bolt again.

" So that's the way Germany is marching! Then I'm afraid the game is up," he said. " Nobody will stand that. We are already at war."

PART FOUR

WAR!

PART FOUR

CHAPTER I

It was our first day in the war, and that train, a favourite with holiday-makers, and bound to a popular resort at the height of the season, had but two travellers in the luncheon coach. There were six waiters to look after Bolt and an elderly stranger; four of them slept. Nothing was said during the journey, except, "Another piece of bread, sir?" and "Here is Yarmouth, sir." Bolt had been sent to wait for an early word of the decisive naval battle, which was inevitable, and would be fought at once, in the North Sea. Everybody said so.

His fellow passenger was a small and elderly man, with a high and polished dome to his head, and a neatly trimmed grey beard. He had other signs of matured intelligence, yet sat studying throughout the journey an evening paper as closely as though he were positive it contained news of his own fate, but with all his patience he could not find the place. He would put the paper down, and make as though to compose himself; then, seized by the doubt again, would reach for it and rustle it impatiently

in another fruitless search.   He could not find what
he wanted.

Now and then he turned as though he would address
himself to Bolt, but changed his mind, and made
bread-pills instead.   The elderly man always turned to
the window whenever the train passed under a bridge,
to stare with renewed astonishment at its guardian
sentry.   Where had these soldiers come from ?   He
never missed a bridge.   He wanted all the bridges and
every man in khaki to confirm whatever thought had
taken him.   As for Bolt, he was indifferent, or else he
was vacant with the apathy which comes when a blow
has put an end to custom and habit.   He sat at the
window, watching England at war with Germany.
Last night at home, oddly enough, his father had
barely mentioned the subject.   He had been quiet.
He only sat, with the newspaper in his hand, but not
reading it, and grumbled that he hoped it would be
over soon.

England, from the train window, Bolt could see,
appeared to be much the same as ever.   A heron had
not heard the news ; it stood there in fixed reflection,
the image of an established order never to be broken.
The war was only a horrid thought.   It was only a
dream he could not forget.   If he could get it out of
his head the world would be all right again.

A venerable man rested on his spade in a garden to
watch their train rush past ; the peasant regarded them
with an intentness so untroubled that Charley felt the

old 'un was sinister and mocking, as though he knew all, and was indifferent while they sped past to what he knew was waiting for them. The hills did something to reassure him. They had not stirred from their ancient sleep. They slept on. The sky was surprisingly blue and peaceful; but the more Charley saw of it the more he felt it was no better than the aged labourer, too old to care what happened to men.

Somehow, bedevilment had come. This was worse than any black trick of an Arabian Night. Where was the catch in it? He saw beside the line a footpath, and the footpath followed the railway over a bridge, and by the bridge the path was thick with stakes bearing an entanglement of barbed wire. Anyhow, that looked as though something was expected. He could see the sea, and over it, at a great height, was a waterplane; the North Sea or German Ocean, as he used to teach the boys in school. Straight across from the windows of the train were the embarkation quays of Emden. Under the lea of the near sand dunes was a cluster of bell-tents, and a gap in the dunes behind them had a breastwork of sandbags.

He scrutinised the scene not quite believingly while it was in sight. The soldiers were smoking and gossiping, and some were sprawled on the turf below the sandhills. On a summit of the dunes two figures stood aloof, having no concern with their idle mates below; they brooded on the distant skyline like statues. When Charley turned to the carriage again his fellow passenger glanced at him, as though seeking in his eyes the confirmation that they had witnessed the same evidence. But he did not speak.

Yet, when he was at Yarmouth, Charley found the same old crone selling coloured balloons to the children on the sands. The shining expanse of waters was empty of ships, so the idlers on the beach watched the incessant patrolling of the aeroplanes instead, as though it had nothing to do with them. In idleness, any object is good enough to watch. The fair on the sands continued its mechanical tumult. In the harbour there was some quiet fun ; a German schooner had heard of the war, and had come to port among the peaceful English to escape from the French.

Charley listened anxiously to the conversation at the hotel table. The diners that night, and for several nights, had much good news to give them a relish. The Germans, he learned, were repulsed in Alsace and Lorraine ; they were at a standstill at Liége, and the Belgians would not give them the time for which they begged to bury their dead.

" That'll teach the brutes," said the man in evening dress on the other side of the table. The terra-cotta shades of the table lamps did not allow the man's face to be seen distinctly, though it deepened his likeness to a handsome cavalier. That soft light, the wine, the ladies, the sparkle of crystal, and the usual rites, were earnest of England's secure tenure of the real good things, and of the steadfastness of virtue. The man

opposite invited his lady to wine. " Armageddon ! "
he said as he eyed the bubbles humorously. " The
Kaiser is sending out ultimatums by picture-postcard."

Anchored close to the hotel in the purple warmth of
that summer night, the pavilion at the head of the pier
could have been a joyous ship sprinkled with
coloured stars. It was musical with its company of
dancing youth. Far beyond that ship of joy, Bolt saw,
in the outer night, a flash of light, and listened for
whatever would follow. He heard nothing. He
heard only, while still waiting for the signal, the
sound of heedless feet tripping to the gaiety of the
music, and beneath that happy sound was the murmuring of a tide he could not see.

He agreed, with other men in that hotel, that he
would keep watch till morning ; the telephone might
call. The word might come while they slept. The
lights of the pavilion went out at midnight ; only the
sea could be heard along the Strand ; mice ran across
the floor of the room where he waited alone. He
went through a row of old volumes of *Punch* he
found there, with their cartoons of the weekly
crises of the past, baffling then with lost meanings.
When the lamp paled because the dawn shaped the
windows, Charley lifted a blind, and peered at a new
day, faint and incorporeal. Midway across it in the
east was a line of gold, so frail that even the mist could
support it. He could make out the grey beginning of
gardens on the sea-front below his window. They

T

were not entered yet ; man might never have entered them. They were waiting for him to come. Then, out of the flawless vacancy of sunrise over the ocean, a number of long black shapes were born ; they crept along the shore as noiseless as a train of dark and secretive thoughts. The destroyers !

THE dining-room of the Quill Club in Fleet Street soon became a sensorium of unwonted hopes and fears. The war was stimulating. They were capricious, those fears and hopes, because born of the air. They dilated and drooped, were febrile and then turned cool, for no known reason but change in the way of the wind. A cheering word would spread from a corner, brightening its confirmatory rosiness as it went, or a whisper would quiver its alarm, and then the tables would deaden to the bare sombreness of the sound of plates and cutlery. The younger members of the club began to disappear, and it was better not to ask about their journey, nor its end ; the bald heads and the grey developed a new sensibility to chance more stimulating than the luck of the card-tables ; they turned anticipatory eyes to the dangerous movements of existence, and became young again in all but the quality for the recruiting sergeant. Maps appeared on the club walls. Its members were often intent, faces to the wall, in unusual geographical studies ; they named places with familiarity which sometimes could not be found on any map, occasionally because the names were not there.

"Where's Chartres ? There ? Oh, yes. I see, I

see. Well, there is something in that story of the Russian army over here. Cossacks. Great chaps, those Cossacks. Kerby, he's knocking about France for us, and he says there's an encampment of them at Chartres. Horses, too. That looks rosy, doesn't it ? "

Beadles, lank and shortsighted, peered at a map past another man's head, his shoulders rounded in his fixed concern. A waiter briskly adjusted an Allied flag some miles nearer to the English channel.

" Whad'you do that for ? "

" The news has just come in, sir."

Beadles removed his glasses, sighed, and slid into a seat at a table. " I can't make it out," he complained, as he unfolded a napkin. " Those damned Germans, they're always being checked and decimated, piled up in heaps, checked and repulsed, and they've been annihilated more than once."

" What's the matter with that ? What are the swine for ? "

" Who said they weren't ? But it does seem funny to me that every victory of the Allies brings the enemy nearer to us."

" Never mind, Beadles. Let me tell you something else. The little British Army is over there now, and the Kaiser is going to get two lovely black eyes. O, what a surprise ! "

" Our army in France ? So I've heard. I hear a lot, but I don't believe much of it."

" You needn't. There our lads are, just the same."

" Our army—our boys are all right—but the Kaiser won't make two bites at that cherry."

" Well, of all the black edged Dismal Jimmies! Cheer up. We're going to have our Christmas dinners in peace, Beadles."

" Think so ?" asked a man lower down the table. " In case we don't, I've just got in two sacks of flour, a side of bacon, and two tons of coal."

" Lucky fellow! Well, I'd like to tell you, and I would if it weren't so public, that if I could do it I'd take the lot away from you, and shoot you afterwards."

The hoarder of domestic stores wiped his mouth and laughed. " So you say now. You talk to me about it later on. None of us will have any more morals than monkeys over nuts before long. I'm going to put my morals in cold storage till it's over. Best place for them. Shan't have any use for them for a bit."

Another voice was raised which turned our ears that way. A member was speaking who so well understood the tactics and stratagems of great soldiers that he could draw simple maps through which civilians could peer into the mysteries. He was pointing a gold pencil at a diagram on the back of a menu card. " What if Brussels has fallen? See here! Isn't the German army within the jaws of a trap? There. Brussels is a bait. The greater the length of the enemy's line the greater his

danger. The French will cut across him to
Liége . . ."

But I was called to the telephone. I had to leave
them hurriedly, and make my way to Victoria Station
and France.

Fleet Street, and all the streets of London and
Westminster, though free now of the anxieties which
till a few weeks before had put over them the cloud
portending dissolution, no longer betrayed notable
signs of adversity. The sky was clear. The streets
were sunny. The crowds accepted the summer in
which there was an inexplicable excitement. Only the
War Office, which once had the quietude of a national
museum, was exceptional with the activity of a hive at
swarming time. Figures in brown uniform clustered
at its entrances, and passed mysteriously in and
out unceasingly. Civilians paused to stare at the
phenomenon, in little groups, curious in their free
world apart from it, as though what was happening
within that building was exotic, and belonged to
another order of life. A kilted piper approached the
War Office from Trafalgar Square, skirling along a
column of young recruits in the dress of their offices
and workshops. They carried handbags and parcels.
Elder men, who paused to watch them go by, raised
their hats respectfully.

My train left at its appointed time. That im-
perturbable guard, the porters at their duties, the
settled aspect of familiar landmarks, were composing,

and checked the anticipations of mischance by headlong thoughts. The common round, with its in-
herited volition, the necessity to button and to
unbutton, saved us. A man should look to his
bootlaces though that night the stars are to alter their
courses.

The crossing to Boulogne was familiar and con-
soling. The steamer was French. The seas of
August with the leisure which comes of an assurance of
a world without end, were canorous and slow. In
that bright plain, where the sails of a few ships remained fixed to the base of the wall of the sky, like
abandoned attempts at the relief of a mass which had
proved too spacious, there was no sign of an evil which
had come to pass a shadow between us and the sun. A
sailor stood near me, watching the waters on our
starboard beam. He shouted, and pointed excitedly.
The thin neck of a submerged monster was rolling
towards us, sentient but heedless. The seaman
regarded it in frozen anxiety, and our steamer swerved
so sharply that I could see the wake boiling as a
semi-circle. Then the sailor clapped his hands in
relief, and ran to dip the tricolour. The White
Ensign had fluttered on that sinister nondescript.
Yet that little incident left me unmoved. A voyager
would not suppose that that object which had risen to
the surface could have been a German submarine.

When our steamer sidled into the jetty, Boulogne
appeared steadfast and unchanged on its ancient

settlement; but strangely there were no gendarmes to look on, and no officers of the customs to intercept us. We could do as we pleased. In such waterside alleys as the street of the Tin Pot, with its foreign smell of fish and drains, the Boulonnais were listless and glum. They looked to the future with a grimace; as for the day we were in, there was nothing to be done now, they said, but take the moon with the teeth. Boulogne was expectant, yet stared at nothing. But yes, it shrugged, you have seen we are abandoned by the military. Why? The Boche is coming. An explanatory arm here was waved to the east, from whence would approach what all good men hated. Charleroi, that is lost; Lille has gone. It is the deluge. Now Calais, Boulogne——!

The highway coming from that eastern region on which darkness had settled was strange with a migration of men, women and children, heedless of us, drifting slowly westward endlessly, weary and apathetic. The refugees from the terror looked as though they had been tramping through the night. They did not pause. Fear had prompted them, and there was nowhere to go. They went on through the town, set adrift from old habits, unable to stop, their household goods bundled on their backs, and in perambulators and handcarts, the children trailing to the skirts of their mothers. They were as aimless and slow as a stream which has lost its channel. A child stumbled and vomited. Its mother, nursing an infant, turned and bent over her sick child, and waited.

The hurry and pother at the hotel, from which so many visitors were departing, made it unconscious of guests who would come in. Madame, in the office, pale and resigned, did not see this wayfarer. She was talking to another woman. " I wake up. I do not know what is there. Something that is of yesterday, something that has changed everything—then I remember. Ah, yes, the war. It is the war. . . . Yes, I have heard, they fought like lions, those British. My father came from Bapaume yesterday, and he told me. But he says the Boche is in Cambrai and Peronne. . . . Ah, monsieur, you have come at a bad hour . . ."

Still, friends were there from London and elsewhere. I could not see Maynard, though, and it was my mission to find him. An American visitor knew of him. " If he's not careful, he'll find himself in Germany, or stuck up against a wall. He was down near Amiens, the last I heard of him. You can't go there. You'd be arrested. It is British Headquarters, or it was. But I'm for Paris. Yeh, that's a great machine, that German army. It's going to run over us all right. She slipped her cogs at Liége, but my God, she's running fine now. She was built for it, and see how she goes. Paris for me. I'm going to be in that siege."

The cool American thus spoke, and then considered,

lost in his anticipation of a sensational future, a
fountain that was playful in the floor of the hall. I
also looked at it, as though the fountain could be
interpretative. It had shabby rockwork, with a
feeble squirt of water at its heart, which agitated both
the sunken distortions of a few goldfish, and a shoal of
floating stubs of cigarettes. At the end of the room a
large picture faced me, a coloured but faded induce-
ment to pleasure, in which a nereid arose from the
bubbles of a glass of wine to prove the virtue of a
brand of champagne.

A TRAIN, next morning, was taking us out of Boulogne. The sunlight was customary. Perhaps day, in its natural innocence, was mistaken about the scene of earth—or else we saw only a midnight brightness, the beguilement of a troubled sleep. Perhaps it was not sunlight. Our destination was conjectural. The train was merely taking us out of that town. It went hesitatingly for hours through a land which hinted that, since men grew wheat and apples, only the weather changed. Its people, who could not be seen, would learn their quiet earth was turning because of the imperceptible blending of the seasons. That was its appearance. But where were its people? The sunlight was bright, but it was merely expectant of the next thing, and that had not come. The land was empty, except for our watchfulness.

By a steep embankment, its tall weeds fixed in the heat of a noon which we doubted for a snare, the train succumbed to the spell. It went to sleep. Time itself stood. A river below was sinuous through its meads, but even that was caught; it had no current. On the eastern horizon was a line of poplar trees, so regularly spaced that they could have been brought to a halt on their march. They waited with us.

As though on an impulse that we must wake up and escape from this, the carriage doors along the length of the train noisily opened together. Women and children emerged and climbed down among the wild flowers, agitating them. Then a near cottage came to life. An old man appeared at its door, hesitated, to convince himself that we were there, then idled over to lean his arms on a fence by the embankment. He touched us from his separation in an illusion. He smoked and talked. He waved his pipe to the line of poplar trees. There! Six kilometres! The enemy is there!

The engine woke, and hissed. The passengers scrambled up the bank and aboard again. The row of trees on the horizon, which we continued to watch, made no sign. They were on the edge of the dream, which resembled an innocent land of summer. Kine were knee-deep in a pool under the shade of an elm; but between us and that picture of placid coolness marched a column of Algerians, disorderly, with improbable Oriental robes flowing. They chanted no northern song. They lifted their rifles to us, and made shrill cries. We saw Arab soldiers by the railway digging a trench, and they grinned their white teeth; the children threw to them their wild flowers.

We came to stations with unknown names, stations

that had no purpose. Soldiers garrisoned each, men of middle age, who frowned in wonder at our intrusion; some of them wore the red pantaloons of a soldier, but a workman's soiled blouse, as if, like ourselves, they were not sure whether they were asleep or awake, but had compromised with the red trousers, to be sure of the safe side of it, whichever way it was. My fellow passengers were women with market baskets and children, a priest, and men who were in uniform. They spoke of a war, yet in doubt. Where was it? They looked uncomplainingly to the east, and accepted the fable in simple faith, despite the repose of the summer hills. The war was over there, behind those hills. They did not know what it was like, but one must believe. It had broken their families; it had stopped their work. The war was over there. They stared at the hills, beyond which were armies at battle, hills keeping the unknown. They stared at the hills as children might at the silent walls enclosing the secrets of a sullen and forbidden house of wrong.

We came to a town late at night where the train hesitated so long that we doubted whether it could move again; we escaped from it. This was Amiens, a shadow told us. "The British are here?" we asked.

"But no, monsieur, they have departed."

The city was in darkness. A few of its people haunted its streets, whispering in secretive and earnest groups. The echoes mocked us in our wanderings through empty byways, where the pale and shuttered houses could tell us no more than the dead whose eyes are closed ; so it was, we recalled, in that hampered flight in a sleep, when what was nameless followed close, in a place where every door was strange, and fast. We chanced into an open space, where a vast structure towered from basal gloom to spires that were faint amid the stars. What was it ? Merely a greater shadow, this cathedral, in a city lost in night, where two fugitives from the pursuing scourge of another era were confused by many shadows.

My companion stopped. He gazed up at the mass. " Edward III of England rendered homage in there to Philip of Valois," he remarked.

I stopped, indifferently. " When was that ? " I asked.

" In May, 1329," he said.

We gazed at the place where kings were crowned or made peace so long ago. We had paused, and so were forsaken even by our echoes. Numberless figures began to people that stupendous berg above us. I could see them now, peering down mutely to us, the wayfarers of a later time, from the shelves and precipices of that settlement of night. A nearer face leaned out of its mediæval niche, and grinned at us. Out of the obscurity of this towering survival of ancient faith a face became plain, with a comment ; it leered.

We turned from the transcendent enigma, which was unable, with all its ancient memories of the aspirations of men, and with its spires amid the stars, to do more than mock ; and came to a main road, which had no better illumination than the white moon-face of the railway station clock.   Along that road, with the heavy deliberation of the last march of all, came over the cobbles an endless line of French military wheels, guns and limbers, ambulance carts, forage and ammunition waggons, with their guards pacing beside them.   The troops, shrouded in cloaks, mounted and afoot, moved bowed and downcast as though convoying the wreckage of their hopes.   Amiens was lost. A scatter of citizens stood in silence and watched the procession through their midnight city ; or at most they whispered.   A covered farm wain went by, its cavernous interior lighted with a feeble lamp suspended over a load of wounded men sprawled on the straw of its floor.   One yellow face, with a thin nose and a pointed black beard, stared fixedly upwards from the floor at the swaying lantern.   There was no sound in Amiens but the dull rumbling of ponderous wheels, like the sombre rolling of slow drums.   A shade moved beside me, and spoke.   " It is another Moscow."

THE shadow of war, like an eclipse of the sun, moved across from eastern Europe upon us. Darkness covered nearly all Belgium and much of France. Day, so far as was known, ceased to shine over there. And the onward sweeping shadow was impenetrable. It could not be entered. The shadow spread. In an hour it would envelop a French town, which had been free as ever one day, to retire on the morrow within the penumbra of the eclipse. Then it was as unapproachable as though in another planet. The flowing shadow of iron extended its obliterating rim, and locked city after city within its darkness. It stopped the circulation of life along roads and railways as though they had abruptly and mysteriously projected into a void, where but lately there was land and people. The void beyond the habitable land stirred with the movements of Eblis and his hosts at large, who could be heard if you approached that rumbling boundary between day and night.

The shadow was slipping down on Amiens; it might sweep over its houses while we watched, and we should be enclosed. The booking-hall of a station of the city, in the first hour of another day, was as cold as the glare of its arc-lamps, and strangely full of people, though there were no trains. Families were huddled in motionless groups about the walls. The sleeping children were sunk into their mothers, and their mothers, with bowed heads, stared at the floor. Men wandered over to look again at the pigeon-holes of the ticket office, but these were shut. They returned to sit on bundles beside their women, propped up their heads on their fists, and stared at the floor. Gendarmes promenaded restlessly, hands clasped behind them, and considered the floor, though its stones were bare. The hollow building itself was brooding in its sleep. With whatever vision it had, it complained and mumbled in its caverns.

Maynard foraged about the baggage office, for he has a way of finding things where Providence has not been spendthrift, discovered two pillows, and a barrow; and we shared the barrow. The slats of that couch were made for trunks not so soft as our own. Draughts moved over the stones. We listened to strange noises, though listening was useless, for the sounds could have had any origin. Somebody was sleeping on the counter of the office, but I could see only a pair of elegant and diminutive boots and one slim white hand; she might have been a body covered up and left for forwarding. A noise brought me out of the uneasy nonsense of a doze, and there, over Maynard's disregarding figure, were two women shaking their fists at an official. The official saw that

U

the dispute had wakened me, and grinned. " Sleep well, les Anglais," he said.   " C'est la guerre, but it is not the shells, not yet."

Then in the emptiness of my mind another sound began, as part of a dream, though it roused me. Maynard was sitting up, listening.   It was three in the morning.   I could hear a quick torrent of feet pouring along the road without, and the voices of young men. The shouting and the babble increased, and then conviction gave form to the hubbub ; out of a gathering tumult of song the defiant Marseillaise arose. Maynard weakly smiled.   " They are marching their youngsters out of it.   They're too valuable to lose."

When the morning was grey a long line of cattle vans was brought along a platform.   We found space in which we could stand in a truck, and at last it moved out of Amiens.   Near me a young mother sat with her two small children on a bag.   They were daintily dressed, but their clothes were stained with travel.   I heard the mother's droning voice as she talked to an elder woman ; it was flat with weariness, but no doubt she found comfort in a good-natured listener. Through the bumping and jolting of uneasy travel now and again I caught a fragment of her story.   " Their papa . . . a cavalry officer . . . we had to leave Longwy . . . I looked back and saw flames. When we went to live on the frontier, after we married, my husband said there would be no war.   Soldiers, he said, were finished.   He said science would make war

too dreadful . . . no statesman would dare . . .
regard Longwy! There is no home . . . then to
Charleroi, but there again . . . if I could get to Paris,
I considered, I would find my husband's family; but
all have gone. Who knows where? Paris also will
go. Then I come to Amiens, to see my mother and
father. But again, nothing. They have gone."

I looked at the speaker. Her children were
listening with grave and indulgent interest. She was,
as the vulgar say, a lady; not pretty, but patrician,
with the self-possession of intelligence and authority.
Her dress expressed a morning thought which had
been bright in a happy summer, but now it was dingy
with strange neglect. She began to tell her grandmotherly friend of a company of Turcos, which
marched up to a corner where she waited with her
children, wondering which road she should take.
The Turcos were laughing at something they carried
with them, but she could not see what it was. They
came to a stand, and an officer was angry. He inspected his men, and drew his revolver. He was very
angry. The lady lowered her voice. " One of them
carried a head. I could see it then. It was tied—
upside down—to his bayonet. Yes, yes. The officer
was serious. It must be buried at once. The Turco
buried the head, but I saw him cut off the fair moustache, for a souvenir, he said for his wife."

The lady for a space maintained her dreary calm,
and her eyes were still absent; then she put her face

into her hands, and her body shook.

The journey could have no end, with our creeping gait. There were long halts, for no reason that we knew. Whenever we waited, all we got was new rumours, which always took advantage of an open door. There was no water, and no food. But the demeanour of the common people of the country through which we passed was the same as refreshment. If they were not undismayed, they baffled the prompting to panic. Tough stuff, common men and women ! An enemy, with terrors which could only be hinted, was at their doors. Yet it is hard to forsake one's door. There are the cows to be fed, and the legumes for the winter to be tended, the sick child, the gates to be watched at the road crossing, the lock at the canal, the barn to be roofed, the railway trucks to be shunted ; therefore the unimportant ones continue to revolve this earth, without knowing why. Wheat must grow. The earth should not cease to turn from morning to night, and back to morning again, until a veritable comet smite it finally from the blue. They paused, these folk, and looked severely to the distance when we heard thunder begin on the skyline. The guns ! They did not pretend that thunder was any better than it sounded ; then they turned patiently to whatever belonged to the hour ; they went about the next job. C'est la guerre ! What could one do ? That incantation covered all, even death. They had been busy so long, while kingdoms rose and fell, keeping the earth turning profitably in and out of the sun, that they forgot to withdraw their hands now the sky grew threatening again. But that? They made a gesture of resignation. It is the war!

The hours crawled by, not by the clock, but in episodes, and whether they were in this day or that, this week or last week, were seen in this vision or another, is no matter when a dread, from which there is no escape, though it has no face, continues close at hand. You have to keep on running. You cannot stop to think.

At the panel of sunlight where the van was open to give us air, Jim Maynard stood, watching the country. He had been sparing of words. Still, his insignificant profile did not suggest the weight of a strong man whose opinion would be sought, and who would have it ready. Then, as though in idleness he had just remembered it, he startled me with the news that the French government had forsaken Paris; Bordeaux was now its seat. He kept one hand in his trousers pocket, and lolled against the car as he still mildly surveyed the trees and fields. Yet his message was enough to sink a fellow, already heavy with foreboding, plump to the bottomless.

I became testy. It is wrong to pass such words, and then no more. Why had he not . . . ?

But Jim remained gentle and pleasant. "A government is always the first to run. But this won't stop the war. It only seems important."

Because I feared the implications of this news I felt anger rising. There is nothing more disturbing than the imperturbability of courage. We never know why it is calm. Jim suddenly was removed from me. I could see he had accepted the change in his life. Leisure filled his soul now war had struck hope from it. The future had been taken from him, so it was easy for him, I suppose, to come to decisions and to leave the consequences to powers he could not control. His head, feminine in its refinement, turned from the landscape. His face had the flush of a good heart, and his light eyes, bleak in their grey honesty, sought the haggard thought in mine with sympathetic amusement. He could read me, no doubt; he saw I was not yet reconciled to the assault on reason and good by brutal circumstance.

"What's the use?" he asked. "You are arguing with the tide. This is the way it goes. We can only do the best thing we know."

"When we know what the best thing is."

"Well, we can't escape from this affair, can we? We've got to be in it."

I thought over that, but trusted, on the whole, that it were better not to be impetuous; it must soon end.

"It won't. You can feel the weight of it. It will take long to wear itself out. What's to stop a continent on the move? We shall have to share the common lot—take our ration."

"It isn't ours."

"Must be. It comes in our time. I hoped we should escape, but here it is, and here we are. Besides," he went on, "I thought you always hated the lie that you may do what you wish if you have the power. Now it is either the end of us, or Germany."

"You know well enough there's nothing to choose between the lot of them. They've been asking for it."

"Of course. But we can't help that. We're on this side of the boundary, and there's no choice."

He did not impress me as a fervid crusader. He again contemplated the country of France as if he saw nothing in it. His unsoldierly countenance was turned to it quizzically ; lines which slightly depressed the corners of his mouth, his usual ironic show when accepting a predicament, said that he was taking one way because he could see no other. "And look at it," he continued, "what is the use of choosing life when all good things have gone, or are going? We'll have to shoulder the pack with the best, and hump it along."

The uncomfortable and stringy quality of the gentleman ; own up, pay up, and shut up ! Our train came to a stand in a junction. Another train was there, composed of cattle trucks like our own, though not, like ours, bearing a burden of the completely living. I gave it no attention till Jim frowned in wonder, and then dropped hurriedly to the ground. A French soldier, trailing a leg with its foot improperly reversed, was escaping from the other train on his hands and knees across the tracks towards us. His twisted mouth was slavering; he made Bedlamite noises when there was an attempt to get him to safety. That train bore a load of battle wreckage, but nothing was near to give it ease. These wounded men had been travelling for two days, we heard, and were not there yet, wherever it was they were going, if that were known. The relentless sun made a glaring desert of the steel lines and the gravel, and the dying men waited in the heavy heat for whatever their country would do with their last hours. They stank. They drew the blow-flies. Their clothes were glued to them with ordure and dried blood. One man on his back near a door, his face that of a child in its pallor, had a darkened hole in his thigh, stuck full of floor rubbish and straws. He opened his eyes once to us in the sunlight, and shut them again. Beside him were two of his field-grey enemies, but he and they were reconciled. One was a boy who stared at the roof, and he was alive, for he blinked at a fly; the other was his senior, with a blonde beard, but he had found peace.

" I think you were talking this morning of Eblis," Jim reminded me as we went away from men we could not aid. " You saw those Germans ? " he asked. " Two of his afrites, my son."

Then presently, somewhere in France, there was a silent street pale in the light of a waning moon. We stopped under one white wall, and Maynard pulled at a handle. An interior bell clanged and echoed in challenging insolence throughout the nervous hollowness of fear. Where was it? A grey-haired woman appeared, and without looking at us, without a word, led us through vistas of corridors till she came to one door like all the rest, opened it, and left us.

I was shaken out of a sleep, and it must have been that same morning, and sat up. " They're here," Jim said, " or they soon will be."

From a window I could see below a group of French soldiers with a prisoner, a big capless German cavalryman. There was a thread of red trickling down his face. In a frenzy he began to resist, but incontinently gave way, and marched. An old man, his jaw dropped, was hobbling away from that group; down the street went that figure of senile panic, in his slippers, pink pyjamas, and with an umbrella.

We took to the road again. Four abreast marched with us a column of men, newly taken from their families, for gun meat. It was a motley consignment of respectable fathers, still smelling of their trades, and raw from the homes they had just left. They were going to their fate with that docility, caused by the enchantment cast over us, which became the mark of most Europeans. One notable figure, with the luxurious girth of the proud whose watch-chains go well before them, and a ruddy forked beard, which, but an hour before, was the mark of his godhead to his children, glanced at me enquiringly, with something of the dumb alarm of an ox who is beginning to suspect that all is not well when on his way to the butcher.

The August morning held aloof in its unconcern. Its brightness was superior to our misgiving, and we did our best to accept its misty blueness.   There were retired hamlets which, from afar, largely called themselves Dubonnet; though others, seen across the fields, were known as Byrrh. It was not easy to believe that repose so established could be broken; but then, why should man feel that he is immortal? There is a place in France called Gournay.   I saw the name on the side of a station building, and so suspect that this is true, and that Jim and I were there, one drowsy summer afternoon.   The station was filled, to the metals, unaccountably, with anxious women. A train ran in, and they had eyes for nothing but the door-handles of the carriages, which they grabbed as at life-buoys in a shipwreck.   They carried with them their salvage, tied up in shawls and handkerchiefs, in cardboard boxes that had burst; and somehow the train swallowed most of them.   When they were safe within it they relaxed, staring and motionless.   One woman then began wailing for a lost child, dropped to the ground again and fled.   A long straight of road approached Gournay from the east, but it could not be seen; it was hidden in the march of a multitude. Somewhere beyond us a region was being emptied of its people, and there they came, an endless pour of fellow mortals, a slow overflow from the hills, congested into a narrow channel formed by cliffs of trees. It was a dark thick flow, though quaking in its mass. The roofs of motor cars floated in it, and the horned heads of bullocks. Great rounded covers of wains were adrift in this flood. Above it, at the edge of a white cloud, two aeroplanes circled. One fell straight, and vanished behind the trees. A grandsire in his shirtsleeves was harnessed to the shafts of a little cart, and he laboured past us with a grey-haired woman sitting on a bed as his passenger.

That train was loaded, but another, headed elsewhere, stood empty and waiting. It was marked for Beauvais. We would go to Beauvais—anywhere would do—and see if one night of peace had been overlooked and left there, by any chance. The conductor, when we told him this, gave us a curious side-glance. Nobody else was going to Beauvais; I felt we were lucky to escape, for an hour or two, from the distressing contact with chaos. Our train, empty except for us, passed through forests which enveloped us in quiet and security. Rest was here; the nameless and infectious trouble had forgotten this patch. And there, in an hour came Beauvais. We began to pass by a row of houses of an earlier century, and had a glimpse of a cathedral in an evening sky. It was about the time for the lighting of lamps in homes—not night, but when folk are coming home for the night. Yet Beauvais had no lights, and its

white road, luminous in the dusk, was empty.   There
were no children and no gossipers.   We went slowly
over a bridge which crossed a river; and below us
was the only inhabitant, so far, a French dragoon,
astride his horse, with a cord in his hand, and he
ridiculed us as he pointed to what was below our
wheels.   He was waiting to blow up the bridge.   A
deserted city, in a twilight, with its long prospect of
a vacant street waiting full of broken bottles and
tangles of barbed wire, is no better than the wilderness.
The dark shapes of the hills stood around.   The
station-master chuckled when he saw us.   He was
glad to get our company.   They had plenty of room
for us there, he assured us.   He stood, garrulously
recounting the local news, but stopped his speech, his
nervous hand arrested as he pulled at his grizzled
moustache.   That was near.   The guns!

Creil, decided the engine-driver.   Creil was eighteen
miles away.   He thought he could get us to Creil.
Then take your engine and these gentlemen away,
the station-master told him.   Off we went, crawling
through the night from signal to signal, and so came
to Creil.   Eddies from the swift and penetrating tide
of war were running into it.   The armies were
engaged outside the town, and a mob of civilians was
besieging the railway station, the doors of which were
made fast.   Bolts and gendarmes kept civilians outside.   The station itself was quiet, though crowded
with troops in their cherry-coloured kepis, and their

long blue coats folded back from the knees of their
red trousers. Their piled rifles and equipment made
unexpectedly solid the deceptive shadows of the place.
The men were unshaven and drab, and fatigue had
dropped them into careless heaps against the walls,
where we saw them plain only when a lamp cast about
them a brief area of light.

That still August night was overcast, and so dark
that a distant signal planet was the one red eye of
all that was without and here below. The heat of
the quiet dark, and its tension, was as if the unseen
sky had lowered, and must soon fall. There was not
a movement, except where white moths were mixing
their giddy orbits round the railway lamps. Officers
stood in a group conversing quietly with such ease
that I thought they were under restraint, resigned,
and affecting a show of indifference. Paris was now
near. The oblique signs were threatening, and
prompted the question of alarm. It was not asked.
The foundations of Europe were moving beneath us,
though moths continued to blunder about lamps on
a hot summer night. A soldier offered us a French
newspaper. He struck a place in it with contempt
as he held it up, without a word. This, I thought he
meant, is past speech. The paper was censored of
the war in France, though the guns were in the
distance, but it was promising with Russian triumphal
fanfares. French peasants, who were satisfied to
learn that their unknown friends the Russians had

won Lemberg, were startled first when from their doors they heard artillery on an evening that had been lying to them with its traditional aspect of permanence.

They dumbly met their fate. The spent troops, retreating from the north, slept under walls now within hail of Paris. They questioned nothing. They blamed nobody. They were silent. War blindly lumbered its brute bulk into the delicate fabric and tissue of their society, trampling to rubbish the work of generations of such lives as theirs; scattered the family, and destroyed the roof-tree; and they turned from the ruin without words, because there are no words for hope and work destroyed, turned in dusty misery, and joined the increasing drift of continental wreckage.

We were expelled from Creil to Paris; I know little of that journey. But an officer dozed in the opposite seat, and the red tassel of his forage cap danced fatuously over his nose to the movements of the train. Beside him was a child, confiding in Jim, who found biscuits for it, and showed it how surprises may lurk in a length of string. Our train, I know, stood on a bridge of the Oise; the cross-hatching of girders outside my window had clamped to it an electrical device to destroy it. Jim looked up from one of his successful wiles, met my eye, and winked. He was engaging the interest of a child. But I had been absently watching him for some time doing that, remembering that he would shoulder his pack, and recalling also the cattle trucks in the glaring sun laden with broken soldiers. My thoughts had caught at his easy and kindly glance, long familiar, now to go adrift in this welter of things hurriedly passing. It would go, that lenient regard, with the host of other faces, which had been real but briefly, which fled past helplessly and without end in silent travail, the questioning gaze of some close and direct, intimate in a look; faces that were bodiless, which turned to move their lips in urgent and warning counsel, in appeal for aid where there was only the haste of bale, and then vanished. Phantoms, the fellow apparitions of a world swiftly dissolving in headlong wrack!

We ran into the Gare du Nord. It was half-past midnight.

Paris ! I had not been there before. It was the very city I had refused to squander meanly in the eager mood of a brief holiday. It had been reserved for the leisure of a mellow and expansive autumn, and that golden season, experience teaches us too late, can be winter before we see that our chance is past.

Here it was, this city, and I was stranded in it, without design, by an eddy of war. Paris, in that first sight of it, was a bareness of flagstones under a high vault from which echoes could not escape. They were trying to get out, but were falling back. Near me was a bundle tied in a shawl, and beside it a canary lively in its cage. That bright atom, then, was the last sparkle of the famous gay capital ? Crouched by its cage was a figure draped in black, as though grief sat beside the memory it owned ; a hank of grey hair hung over an arm on which rested its bowed head.

It sat apart, as grief should. Crowded together at one end of the great hall was a concourse of refugees from the north who had nowhere to go. Many of them slept. The gathering was subdued. It was surprising that so many people should be so

quiet.   Paris was abandoned.   Its fortifications ? But
this was an untimely joke.   Again the Prussians were
coming !

Jim, at his ease, but a little romantically dishevelled,
who attracted, without knowing it, the attention of
two young Parisiennes at the next table, listened in
sympathy to the logic of a venerable iconoclast sitting
with us, whose head wagged in frequent and mournful
negation, in part because of the irritating attentions
of a fly.

"Ah, yes," he assured us, "the Prussians are
coming. Why not ? This is to be expected, when
the French forces, as we all know, were concentrated
against the eastern frontier.   Naturally, the Germans
have come through Belgium instead.   Everybody
knew they would, except the Catholic oligarchy of
militarists which controls the French army.   Why
should the Prussians choose the most difficult road,
between the fortresses ?   For years it was seen they
would march on Paris through Belgium.   Yet the
military art, monsieur, with famous soldiers, is occult.
We must suppose they beseech the saints.   Strategy
is revealed to them in dreams.   It is thus they divined
that it would save France to concentrate on the
eastern frontier. The saints allowed them that sacred
intuition. You see the consequence. We should
not leave this matter of guns and bayonets to the most
superstitious yet most arrogant men in the community.   Their ideas are mystical.   They throw dice,

W

and trust in God. Then they know they are right. But the Prussians are here, nevertheless."

His discourse was stopped by a sudden commotion. Chairs overturned. People rose hastily to stare at something behind us. Glass smashed. We turned, and saw an isolated group of men in khaki gazing indifferently about them. "Les soldats anglais!"

They were men of the Essex Regiment. Appearing abruptly as they did, in that place, at that hour, was testimony enough of what night was hiding in the north. But these men knew nothing of it. They wanted sleep. Their eyes were half-closed but their mouths were open. They were dumb. They walked as if a little drunk. Something, whatever it was, had ended for them at Senlis. Senlis? That was near the suburbs. What, then, had happened? But they could not say. They would not have cared then if we had told them the earth was about to blow up. Time it did!

The heart of the French capital gave hardly a sign that it was beating. The government had fled, and the roads out of Paris were slow and distressing with a migrating population. Many of the villas in the suburbs were deserted; toys, packing cases and books, scattered their lawns. The midday streets of the city were hot and empty. Famous boulevards were avenues of closed shutters. There were no assemblies of its citizens, save before the official notices, which were regularly displayed, laconic and cryptic, without any light on them but that of the sun, which was insufficient. Whoever then was in Paris must stay because they could not get out; the exodus had ceased. The city waited. The roads to the coast were so littered with the wrecked cars and cabs of those whose flight had been too fast, or with insufficient skill, that now, if one would, one must walk.

The newspapers also were shuttered. They were reduced to one sheet; which was enough, because the events that had paralysed a capital amounted to only a dozen words a day, after all, and those words had no meaning. Paris waited. It was left undisturbed, except by a German aeroplane which dropped insolence and a bomb, mutilating two women; or sometimes a spy—or so he was called—was caught, and a frenetic commotion swirled round him while policemen hurried the crumpled object within doors. It was natural to let emotion expend itself on a subject so solid as a spy, because there was nothing else to account for a common affliction; there was no news, and there were no rumours, except the fearful sort. The city, forsaken by its important people, looked to the sky, which was still as serene and blue as when the war began; the sky, too, was bare.

Sometimes we learned a little more than official notices vouchsafed, but it was enough. The British Army was near, yet von Kluck, who never slept, was across the Marne. The shadow was not only resting on the northern outskirts of Paris, but to the east of the city it had crept down below La Ferte sous Jouarre. Still the allies retired. The British were— or they had been—at Coulommiers; they were certainly at Melun, and that was well to the south. Yet General Joffre, the cynics were sure, would not fail to make his stand when he had Marseilles at his back; tout va bien!

The war therefore remained as inscrutable a mystery as the problem of evil. All went well, because, though the hotels of Paris were staffed and equipped as hospitals, there were no wounded. The hospitals had nothing to do. To save citizens from anguish, or ministers from the evidence of their folly, the wounded made longer journeys. Soldiers, we were to suppose, were not even wounded in this war. Its only sign was a drunken and boasting Zouave in a café. Beyond the closed buildings of Paris and the braggart, the earth was dumb; the living world stopped not far from Paris, at the point where a bored sentry stood with a fixed bayonet at a barricade on the road to the east. Beyond him the empty road went round a bend, and reason failed. Sometimes there was a fluttering or a rumbling in the air; that was the only authentic news which came of the collapse of the ordered and civil existence of Europe. It might have been a secluded housewife beating a carpet. The sentry met your eye, and grimaced. He looked to the distance in the direction of the sound. Only the hills and trees and tranquil white clouds were there.

Those millions of men at battle, to which the road led round that bend, were no more real than a conflict in Asia. That flutter had been conjured in the air by a few of Europe's dedicated magicians. Into what dread now it had grown for all unimportant people was as obscure as the welfare of the dead; and, it was beginning to appear, the fighting legions themselves rarely knew where they were, and never what they were doing. The movements of the battling hosts could be as leisurely as meandering streams of undirected lava, or as abrupt as a volcanic outburst; and nobody knew why, not even the eminent ones who wore the more inspiring signs on their uniforms. The confident mind of man, assured of its knowledge, had set forces moving which now went their own way, heedless of high rank, the speculations of patriotic purpose, the science of human material and devices, and even of prayer. Because of this, and to keep supported still our faith in the actions of our elected and energetic persons, wounded men made prolonged journeys to avoid the surgeons.

The tardiness of the crisis became suspect. The Prussians approached no nearer. Would they come? The Avenue des Champs Élysées, from the Arc de Triomphe, surprised us one afternoon of the first week in September. It was without note, except for one boy on a bicycle, and the rays of the sunset, which signalled on the chestnut trees the coming instead of autumn; and those trees, as if cheerful through an intimation withheld from us, had lit their candelabra anew. Was there a war ? If a fallen leaf had turned we should have heard it, but the air rested. There was only light. The sky was radiant. The towers and parapets of Paris had no base in a city of fears. They soared above us as another and an unattainable city, glowing in a joy removed. The aerial tracery of Notre Dame, in the triumphal loveliness of its ascent, was an ache to those who looked up to it, but must share the common lot below, and thus come to nought ; for what was it to them that remote beauty is imperishable ?

In the morning, by a slant of air, by the opening of a door in the sky, plainly we heard the guns. They were coming at last ? Jim and I listened. We waited for that sound to grow louder. A stranger was at our table, who took his ease severely and fastidiously ; he had a head similar to that of Blake's representation of the Deity, only his complexion was that of a pale gas-globe, and the black of his whiskers was ambiguous, because his hair was white. He removed his clips from his nose, trailed his newspaper, and slewed sideways to listen. He played a nervous tattoo on the table with his fingers.

The ominous thudding did not increase.   At length we agreed that there was no doubt of it : that sound lessened because the guns were more distant. We did not know it, but we were listening to the guns of the Marne.

In London, when we reached it, nothing had visibly altered. There still, unaware of the change in the earth, was the smooth continuity of age-long rectitude. We stood in surprise looking about us at Charing Cross. We made an effort to credit it. The traffic was at its accustomed gait along the Strand. The shops displayed their wares. London was unperturbed. We could hardly believe that what we saw before us was there, for the transit back is not so simple, the return to what is gone, the re-entrance to an old scene in a departed yesterday. This was the London we had thought we should never see again, because it was in oblivion with an order that had ended; but we recognised men we knew who plainly had never left it. Possibly their presence kept London in its place. An engine puffed out the usual cloud of white smoke on the railway bridge about Ludgate Circus, and the cross of St. Paul's floated on the summit of the smoke. Perhaps the apparition must persist with its ancient look until the dead men within it understood that they were one now with the Babylonians.

"What," I asked Jim, "is reality?"

317

" Don't know. Better say we are, I suppose, and chance it."

That might be it. Keddy's, however, that eating-house in an unfrequented alley where the roast and the boiled were the best in London, and its ale coeval with old folios, made us glad to sink comfortably into one of its antique pews, with even a *Morning Advertiser* folded undisturbed on the back of it, and shuffle our feet in the sawdust of a floor that deserved to keep its place if the rest of London thought itself righteous and unwarned. Jeal, its head-waiter, too small to be seen in the shop at the busy hour, and too quiet and wizened to be noticed by strangers, saw us at once, and conducted us, signally favoured, to a small and upper apartment he reserved for those he thought merited it. " I thought you would like to know Mr. Langham is in there," he said. He let us in, and closed the door.

There Langham was. " Are we downhearted ? " he cried. He beamed on Maynard. " Haven't you just come across ? You're the very man I want to see. Come over here. What about this great victory ? Are we being lied to as usual ? This is my brother. He is going over to France to-day to save souls ; isn't that so, Francis ? "

His brother did not reply, but gravely disapproved. The Reverend Francis Langham might have been in the dress of a British officer, to a careless inspection, except for the collar he was wearing. His uniform

was so very new that his leathery complexion of aged
and meditating sorrow appeared to be a mistake in
his embellishment. Soon, and with easy authority,
he rejected a few of Maynard's more pointed allusions
to the things to be seen in France, as of little consequence. They were hardly relevant to the great issue.
Maynard turned sharply upon him.

" Then you don't think we need bother about this
casual slaughter ? "

" No. Isn't there something more important than
that ? "

" And you are going to attend to it ? "

The new chaplain was silent. It could be inferred
that so much was manifest. He broke bread, and
continued seriously to chew.

His brother laughed uneasily. " Francis really is
for salvation. We're only for death. He knows
their souls cannot die, so nothing can happen to them,
if they are Christian soldiers. Isn't that so, Francis ?
That's all right," continued the elder Langham cheerfully to us. " We can't lose this war if we can only
get men into it like my brother." He patted him on
the back. " The more we have killed, the more
intercessors we shall have with God. Now let us
come down to the paltry guns. Where have you
been ? "

Maynard indifferently indicated a little geography,
and its latest interest.

" Over here," Langham told him, " there have been

some terrifying stories. Is it true the French have been running like rabbits ? One nice Sunday morning recently *The Times* came out with a special edition to announce the scattering of the little British army. London had no appetite for its breakfast. Kitchener was tearing his hair over the French plan of campaign."

"The French have been running, chiefly from the places where they ought never to have been sent to where they were badly wanted. It was what anyone might have guessed—they were misled and wasted. The men are all right."

"I thought so—French politics again, and the recovery of the damned lost provinces. Mustn't say the men were wasted, though. The duty of my department is the issue of encouraging information."

Langham, as occasionally happens with men who when young are of an earnest, ascetic, and intellectual cast, had changed his lean and hungry look for one that had been made plump and comfortable through the easy adaptability of his mind. His dark eyes sparkled in their observance as brightly as ever, but cynically now, in good-natured mockery. He poured out more Burgundy for himself.

"Of course, our soldiers will never run for any reason except a gallant charge. Isn't that so, Maynard ? So far as we are concerned, only the treacherous and cowardly foe is misled." He looked over at us, and chuckled. "If my brother weren't here—we mustn't worry his high emprise with our low cunning—I'd tell you that what I really want from reliable witnesses are stories to make this mighty and puissant race spread its wings anew. Sacrifices must never be in vain. We shall not sheathe the sword, which we have not lightly drawn. . . ." He quoted the Premier's words with gay unction.

Maynard was troubled. " I'm afraid I don't get it," he said.

The rebuke checked Langham. I saw the quick shadow of his annoyance. He did not enjoy the hint that though the finer cause might miss the support of his idealism if he did not like the look of it, yet that other men would quietly take the way whose narrow gate he had recognised as quickly as they. He met at once the mood of a friend who was tired, and so unresponsive, just then, to his banter.

" Yes, you get it all right. I know you do. But you had better understand a little better." Langham, who had grown to be at ease with cabinet ministers, and who could indicate, if it served his purpose, enough of a secret of state to show that you did not know what you were talking about, became serious. He sat back and overlooked us. His force and definition reduced Maynard's gentle meagreness to still less significance. He gestured slightly and agreeably. " It is going to be an infernally long way to Tipperary, and unless we recognize that fact cheerfully we'll never get there. For a jolly long time to come virtue and truth aren't going to be what they were.

It won't do to be too particular, if you will allow me
to offend your nice perception of things. You'd be
called a pro-German pretty quick if you were fool
enough to mess about openly with the truth. I know.
I've had some. You see what we're in for, no doubt,
but it is rather worse than you suppose. You think
it's a straight game. Get that out of your head. It
can't be. We've got to win, and that means anything.
It means, among other things, the law-givers and the
other playful dabblers with the dynamos at Westminster, and you don't know them as well as I do.
They're more concerned still with what Northcliffe
will publish about them—he can shift the biggest of
them by singing out Fire when we're all in the dark—
and whether Lloyd George will jump this way or
that. They're busier than ever getting jobs for themselves and their friends. The fact that Ostend is an
enemy naval base and that the Germans are still within
a short ride of Paris doesn't worry them. They're
not in Paris or Ostend. They're all as busy as bees,
and they enjoy the exciting activity. There is just
one thing that jolts them into a sense of reality—they're
afraid, sometimes, the Germans may paddle ashore
at Yarmouth. That's their only nightmare."

"Invasion ? But what's the navy for ? "

"Oh, they've forgotten the navy—they can't see
the ships as plainly as their private interests ; or else
they don't trust it. You know well enough they've
always regarded the Admiralty as a sacred grove.

Perhaps they're not sure about their joss now. I won't say I am. He hasn't done anything in our lifetime."

"Well, Langham, I can't see where I come in with these people."

"You will, though. They're going to interfere very strenuously with you without knowing what they are doing."

"But does anyone know now what he is doing? This chaos gives the chance of a lifetime to every humbug who wants to appear busy and important. The busybodies will make things worse, I suppose. They'll make us sick if we think about them. But they are an inevitable part of the affliction, and we can't stop them."

"Well, what are you going to do about it—your king and country need you, as the posters put it?"

Maynard did not look up, nor answer. He contemplated, as if for an augury, the pattern of the froth floating on his beer.

"Something else, Maynard. Do you realise who is in charge of our part in this show—and I suppose it is the same in France, and I hope it is so in Germany? Just luck. Only luck. We haven't a man for the business, either at home or in the field, who looks more likely than an old woman in a runaway bus without a driver. Nobody good enough. That's the fact. In the field, the generals have nothing better than Aldershot. And we know Aldershot, don't we?

At home here, Kitchener is as impressive as Krishna
if you happen to have any faith in Indian mythology.
I haven't.   Anyhow, nobody could ride this storm,
which will get worse as it goes on.   Events, as they
fall out, will change the situation, and the only thing
we can do is to snatch what opportunities accidents
offer, if there is anyone about quick enough to see
them in time.   And we'll have to make up our minds
to be unscrupulous about it.   We've got to come
out on top, if we can.   There's no doubt about the
issue in the popular mind, and we must keep that
moral purpose straight, anyway.   It is wrong to make
war without a moral purpose, and we've got one.
It's our only asset.   Isn't that so ?   However it all
came about—and you don't want me to remind you
what Europe has been like since 1870—Germany was
fool enough to put herself in the wrong.   We know
it had to come, but she began it.   She refused to have
it arbitrated.   It is launched, and it isn't our doing.
If we can, we'll make it go our way.   Between the
two of us, call the war what you like, but don't forget
that we're making the world safe for democracy—
say we're putting an end to militarism—a war to end
war—any damned thing.   Anything that will work.
We've got to win, you must admit that.   The war
won't be won on points, my son, so we'd better
smuggle horseshoes into our gloves for luck.   That's
common sense, isn't it ?   We're supposed to be in
it to save Belgium for God, or something.   It doesn't

matter. The important thing is to hold up France so that she won't let us down. Do you know the leading French politicians? They've been waiting for their revenge for forty years, and we're in this to get it for them, but you'd be safer with welshers on a racecourse than with those fellows. As for the Russian steam-roller, it hasn't got a boiler, from all I hear whispered. We're in for it all right, and, Mr. Maynard, you'd do well to hit below the belt, or anywhere else that will hurt most."

Jim, maybe satisfied with what he could read of the chance lace-work on his beer, pushed the tankard away, and rose to go.

" That's the sensible view, the view forced on us, don't you agree? "

" Well, Langham, I'm not looking for a sensible view of a calamity. I'll agree with you that we're getting what we ought to have expected. What the busybodies will do about it I don't know and don't care to know. They're part of the trouble. They will do anything to dodge their share of the punishment, that's all that is certain about them. But I've nothing to do with them. There are others who will certainly not take the sensible view, because they won't be able to. They're going to be offered up. Well, they're not going to be offered up for me."

He went out leisurely, without looking back. There was a long and awkward pause, and then Langham remarked that one of the great difficulties with the

English would be their virtuous fools. But his brother, the new army chaplain, approved Maynard heartily.

" Stout fellow. He means to fight. That's the way to look at it. Good man. He sees the right thing to do is to kill Germans. They are the enemies of God and man, and he knows his duty. He's an honest fellow."

I went over to the office with the bewildering sense that somehow we existed on two levels at once, or else that time itself was tricky with us, so that truth was good if you looked at it behind the clock, but turned to evil if you brought it round to the front.

Where was Bolt ? But nobody in the busy place knew anything of Charley, nor was concerned to find a reason for his absence. " There's his hat," I was told. " Must be about."

On a peg in a corner of that room which had altered in no particular, there was his hat, but with its pose and dust it suggested that it had hung like that for a year. The key was in his locker, and inside, thrown on top of his papers, were scattered the pages of his unfinished book.

Charley had forgotten his key. I turned it on the little our room still held of him, and put the key in my pocket. The office, when I looked round on its familiar gear and figures, was as I had always known it. Yet I felt I was not in it, and could never enter it again. It was estranged, and evaded me. My colleagues were friendly, but something invisible had come between us. The very words they used had another value now, and were queerly inapplicable, though I dared not ask them whether they knew that. The square of carpet on which we stood and conversed had been transmuted ; it was an abysmal ocean across which, unavailingly, though with the same goodwill, we tried at a distance to understand each other. No good. And they were too busy to waste much of their stock of past time on me. It was valuable. Moreover, I suspected there were two wars, the one in France, and another they knew so well that they assumed I, too, must know it.

If only I could have seen Charley for a moment I felt sure I should have got back into the place where rightly I belonged. He would have let me in. He was the clue to it. I sought him, that evening, at his home.

Jim was there already, as I suspected he would be. I could hear his voice, but the room was dim, and his voice was all I knew till Annie, moved by my arrival, lit the lamp. I saw Mr. and Mrs. Bolt, and the two daughters, and Maynard. The room and its company was coldly incomplete, but I betrayed no curiosity over those who were not there just then. They would come in.

There was restraint upon us ; there was a noticeable avoidance of one subject. Mr. Bolt was subdued and taciturn, and his wife, now there was light, used it for

x

needlework in her lap.   Her hand never ceased then
to ply briskly back and forth, nor her gaze to lift
from it.   Jim leaned forward, tickling the cat, and
talking in undertones to Annie.   Polly was pensive
with a book, at an evident distance from us.   The
rhythm of Mrs. Bolt's unremitting industry put a
weariness upon me which I thought a solitary stroll
would help to lift.   And it was getting late.

Jim, too, rose to go.   Mr. Bolt stood, and looked
straight and steadily at the two of us.   He pouted
his underlip.

" Here we are," he said, " here we are.   But the
boys have gone.   Jack and Charley have gone."

His wife did not look up ; she kept her attention
bent to her duty.

THEY had gone. And now Maynard was missing. One's friends were missing from the places which knew them. Nothing rare that might confirm the well-being of the world, if one became doubtful, remained where one had been able to find it. The very landmarks which we had thought as good as the everlasting hills shifted in the stream of an invisible tide which was taking us into a new routine, into another era, amid circumstance that had the bleakness of the unknown. Our outlook was mutable and mocked us ; it hurried like the flow itself, which was carrying us whither we would not go, but must, to an end that was as nameless as the haven in the seas where there is no land.

Friends were parted, and there was no way of meeting again across the welter where all was adrift. We had to keep to the direction set by fate, and out of hail. There was one letter from Charley. It was from a Sussex camp, but I could not answer it, for he had orders to pack up again, and where next he would be he couldn't say. His letter was buoyant.

" . . . I had a dread of this, and used to worry more than most over the signs of its advent, but now

it has come I would not have missed these days for
anything. I like the emergency, in a way. It will
test which dyes are fast. The people left at home
will feel it most. Did you know that once I was
writing a novel? That makes me sad when I think
of it. I knew nothing of reality, but was sure I did,
and now I see I didn't. Something gained already,
eh? . . . Jim said once that men and women are the
silliest creatures God made, though one cannot help
liking them. You would say so here. I have
learned a lot about them. Under the stress of war
they have not only undressed, they have got out of
their skins. They don't care if you can see through
them. I think the girls about this camp are crazy,
the dear little anarchs, and the men desperately snatch
at the life they are afraid they are going to lose. That
may be it. You never heard such loose and rollicking
talk. All the old fences are down, and we rove, and
we don't care a potato peeling. I could laugh when
I see these fellows in church, and remember their
bawdy anecdotes, while the padre, who must have
been kept in a cage at Oxford and fed on print through
the bars, talks to them as though they were angels
of light banded against fell Apollyon. There in the
pew in front of me yesterday was the bull neck,
blotched with freckles, and the brassy hair, of a stout
lad known as Ginger, whose language and story the
night before would have made Benvenuto Cellini feel
like a timid adolescent. I should like to see the two

respectable sisters of Ginger's story; I should like to know whether one could guess it of them by looking at them, though I suspect not. I doubt if I could, anyway. It makes me wonder whether I myself am alive, though I shall continue, because I must, to assume that I am. Why do I doubt that I'm alive, when I hear of these features of the wayside, so ordinary that men enjoy them and joke about them, such as Ginger's adventure of last Saturday night? Because, though I know they must be there, I myself never encounter anything of the sort. What was it you told us once? Some stuff about there being no world except the one a man sees, but that every man sees a different world. I shall not try to get into a world I cannot see, so don't worry about my immortal soul. It is safe, because not always aware of what is about it.

" . . . is there a War Office? Or is it a Public Joke? This is highly important, as there is a war on. I want to know. You would think the great brains over us were doing all they could to arrange for the damping of our fires. That has been done, most effectively, in a large number of cases. Stamped our fiery ardour right out. Discipline, that's what it is. I suppose the idea of discipline is to make us more afraid of the gold braid behind us than of the enemy's guns in front. We would rather meet the furious Goth and fiery Hun than face old Brigadier Chutney. Lots of poor devils never get a chance of

killing Germans—our War Office saves the enemy
that trouble. When the chaps try to join up, they
are kept waiting in queues in the rain—they're ticked
off—they're told to come again—then they're kept
standing in the rain again—then they're sent to mess
with microbes in insanitary hutments. If they dare
ask what about it they get it in the neck. Those
fellows want to have a cut at von Kluck, but General
Pneumonia does them in before they cross the water.
But are we downhearted?   I tell you I can face anything, even the cooking and the corporals. Young
Jack is in it somewhere—the Lord knows where—and
I could not let that kid go alone.   That boy is burning
with a zeal for battle that he never felt for religion.
I can't say I'm as good as that, though I'm cheerfully
interested in what is going to happen. I really want
to see France and to find out in the thick of it what I
am made of; but of course I hear we may go to
Egypt. When Jack left home to join the ruction,
why, that settled it for me.   How I wish I could do
his bit for him!   That's the part that hurts. I don't
care anything about me; but I had that child out on
the Surrey downs not so very long ago, showing him
the difference between a rampion and a sheep's bit
scabious. There were lots of tiny butterflies about
of the same shade of blue, and the sun was hot, and
the thyme was strong. But that's all over. It seems
frightfully remote, now. We must not think of banks
where the wild thyme grows.

" . . . the imbecilities absolutely essential to drill
and discipline make me feel that my old more or less
reasonable existence must have been a dream I had
once, and had better forget. Blast the blue butterflies.
I tell you this will do me good. It is sorting out the
elements for me. It has poked its ammunition boot
through a few old picturesque illusions. I never
wanted to fight, and I'm shocked still when I stick a
bayonet into a stuffed sack. I could always oblige
the other chap, if he insisted on a scrap, but a bayonet
looks so final.

" ' Oult ! ' shouts the sergeant. ' Call that
fightin' ? You there—are you a bloody 'ousemaid
tickling the china with a feather duster ? You got
steel. Feel it, man, feel it. 'Shun ! At the word—
quick for 'is guts ! '

" The sergeant meant me. I fear I was not made
for it, but I respect that sergeant, and seeing as how
I've got to do it, why, by jingo if I do. Gimme
that baggonet ! Besides, we certainly went into this
war with clean hands. Our case is clear. Germany
has gone balmy, and must be stopped somehow, and
talking to her won't do it. It is a dirty business, but
it ought to be done, like the Augean stables. It was
the burning of Louvain that settled it for young Jack
—he left home without a word to his mother and
father ; and that raised the issue for me. I'd had it
on my mind—whether might is right—whether con-
tracts mean anything—whether promises are pie-

crust—whether the civilization of Voltaire and Anatole France must perish—whether that brainless bully in helmet and jack-boots whose idiot sword has bossed everybody so long had better not be properly handled once and for all. This fire ought to clear the world of a lot of old lies. It may be the beginning of the new earth we have dreamed of. We'll get this job over, and make another start on cleared ground. And yet, the more I see of the army, the more I wonder whether I've changed one illusion for another. My God, is there more than one Prussia? That's the point. Write to me, and make something certain. Tell Jim to write. One must have something to grasp. I'll give you another address in a day or two. . . ."

His next address did not come, and so I could not give him anything to grasp. Whether he went to Egypt, or India, or France, perhaps I should learn in time, and with good luck. For the year was running out quickly, and the war, as the more expert and hopeful observers explained to us, was becoming stabilised.

That word meant merely that the desperate gambling by the generals with surprises was over. The rapid battles in the open with victory or defeat dependent on chance were at an end, and generals could no longer manœuvre their men, because the troops were crouching in trenches, below the level of the ground. Their men dared not even stand upright. The lines of the ditches into which the armies had drained, and were stagnant, began at the Swiss mountains, and meandered as though they were raw interminable wounds in the green of the earth for hundreds of miles, over the hills and through the valleys of France, having no design in their positions anywhere except the ruthless truth that the war was stabilised because men were worn out, or had been killed on both sides in numbers so great yet equal that the survivors tried to find rest where they were and under cover, which only spades could give them ; for their commanders, whose theories of the right conduct of war had suffered such awful casualties that not one sound and traditional principle was left to them, knew of nothing more that they could order except that their men should dig. The teachings of the historic military academies of Europe had been reduced in three months to the shovel of the navvy, and therefore these trenches and breastworks continued across marshes, where men stood to their hips in frigid mud while bending their heads below flights of bullets which cut the grass, and through churchyards, where the shovels of the last resort of the science of war burrowed into the catacombs and cast out the sheeted dead to instal the living in the graves ; cut through farm buildings, and round the black refuse-heaps in the coal-mining districts, turned the streets of villages into barricaded gullies and their houses into nests of machine guns, converted brick-fields into forts, dived under the banks of canals, and ended at last among the sandhills of Nieuport because of the waters of the North Sea.

The troops went underground to live, if they could, and died of mines and counter-mines, grenades, and of hopeful yet credulous artillery fire, which not seldom was that of their friends. The whole library of military science and history was as obsolete by the end of November of 1914, as the runes of witchcraft. The generals, though they kept their expressions of stern absolutism, did not know what to do. An army no longer had its legs to use, and it had no centre to be pierced and no wings to be outflanked; and that left the generals as were the theologians when the gods ceased to be. An army had become, for the first time in history, a continuous ditch of hidden men, quite unnatural to the theories of commanders in the field, yet still a fact, for it baulked them. The great soldiers had millions of men to command, and nations behind them occupied solely in supplying whatever they required, and the population of the planet as audience to the display of their talents. But they could do nothing more. The head of a modern military genius, gifted in the waging of successful warfare, firm in its resolution, wise in its knowledge and theories after a profound study of the battles of the past and the science of the latest arms, was really as empty as Napoleon's old hat. The great soldier could only retire to the end of a telephone wire so distant from bursting shells that he could not hear them, among the typewriters, secretaries, clerks and teapots, of a factory office, and there order his men to kill the enemy troops under the hedge of barbed wire on the other side of a field, whenever they got the chance. That was all, except that he demanded more men, and still more men, for though nothing happened, men died.

The war was not only stabilised. It was better than that, for beyond the immediate sense of relief afforded by the repetition of a novel and abstract word that exorcised the harsh verity which kept us from victory, the war was now seen to be, as were the hills and the parish church, a settled fact of life which next morning would show unfailingly to be in its usual place. Already the accommodating prudence of man was classing his self-imposed affliction with the state of the weather and other natural wonders beyond his control; therefore the conflict might end only when the last Patagonian died on the strangled body of the last Chinaman.

It might indeed die down finally in Manchuria or Tierra del Fuego, after Europe had put on once more that forbidding prospect of sterility which came over it when long ago the glaciers descended from the North Pole to bury the earlier enterprises of the cunning makers of arrowheads. The erosion of the war was beginning to have the same effect upon Europe. Man there was turned nomad again, migrating, if he had the time for it, before the invasion of the destroyer he himself had loosed. This time he could not blame that wobbling of the eternal spindle of the earth, which brought the glaciers down upon him. Across the central plains of Europe, communities of tillers and herdsmen, and their granaries and cattle, disappeared under the trampling of hordes of Teutons, Bavarians, Hungarians, Czechs, Poles and Slavs, who were locked together in struggling masses. The masses of men and artillery swayed to the west for weeks, and then to the east. They were defeated, and recovered; they passed over the ruined land again, from which towns, railways, roads and bridges had gone, to victory on the other side of it. They occupied the Carpathian forests instead of the wolves and boars, and killed each other on the shores of the Baltic. But they could come to no decision. In this war, words like victory and defeat had the same meaning as stabilisation or the signs of the cabala. The anxious taxpayers of Ancoats, Dundee, Bruges, Dijon, Penzance, Marseilles, and Belfast, all became concerned with the fortunes, now of supreme moment to them, of other cities which now they heard named for the first time, with varying pronunciation, though usually it was hopeless to search for those strange cities on the map—Przemysl, Jaroslav, Sambor, Rzeszow, and such. These suddenly discovered cities, avowed the public oracles, whose explanatory diagrams were published in the popular newspapers daily, were as important to us as the signs of the zodiac; and they were important to some people, no doubt.

The Austrians were defeated in Galicia. The Russians were advancing on Cracow. But the Germans threatened Warsaw, for they were crossing the Vistula and the Sau. Battles were raging near Riga, and in Poland and Silesia, and across the Danube into the Albanian mountains. Yarmouth and Lowestoft had their bathing machines, hotels and lodging houses, shattered by German cruisers; historic coastal settlements in Algeria with Roman names were visited by lyddite from the Mediterranean about this time. In the Ægean sea, by Samothrace and Lemnos, the ironclads of France and England shelled the site of Troy. To balance this, Odessa and Theodosia were tumbled by the enemy from the Black Sea, for Turkey was now an enemy, in spite of bribes and promises. Italy, however, still looked peacefully across into Tyrol, not sure yet what she would do. The airmen of the Allies flew to Dusseldorf on the Rhine, and dropped bombs on it; and a London newspaper heartily congratulated its readers that their men had " laid the first eggs." It forgot that the first eggs are only the first.

Russians were hurling Kurds from the slopes of Mount Ararat. And at Basra, that port of the Persian Gulf for which Sinbad set sail, Sikhs had arrived from the Punjab, and Gurkhas from the Himalayas; and these men, moved by the new zeal which would free us from the tyranny of obsolete and ruinous dogmas, and led by young men from English public schools, marched to dislodge Ottomans who were entrenched in the Garden of Eden. The coconut groves of New Guinea were stormed by Australians. In those days, while steaming at sunset under the snows of the Andes, British ships were sunk by their foes; who, but little later, were sunk by British warships off the Falkland Islands. Merchant

vessels and their cargoes foundered in the Bay of
Bengal and off the Cape of Good Hope through the
explosions of torpedoes. It might have been thought
that Penang, that city of light and colour with its
smell of spices, would have remained inviolate, if
only because it was on the Strait of Malacca, yet a
German cruiser appeared there one day, scattered its
anchorage with smoking wreckage, and vanished
again, leaving on the waters the bodies of a number of
Japanese girls, which had floated out of a sunken
Russian cruiser. Indian troops who were stationed at
Singapore, moved by nobody knows what impulse to
make things better, shot their white officers, and then
fired into the gardens of bungalows, and waylaid
merchants and their ladies who were motoring into
town. Far to the north of Singapore, by the Yellow
Sea, the Japanese landed in Shantung, and attacked
Tsingtau, a Chinese city, though occupied by Germans,
who were ordered by their Kaiser never to surrender
that symbol of Germanic honour. The Japanese took
the Chinese city from the Germans, and remained in
Shantung.

It was already becoming clear for the first time to
many onlookers that the earth is not two hemispheres
as we had thought, but one simple and responsive ball,
and that happenings on the shores of the Yellow Sea
and elsewhere may cause disturbing noises even in
Washington. That decision to assemble his army
made in St. Petersburg, not half a year before, by the

Emperor of Russia, and the edict he signed, was provoking events undesigned by him yet engendered by his act. Its inherencies were not yet fully noised abroad, for Lenin was still of no consequence in his cellar, yet very early its reverberations were heard in the twilight aisles of the forests of the Congo. There the pigmies knew of an ominous stirring among the leaves, by a terror unknown in their simple lore. Negroes fought each other because of it on Lake Tanganyika. White men died on the red-hot iron of burning ships sequestered in the mangrove swamps near Zanzibar; they pursued each other, with black levies, through East African jungles, and across the waterless sands of Namaqualand. African tribes, that had forgotten raw head and bloody bones through the gentle persuasion of the followers of Jesus of Nazareth, were dislodged from their mealie fields and hunting grounds because the Emperor of Germany had invaded Belgium; so those simple black folk, shelterless and without food, hopefully followed the troops from battleground to battleground; after a battle, they drove off the hyenas, and found abundance wherever Christian machine-guns had mown a harvest for them.

Our friends departed for that universal Labyrinth. Behind them fell the censor's iron door. Sometimes a word came back from them to the land of the living, but we could see it was a guarded word; they could not confess what they knew. The truth, whatever it was, remained on the hither side of the iron door, yet at least we were sure the minotaur continued to flourish, for sometimes we heard his distant bellowing. It took a long time to kill him, in this affair to end gross and obscene beasts that too long had troubled mankind.

Across into France our young men were flowing in a steadily increasing host, though France over the channel had become to London as mythical and monstrous as Knossos to the Greek tribes who were forced to send tributes of their young men and maidens to King Minos. France was as dark as that, though so near to us, as dark as was Cathay to Marco Polo's folk at home. Occasionally there were brief disclosures of what was hidden there, stories to compose our doubts, to hearten our fearful impatience. It was then we learned that all was well. All was well; our absent men were happy. The stories we were allowed to know were hearty and marvellous, and made light of wild beasts, of earthquake and eclipse. We read them in fond hope, because when Munchausen reveals what is kept from common and ignorant eyes he may range at his pleasure. His instinct is his sure guide ; that tells him what we would prefer to hear. He need not be hindered, in his desire to please, by the facts, which do not always accord with a likeable story, and are sometimes hard and unsettling to readers who would have their faith in wonders confirmed. Munchausen and his like, those fortunate narrators, are free of the conditions which hamper sober witnesses who foolishly suppose that what the people round the home fires prefer to hear is what veritably is extant.

Yet as to the truth, whenever we would look honestly and squarely about us for it, ignoring Munchausen, Ananias, Judas, or any other witness whose anxiety to interest us we may suspect, who else would be near us to reveal it? There surges the tragic event that is the inevitable crisis of evil begot long ago ; and who stands near that could put his healing finger upon the sinful heart of it ? Too late ! When the multitude begins to clamour for sacrifice, and High Priests and Pharisees in the midst of the clamouring voices use the potent words which keep full the springs of a people's righteous anger, what is there for Pilate or any just man to do ? He can but ask his sad and unanswerable question ; wash his hands ; and let the matter go forward.   Thus it was willed before his day, and ours.   Truth is silent.

And for such a reason it happened that along the line of Belgium's River Yser, in the first October of the war, young German volunteers were hurriedly assembled.   They had come from school to war because their Emperor and famous soldiers had failed to take Paris, and had not abolished the French armies ; winter was at hand, and the confident theory of a rapid overthrow of Germany's enemies somehow had disclosed a fault in its calculations. There was no longer a French centre to pierce, but there was still one flank that could be turned, and so along the Yser German youth mustered to do it.   The German High Command, compelled to the next thing, knew it should send its men across the river, take the Channel ports as a threat to England—which Berlin, in all the popular cartoons, knew as the obdurate foe of good Teutons—and strike at the communications and the rear of the Allied forces in the north.   The young levies were marshalled for that emergency ; they were ordered forward, they clasped hands, and advanced chanting national songs.   But the land was a swamp, and their masters did not know it. A flood was rising ; the sluice-gates had been opened by the sea.   Belgian machine-guns stopped the singing ; and the lads moved towards the Channel, in their threat to London, only as flotsam on the drift of sluggish waters.

Yet men who have staked much in a gamble always see it would be wrong to confess failure because dice are inconsiderate. They must double the stakes. The flooded country of the Yser, though men, guns and stores had sunk in it, was an advantage after all, for the German generals saw well enough that if it defended the left flank of the Allies it also defended their own right flank. It freed their men to make elsewhere a successful spearhead. The German forces therefore gathered more to the east and the south, and struck at the approaches to Ypres. Germany would reach the sea along the Menin Road.

It was in that pass that the remnants of the British army stood. Upon it, desperate through loss of time, with winter at hand, Germany hammered. Thin companies of men in khaki, the rags of battalions, haggard with weeks of battle, and none there yet to relieve them, numbed by continuous shell-fire, sheltering among ruins and beet fields while existing on rum and biscuits, resisted the renewed attacks, and melted fast. The survivors did not retire. No orders had been given to them. They dragged their wounded behind hedges and broken walls, if they could find any, and left them there to wait for water and aid which could not always reach them; they tightened their harness for the next bout, not knowing that they were all that remained between Germany and Calais. They knew nothing except that their enemy would give them no rest, and that soon none of them would be left; most of them did not know where they were. They kept free the bolts of their rifles, and looked for the signs of the next attack.

And the German commanders were perplexed, when their next attack, fashioned hard and heavily with new men, awakened steady volleys from ground where they thought all must be dead under renewed bombardments, and when their new troops were met in the open by scarecrows in khaki whose desperation to have done with this was all that flickered their bayonets. The German commanders considered so unreasonable an obstinacy in the light of military science, and the solution was plain to them. They had no doubt that the British must have heavy reserves. There must be a trap prepared in the woods to the west, for otherwise odd and ragged groups of men would not resist properly constituted brigades. They hesitated. They reformed, and planned anew. Yet nothing was between the German army and the sea except tired men who guessed that life for them was over, and the wounded and the dead, and the staffs of headquarters; and the last indeed were puzzled themselves, while waiting for the signs of the approach of the foe, to hear British rifle fire break out once more on the road ahead. Some men were left?

In mid-November, in the morning mists of the first of winter, the Kaiser himself announced his presence, and brought up his Prussian guardsmen; and this time there should be no doubt. Those stout soldiers suffered, but they broke the thin barrier, and advanced into the woods beyond. There they paused. They did not know what next to do. Nobody was there to direct them along the road to Calais. And there they were found by casual detachments of the British, who learned, when they tried, that they could butcher these formidable Prussians among the trees like pheasants, for they were leaderless. The road to the Channel was closed because the Germans did not know it was open.

That evening of November the eleventh, 1914, when the gun-fire of Germany's last attempt to break through had died down, storms of rain swept the battle-ground. The British lay in the mud, listening to the voices of the wounded, knowing no help was near, and waited for light. That would end it. The next lot would finish it. They could not know the last serious effort of the enemy upon Ypres had been made. They would have to face it at daylight. Their sentries, too weary to feel hunger, watched the fear of the battle ground after dark, the sudden threats of odd shapes in rain and quick gleams, the fitful lights from nowhere, and the desultory explosions. Their shallow trenches dissolved in the runnels and drainage.

They were abandoned to rain in the dark. The only reality for them was a night of ill-omened phantoms and the cries of men dying in the mire. There it was. The many inventions of years of Downing Street and Whitehall had come down to mud and havoc. The road paved with the good intentions of sage ministers was the Menin Road. But those soldiers who lay in the filth, expecting to be on the morrow what their mates were whose groaning grew less towards daybreak, who were of no importance, Tom, Dick and Jim, without knowing what it was they did, had stopped with their bodies on that road the coming of retribution to others far from it who had devised elaborate evil, sure that in its patriotism and cleverness it was good.

In London, on the morning of that same November day, Annie Bolt was early awake. She was thinking of the postman; there had been no letters from her brothers for too long. She found the sitting-room door open, mud where it should not have been, and her father, in his grimy overalls, fast asleep on her mother's cherished sofa. He was collapsed in an excess of weariness on his back, with his mouth open. She was alarmed, and was about to rouse him, if she could, for his face was drawn and grey. Then she guessed what it was, and stood looking at him.

Mr. Bolt, or Old Bolt, or Old Tom, as it was in the years to call him, had been shaping a liner for sea even while she moved down river. He and his gang of men had laboured for thirty hours without a break. They had been put ashore, their job completed, where no rest could be had, and no refreshment. There had been the usual heated dispute beforehand with the shipyard office about money for overtime, which Mr. Bolt had thought just for his good men; but the owners, who were the Carroll Line, had behaved as though expedition in an emergency, if properly considered, was its own reward. Old Bolt, ponderous, tyrannical, and energetic, against his sense of justice, had bullied his men through it; it was finished; and his overalls sullied the choice brocade.

Mrs. Bolt came in and stood beside her daughter. She moved at once with an instinctive protest to remove this outrage from a piece of her best furniture, but paused with her hand at her mouth. She was quietly withdrawing her daughter, when her husband roused, and sat up, gaping at them.

" Hullo, my dears." He glanced round vacantly.

" All right, dad. You stay where you are. Here's the *Morning News*. We'll get you some tea."

He took the paper obediently, and searched it, in another habit he had acquired, for news from the front. There was hardly a word of it. " Enemy attacks were renewed yesterday east of Ypres, but were repulsed with heavy losses."

Then presently they heard his exclamations, even in the kitchen, and returned hurriedly. He had crushed the paper into a ball and was trampling on it.

" Well, look, look, if you don't believe me. It says so. The paper says so. I don't work. I drink. It's in that rag. They've got a sermon about it. We're all drinking. Drinking and striking . . . while our boys are dying . . . it says so."

" Don't take any notice of them, dad."

" All right, Annie. You don't know. I tell you I bullied my gang all down river—got it done— damned good men I say—I gave them hell—drink—

not a coffee for them and cheated out of their pay—I'll
see about that blasted overtime now."

" Dad, I shouldn't bother."

" I'll see about it.   I'm going to that office.   They'll
hear about the drink."

" It doesn't matter."

" Boozing, lazy swine who won't work when their
country's up against it . . ."

" They don't know.   It's only the newspaper."

" Loafers who booze and strike, that's what we are.
Carroll says so.   It's in the paper.   He's been telling
them.   I'm going to that office now.   I'll give 'em
booze."

He had some tea, and he went, refusing at first to
get off his overalls.   " Not me.   I'm going straight
from the job, like this."   But it was pointed out to
him, by Annie, with her mild and cunning discernment,
that a prevailing argument is difficult for a man when
his opponent wears superior dress.

Old Tom Bolt did not know, when indignantly he
set forth on his errand to insist on the truth, that the
King was opening Parliament on that day.   He was
kept at a road crossing by the waiting crowd.   He was
jostled.   He lost his spirit in an impressive scene,
which was heedless of men of no importance who make
a transport ready for sea while the pilot is navigating
her.   The day was heavy and overcast.   While Old
Bolt waited, with his purpose weakening, he heard
martial music, but only drowsily, and with nothing of

his usual elation when there passed the pomp of drums and brass. He saw Lord Kitchener ride by, huge, grim and dark, and Mr. Bolt felt small and mean. His strength had gone. There were too many people; they were all cheering. He was getting old; getting past it. Damn the war! Spoiling everything. Tired, he was tired. That's what it was. He would go home to the old girl.

And on that November night, because everybody on so important a day was in town, and at the hour when the British sentries by the ruins of Gheluvelt looked eastward beyond the Menin Road for what was to come, there was a gathering at Lady Carroll's house. Langham was there, and several Ministers of State. The occasion was not unhappy.

The war, everybody there thought, had taken a better turn. The tension of the previous months had eased. The battle of the Marne, which ended the battles in the open, had restored their confidence. That first rush had been breathless and haphazard, but now, they supposed, England could settle down and put her weight into it. She could last it out. The legendary might of the German army was no longer an incubus, something with powers which the wit of man could not confine. It was proved mortal. The name of Ypres was familiar at the table, for it had appeared more than once in the official reports from France, but it had no particular significance for the diners. There had been so many strange names.

One could not remember all of them. It was good, the news, as far as it went.

" What exquisite roses Diana does manage to find in November ! " exclaimed the young lady beside Langham. Her eyes satisfied themselves with the fresh elegance and colour before her. " It eases one's mind to look at them. I had such a bad morning. I have a beautiful etching by Brangwyn of that town mentioned in to-day's paper—what do you call it ?— Ypres ?—is that the way to do it ? Beautiful. One of the best things Brangwyn has done, I think. You know, I looked for it on the map. I thought after all this time it must be near Germany. Wasted nearly an hour. And then I got a shock. Really, it is unpleasantly close."

" It won't come any closer," Langham assured her.

" It had better not. I suppose it is one of those wretched Flemish towns, but I'm told they are so picturesque. I hope it doesn't get damaged too badly. I should like to see it, some day. That etching is a dream."

Langham, who was tired and did not wish to talk of the war, said he knew it. He said that Brangwyn was a friend of his—a square, forthright little man, who might be a sailor, by his bluntness and dress. Brangwyn's etchings of those choice corners of Flanders, some of his best work, had an added value now ; they might be all that was left of them, if this awful business went on long enough.

" Oh, let us hope it won't last all that time. Do you know, I've made up my mind to join up. Yes, I have." She indicated the attractive table with its roses. " This sort of thing makes me feel rather uncomfortable when I think about it. So it should, don't you agree ? With so much going on I can't rest in London. I'm told the wounded often go for days without proper attention. I must—I will see something of it. We're only half alive here. I'm going to offer myself. Drive a car. Do anything."

" There you are, Langham," admonished the man opposite. " That's the spirit. The women will shame the shirkers into doing their duty. You'll have to drop your Radical notions of liberty. They won't do. Germany won't wait until our men have made up their minds whether they'll go or be fetched. My wife is in Boulogne, and she says the casualties are frightful. From what I'm told we can't have much of an army left. Why don't you tell the public the truth ? You'll have to come to it—conscription, and the sooner the better. The beggars must be made to go. Comb them out. As it is, it isn't fair to the others."

" Who are the others ? " asked Langham slyly. He had noticed that Lord Carroll was listening, and was nodding approval.

But laughter elsewhere prevented a ready indication of their nature. The table glanced with interest to the cheerful group. What was

the joke ?   A Minister there waved in slow grace
a rhetorical hand.

"It is merely this.   I asked, and now we all want
to know, where are a cow's ears, before or behind its
horns ?   We have referred the question to our friend
here, who was for so long the chief ornament of the
Department of Agriculture."

His lordship flourished his hand again, and a man
with a vacant but ponderous face, the lower half of
which hung in the loops of senility from a rigid eye-
glass, bowed to the company in mock gravity.

"We have asked our respected friend, our agricul-
tural friend," continued his lordship, "and he cannot
tell us.   What, I ask you, is the position of a cow's ears
in relation to her horns, if you please ? "

SUMMER returned, but not our youth, and with summer came the Zeppelins. One night they made their first visit to London, and so England's repose on the sea as her heritage went to join the legends of the Phœnicians. The man on his way to the morning train saw in the tranquil light of another bright day that there were gaping wrecks in the order of the new suburban villas, and understood that the inviolable ocean no longer kept his island and his rose-trees. Around him somewhere was war, certain as the privet hedges, milk cans, and bombs from the stars, yet still as abstract if as inexorable as death and time.

What could he do? He could but go on to his train as usual, and pray for a wet and windy night. He doubted for the first time in his life that even the calm morning sunlight was truthful to him; he began to suspect that it was of the same nature as the news of the day. Anyhow, there were the bedrooms of his friend Robinson, with no front wall, their privacy exposed to all eyes, and the bedchamber vesicles lying in the front garden with tiles, counterpanes, and part of the roof. He knew it was better not to ask after the Robinsons, and he was right. He accepted this drastic variation of his existence, and caught his train ; for if man is the most ferocious of all animals, he is also the most submissive.

On his way to town he read the news—if more news of it were in his daily journal—of a place, strange in geography, called The Front.   The Front, to him, to most of us, was as airy as a mathematical reality.   It was worse than that ; it could not be demonstrated. It was known to some of our friends, but they were overcome by shyness if we questioned them.   They changed the subject ; we could only infer from their manner that it was useless to tell us anything about it. The Front was not for us.   It was taboo.   It was as viewless and ineffable as a holy place to the vulgar. The air of this place, we did know, at times burned out the lungs of those who breathed it ; the ingenious mind of man had devised a means by which he could surprise his Maker with an appearance before the Judgment Seat in a gas mask.

A day came when it was necessary for me to see this secreted region to which our younger men were drifting, and at once it was doubtful whether or not I was good enough for so reserved a privilege.   The War Office wanted to learn that, and sent for me.   I waited for that audience in a large hall, with each of its many doors sacredly kept ; one of the doors opened and a woman came out and stood there with a hand covering her eyes.   She began to wail, and then another door opened, and she was taken within hurriedly. I was called to a door, and was allowed to enter. A handsome soldier, easily maintaining a monocle, stood reading a document, unaware for some minutes that I was in the room with him. Then he re-established his eye-glass, and regarded me without surprise, without even interest. He waved his hand deprecatingly at my testimony on my own account, and reached to a pigeon-hole, and withdrew a sheaf of papers. " We know all about you," he said, sadly ; and it was plain he knew something, and that it gave him no curiosity. He stroked his face, and at length agreed, in almost a friendly way, that he knew of no reason serious enough to keep from me the privilege of being shot at or choked by chlorine gas.

Presently I was once more in Boulogne. The change in the fortunes of that town was manifest. It was developing a new commerce. Stored near the water in one place were shells in such abundance, stacks of cylindrical solids of all weights, that the new commodity for intercourse between men suggested that Peace had retired, like the Early Fathers, to a place remote in time. Elsewhere I saw a hospita train busily discharging its freight ; there, in juxta-position, were Boulogne's new exports and imports.

Yet outside Boulogne, beyond a farm-wagon which was drawn across the road to block it, where a French sentry emerged from a hut of straw to prove the mission of the staff motor car in which I sat with a sad, reticent, and gigantic officer, the land sank into the

z

familiar aspect of summer. There was a smell of
bean-flowers. The white road diminished over
smooth and rounded downs whose bold and easy
outlines assured us of the magnanimity of continuous
days. Those hills once had been occupied by the
bowmen and knights of Edward III, and the host of
Napoleon which was to invade Albion. The bowmen
and the knights had gone, and Napoleon's ambitious
project had gone, but the clouds of summer persisted,
and the smell of bean-flowers. The shadow of the
cloud which Napoleon's men had seen was still
travelling over the same hill as we approached it.
We smelt the wood-smoke of a hidden homestead,
and I fancied that somewhere near us was a mild and
aromatic flame which could not be quenched. An inn
was retired under a walnut tree. It had outside
benches round its old red walls. Standing beside it
was a London motor-bus, not at all out of place
there, for it was disguised in the dust of ages. Sun-
burnt Londoners in dust-coloured uniforms were
idling near, and their rifles and packs could not keep
them from merging into the fulness of June. We had
left the war behind us, I imagined, in London chatter,
or stored at Boulogne. A yellowhammer called from
a telegraph wire. It was calling there, whatever our
speed, as the wires beside the road soared and sank, as
if a thought of my past accompanied me, and was
vocal. I supposed the note of that bird was only my
own melancholy affair, but once, when it called, the

huge and silent officer in the car, who was a stranger to me in all but his famous name, turned and looked at me fixedly, and smiled bitterly. He had heard it, too. We both had heard that voice of a spirit familiar to the dusty highways of home and the smell of bruised nettles.

We passed a long train of English motor lorries parked by that roadside of Picardy, their men asleep in the heat of the day, or peeling potatoes, or writing on upturned boxes within the wagons. Slender posts painted blue and white carried wires across the cornfields; the nerves, perhaps, of another and an alien organisation imposed on the land. We entered the long street of a drab village. It was occupied by the British, who were in their shirt-sleeves, and brisked about on domestic duties. Over the doors of a few of the houses and barns hung various pennants, to designate military mysteries for those who understood the signs. Perhaps, in spite of its appearance, a spell had been laid on the summer, and here were its warnings. One might not be able to trust the look of things. A field beyond the village was bald with the traffic of horses, which were tethered there in lines. Kine were browsing on a distant slope, and a windmill was uplifted in stark simplicity on the clear ridge above the herd. The cattle were grazing; and the mill continued its ancient task, not deliberately deceiving us, for it had not learned of any change in the winds of the world.

We left the mill behind, and saw ahead, over our road, a balloon hanging from a cloud, as though it were a black sausage suspended for us to laugh at. A minor cloud, a livid blotch, formed on an instant under the sausage, and another above it. The grotesque object above us became the centre of a gathering of balls of lurid smoke. The sky was snarling. I did not think this had anything to do with me. Our driver increased our speed, but as we shot under the balloon there were more dull reports, and a tradesman's horse by the roadside fell kicking in the shafts of its cart as we passed it. A horse received what was meant for a balloon. We came in a few minutes to a town, where women were gossiping at their doors, children were at play, and only a turbaned Indian trooper, as odd there as the balloon in its constellation of bursting shrapnel, stood and saluted us, and was accepted as one accepts whatever one sees in a dream.

CHAPTER XII

WE went through this white town, which was old and sleepy in the early afternoon, and then the road continued till it brought us to ornate iron gates. We drove through them, and over a drawbridge. I did not know who lived there, nor even where it was, but we have to take, on such an occasion, whatever we find within the gates of iron. There my officer abandoned me. Whatever was to follow was for myself alone.

The French house was seen, as I turned a corner of the drive, remote in a diminishing avenue of noble trees. Below the hush of midsummer was the vibration of many wings. The bees were in the limes. I could smell the nectar of that tree ; it is full summer when the limes are in flower and the bees get drunk. That was a pleasant confirmation of the season, for the summer to me was doubtful. The house was set deeply in a perspective of rounded foliage, as though I stood in the June of one year, and saw distantly the pale ghost of the old chateau in a June that was silent, for it was past. I wanted to reach that house, but it seemed as though I could get no nearer to it than the murmuring summer in which I stood. I could only look back to where it was secluded in the silence of a forgotten year.

That was a confusing idea ; but then it was a confusing summer, a summer dubious with its immemorial aspect of continuity, yet suggesting bleakly a subtle yet disastrous interruption in the life of the earth ; as though common and pleasant things had their accustomed aspect, yet a suspicion had taken us that now we saw only the bright illusion of what was familiar. What had been behind everything was gone. If in one of the arbours of that estate, where stood white statues pensive with ancient secrets they would never disclose, I had surprised a furbelowed lady who ought to have been nowhere but in a picture by Watteau, she might have been more startled than myself. I should have felt that I was the intruder, and should have withdrawn at once from a June which did not belong to me. Not my June ; and that was not a lady for me, but only for a gentleman in satin breeches and a brocaded coat. And from one of those arbours, in a vista which was still and suspect, a figure did suddenly emerge. It came out quickly, gave me a direct but not a startled look, and turned towards the chateau. It had a cockney face, and its khaki dress was unrelieved by ornament except the blue and white armlet of a British signaller. I could see it had no doubt whatever about its year.

I had to believe, after all, that I had not wandered into another age. If I had, others of my own time

were lost there with me; or perhaps in a celestial
dreaminess the gods had become careless, and had
muddled the sunlights and affairs of far different times.
For a Sikh, with a rifle that was only a toy in his giant's
grasp—a giant with a divided black beard the ends of
which were curled up behind his ears—was patrolling
the balustrade of a terrace of that French house;
below him was a moat in which waterlilies floated.
The Indian sentry reached the end of his beat, and
paused to look down at the white body of Aphrodite,
who stood there with a foot coyly poised over the
water she had been about to enter since Louis Soleil
was king. War? Not even though a Sikh with
fierce whiskers were considering Aphrodite. There
was no war. There was only an occasional and
inexplicable flutter in the air. The air sometimes
shook; the summer day was quite peaceful, but it was
not accurately fitted to the earth, it was not quite firm
on its base. It gave a sense of insecurity, as though it
might be withdrawn from us because it was a mistake,
being the misplaced summer of another age and place.

Nor was the interior of the chateau reassuring.
The frail furniture was right, and the ormolu, the
crystal candelabra hanging from the painted ceiling,
and the tapestries; they were in their place in the
serene continuity of pleasant human things. The
ladies of the house looked down from the walls out of
their frames of heavy gilt, and one of them, a girl of
1779, seemed as surprised as I was to observe soldiers

below intent upon typewriters, and the coming and going of British officers.

One of the officers came to me.   He knew my name, and met me as if I were one of that household, though I had never seen him before.   " They telephoned from G.H.Q. about you this morning.   We were thinking you were lost.   The battalion you want is somewhere near Neuve Chapelle, but the ground is rather altered up there since the attack, and its an unattractive corner. But we've got a guide for you—here he is, too. Lieutenant Jones . .."

The lieutenant was boyish, and had the brusque candour of shyness.   " I offered to take you before I knew where you wanted to go.   Shall we start at once ?   It's fairly quiet there now, so we'd better get it over."

We had a brief run by car through an uninhabited country, and then, for no reason that I could see—but perhaps reason was not there—the young soldier hid the car by a hedge, and said we must walk.   We took a straight road through an avenue of poplar trees ; on each side of it was a stagnant ditch, and peeps over flat meadows.   The sun was on it, but if his light had been blue, and so the land had had that sinister complexion of the spectral vista we get through a tinted window, it could not have been more forbidding.   It was an earth changed in nature.   We were alone in it.

This region was enchanted, without a doubt, but it offered us no clue.   Cavities that were raw and deep were frequent in our road. We came to a footbridge, and the ditch there was widened into a circular basin of black slime as smooth and polished as glass; its duckweed and rushes were plastered fanwise across our path, and had stuck to neighbouring walls. The muck was new; the water was still draining from it as ink. We approached a large pool of blood, and separated to walk round it. Its extravagance alarmed me, but, except that my guide must have seen it to have avoided it, he gave no other sign that he admitted its existence. It spread in front of an estaminet. The door of the inn was open, and beside the door was a chair; but nobody was in the chair; nobody sat in it contemplating that mystery in the middle of the road. The estaminet was deserted. There were houses, sunlight, and blood, but no people.

The distance was thudding heavily. The horizon was loose, perhaps, and was bumping on the earth. Ahead of us, almost lost in a clump of trees, were the red roofs of a farmhouse and its sheds. There were ragged gaps in the tiles. As we neared the farm there was a crash, as though a boiler plate had dropped from a great height to paving stones, and was at once still. Two columns of black smoke, which had not been there before, stood over the farm. Nevertheless, the road continued with indifference, though a tree had been lifted by the roots across it. There was a row of trees that had been reduced to bundles of white splinters, and near them we found the first men. Six of them lay in a row by a wall, and two others stood over them.   The faces of the men on the ground were averted, and their eyes were closed.   They did not want to look at us.

The ugly but intermittent sound of unseen bodies lumbering through the air was more frequent when we reached another group of buildings, scattered among trees at a road crossing.   The trees were motionless in the sleeping afternoon.   The walls of one of the barns, a structure so weathered that its rufous brickwork had the surface of crumbling grey stone, were riven, and the raw edges of the gaps were bright red.   From somewhere came a noise which might have been made by an idle boy rattling a stick along a fence.   An officer, to my surprise, then appeared at the door of a barn I had thought was empty.   " Come in," he urged us.   " They spray that road with a machine gun. Can't you hear it ? "   But for that distant rattling the silence was so deep that I imagined I could hear a frog I saw flopping across the road.   A pair of swallows were circling about, and their familiar celerity and accuracy, as they pitched on their nest built under the eaves of a house on the point of collapse, had been regarded by me in confidence as tokens of the world I used to know.

Under the rafters of that partially dismantled barn was a man who laughed when he saw me.   His amusement was caused, most likely, by my unexpected appearance, which he had to take as another absurd feature in a phantasy. He himself, an Oriental scholar, as a soldier in that place, was not easily believable. He laughed again because his quizzical temper, I suppose, thoroughly relished the waywardness of this coincidence.

" What brings you here? Have you gone potty, too ? " he asked. He gossiped disjointedly about our circumstances. " You may have noticed there is a war on up here, but who is making it, except ourselves, beats me. It's between us and the spooks, I think. You haven't noticed any so-called Germans hanging about, have you? I haven't seen one yet "—he flinched and grimaced at an explosion outside—" but that sort of thing all day has to be accounted for."

We left that barn. We set out together for his own place, which he said was near, though long before we reached it—mainly through a serpentining trench— my sense of direction went dizzy, and was sure only of up and down. The earth was crackling in the heat ; that was rifle fire. The deep drain meandered aimlessly, with charlock and poppies vivid overhead against the sky. We climbed out to hurry across a road, and entered another drain, which burrowed among the ruins of buildings, and then we waited, on hands and knees, while the brickbats ahead of us were smashed a little more. When the dust and smoke were clearing we hurried along, and soon came out into a village.

It was abandoned. It was acrid with smoke and

smouldering fires.   There was a smell of damp earth
and mortar.   Some of the houses had fallen across the
street.   That village had come to its end, and the only
proof that life had even known it was a child's doll
sprawled in mimicry of wanton grief near the mummied
carcase of a cow.   We crossed the churchyard—one
Gothic arch of the church was standing to frame
daylight—and strode over grey rubble, splintered
coffin boards, and a few resurrected sleepers in
nightgowns who had risen from their graves indifferent
as to where they slept.   A spasmodic growling flew at
us through the quiet and ended in a great clang by the
Gothic arch.   We descended hurriedly a long flight of
stone steps to a cellar.   My friend Upcott then sat on a
packing box and laughed again, a little too long.
" This is my home," he explained.   " I share it with a
surgeon.   I think he'll lend you a bed for the night."
Upcott pointed to a stretcher in a corner.

The cellar was spacious and gloomy, and our
privacy was a corner of it, screened by some sacking
from what Upcott named the Battalion Aid Post ;
that was the remainder of the cellar.   We had the
cellar to ourselves, then.   Upcott was eager for news ;
yet even as I began to recount some to him our cellar
began to shake in a series of spasms.   A tin bowl on
the floor trembled and whined.   We waited, and soon
the cellar sank deep into the quiet earth again.

" We're all right here," Upcott speculated
doubtfully, " because if that stairway goes there

is another way out. Perhaps I'd better show you where it is."

We had a look round, and saw the other stairway, a pile of bandages, and wine bins containing nothing but a cat, which was pleased to meet us. Then there was no more to do except to return to the kitchen table. That was loaded with neat piles of documents, each pile under a shell-nose. Upcott took off his tunic, inspected a document, and filled his pipe.

" Now you've seen this place, perhaps you'd hardly believe the trouble I took to get from India to it," he said. " We heard that men were badly wanted, so I thought I ought to be quick, and I was. I got away from the mark in style, but the results surprised me. My patience had to mount a lot of monuments—it was patience which sat on a monument, wasn't it ?—anyhow, I was kept waiting a devil of a time on each one I came to. After all, there was no hurry in this war. What a rummy old dear Authority always is ! It tried to keep me from the delights of this beastly hole as long as possible. But one day I got to France. I was peeved, for I thought the war would be over before I could have some. Whelan ! "

" Sir ! "

" Whisky ! Have you seen Major Weston to-day?"

" No, sir. He was killed last night, sir."

Upcott rose and stared at me. Then he sat down again. " Bring the drinks, Whelan," he said.

He sat, turning his pipe round and round, as though

examining it for a defect, while he frowned.   Then he
spoke to himself.   "I suppose it's right."   He
muttered across to me in doubt.   "I tell you I spoke
to him last night.   I spoke to him."   He appeared to
invite my confirmation that a little conversation with
another man might at times fail to render him invulnerable.

The servant returned, methodical as at a London
counter, and then vanished as though he had passed
though a wall.

"They end like that," said Upcott.   "There they
are, and then they're not; but the war goes on . . .
for how long, do you think ? . . . I say, I wish I had
no sense, then I might enjoy it."

Upcott remained pensive for so long that his pipe
went out.   Then he walked to the other end of the
cellar and back.   He lit his pipe again, and sat down.
"I came here in such an infernal hurry, in case I missed
it.   You might as well worry over not being late for
your funeral.

"They shunted me about France for weeks in trains
and lorries—I couldn't find my lot—I thought the
battalion I'd been sent to didn't exist.   Everybody
knew at once where it was, but it was never there,
though sometimes it had been.   At last I did find it,
and reported myself.   The adjutant said, ' But where's
your sword ?   You can't parade without a sword.'
So I went to a farm, and sent to London for a sword,
and slept in an outhouse under the chickens while

waiting for it. Then the sword came, and I reported myself again. 'You've got a sword,' said the adjutant. 'You cannot parade with a sword. The order is to return all swords.'

" That's what it's like," Upcott assured me. " It's all like that. I tell you there's only one thing to do here —shut off your intelligence. Kill your memories. Forget everything you ever learned, forget your friends, write them off. They don't exist. Hope the next thing to happen won't be as silly as everything that has happened before. If you try to be reasonable here you get into a frightful mess. One day one of the headquarters—I dunno which, brigade, division, corps, army, or else the holy of holies—wanted to know why we were using so much chloride of lime. I suppose they thought we were eating it. Perhaps head-quarters don't have to use chloride of lime. Anyhow, I wrote across the requisition, 'latrines and drinking water.'

" Lord, we wanted a disinfectant then, my son. My truthful reply tore it. Believe me, there was a stink. The colonel got worried. He said I'd better send an officer to the latrines just to satisfy the holy of holies with a nice report. That officer was gone too long about it. I got nervous, and had to go after him. There had been some nasty shelling, you know. His runner was lying wounded by the latrines, and there was the subaltern . . . well, we wanted more chloride of lime, then."

Upcott's narrative was interrupted here. I heard a scuffling on the stairs, and a whispering.

"You take 'is legs."

"I gottim."

A little group of Tommies then moved across the cellar, and laid one of their number on a bench. The others arranged themselves along the same form in various attitudes of lassitude and indifference. They were muddy, gaunt and unshaven. Several of them attempted cigarettes, yet with a sluggishness which allowed a match to burn out before it was used.

Upcott, after a steady glance at that array of cripples now composed, lax and still, called out that the medical officer was expected back at once. One of them lifted reproachful eyes to us, but none of them spoke nor moved. Other footsteps sounded on the stairs, hard and deliberate and the M.O. and two men entered. Upcott adjusted the canvas screen, watched round the edge of it for a moment, called out that if help were wanted we were there, and then came to sit beside me on his box.

"That goes on all day, off and on. When they're really busy it's no place for me—I can't stand being looked at like that. I don't care for the colour of that fellow on his back, do you? His feet are too loose. Sometimes a man's feet tell you more than his face."

We heard groans, and Upcott paused. We sat, looking at the floor.

"No." (It was the decisive voice of the M.O.)

" No. Leave that man. You men all right now ? Feel you can do it ? Then make your way out while it's quiet. Lucky beggars. Hop it. Off you go."

The shuffling began anew, and when it had ceased we heard the M.O. coldly instructing his assistants where they were to put the soldier who had to stay. The doctor came over for a gossip before venturing forth ; and then again we had the gloom to ourselves.

" Can you make anything of it ? " asked Upcott, with an inconsequence which was not quite innocent.

" It is a little queer."

" Queer ? You may well say it. Queer, eh ? There's no sense in it. We're all daft. We're all up in the air. Those fellows who have just gone out to hobble through shell-bursts trusting to luck—what do they make of it ? What patient lads they are. They never say a word. I shouldn't have thought men could be so patient, but between you and me they're damned fools, and it's a good thing for us they are. We'd be in a fix if they had any sense. It's all our doing, you know, all this. We're the governing classes, aren't we ? Sorry; I don't know whether you belong but I do. I'm one of the rulers of India, in case you haven't noticed it. I tell you I wonder those fellows don't round on us, for the bungling duffers we are. That would stop it. They ought to right about face all along the front, and march on London, Paris and Berlin. That would be fixing it where it belonged; but they'll never do it, never. No, they never say a

AA

word.   They'll never do anything except kill each
other.   When I see what good-natured lads they are,
and the way they stick the worst of this job, I feel I
could hug them first and kick them afterwards.
They're like the horses.   Do what they're told.
Never say anything.   But some of the horses sweat
through funk.   Once a horse has had a dose of it, he
begins to sweat whenever he hears a bump.   Trembles
and sweats.   But he goes into it when ordered, all of a
lather, and so do we—all of a lather.   Heroic fat-
heads ! "

"When I was getting here to-day," I told Upcott,
" I got the notion that the whole thing was an illusion.
The country is hardly real.   I began to wonder
whether it was there, or whether I was there.   Perhaps
these men . . ."

" I know.   That's what does it.   Most of us feel
that way.   We reckon we're in a dream, and can't
wake up because we are awake.   But you'd better not
be fooled by it.   It is real—as real as this cellar.   At
first you think it's rather a silly joke.   You laugh at it.
That's why some of the best of the young 'uns die too
soon.   They hardly believe it.   They go about
showing it no respect.   But there it is all right, and it
gets them.   It may look like moonshine, but we're
caught in it all right, and so you'll jolly well find.
Look, here comes its Hermes."

A despatch rider entered, saluted, handed out of the
blue his token, and went.   Upcott read the message,

sighed, and placed it on one of the neat piles. "You get the notion," he said, " that anyhow you are lost in it. Nobody knows where you are, and nobody could ever find you. Wrong again! The gods have got us taped. They know where we are, and all about us, and if they order you to put your head in a bag you've got to do it. You can die here for two reasons—for being an idiot, and for refusing to be an idiot.

" The things that happen here—there never is any sense in them. They just happen. One day, when we had got back to rest billets—our rest was shelled to hell most of the time—the colonel came to me. ' Look here,' he said. ' Here's something from the general. It says a French colonel is going to visit us, though it doesn't say what he wants—just to see our little lot, I suppose—and we've got to treat him mighty fine. Look here, we've got no food fit to eat, and he'll be here to-night. Just scout for something tasty, will you? Luckily we can make him drunk, if he's that sort of chap. And I say, I wish you'd let him have your bed. His adjutant will be with him, and he can have mine, as yours is the best.'

" I tell you, we cursed those Frenchmen for nuisances, but we made ready for them, and our mess cook turned out a really presentable table. Then we waited for them, wondering what was the correct form for such an occasion, because we'd seen nothing of the French in the war, so far. Immensely impressed, of course, by their reputation, and all that. They were soldiers, and most of us were only civilians trying to be. Our adjutant was the most likely specimen we had. Even our colonel didn't look like a colonel—a stout man, though. We were a bit nervous about this visit.

" Presently he rolled up, this French johnny—a big fellow, with a tummy on him, in a blue uniform and brown bulging gaiters. Behind him was a slender young officer, very stiff and correct. The French colonel had one of those hunting horns round his shoulder—you know the sort of thing—you see it in comic prints of French sportsmen—a curly trumpet— they go out after partridge with it, don't they ? Well, he didn't take that trumpet off him. Only his cap. His bald head was pale, but his big round face was rosy and very happy, with lots of chin, and a long grizzled moustache which would have been straight and fierce if he hadn't laughed so much. He did laugh. He stamped with one foot, and patted his tummy with both hands, and laughed very free and hearty, and then hummed and pulled out his moustache. A cheery card. But his young officer was prim. He didn't laugh at anything. Never said a word. Smiled faintly and loftily when spoken to. ' Yes,' he said. Only that. He was supercilious. Thought we were rather a bore, I believe.

" Not a word did they give us about the object of their visit—just rich laughter from the colonel over nothing in particular. We began dinner. The

French colonel wore his hunting horn. Of course, we pretended not to see the thing—sort of behaved as though we were used to that at dinner—custom of the country, you know. The young officer, he hardly looked up, or if he did it was only to screw his eyes at the wall over the head of the man opposite. That chap ate our food as if he had to do it. Duty was duty, and we were only British, and didn't know any better.

" But his colonel was all right. He was different. He enjoyed himself—we happened to have a Burgundy of a good year—and our fellows played up to him for the good of the regiment. After one burst of merriment, which was so hearty that we all joined in, that big Frenchman rose, put one foot on his chair, and tootled his hunting horn.

" Not likely we took any notice of it. Not likely. Too well-trained. Pretended we heard nothing. The young Frenchman, he took no notice of it. I supposed this tootling might be the custom of the regiment of our visitors, an ancient right won in battle. It was the proper thing for the colonel of that regiment to do—blow his blessed horn at intervals during dinner. He had to maintain a link with the glorious past.

" He was a lusty chap, our important guest. Full of beans and funny stories. At the end of a cheery one, when he'd got us all going, he'd rise from his chair, and solemnly let go a tantara. Our servants were good lads—they did seem a bit surprised, but they never laughed.   As for our own old man, he was so polite that he might have been as deaf to that hunting horn as the young French officer.

"After dinner the fun got very lively.   I must say our youngsters thoroughly enjoyed this Gascon, who certainly was enjoying himself.   He approved our whisky.   Then he got into a sentimental mood; he mentioned his wife.   Ah!   He would show why France would fight, gentlemen, till not a German was this side of the Rhine; that or death.   He became serious.   Gentlemen, you shall observe this.   He put a hand inside his tunic, and tugged at what I thought was a pack of cards.   But the pack was tight, and he tugged too hard.   The cards shot across the table. Well, I was a bit shocked.   I'll admit it.   Photographs of women!   And some of them!   You never saw such a collection of bosoms and behinds.   Do you think that fine old fellow was embarrassed?   Not a scrap.   It was the sort of thing that might happen to any good man, if he were clumsy with his pocketbook.   He began to sort them, coolly and indifferently, sort of shuffling the pack, perhaps looking for the queen of hearts—I dunno.

"Then for the first time that evening the severe young Frenchman condescended to take an interest in what was going on.   He rose, and leaned over the table, intently inspecting the pictorial assortment of ladies.   His curiosity was genuine.   Suddenly he pointed sharply at a

photograph. He spoke at last. ' That is my wife,'
he said to his colonel.

" He punched his colonel in the eye. The big
fellow collided with a chair behind him, and over it
went, and so did he, with a frightful banging of
brassware on the stone floor. Our own colonel was
horrified. We were all alarmed. We stared at one
another. What happened when a French officer
punched his colonel in the eye ? What ought we to do
when they were our guests ? There's nothing in the
King's Regulations about that, is there ?

" One of our fellows was assisting the jolly Frenchman to his feet, but he sprang up, shook with laughter
as he pulled his tunic straight, and went out into the
yard. Outside, we heard him play a bold fanfare on
his horn—a salute to all stags, I suppose. He was
soon back.

" As he entered he was met by his junior. They
embraced each other, and kissed. I looked away at
our colonel. I didn't know where to look. Our old
man stood as if he were frightened. He stood at the
fireplace, fumbling badly at his moustache. Fact is,
the lot of us supported the old country pretty well, I
think. Nobody acted as though he'd seen anything
out of the way—sort of thing which might happen in
any well-regulated mess in war-time, don't you know.

" I lost count of the time that night, but I remember
helping the big fellow to bed. When the pair of them
had gone none of us said a word about the evening's

performance. Oh, one of the young 'uns did speak. He said to the colonel, ' Do you think he plays that trumpet in bed, sir?' But our colonel said nothing. We put out the lights.

" Next morning at breakfast we were very moody. The Frenchmen were a long time coming down, but nobody said so. I rather think we were in doubt. What had happened the night before? After a bit our colonel called across to me. ' Look here, Upcott, I'm right, am I not? There were two Frenchmen with us last night?'

" ' Yes, sir, I think so. I had that impression myself, but as nobody else owned up to it I thought I'd better keep quiet.'

" ' Right,' said the colonel. ' That settles it. If they were here then, they're here now. Come along, Upcott, come and greet them.'

" We went to our colonel's room first, where we'd put the adjutant. He wasn't there, though the bed had been slept in. Then we toddled along to my room. No French colonel, either. Nothing there, except a hunting horn, hung round a knob of my bed. ' Well, I'm damned,' said our old man.

" And it's a funny thing, but none of our orderlies saw those fellows go. And we never heard any more about it. Not a word. What do you make of it? "

I did not attempt to make anything of it. As an episode of the war it was as meet and proper as an Oriental scholar making British reports on the local use of chloride of lime in the cellar of a French farm. While Upcott and I sat smiling at each other, filling our pipes, the tin bowl on the floor woke up ; it began to complain again. It trembled and whined. The cellar became convulsive. The cat galloped up to us, and stood staring, in alert suspicion, at the bare wall behind us. Somebody fell headlong down the stairs.

PART FIVE

THE YEARS
1916 TO 1919

PART FIVE

CHAPTER I

THE two new subalterns, joining their battalion, paused to take in this region of the Somme. It was strange, though the battle-line to both of them was now more familiar than home.

This country is an improvement on Hooge, thought Jack Bolt. "I say, Webb, I like this," he said to his companion. "This beats dirty old Flanders."

They both approved. Real bold hills and dark copses—something like hills, these. They had a notion these hills were more friendly than the slag heaps about Loos, which bossed you like black ogres, and those hardly-to-be-seen yet filthy blisters on the mud of the Salient.

"There's Albert down there!"

They tried to make out the Virgin and Babe, for both had heard of that miracle of the pendent gilt images of Albert. The war was going to end, the legend went, when those images fell. They could see only a diminished dim tower. It was too far, and it was in a hollow. It was dusty, too, or hazy, down there. It was hot—beastly stuffy—hardly any air.

They were going into the jolly old line once more, but they were not in it yet. They need not think about it before they had to. They did not think about it. They pushed down unpleasing speculations which rose. They could hear The Front. The smallness of the noise surprised them. There was nothing in that. They had heard it a lot worse than that. From where they stood, they judged, hopefully, that the dire intensity of the latest gun-fire had been rather exaggerated. Over the broad landscape far away they watched noiseless and unauthentic clouds bulge, black, and sulphur, and sometimes, when a gleam of sun made solid and lustrous the bulk of one of them, vermilion. Up went some house, then! That was the new battle, the Great Push, with its odd names, added so recently to the names which worked like a spell on those who knew what they stood for—Gommecourt, Thiepval, Fricourt, Mametz, Trones. It didn't look too bad; and after all the hectic stories they had heard about it! Of course, the other fellows had been trying to put the wind up them in Amiens, trying to take the nap off their new uniforms. Trying to make them feel they'd got it all to learn. Can't be worse than Hulluch, thought Jack, can't be worse than Hooge! What was the good of listening to what other men said? The thing itself was always different. That country ought to have plenty of cover. It would be useful for artful surprises.

And in truth the Great War was almost as many different wars as there were men who were in it. Jack's mind, on that hill of Picardy, was at ease in a respite, and it wandered. He'd had a long dose of it, before he got his commission. He thought how beastly pretty Webb looked. Just out of the tailor's shop. Well, that was it ; so he was, just out. Webb looked as if his mother ought to brush him down and kiss him ; but he had seen Webb giving water in the open to a wounded Jerry when the shrapnel bursts had made everybody else shrink under their tin hats. He supposed he looked the same. He was right. Both of them, slim and limber, smiling and in good health, had complexions as proper as the flush on peaches, to which dust only added a bloom.

This hill reminded Jack of Coulsdon. The country was rather like Surrey. Honest chalk and marl ! No wonder he thought it was like Surrey—he stooped to pick a scabious. The very flower ! Where was poor old Charley these days ? It was a hillside like this ; the same sort of stuff growing. Charley lay on his back, hat over his eyes, and the stalks down the slope moved in breaths of wind, just as they did here. The same sort of day. Was Charley's lot over there, in this Somme show ? Almost sure to be. It must have been a sticky business. The traffic on the roads showed that. Everybody would have to have a cut at it. They must get it over. So the worse it was, the better for them. After that they could go home.

He felt no elation, and very little curiosity. He was going into it once more, but he was not in it yet. The Germans had to be shoved out, and now it was being done. He was there for that. This show would settle it. It had to come, and here it was. If he had been reminded of his keenness when first he strode over the corduroy track through the haunted wood at Plug Street towards the breastworks, and even paused to look up in interest to the funny honking of shells in flight over the tree tops, he would have been perplexed. Why, yes, so he was green, then. He was a kid. But lots had happened in a year. There had been hundreds of miles of trenches everywhere. The same old fag over and over again. Those first months were in another life. Now it was business. You just had to get on with it, and not stop to think about it . . . Croydon High Street, and a Saturday morning. A day off and nothing to do. Dad reading the paper. The mater putting the ornaments to rights on the mantelpiece; watering her old pot of musk on the window-sill, touching the leaves with her finger, bending to smell it, not knowing he was watching her.

"Come on, you shirker!" Jack shouted. "Step it out. We've got to find the transport lines or we shan't get a seat at the show."

Any reader of the news that morning in London knew more of what was happening there than those two care-free young officers. They always had to

wait till they saw a London paper before they knew
what was going on about them, and yet when the
news concerned their own exact spot it was bilge.
What fool wrote that stuff? He ought to be strafed
in a shell-hole all night. Young Bolt and young
Webb had heard this Big Push was to end the war.
They were mighty glad of that. The tide at last had
turned. Everyone said so. And they had heard of
a Great Victory. Everybody talked of it. The
papers had been full of it.

Was there a snag in it? There had been time for
other stories to reach the most remote messes. There
were confidential whispers. " It's another muck."
" They're telling the tale again."

Well, some fellows always thought they'd pulled it
off, they'd done the trick, if they got out of a dust-up
on the cheap, and other men thought it was the usual
wash-out if their lot got scuppered. You never knew
what to make of it.

Anyhow, by the best accounts they ought to be
getting into Bapaume soon. Bapaume, that town
clean out of the map! Open country then, and no
more trenches; nearer home by miles and miles.
But there was that lieutenant of the London Rifles at
Amiens. Jack could not forget that chap. He had
listened to the talk about the great doings, and then
he stood up over them, very sad, and they shut up.
He had a queer look. Then he spoke. He wanted
the blood of all war-correspondents—seemed to want

to paddle in it. He hated them—he said they were decoy ducks. They thought he was going to make a fool of himself. He was old for a lieutenant, too. He was white with fury over something. Then he pulled himself together, looked at his knuckles, about turned and went out. Most likely he'd had a rotten time. Poor old perisher. But it took the shine off the talk.

When the two young officers were on the road below, if it had been thundering nobody would have heard it. What a jam! British lorries, motor-cycles, guns, limbers, French horse wagons, ambulances, troops singing, all trying to get somewhere, in drifting clouds of dust. The dust made the eyes smart and crunched in the teeth. The trees and buildings were drab with it. Perspiration streaked the faces of the men, yet they sang. They were in good fettle. "The bells of hell go ting-a-ling-a-ling for you but not for me." Songs, rumbling of heavy traction, jangling of chains, clattering of hooves, shuffling of feet, backfiring of the buses, honking—something was doing, something was really up! This was some push! On a rickety barn door was stuck a placard of Horatio Bottomley's rag: "1916! Thank God!"

The two new subalterns found themselves in a valley. It was known as Happy Valley. They were at once lost amid the activities of a monstrous fair ground. Everybody was going to the fair. There was no mistake about the guns now. Their shocks

displaced the air. It was not gun-fire; it was a
continuous eruption. The blasts blew down that
exit from the valley towards the north-east. That
led to the unknown land, to the woods and villages,
not so distant, whose names were new and dreadful—
Montauban, Longueval, High Wood, Devil's Wood,
Bernafay Wood, Lousy Wood, Guillemont, Ginchy,
Combles. Those names were the gossip of the fair.
They were the acute points on the fluctuating line
where the earth was blowing up, and the flames
consumed more men than could be sent to feed them.
Sausage balloons hung in rows in the sky; as if they'd
got up there to see the show, and their big behinds
sat where there was no gallery.

Happy Valley was a desert. Its surface was
pulverized by myriads of feet, hooves, and wheels.
Restless brown lakes could be seen in it; they were
congestions of horses. All the trees of the valley
were dead or dying because the horses had gnawed
off their bark. A great carnival was being held in
the valley; excitement and energy stirred its life,
without joy. Its slopes were blotched with the dis-
coloured canvas dwellings of the hands in the new
industry of war, surgeons, and craftsmen with rifles
and cannon, and their hosts of qualified attendants.
The broad valley crawled with humans, cattle, and
machinery, and distance merged horses, men and
engines into a ceaseless stirring on the hairless hide
of the planet. The interest of man had settled on the

valley, and had worn it as dead as an ash-pit. From a distance, it was not an army of men you saw there, but merely an eddying of clusters and streams of loose stuff. It was not men, but man-power, which moved into that valley without ceasing, and the power was pumped into it from the reservoirs of distant cities to keep revolving the machinery of war. If life clotted, it was deflected into those hospital tents. The streams had to be constant and free. The flies of all the plagues were in the valley, more flies than men and horses, because every dead man and horse bred an army of flies; the flies darkened the food, shimmered over the ordure, and swarmed on the clotted life in the hospital tents.

The land around was terraced with massed batteries and howitzers. Their crews laboured at the ranks of glistening steel barrels, stripped to the waist. They fed them glumly and methodically, as in a universal factory where overtime was compulsory for a greater output of death, which nobody wanted. The machinery had been set going, and the men were its slaves. They could not stop. The engines compelled them to continue as they had begun. They were being broken on the wheels they had started. The wheels and cogs of the age of machines had taken charge of their inventors, and were grinding them and their earth into powder, for the increase of the flies. Work did not finish at sunset. Night was in abeyance. Darkness was an intermittent day; it was tremulous with an incessant flaring and glittering, and the very clouds flushed phantom-like with the red reflections of earth's sinister activities. It was the Battle of the Somme. Giant automata hammered ponderously on the old horizon, breaking it up. The earth sparked and flashed under their poundings. They hammered with a violence so rapid that you knew only soulless bodies of steel could be so powerful and tireless, so blind to ruin, so unheeding of the dismay of listeners. You had a dread that evil had been freed. It was beyond control now, leaping huge malignant rapine over cornlands, orchards, and altars, turning the ancient establishment of prudent peace into dust and corruption.

As for Jack Bolt, he was a new officer, and his thought took no such turn in Happy Valley. The noise and the impersonal movements only subdued him. In the transport lines after dark the flaring and crashing beyond, through which he must pass, awed him a little. This was the limit. Golly, this was something like! Now we shan't be long! He felt even a little grimly sorry for poor old Jerry. Jerry was being blown to hell. Stuff to give him! Now he knew what it was like. Jerry was getting a bit more than his own back.

" Where's your pal ? " demanded the transport officer. " We're off."

Jack was taken then by a momentary panic. In that pandemonium of darkness, flashes, shocks, and confused activity, a fellow could be lost, and never found again, and nobody would ever know. Worse than the Hohenzollern Redoubt!

Good! There was Webb, brought back by a gun-flash! Jack did not want to go up into that sort of night without a pal. This was the end. It was stepping off the edge. In those other raids and shake-ups he had been somebody, if only a number; now he knew he did not matter. A fellow could be missing, and nobody would bother because it would be no good bothering about anybody.

That journey gave him the impression that it was good-bye to all. He could never find his way back, even if he had the chance. He was going beyond the limit, and maps could not help. There was no way back. He blinked at loud lights bursting out of nowhere. The earth existed only here and there. You didn't know how long its pieces would last, either. The chunks of the blessed old busted world jolted and sank and upended under your feet. The sky was bursting and tumbling and the ground was broken darkness. He saw in a bright instantaneous heaven the head of a terrified horse thrown up for a second, and a man's head in a tin hat. Then they were blotted out. There were angry voices and no men. There was a long flame and a roar alongside which made him fall over the belly of a dead mule. The belly was tight as a drum. He was thrown about among panic-stricken horses. A cooker went into a hole; it toppled over. He heard the grief of the cook : " It ain't 'arf a bloody stew now." Somebody caught his arm and began to laugh. That was Webb. Webb couldn't stop laughing.

Daylight came thinly, as though reluctant to show what it must. The things about Jack had no substance, and he was glad of that. They were better that way. He didn't want to think. He didn't want to believe. He had shrunk within himself to a mere point, and had no fear, only a still and alert doubt. He watched. He held himself in. Only his eyes were there; he did not want to be sure that he was any more real than the shapes he could faintly make out about him. There was, around him, only a vision of the last day, which a wind could disperse, it was so grey and thin. It was not a surprise that the scene trembled in the blasts of the British guns. Their light was brighter than the faint daylight.

A vivid flame burst beside a gun a little ahead and to the right. One of the gunners spun a cart-wheel in the air and flopped on the track and stayed there. Jack passed that object as though it were at a great distance. He was apart from it. Well, those gunners were asking for it. There they were, in the open, all over the shop, and going it so hard that Jerry had no time to find them. It was an audacious scene, new to the war, and Jack was cheered. One shell at all those guns! A battery of field pieces stood blatantly amid the rubbish of broken walls and slammed away into the morning; those guns might have had nothing to fire at, but were merely emptying their dumps into the sunrise. Tiny aeroplanes, meteors in the upper light, passed leisurely eastward to the dawn. Anyhow, that proves right one of the fairy tales, Jack supposed; our fliers really have got the German airmen cold. He was pleased with any promising sign.

He tripped over wire, while eyeing those shining birds in easy flight. The ground was an awful mess; a confusion of silly wreckage, brickbats and beams, lathes and plaster, huddles of grey sandbags, flattened trenches, the entrances to old dug-outs blown cock-eyed, craters, and red thickets of wire; broken rifles, helmets and shell-cases stuck out of the piles of grey muck like fossils.

My God, Jack was glad he was out of this when it was going on! This job hadn't been easy. Fright-ful! Could a man live through it? Had Charley been here?

They were met, in the empty world beyond the batteries, by men of their own battalion. It was a comfort, it was like a miracle, to find the right sign, in that chaos. But Webb and Bolt were hardly observed. These men were in a hurry. They carried petrol tins. They were there for water. They were very dirty, quiet, abrupt and quick. Jack was ashamed of his new uniform.

No time to lose. Jack saw he was on the edge of it. The land beyond was dead and waiting for the next thing to happen. It was a tumbled sea of brown earth, shockingly bare to the hot sun, thrown up into waves by an infernal storm, which had destroyed all life there and had passed, and the waves were fixed in their last crests and troughs. These fellows perhaps had been in it, and were afraid the storm was coming back. Nothing moved in that world ahead—yes, fountains of earth! The damned sea was trying to get going again. Little clouds with claps of thunder and sparks in their hearts appeared over the ridge beyond them. The officer in charge looked that way keenly. He was shabby, grey, unshaved and nervy. " No shelling ? " he blustered to Webb. " My Christ, they've no time for people at the back. We get it all. Keep low—they'll have a sight of us up there."

Jack would not have called that a trench. It was a raw brown furrow. In some places it had no sides. It ascended the shoulder of a low rise, and that horrid bright sky at the top would give them away, he knew, to whatever power brooded over that landscape. They had to go into that light. A geyser banged ahead of them, and rained clods. Any more ? He crouched. A clean beetle scurried under his nose in the loose earth. In that pause he heard the blood pulse in his ears. Overhead passed the tearing rush and wailing of shells. His back was too big for that gulley. The sun could see him easily—it made his back hot. His back was as big as a barn.

They got over the bright horizon, and crawled through a corroding waste, a poisonous welter of drains and stinking shell-holes, some of them still smoking. In a recess a number of men were cast down, in careless attitudes, as though they had been caught by sleep, and friends had covered their faces. Jack hardly glanced at them. He was not thinking now. He had arrived. Nothing had happened, after all. Jack felt suddenly a little jocular because of that. " I'll never learn this patch," he said to the guide.

" You won't have to, my son. You're supposed to take another."

The officer pointed then to a spacious distance which could be seen when he peeped over an edge of muck. " Over there." Men stood leaning against that slope of raw earth, clothes and faces the colour of it. Only their steel was bright. They gave Jack the impression that they had lost something and were hopeless about finding it. They did not look at him, but they must have known he was passing them, for they squeezed into the dirt as he went by.

He was sure he had forgotten all he had learned, but he was pushed into his job at once. His captain, Gillow, was a comfort, if there was anything in the signs. Gillow was tall, slow, solid, and wise to it. He was covered with rusty earth, and had a cut on his forehead. " I'm not always like this. We've had a bit of shelling. They've just dug me out." He blew his nose. " What is London doing ? "

Sergeant Worswick accompanied him to a post. He peeped over the land beyond, and heard the names of it from Worswick. They were near the bottom of a shallow valley. It was fallow, dead, and still, like the rest of the world, and the opposite rise was crested by a line of black jags. That had been a wood. On their right was a leprous patch of grey and red in the brown waves; that was what was left of a village.

"Jerry's still in the village. The Downshires are trying to take it." Worswick stated that, his eyes fixed. Machine guns were stuttering down there. Nothing moved, except spurts of dust from the ruins. Jack heard the clanging of metal where nothing could be seen, and the earth was jolted and rocked.

"They're off, sir. Our guns are at it—that ought to stop their reinforcements."

Jack felt it under his feet. It started the clods rolling. It was as if the cranks and cogs of the earth's guts had broken loose, and were banging about. The tree stumps on the ridge before them disappeared instantly within a long ominous cloud. It billowed, rocked, and throbbed. The wrong sort of cloud. Jack, in his interest, slipped and struck his face on the parapet. He wiped the filth from his mouth. He watched the scene again, but slipped. Damn! Greasy ground. He looked to his boots. He was standing on the pale breast of a man, which formed the bottom of the trench just there; young Bolt side-stepped for a firmer foothold.

Where the tree stumps had been on the opposite ridge a volcano had burst. The earth was rent. Flames and smoke jetted and bulged from internal fires. The venomous cloud increased and mounted, black, sulphur, and dirty green. It did not lift. It was fixed to the hill, but it was convulsive, leaping and ballooning as if trying to burst. It was threshed within by incandescent flails. Sometimes in places the cloud thinned; it became translucent, and the tree stumps appeared again in a bluish fog. Then the raving cloud and the darting flashes rolled back over them, and some of the stumps shot revolving out of the smoke. One end of the eruption rolled down the hill to the ruined village in desperate bounds. The ruins vanished. Where they had been was a cruel storm with fire jumping in its belly.

" Made a muck of it, sir, I'm afraid," said Worswick. " That'll mean we'll have to have some more."

THAT night Jack's battalion advanced its line slightly and without hindrance, into a worse place. It was said the Downshires had taken the village after all; they had been strafed by their own guns while they were in it. Jack was told he had better get a sleep in, while there was time for it.

Gillow had a good heart. If ever a man seemed to want a rest, it was Gillow. He was worn out, Jack could see. His eyes were red, his skin was papery and wrinkled. He might have been deliberately standing back a little from them, the better to see everybody properly, to see how they shaped. His glance was quick but his movements were cautious. Nothing hurried him. He had quiet words for the men. It was a relief to see him coming along. How was Webb getting on?

Jack felt all in; he curled up in a corner Worswick found for him. Just five minutes!

That was a nasty bump somewhere in the line. He sat up again. There was no sign and no sound for a spell, and then a yowling. Like a cat. Funny noise for a man to make. The fellow kept it up, quite calmly; he was imitating a cat. Jack wished he would stop it. A creepy noise; no cats there.

He drowsed. He sank out of it. He was sinking out of it. It was easier than he thought. Right out of it. There was nobody to stop him now. It was all over. He could go. He was stumping out of that trench. Nobody was there, except the dead. It wasn't day, but he could see them, curled up, and sprawled on their bellies, and on their backs, knees up, helmets rolled off, yellow hands and faces, with their black mouths open, and eyes open, soddened with weather. Nothing moved. Poor devils, they would have to stay. But he was off, he was getting out of it. He hurried on. He must get out of this.

He wished there was a better light. It was only an evening light. Everything finished, everybody gone. It wasn't light, but he could see the dead. It would be morning after this. This trench led out to morning, and people, and the grass, where you were not alone. He must meet someone soon. He looked for a pal on the move. Nothing moved. Round and round the corners, always the same trench, and the men huddled on the bottom of it, and nobody there. He must hurry on. He must keep going. It was the only way out. Nobody was there, all was over. The end of the trench must be somewhere. It must let him out. He began to run—round the traverses—he must get out—but it was the same trench everywhere, with the dead whose eyes were open. Nobody but himself. Everybody had gone—they'd left him behind. He fell.

Oh Lord! Just slipped on the earth. Here he was, in the trench all right. He looked at his watch. He had been asleep no time. He listened. That cat! There it was, yowling again. It was worse than the guns, that noise. It would take the stuffing out of you. It was the only sound now. What on earth! Like a horrible wild beast! It filled the night.

Some feet pushed near him. He heard voices. That was Gillow. "That you, Worswick? Poor young devil. He's unconscious . . . got him in the crutch. Can't do anything . . . shot away all he'd got. Can't last. Unnerving for the men, that noise. It'd be a mercy . . ."

There was a muttering by Worswick. Then Gillow again. "Yes, only just joined . . . yes, Webb . . . must put up with it, I suppose. Bad for the men."

Jack sprang up, but the captain and the sergeant had gone. There was no yowling now. Webb! Which way was it? It was all dark. He ran a little way. Steady; wait. This won't do. A figure rustled near him—one of the men—the sentry shifted his rifle on the parapet, and spat. Jack returned to his funk-hole, and tried to get his thoughts lined up. Steady does it! Webb. Bill Webb. Old Bill!

Jack waited, listening in fear for the yowling again. He must stay where he was. He must stay where he had been put.

There was a droning overhead and then flashes
beyond. The parapet danced in and out of the night.
He looked out over it. Machine guns were jabbering
away on the right. A screaming came at them out
of the darkness, and livid clouds began to flash and
clang along their front. Shrapnel! Now and then
there was a heavy shock and a burst of flame. The
trench went slithering under him. The night split
open wide in brilliance before him, and swallowed all
the noises. It was dark—an iron shutter had dropped.
Buried! He gave way to it.

More stuff was falling on him. He wouldn't stay.
He heaved, and presently stood out of it. It was
loose. His ears were ringing, but he heard no other
sound. The trench was a line of bright smoke, a
luminous surf of fire breaking over them, a high
bluish surf darting with crimson jabs.

Men stumbled along the trench, bringing something. Gillow was with them. They had a Lewis
gun. Gillow put his mouth to Jack's ear. "Bolt
. . . good. You're the man. Here . . . here . . .
sit tight. Look to it. They're coming back. Mustn't
come back."

The men humped themselves. Nobody came back.
The shelling died down. That was the dawn begin-
ning over there. Time the bloody sun did come.
He didn't care now. He could begin to see things.

Jack felt he was no good. His name was Mud.
He wanted to see things. He wanted to see them

plain. They were taking shape now. He stood over the men, head above the parapet, a faint light on his face, quite still, watching.

A boy of the crew looked up at the officer. Young Gladwish, squatting below, looking up at the officer, wanted to be sick. He kept his eyes on his officer. He hoped nothing would come. He wanted to be sick. Could the officer see anything? There was nothing to show on his face, no sign, only the morning on steady eyes, and an easy sort of mouth. Young Gladwish began to feel better. This officer was no older than himself.

Jack gave a start, and slipped. He was up again in a hurry, and peered out with a frown. He turned and gave a range and an order. He held up one hand, keeping them as they were with little movements of it. In the murk of daybreak, figures like men bobbed about before them, loosely scattered, bobbing about slowly. Here they come!

"Now!" shouted Jack. The gun became agitated. It spoke in a skipping falsetto, like the heartless titter of a mechanical man of brass. The approaching shapes, which had grown to big-headed Jerries, fell aside limply, suddenly tired, for no evident reason. In twos and threes they sank languidly out of sight. Some came on, bobbing along, growing still larger. Then there was only one of them. He was near, striding at them over the heavy ground, an officer with a baby face lost under a big green helmet. Must be mad! He carried nothing but a stick. He stared up at Jack openly and gravely. His head dropped forward and his knees gave way. He was down. His helmet lived a little longer. It wobbled when he was a heap.

WITH the leaves of that autumn fell the bright promise of the war. The dove did not descend to us precipitously with a laurel crown in its bill. It did not come at all. It was rain that descended. The jest that the first seven years of it would be the worst failed to amuse us as much as when it was new, for we began to suspect it held a secret too serious for merriment.

The urgent battle plans of the Somme turned blind ; they went astray and were lost in autumn's unfathomed mud. The soldiers settled into the mud, and occasionally sank out of sight in it, helmets and all, wherever they were benighted at the time when their generals decided that no more progress could be made towards whatever prize they wished the troops to win, an object which had been as vague as the desire which is behind the sacred mask of stone of a heathen god.

With the disappointment of the public came the need for the politicians to shake despondent heads over the generals, and for the generals, who did not know what next to order, except again the thing which had failed, to declare that it was only ignorant civilians who would have expected victory; their aim had been misunderstood. This, they explained, was "a war of attrition." They had been fighting "a wearing-out battle." When the matter was so considered it was clear they must have been as successful as they had expected to be, for it was certain the attackers had lost as many men as the defenders. Attrition had been achieved.

Yet the people at home, whose street lamps were funereal at night, shrouded and ominous, whose food was poor and allotted in measured doses, and to whom a fair heaven by day was a sign that they might die after supper through bombs from the stars, could not understand why the triumph of their cause should be tardy when it was just. We began to repine for our customary ways. We wanted the lights to go up. We still wanted victory, but now we also wanted peace. It was therefore natural for us to suspect that treachery was about, secret and devious, never to be seen but always at work, and that it obstructed our honest path with cruel hindrances. Something was wrong, yet we knew we were right, and this sense of our virtue made us suspicious of others, and especially of men whose opinions were different. We sought for a solid body to punish for the dreads which were invisible but unescapable. Now, too, the lists of the slain were not published, and for a reason which was worse than a scarcity of printing paper; and yet we surely knew, without being told, that the shadow of the battles of the Somme was of a nature that no radiant May morning of a better year could ever lift. We faced a world that had an aspect changed and obdurate, that would have a future we could not guess; even our standard roses would never bring summer in the old way; and life faltered within us. We began to surmise that the world we had known, which was fair, had gone the way of Eden and youth, and that it would not return. It was even said by some men, so accustomed to the attrition of the battle-line that they feared the engine had struck once and would strike no more, that God was dead.

We waited, and out of these doubts we complained. How long now? Even the dug-outs and shelters of the dread region in France had a changed air. Winter fell over the front in accord with its prospects. One day I went a journey there. At the end of a long ride I tramped through what had been a village, and down a trench, and then over a road, and across a field, in an unnatural silence. I saw Ypres in the distance, the skeleton of Ypres, pallid and ghastly, still haunting its abhorrent plain. I was led through roofless houses and by broken walls, traversed a back-kitchen and yard where there was nothing but old bottles and a perambulator without wheels, passed a dead horse, and then met an aerial torpedo. Beyond the torpedo were two dogs, interested in each other, and a sign in the trench, This Way to Cookhouse. We came to a turning with a notice board, Don't Use

This Trench in Daytime. We did not use it. A little further on was an arrow—To Bomb Store; and near it a notice, Service in Crypt Sunday Morning. We passed another and a narrower trench—To Mortuary—and came to the entrance to a dug-out.

Its entrance was deep in mud, its casual roof a heap of corrugated iron and sandbags. We stooped low and sideways, and descended steps which also were mud, though they were fairly hard after one's feet had sunk a little. Underground, but insufficiently underground for that silent country with its tendency to sudden uproar, the ceiling was upheld on grimy wooden beams. From nails in the beams hung sullen military gear and coats. There was a table, with several lighted candles stuck in bottles, and some shapes of officers who were so much the colour of the shadows that they were seen not to be fixtures when they moved. They did not say they were glad to meet me, and they did not say they were not. There was a smell of cellar, leather, and warm bodies.

When the umber gloom thinned a little, as I got used to it, I could see no visible change in these men. They pushed an enamelled iron mug at me, and enough stuff in it for a powerful man.

" Hello, hello ! "

" A long time since you blew in last. Where was it ? "

" Near Sailly-Saillisel, I think."

" Then cut it out."

" You seem quieter here."

" Rather, just now. Though that reminds me. I say, Landles, do you know what our friends across the way are doing to their trench by the big mine crater ? A contraption like a beehive. What frightfulness are they plotting ? "

" Don't know. The trench-mortar expert is coming down to-morrow afternoon to strafe it, whatever it is. So you're earmarked for the show."

" Reply paid. How nice of you to think of me."

" We don't wish the Trench Mortar bunch any harm," I was assured, " but after they've bumped Jerry about a bit, it takes us all night to shove up our parapet, and most of next morning to polish off the funerals. Then the T.M. man is home drawing up a virtuous report of his success."

" Poor muddy infantry. It has no friends."

A young man, who once had shown me the lurking vices of St. Pierre Vaast wood, sitting on the table swinging his leg, addressed me with pretended curiosity.

' You've come from the place we don't believe exists. You know—where heaven is—where a marmalade wallah to a staff-brigadier is a better man than a colonel in the line. I'd love to see G.H.Q. Really, what is it like ? Is it true you have parlourmaids ? "

" And is it true," added another fellow, " you don't reckon we are men, but only insufficient numbers ? "

I did not answer at once, but used their enamelled mug; it was a chilly day. I knew them. They always rubbed it in like this. It was a privilege of theirs. They always enquired whether we had any vacancies for secretaries at our chateau, and would I speak for a pal; and yet I was sure that if I could have taken one of them back with me, no bribery would have moved him from his mud, not even the promise of a distinguished decoration in addition. They preferred enduring in their comradeship to easy association with us.

"You mustn't make faces at me through the bars. I can't help it, being outside."

"Bet you can't. Have another drink."

These young Englishmen joked allusively of their part in the war, as though accidentally they had got mixed up in a perfectly absurd affair with which they had no personal concern, but from which they could not get free, for an unexplained reason. I had failed to notice the fact, but they did not refer to the past. I was with them last when the Somme affair was losing its go, and knew they were most of the survivors of the officers of that battalion. That was why I blundered and asked after one man. They acted politely then, as though an ignorant visitor may, while meaning no harm, infringe a rule of the house.

"He's gone home!"

That did not mean he was on leave. I maintained an innocent interest in this captain, a droll and mocking

Scot, whose beam showed his endurance, and his dark eyes his vivacity ; he had a mellow bass voice which rendered Falstaff on the subject of honour so ripened by wine that we had ordered him to do it again. " Was he wounded ? "

" Well, he was, in a way."

Something here was reserved, certainly, and I would not have asked for more, but one of them turned towards me quickly after too long a pause, in rather a challenging manner, but he was deliberate with his words.

" Of course, you don't know, but Mac had an accident. He was crumped—no, not that, not what you think—he wasn't hurt at all. He doesn't get a wound stripe because he was only blown head-first into an old fat Boche."

I nodded sagely, not caring to hear exactly what this meant, though still uncertain of the nature of the accident.

" And the old Boche was considerably dead. It wasn't his fault you know. We pulled Mac out."

" Cheerio ! " murmured a shadow reclining in a bunk.

" And after that Mac never sang. He wouldn't eat. He only wanted to wash out his mouth with neat whisky. He became beastly unsociable. He only talked to himself, in his sleep."

There was an interlude with a gramophone, for which I was grateful, but before the disc was ended a voice required us to put a sock in it. "That's all ancient stuff—do chuck the things away."

There had been a year when it would have been easy for a visitor to have had a place in such a community on the front, but on that day I learned I was definitely out of it, though the men were as friendly as ever. We now belonged to different spheres. They did not cherish, because, simple souls, they did not know they had a proud resentment. The war was getting old. We had drifted apart. They knew no man would share their destiny who could dodge to another track. Somehow, as I watched them in that brown gloom, I felt they were with us no longer. They had passed over. They could look back at us, and grin ironically, with thoughts they would not display; we could not communicate with them, though the gramophone droned, and they filled a mug for me, a visitor from the land of the living. They were young, they could be frivolous when the subject was not amusing, and they were only faintly satirical, and I wanted to make the right gesture, to say the right word; but there was no gesture, and no word.

"You're not drinking anything."

I had forgotten it. I remembered the mug with gaiety. The talk helped me, and I told them stories of General Headquarters, that they might know it indeed was there, though hours away by car; and what the gods were like on Olympus, and how They fared. It must have seemed remote to them, Holy Ground that was beyond Brigade, beyond Division, beyond Corps, more distant even than Army, which itself was legendary. They had faith, though never had one of the high gods descended in light arrayed to their lowly plot.

"We ought to say for the Brass Hats that they're soldiers in a sort of way, though for all they know about war they might be blotto," commented one calmly, whose age could not have been much more than his majority. "I don't mind them so much, don't you know, because there's nothing the poor beggars can do, that I can see, except mess us up. It isn't their fault, don't you know. It's all a jolly old muck, and we're all muckers."

"Rather. Isn't the child learning? Brigade sent a chit to-day asking whether we could get that sniper for identification—the one who fell into the water of a crater when he was pipped. Pa told us to say we could, if we had some salmon flies. Shouldn't be surprised if Brigade indented for some flies."

An elder whose hair was greying sat nursing a long boot of remarkable dimensions ochreous with clay, and pulled at his pipe. He had not spoken. He had merely looked upon us benevolently. He nodded to me.

"Tell me, have you been home lately?"

"No, sir. Not for some months."

He mused. "I was there a week ago. I was glad

to see the first shell-hole on my way back. What is the matter with London? I didn't know the place. We can talk here, so you needn't take any notice of us. As you know, we're bound to let off steam, and it doesn't matter. In my London club, though, I wasn't sure I was a member, after my first visit. I'll admit they didn't turn me out. Everybody was so hearty at first about seeing me again. Then they left me alone. I suppose I didn't say the things they wanted to hear. I only talked to them cheerfully, as I might to you—I forgot it was different. I didn't know what to say to them. I didn't know what they expected to hear. There would only have been a shindy, I'm afraid. The fact is, I was unpatriotic, if you please, and I hadn't known it. One has to go home to find that out. It was quite a relief when my dog took me on level terms. I think my dog was the only man at home who knew me."

" Shame! Poor old Pa!"

" That's a good dog, sir!"

" I met in Piccadilly one afternoon a sergeant-major of ours who got a nasty one at Ginchy. He told me a tale I thought was extremely doubtful—one of our own men, with two wound stripes, was imprisoned in a political concentration camp. I tell you this because you're a member of the Intelligence Department. A fact or two won't hurt you. I wasted time going into it. It was quite true. I found there is a fierce witch hunt on in London, and this boy, who had enlisted in 1914, was a victim, because his father was of German origin, naturalized, of course, and had lived in London for an age. When that youngster knew who I was he cried with mortification. One of my men. The joke is, he has a brother in it too, yet his father's shop has been gutted by the mob. After that I noticed what some of the newspapers were doing, and it was easier to get a better view of London. Those papers were the witch-finders. They appear to be scared stiff. I was foolish enough to suppose I could easily get our own lad's case put straight. The boy wanted to rejoin us, naturally. I saw them at the War Office. Nothing doing ! "

" Is that a fact ? One of our men, sir, when we haven't known where to find 'em ? "

Their senior tapped his pipe on his boot. " Oh, yes. It's all correct. If the witch-finders were really logical they'd take care that lad was kept in the line till he copped his packet, as the men say. They don't see that. They put him where he won't get hurt any more, though they're perfectly frightful about getting every other boy under fire. It's hard to see what is the matter with them. It's like lunacy, for the greybeards at home glower at any youngster they see about. They make enquiries about his age. They set the girls at him, instead of the dogs. They want to know why he isn't in it. They won't feel safe till there's a rampart of all the chosen young 'uns between them and the cruel Huns."

Somebody laughed.

The senior rose, unfolding slowly, a bony length of giant, his towsled and grizzled summit bent to miss the top of the dug-out.

"It isn't clean." He got his pipe alight again. "It's horrible.   Europe is eating her own young."

That sounded serious.   Nobody moved or spoke ; then a tiny voice piped :

"All right, Pa, we don't mind."

He ignored them.   He was talking to me, and I fear as one who was, in a sense, an enemy, a representative of the outer world.   He rarely met one, and now he had a chance.

"I'm beginning to hate men of my own age. There is something nasty about it.   If all the young 'uns suddenly revolted—turned round and began to exterminate the old 'uns behind them instead, it would be all to the good.   Don't you think a biologist would agree ? "

I surrendered cheerfully.   "If he were a young one."

He lowered himself into a chair, and his eyes twinkled.   "You seem to have hit on us when the wind is in the wrong quarter.   It's because it's a slack day. Another drink won't do you any harm before you go. Don't you want to see one of our men ?   Lieutenant Landles will take you along as soon as you're ready."

The Lieutenant and I set forth. The afternoon
was early, but the light would soon go, and I desired
that darkness should not catch me in that country.
We meandered through deep and narrow ditches,
with banks, for the most part, built of grey bags of
earth, like mounds of monstrous slugs, dead and limp.
They oozed slime. There was a drainage underfoot.
The Lieutenant squelched ahead. The drains we
followed were so narrow that one had to touch their
repulsive sides. We dodged cavities where men, up
to their waists in water, were attending to pumps.
My guide paused to scrutinize this work. " If we
could only widen this canal," he said to me, " we
could bring the fleet up." There were occasional
caves of timber in the base of the dissolving huddle
of bags of mud, and protruding from them, almost
lost in the slush, the legs of men either asleep or dead
and improperly buried. We stepped over the legs,
if we saw them in time. No brightness was in those
half-liquid gulleys, except bayonets, and the whites
of the eyes of men, and the reflections from the bottom
of the drains. We bent double and hurried where
the parapet was low. Sometimes a rifle cracked, or
a bee buzzed, or a harp-string broke and whanged,
or a frightful whip-lash smacked viciously near our
heads. We found a dubious shelter under corrugated
iron with the usual protection of a pile of wet grey
slugs, and my mission was reported to a captain within.
He frowned, but he was friendly.

" Bolt ? I know the man you mean. Oldish for his job. The most enterprising Lewis gunner I've got, and a sticker. Do you want to loot him ? "

I owned to it shamelessly that I wished for more than a sight of Private Bolt—that I would loot him if I could—but that I thought my chance of doing so was slight. I did not explain to his commander that Charley had been gassed, and was certain to go on till he dropped, saying that it was only a cold. I did mention that it was not easy to move him, against his desire.

" All right, I hope you have no luck. If not, drop in on your way back and loot me. Afternoon ! And please don't forget that my beauty sleep depends on good Lewis gunners."

We continued to follow the icy gleam of pools within a dim and confined morass. We turned several corners, thinking each was the final outlier of earth forlorn beyond the end of time under a sky of everlasting lead, with no light below but the glassy pallor of this sick planet's confluent ulcers ; and there I saw my man before he saw me. As we moved towards him circumspectly, trying not to wake the dead, or whatever might be about, through our clumsy feet making too much noise in the slough, he glanced over his shoulder. Charley's coating of mud, and his steel helmet topping a face framed in a scarf, like the living head of a soldier of Agincourt, and that outpost, so uncertain in its place and its

century, made his identity the more improbable, yet
veritably there he was. He stiffened correctly, and
saluted the officer with me, who then left us.

Charley stood regarding me, trying to believe this
extraordinary fact, while the beginning of a smile was
his only expression of faith. Each of us must have
concluded that the other was alive, and was even
present. Charley curled his finger over his crooked
nose, and surveyed me silently, making quite sure
this was true. Then he called to several still figures
of his own sort who were already half merged with
the liquefaction of the ramparts, and indicated me.
They were to be on brotherly terms.

He took me aside. He looked older, with those
crows' feet to his eyes. His voice was subdued. He
spoke hoarsely. No, they'd had a pretty easy time
there. Not too bad. He thought it was too good
to last.

He rubbed his nose and smiled artfully. Did we
want a bootblack at our chateau ? He knew a man
who could do with it.

Any news of peace yet ? Jerry seemed quiet.
Yesterday was the worst day. It was rather funny.
Jerry got windy about something. He sent over
a lot of stuff, and it did no harm, but they got fed
up. Their tea was filled with dirt. Then their guns
retaliated. They found Jerry, too, good and proper.
Things bounced, over there. Charley was unaware
of the truth of it, but he supposed Jerry demanded

of his gunners what in hell they were playing at.
Anyhow, Jerry's shelling ceased. So did theirs.

Charley spread his hands and chuckled, and medi-
tated a brass canister suspended from a gallows before
him for sounding the alarm should poison-gas roll
over us.

"One minute there was an awful din, then you
could have heard the fellow in the next bay shift his
feet. While we were waiting for what would happen
next, one of our fellows sang out : ' Don't you wish
you was 'ome, Jerry ? ' We got an answer back
at the toute : ' Not 'arf ! ' It doubled our fellows
up laughing."

I was amused, but there was no time to waste. I
took his arm.

"I haven't come just to leave my card. Listen.
Nothing can be done unless you take a commission.
Then we'll see about that bootblack's job. I'm
unscrupulous."

He did not say anything to that. Time might have
been nothing there. He glanced down the trench,
wasting the minutes, and so did I. The curious gaze
of one of his new friends met ours, held us for a
moment, and turned away, shyly. Charley inclined
to me. His boots made a sucking noise as he took
them out of one hole of the paste and put them in
another. A bullet sped with a thin whine over our
heads and went into the distance. The guns were
grumbling about Ypres.

" Can't be done, old son."

" It might be easy."

" Not a bit.   Look here, don't say anything more
about it.   These are good fellows.   They're only
boys, most of them, and they don't know much.   I
like them.   If I go for a commission, I must be a
corporal first.   Not me !   I'm not going to order
other men to do what I don't want to do myself."

He was going to put up with it.   He would not
allow me to try to change his fate.   Our talk, therefore, became desultory, even a trifle desperate.   I
could not think of the things I wished to say to him.
What were they ?   They whirled in the memory so
fast that they were mixed up.   Too many things to
say to him.

I made a movement.   It was time to go.   I stood,
not looking at him, but at a sloughing wound in the
sand-bag behind him.

" Well, Charles . . ."

His voice instantly was the less subdued.   It had
the quickness of alarm in it.

" You're not going ?   I say, don't go, old man.
You haven't got to go yet, have you ? "

Yet I had to go then.   It was so ordered.   There
was a long tramp, and a run of hours for my staff car,
over bad roads, and after dark ; a staff car is valuable
property, for which there must be a strict account.
I met his eye.

It seemed to me he was troubled, was even dismayed,

as if he now saw he must be abandoned. Into his sombre land, where hope could not live, a surety unexpectedly had come to him. There I was, a sign of another existence, a life familiar but removed, and once upon a time he had shared it ; now its sign would be withdrawn.

We said no more. Each of us took a good look at the other. I knew I was fated to remember these seconds. In a few strides I was alone in the next bay, and its parapet was down. Charley was in the past. That frightful whiplash began to crack over me, and I abased myself to the dirt.

It was a gratifying landmark on the return journey, that backyard where nothing survived but a limbless perambulator. I found a way through the echoes of the broken walls. I gave a side glance to that dead horse by the roadside, whose horrific grin was apocalyptic; he was chrome yellow and crimson, for his skin had gone; his anatomy was uncovered. His smile of teeth almost broke the silence. Even when I reached the point where my car was hidden it was well within the hollow resonance of an abandoned region where solitude was mournful when more stones fell in their decay. Mud weighed me down, without and within.

My driver! Where was he? I sounded the horn —it was as peremptory as the awakening clarion of Gabriel. My man resurrected at once, spruce and animated. He arose by the wayside, out of the lowly opening to a sepulchre. He came from the underground through a door, wiping his mouth hastily. He saluted, and off we went.

In less than a mile we approached a figure, which I imagined would check my car automatically; but it did not. It was not easy to accept that wayfarer who was drawing near, and as our car shot by him my mind failed me. The shape did not look at us. It was an apparition of an aged man, in evening dress, with a white tie and a bowler hat. It wore no overcoat, though it was bowed to the cold. It was embellished with a blue silk sash. I turned instantly and disbelievingly to watch it go. Beyond it suddenly flashed and thundered a siege gun. The figure took no notice of the gun. Our car maintained its speed; so I stopped it. The driver turned on me enquiringly, but with respect, to get his order.

" Did you see that man pass us ? "

" Yessir."

Then it could be seen by others. Well, let every pot be cracked.

My driver was solicitous. " You all right, sir ? "

" Quite. Carry on."

" Yessir."

We carried on. There were luminous watery patches of lemon and pale green in the darkening sky, and rafters of iron. Night would soon be at hand. It was upon us when the car brought up by some ruins. I should have guessed a church once stood there. Night was come, but the raw and tumbled masonry had its own pallor. The driver spoke to me in a low voice, which hinted that he had sinned beyond redemption. His petrol had failed. He then got out of the car, and faded. He went. He was lost in the shadows.

Nothing moved. I could hear my trench coat rasp if I breathed deeply. There were only strange noises afar, as though desolation were communing with itself, sullenly. It grumbled in cadence. Now and then an object pinged in flight and I thought of night-flying wasps, headlong and sinister. Occasionally a bird poised over us in mid-air—wee-weet, wee-weet! The machine-gun bird. I do not know what the haunted seclusion of the poet may be like, but mine was unfit for the worst of bad poets; and in it, amid all that was extinct, or would soon die, nothing was more dead than my car. I remembered that broken buildings, especially the ruins of a church by roads which cross in Flanders, are certainly haunted. The grisly spectre might show at any moment.

Where was that driver? The obscurity thickened. Darkness welled from the vaults of the wrecked church beside me till it submerged all but the upper jags of the outline of what, in the good days when the world was right, was a steeple. The dead, however, are silent. That is the strangest thing about them. A Verey light mounted, as if pale fear had sprung up behind the car. The slavering greenish face of the rocket stared down at the ruins, and they stared up at the light.

The staring light sank to earth, followed by darkness. Where was that driver? The car was much too still and quiet, and so I got out of it. It was easy to suppose so silent a corner was expectant of some-thing. A strand of wire near me twanged, and I listened, but could hear no more except the hornets. They flew. One of them, perhaps, had flown into the wire. Had one stung that driver? This was like waiting for a morning that had been omitted from the almanac.

Something was coming to the church. I heard its vociferation increase on its way. A meteor exploded into piercing rays and fragments near the ruin. The night which followed was blind. But I was still there, for I could hear myself sighing again. I retreated a little farther from the car, which had stopped so foolishly near a haunted cross-roads, and had given up hope—had accepted the fact that I was lost infernally—when I heard a confident voice at my ear.

" I gossum," it said.

" All right, get on with it."

Nothing was to be seen. I could hear the reviving spirit being put to the cold lips of our car, and the driver, his efforts presently suggested, was trying to raise the listless thing to its feet. He grunted. He did his best. Unexpectedly the car sprang into immense and eager energy. We moved. We got out of it.

Thereupon I gave myself to the northerly wind, which our speed secured to my face as a mask of ice; but what was that trifle in the sum of glory which I must share when nations would come to a decision on the eternal problem of good and evil? We entered the

centre of a Flemish town. It was the hub of one of
the numberless wheels in the continental machinery of
war. It was much as were all other towns of Flanders,
Artois and Picardy at that hour. The town square
then was no more than a few lower windows of orange
in a wet and hollow murk. Guns and wagons
lumbered over the cobbles, slow shadows with a
ponderous din. A military policeman in a cape,
black and magnified because one of the bright panels
of orange was at his back, was a mythological giant
directing the nebulous traffic of war, though his
leisured gestures and voice were only as if to-morrow
were another market day. Were the gods already
preparing for the spring ? It looked like it. There
was plenty of traffic here. With the hawthorn buds,
we knew, must come the new crops of emplacements
for guns and gas cylinders. Here again there appeared
to be signs of it, though Easter was far away. Those
signs were becoming familiar to us. The " Spring
Offensive " was our name for the new interest of the
vernal season ; it was the adventual efflorescence, for
us, of surgical saws, bandages, and suppuration, as
natural as the wind-flowers and little blue eggs in the
shrubbery.

My driver turned to me. " I may not be able to
get you home in time for dinner, sir."

" What's that ? Oh, all right. Go on."

We had settled down to it. All France accepted the
weird as it did the seasons. The war might make us

late for dinner, now and then. The wheeled traffic
paused to allow a regiment of infantry to pass through.
Those armed men were as impersonal as the vague
masses of halted transport, as the urge to a spring
offensive, as the night itself. They knew no more
why they were marching in that direction than migra-
tory marmots know they cannot survive the sea.
They flowed along, those Londoners, a steady and
irresistible tide, the sound of their feet the rhythm of
inexorable destiny, moving to the same necessity as the
wheels of the transport and the stars in their courses.
So in lighthearted rhapsody we had willed it, and so it
went. Men and mules had merged as one body into
the slow monotony of war. The monotony was as the
universal mud, stupefying as an endless morass of
black batter, and reason, youth, good will, commonsense, and one's dinner now and then, foundered in it.
If any man there could have got out of it, could have
crept away home, could have washed off the last stain
of it, and not be missed, and not be asked for, he
would have done it; but the mud and the monotony
held like death. Men were as helpless as the transport
jackasses, and gave less work to the whips of authority.

My driver saw his chance. He swerved and missed
guns by the width of his paint. He shot free of the
congestion. Our headlights soon showed only pale
trees and hedges leaping at us, but never touching us.

" We might do it yet, sir."

" Do it ? "

" Yessir."

A good man, that driver. To him the historic conflict for right principles in human conduct was as simple as getting me home in time for the soup, if God so willed it. The great war at the moment was that to him. He knew his duty. We all knew our duty, and it was absolution for us to obey. In our obedience we put out the light of reason ; therefore, with loyal eyes fixed on the arrangement of another man's knife and fork, or some matter as near and just as that in the imminent vast ritual of cryptic powers, calamity was free to expand its corroding radius.

Our motor-car again came to a stand. Its lights shone on closed gates where a railway crossed the road. We must wait. My impatient driver, remembering that the stroke of the dinner-hour at our headquarters was despotic, sounded his horn so loudly and imperatively that I feared a neighbourhood not concerned with my dinner would be retributive. Only a train approached us. A column of box cars drew slowly athwart our path, and jangled to a halt. They were monstrous and prognostical cars, for no end to them could be seen, as though they were inordinate but appropriate hearses that stretched the length of France, too grave with their import to be revealed by daylight, so making their furtive journey under the cover of night. We heard voices within the cars. We heard muffled and lugubrious chanting. Perhaps the enclosed departed, because they had no mourners, and

because there was no witness to their transit to
nowhere but the chance eyes of my driver and myself,
raised their own lament, voiced their own last hope.
That train in France, somewhere in its long belly, was
singing "The Church's One Foundation."   Then the
nearest great box on which shone our headlights took
up the singing, and we heard within it the drone of the
sacred air to these strange words :

> " We are Fred Karno's army
>   Just come a—cross the sea—a—a,
>   We can-not fight we can-not shoot
>   No blood-y good are we,
>   An' when the war is o-ver,
>   The Kay-zer he will say,
>   Hoch, hoch, mein Gott,
>   What a bloody fine lot
>   Are the Brit-ish In-fan-tree."

The jangling recommenced, and hearse after hearse
complained under the renewed compulsion till the
whole length of the procession meekly submitted to its
former direction.   The singers were withdrawn into
the outer dark ; their chanting diminished and was
lost.

My driver stooped and briskly prepared to start.
The white gates swung open.   He looked round at
me, and smiled.

" Those fellows are all right, sir."

OUR motor-car sank down a valley to the bottom of a thickening of night, which I recognised as the woodlands about our headquarters, and at the end of a tunnel through it—which by day is an avenue of tall trees—stopped at a blurred porch. We were in time for dinner.

That porch was nearly all, after dark, that could be distinguished of our section of the Intelligence Department of the British Expeditionary Force. Only intimates were vouchsafed its name and whereabouts, for though in the nature of war it is right that some men should be killed, it is as proper that other men should live in whatever quietude the field of war allows, for otherwise the killing could not be intelligently supervised. We were kept by the woodlands of a secluded estate. In the grounds of our Chateau de Rollencourt, on fine mornings, the trout could be watched in the Thenoise, a stream forded by Henry on his way to the adjacent field of Agincourt; and, unless the wind were east, then the men about Ypres were as distant from us as Henry's bowmen. But if the wind changed, went round to Sheol while you were watching the image of a big fish set in crystal under the roots of the alder, then a thought would cast its shade around, something would pass between you and the sun, the air would mutter, and the very trees in their stillness would seem to be listening. They, too, appeared to hear the message.

You forgot the shape in the crystal, became one with the trees, and listened. There it was again. The day was throbbing, throbbing. The guns!

And indoors, as far as the remotest bedchamber, with its silver crucifix so placed that it could watch the head of one who would persuade sleep and forgetfulness—though you withdrew to it, at midnight, shielding a candle, to escape from khaki in debate, maps with their critical points, crises, and desperate but unknown quantities, you were followed—you were caught on the dark stairs—you were checked in the unlighted upper corridor where the windows shuddered though nothing could be seen without, nothing but the dark—you were aware of the tremor when the house was silent, and no more could be heard of its debate below for this good policy or for that; the omen followed as you entered the privacy of your own heart. The chamber window fluttered, when the candle was out, as though to the rhythmic beat of monstrous pinions. When would this end? When would it end?

Not with morning. For at our chateau, the Olympians, who held the thunderbolts and were destiny to us, used to meet. Sir Douglas Haig and his generals, not one of them less than a commander of a Corps, came at appointed days to ordinate and fashion earthquakes. A salon of our house was theirs, its doors impressively insulated with green baize, because there are some things the gods decide to do which it is better for us not to know too soon. It was in that chamber, next to our common room, that the conception took place which afterwards was called the war of attrition, though its first hopeful name was the Battle of the Somme. And there the resplendent ones might be, their cars majestic in the forecourt, any morning when you looked out wondering in innocence whether there was any chance of that dove.

A staff officer of ours met me in the porch. Oakley adjusted his monocle to survey me from a cool height.

" Anything interesting to-day ? "

" No."

" You're late, though."

" Yes."

" Well, we've some important guests to-night. Don't be long. They've popped over from London to enjoy the horrors, and the soup must not get cold."

The door of the inner salon was partly open, and voices different in their strong emphasis and innocence of doubt from those I had listened to amid the grey sandbags, met me before I reached it. I paused to look within, for one incisive voice was familiar, and saw, by the logs burning cheerfully within their recess, a civilian whose ample figure was in easy accord with a couch. Langham was quite at home. An elderly general stood stiffly near him, poising a cocktail. The general was bending a polite ear to what might have been a vivacious lampooning of the ways of God to man. Other officers and guests formed a pleased audience.

" Not at all. I don't mean that. I'm sure the plans could not have been better. They were as good as possible. All the same, the people at home are disappointed with the Somme. After the millions of shells they'd made, they expected you'd buy something better with them."

" My dear sir, what are the expectations of civilians to do with us ? Surely nursing them is your job ? "

" Well, yes, but we can't nurse them with field punishment, you know—only imprison an example or two if they won't work." Langham looked happy but wicked. Then his smile went out. " We have to keep it in mind at home to some extent, so why shouldn't you remember it out here ? The rabble which feeds you with ammunition really has its feelings. There they are. It is possible to disappoint it. It is likely that the country whose civilian riff-raff gets the most grievous hacking about of its jolly expectations loses the war."

" I hope nobody loses it," commented a young officer cheerfully, a major and a stranger to me,

EE

whose lack of decorative colour and honours suggested that he belonged to the trenches.

" Nobody ? " asked the general, turning to him mystified. " One side must win ? "

" I suppose so, sir, and I hope it's us. But sometimes I think it would be better if nobody won it. It's sure to be a beastly business if one side can get glorious over victory. I think it would be nicer if the whole war jammed into a complete silly stark foozle. That would give everybody who wasn't dead a chance to sort it over in a sensible way."

Most of the poised cocktails shook in amused approval of the idea. Even the general smiled grimly, as though never before had he glanced in that direction, but now could make out there an item of remote and impossible good sense. I went on to my room. If the walls of that salon could have repeated, when invitingly tapped, all the words in their due order which they had registered on the subject of war and peace, they would have convinced a startled listener, till then merely solemnly aware of the wonders of the mind of man, that this celestial ball called Earth need not have been ashamed among its peers in the heavenly hosts if man's nascent mind had been left in the treetops, unreflective with its nuts and instinctive desires.

I had the luck to slip into a seat at dinner beside Houghton, a junior officer of the department, though white-haired and in middle age. His eyes of onyx rarely told you more, in their direct glance, than that he was a gracious listener. Whether he smiled when he turned away you never knew, but probably he did not. His face was accustomed to the fact that his emotions must not be shown; it had been patient too long to need further training. Its hardened surface merely changed to mauve in frosty weather. A poet and a scholar, he had served as a sergeant in the line, and continued to mortify himself with the punctilious saluting of brigadiers who would never reach his exact knowledge of English drama and the use and abuse of hand grenades. That gentle and ascetic officer was not likely to speak unless he wanted pepper, or thought I needed wine. Phipps was on the other side of me, a war-correspondent, slight and nervous, whose passionate measuring of barbed wire by the standard of Nazareth was a happy feature of our departmental routine; the prickly difference he never failed to find, most surprisingly, between war and the Beatitudes, made him regard our enjoyment of his sorrow with the eyes of a bewildered bird. He had with him then a friend of his, a padre, and I was just in time to get the point of a funny story by the chaplain, who was relating to his immediate neighbours, while the soup went round, the amusing case of an Irish navvy in his battalion. That navvy, in a straight and narrow pass, discarded his proper weapons, and with a trench spade gave it in the neck to five Germans in succession who would have pushed along.

Houghton might **have** been deaf to the story.

Phipps was embarrassed by the infelicity of his simple
clerical friend. There had been a year when such a
story would have delighted that table—the insolent
confidence of our men !—but this was the first month
of 1917. The spirit of the times, on the way to
Tipperary, had dropped the padre out of sight.

At the other end of the table, Oakley, who was
occasionally mistaken by newcomers for a fine example
of a leader of Indian cavalry, was flattering a civilian
guest with his urbane curiosity in socialism as it
concerned leadership of the trade unions. The
civilian was teaching him.

" Houghton," I asked, " tell me, who is that
guest ? "

" Dodgson—a miners' delegate, I fancy."

The earnest civilian was concentrating a lesson in
the palm of one hand with a deliberate finger of the
other.

" It isn't fair," murmured Houghton. " Someone
ought to tell the poor man that our aristocratic soldier
is a student of Bakunin and Pareto, and may get the
sack in consequence, before long."

Langham was watching the same little interlude with
inquisitive interest. He was solaced. " Dodgson,"
he called across the table, " our friend is too chivalrous
to tell you so, but I think he wants to say that your
extreme political theory is about as old-fashioned as a
wheelbarrow on a motor-track."

Oakley made a discreet inspection of Langham

through his diminishing eyeglass, but he did not divulge his idea of what was a wheelbarrow as a vehicle for the burden of government. It was not his way to divulge more than a hint of a notion he might entertain of the art and science of administration, though usually it was enough to make you wonder whether you had heard him correctly, or had better give the problem a more searching overhaul without more talk. But in France we had grown used to opinions which, had they been exposed carelessly in daylight to civilians at home, might have caused alarms from police whistles. London had not arrived at the point where we were ; not yet. It no longer shocked us to see Law and Religion derelict, as were other honoured things, on the flood which had left traditional bearings below the horizon of 1914. The talk at most mess-tables in France wandered freely and with slight deference even to the presence of august military rank. Generals were generals, with the privileges due to their degree, yet even they shared the common lot of a day wherein the wreckage of Society's moral safeguards was like the policeman's battered helmet in the gutter the morning after the joy of Mafeking night. We were looking for clues to a new order, if there were any, because a new order might not be easy to find since most of Europe's younger men had a duty, as good soldiers, to deride and destroy all that priest and schoolmaster had once advised them was of divine ordination. Our elders, in the desperation of their fears, had allowed youth to see how much society had ever deserved its respect and fidelity. That peep, as into the interior of a hitherto revered and tabooed family sarcophagus, made even the enemy's machine-guns the less terrible to face. Before the last shot was fired, ancient thrones and altars would be tottering through the work of worms unsuspected. We already knew, out there, that we must begin anew, but nobody knew where, nor with what.

The deep interest of those strange days, in which the value of so much had gravely altered, and even old common-places were hardly recognisable, swept our table. The talk was eager, as though we were alert to a new time in which suffering had become an honour, and abhorrence of evil a joke. It surprised me that Langham's banter, springing as it did from a cunning man's acquaintance with news withheld from vulgar eyes, though still a pleasant addition to a dinner-table, was quite alien now, with its London origin, in the common air of France. He was merrily unconscious of it. He did not know he had become inapplicable. The most miserable example of a Hun prisoner in a barbed-wire enclosure was more akin to some of us at that table, than that sprightly and well-informed administrator fresh from Whitehall. The general, it was evident, listened to him at first in hard-featured doubt, for Langham was a clever Radical, and then in surprised approval.

" When I was a nipper," Langham was telling us—
to illustrate his good news of popular British trust in
our Premier, Mr. Lloyd George, and of his own faith
in his chief—" when I was a nipper, there was a cheap-
jack who used to visit our market-place every Friday.
I learned as much from him as ever I did from my
schoolmaster.   I had little to learn at Westminster
afterwards.   Half that fellow said I was too young to
understand, and perhaps it is better that I was.   But I
saw how he gathered a great mob about him, whatever
he had to sell—old umbrellas or whatnot—opened
everybody's mouth wide with interest, mesmerised
them, and then unloaded anything he had.   Lincoln
was partly wrong ; most of us are willing all of the
time.   That cheap-jack was a sympathetic orator with
a gift of drollery.   He might have a barrow-load of
bedroom crocks.   You didn't want any.   But something you heard him say as you were passing made you
stop to listen, and if you stayed long enough, and
weren't careful, you'd find yourself wandering round
the next corner short of half-a-crown, and wondering
what you had better do with a chamber vessel you held
in your hand.   If I knew where he was to-day I'd send
for him.   He'd be a useful publicity man.   Very
useful in war-time."

The general was only partly edified by this.   It was
funny, but was it true ?   He demanded some evidence
of genuine power and resolution in Whitehall.

" Oh, don't worry," said Langham lightly. " Lloyd

George means it when he talks of going through to the bitter end. We shall get there."

He outlined for us, partly in raillery, the present trend of the policy of the Allies, its hindrances, its possible dangers, but the almost certain consequence of our assembled powers for good, unless we became softened by our humane instincts. There was a new and insidious gas becoming more and more noticeable —crafty discharges made on behalf of peace. It was well to keep sniffing the poisoned air. The success of his own department, though it started inauspiciously, he knew could hardly be avoided.

Houghton, stiff and upright as a sergeant of the Guards, appeared to be interested in the table-cloth, but he glanced at me slyly because he knew I must be fretful.

" Yes," he whispered. He then quoted absently to himself: " A man's heart deviseth his way; but the Lord directeth his steps."

A civilian guest desired to learn from the young major, who to-morrow was returning to the trenches, how the men were faring. Were they in good spirits?

" Oh, yes." The major was shy. This attention made him nervous.

" Standing up to it as good as ever, eh? I heard them singing on the road. They seemed all right."

" Oh, yes."

" Better ask the war-correspondents," advised

Langham, a little sardonically. " That's their job, courage and cheerfulness. Isn't that so ? " he enquired of Phipps.

" There's nobody else to speak for them," Phipps expostulated, though a little flushed. " They mustn't speak for themselves."

" Slaves, you think ? "

" That's what it comes to, from the time they land here."

" Are you quite sure a lot of them don't enjoy it—I mean enjoy being slaves ? " asked Langham.

" You've never seen a casualty clearing station on a bad day," Phipps reminded him.

" And I don't want to. There must be hospitals. Apart from bandages, aren't they having the time of their lives ? I believe some of them like it. It's a great adventure. The coal mines and factories have let them off—they've got away from the iron yards and office stools. After all, weren't some of us agreed that the factory system made harder going than a beach in the South Seas ? Isn't that so ? "

" An adventure ? " It was a new and sharp voice which fired at him. " The bloody war and its pus is just the outcome of the factories and the laboratories— an interlude, to fight over credits and customers—the serfs go from one part of the great machine to attend to another, by order. And listen to me, Mr. Langham, if everyone not in the trenches got continuous neuralgia till the last shot was fired—if you and Lloyd George and the Kaiser and Clemenceau got fire in your teeth which wouldn't go out till the guns had stopped—or suppose someone important at home dropped dead in the street every time a chap was killed here—how far off would the bitter end be ? "

Langham turned to the new speaker, who was in uniform, and laughed. He addressed himself to the general. " You seem to have a nice lot of anarchists wearing the king's uniform. We don't let them talk like that at home."

" We don't mind," said the general, " while they do what they're told. Besides, our friend Jerry keeps them up to scratch. He keeps them busy, if they want to live as long as possible."

" That's it. That's what I say. They're having the time of their lives, lots of 'em. They know they're alive now, and they're not responsible for anything, not even their homes. Not a blessed obligation, except to carry a gun. Why, they're free of their wives—they're not expected home—and the women have got a happy release. The women have heaps of nights when they know for certain they need not worry because of the moral warning of the legitimate latchkey. What about it ? Isn't that worth having ? And the men have got no job to hold down, no fear of the sack, no landlord. Fed, clothed, and told not to think. Everything done for them, right down to funerals. It's ideal. Isn't that so ? " he jollied of the general.

But the old soldier was not quite sure of his ground. He fidgeted, though he faced the free talk like the gentleman he was. He was used to unexpected things in war-time, because he had spent most of his life on the Indian frontier, and looked all the better for it, for though his short moustache was white, his face was as rosy as a child's, and his eyes had a child's innocent interest and alertness. He was also a favoured general, for he was of the cavalry, and British headquarters never questioned the ancient truth that a family tradition of horse and sword bestowed on a leader a power of second sight amid the confusion of battle never granted to engineers and others who did not begin with spurs. Our general was of the ancient knightly caste, simple, candid, and courteous, with not a doubt of its seigniority, a caste which had survived in the army, where it was venerated, though its bowers, towers and tilt-yards were long forgotten under slums and steel foundries.

"I wouldn't say my men enjoy it," he declared, wiping his immaculate moustache. "It's a hard life, but they know and do their duty, and that's all I ask of them."

His high seriousness got the discussion aground. It was stranded. Dodgson asked him presently whether there was any chance of the enemy ever breaking through the Allied lines.

"Breaking us, sir, breaking us?" he exclaimed in amused indignation. "Not a bit of it. Break us!

Not after the gruelling we gave them on the Somme. No, they want us to leave them alone, and they'll be disappointed. You fellows at home talk of No-Man's-Land. It really doesn't exist. That is our land. My men's country extends to the enemy's wire. No, sir. We have their measure. If you at home give us the support we want, and do not scatter any of our forces to other fronts, you'll see who'll break through. Remember that. You'd better tell Lloyd George that the war will be won here, not in Salonika, nor Palestine."

Langham had a crafty eye. " I don't suppose your lines will ever be broken, but what about the enemy's ? I wonder whether the power of resistence, with machine guns behind barbed wire, is not always greater than that of attack ? "

" Oh dear no. It depends on the strength of the push. We are learning all the time."

" That is so, but vast experiments cost men, and I happen to know that it is easier to make good guns than fit men. The supply of shells is all right, but the men are not inexhaustible. Now tell me, how long will it take, do you consider, to gauge exactly the power which will overcome any given number of machine guns in a well-ascertained trench system ? Now and then I think there is a competition between our head-quarter's staff and the German's as to which will first solve the problem of modern warfare before their last reserves are drained dry."

The general considered this, or the colour of his wine, fingering the stem of his glass.

"As things are," an officer explained, "a consumptive machine gunner, too scared in an attack to bolt, can sit in a lucky hole in the ground and scupper a company of the best as they advance. Courage isn't what it used to be. The machine runs over us and we can't stop it."

"Never mind," Oakley said, "the Americans will soon be in it, and they've got lots of fresh men for the machine to grind up. When we're passed through the spout they'll be going into the hopper."

The talk continued round the logs in the vast and bleak sitting-room. Houghton secluded himself in the coldest corner he could find, to read there, stiffly as on parade, the newspaper which liked him the least. A war-correspondent tinkled " Little Grey Home in the West " on the piano for his own amusement. A young lady of the house, who was executed at Arras during the Revolution, looked down on us from her gold frame with a trifling smile which only just touched her beautiful mouth. A servant came in to inspect a side-table, to see that it was supplied with the right bottles and glasses. The general stood, and very seriously was instructing Langham.

I retired through a door into the next room, which was empty, except one candle to its immensity of darkness. Its baized door closed softly on the urgent talk. Another candle held its spark by the stone staircase, which ascended far beyond its light. Portraits of men which had been watching that staircase for two centuries saw me mount to the upper corridor, where it was quite dark, except for the vague panels on one side of it, which were windows. I thought someone else was wandering there, and stopped to listen.

Was it my own footsteps echoing? No. The windows. They had fits of shuddering. The windows were looking out on night towards the guns; they shuddered.

I turned into my own room. That was not the wind. There was no wind. The glass was responsive, and trembled.

Perhaps a book could help. But presently, when there could be no mistake about that sound, I laid the book on the coverlet, and waited. The door opened, and Oakley entered, a tall figure in pyjamas, who had a cigarette in one hand, and a glass of whisky in the other. He sat on my bed, and smoked, and sipped, and smoked. Presently he spoke.

" Have you been listening to the talk ? "

I admitted it.

" Could you make anything of it—that general— that politician ? "

I admitted also that I could make very little of it.

" What is there to make of it ? When I hear that sort of talk, and think of the millions of people at home who are waiting for men of that kind to save what is left, and when I think of the fellows in the mud and wire, waiting to be got out of it somehow, by those same men, I come up to bed, and say 'Well, God, it's up to you.' "

THE war had fallen from its high estate. Noble chivalry in a crusade against a dragon, whose bestial maw consumed virtue and maidenhood, had sunk to vulgar hardships in cold mud. To what end? There seemed to be no such ugly reptile after all ; or else the dragon was common doom, and doom cannot be struck at. The foe was invisible. Its name was Legion, because the dragon had as many hearts as there were people who wanted it to live. Therefore it was invulnerable. The war was no better than a mania that had ceased to be heartening through its unvarying vacant seriousness ; and weather, and boredom ; and the trampled mire and black clinker surrounding the self-grinding and ubiquitous mill of death we called " the front." I looked out from a room in Amiens, to see what another morning of it was like, and noted in surprise across the Rue de Noyon a café with a name that had been noticeable on a night of an August long ago, when Maynard and I watched the retreat of the French through the city. There the café still was : " Tout va bien ! " All went well, and to-day was almost spring in the third year of it. All went well, but the soft sky and the phase of the moon hinted that we should be visited by the enemy's airplanes to-night again, in their routine of blowing the city's upper bedrooms down to basements. Who to-morrow morning would be missing?

For the war also was lengthening memory. Our friends disappeared. The French mud held them, somewhere. The war was ghostly with them, and the land of France was nostalgic with the names of hamlets and odd corners that never had been important, and meant nothing now except to men who once had foregathered there; often the very places had gone. They were now but names and rubble. The names had no meaning, except to survivors, though for them the shades, when evoked by this magic word or that, must arise and move with them through life; yet the word could not be mentioned, even to one's folk in England. It would have no magic for them. They would see nothing in it. For what was its magic? It might be only the memory of wind and rain and a mound of wreckage; and in a cave under the splintered beams and the brickbats, seen by candle-light, the face of a pal, who was most of what was left of fellowship, and he as flitting as the candle. The next bump could blow him out. Did his light still flicker in the winds of desolation? Soissons, Laventie, Festubert, Vermelles, Hulluch, Boesinghe, Kemmel, Notre Dame de Lorette, Souchez, Hebuterne, Beaumont Hamel, Longueval—there was no end to them now—the very map of France was full of stabs.

And Amiens! That city was still lively with Australians and British; a ride in a lorry could translate a boy, who had been given a few hours' respite from the explosions and the bones, from the Somme to a survival of women, drink, and tables civil with linen and glass. They came there, the young men, to snatch violently at life before it passed, and at sins they might never get another chance to taste, before returning to their burial. Yet life in Amiens had been too deeply roiled. Any draught of its sin was compensatingly poisoned, though that was nothing to droughty and desperate youth, who might have but another hour in which to peep at day from under the black extinguisher. I left the city's main street, and was enlarged presently from narrow and indeterminate side-turnings, and had more daylight around, and the august mass of the cathedral over me.

I looked up at that masterpiece again. I had never been certain that I admired it. The riot of its abundance was disturbing. Man's fertility can be disquieting; he is so versatile, and yet his energies may be only turbulent restlessness. The walls of the cathedral crawled with monsters, were populous with grotesques and wry faces; sometimes the lines of its ascending stones leaped upwards impatiently from the body of it, and spanned the air in curves, abutting after a dizzy flight. It fascinated and appalled, this cathedral, like the spectacle of humanity itself. With his hands clasped behind him, standing at his ease, an ordinary captain of British infantry stood near the piled sand-bags which protected the base of the west front from bomb-splinters, considering the fervid and various masonry. I went and stood beside him on the instant, staring with him, but did not speak. Jim Maynard gave me no attention. He was too shy to glance at a stranger who acted as though the cathedral were everything and a British officer were hardly noticeable. He had to hear me before he turned.

We passed through the base of that cliff, even before there had been more than two words between us. Perhaps we both felt we ought to go apart from the ambiguities before we spoke. We pushed through a muffled inner door; and then we could have been back in an earlier morning of the earth, which would be long in coming to noon, and would not abate to night. We had changed our age and place. The silence of this lofty interior was the calm certitude of another disposition of the mind of our fellows. If the show of men without was monstrous and turbulent, if the outer part of that Gothic mass was a mounting vortex of grotesque fancies, dark, gibbering, awful and meaningless, rollicking up to an abrupt poise of haughty pinnacles, yet within the heart of it, looking through the grey quiet of the nave to the sanctuary, Jim and I could come together again.

There it was simple. We had nothing to say to each other now. All had been said here, long ago. Jim's uniform was stained and threadbare, yet the war had left upon him no other visible mark.   He and his stained tunic and muddy boots were in place in the lucent calm of that retirement.   His eyes were of the same nature as the patience of that grey light.   He no longer appeared slight and of no significance, nor even shy and reticent, for his communication had been made, when the world was young.   The world had changed, and was changing still in a loud continuance of the trial of its errors, but whatever light Jim kept would not go out, though these walls fell.   In that interior, with its triumphant magnitude and soaring pillars, there was a human aspiration which was spacious but composed.   It seemed without bounds. Not only the walls kept it.   It went beyond, in a dimension no catastrophe could reach, its distance veiled by a prismatic screen which fell from the rose window of the south transept athwart the high and slender shafting ; and it ascended beside us straight to the vaulting in cool lines as direct as a simple cry to whatever might be.   Man, too, had done this.   This was his work.   Jim's own ease was in accord with the lift and sober light of these stones.   It might be hard to name the tradition, but that did not matter, for it would live.   Jim himself did not know that he kept it. He was like the other good fellows.   They would shield through the disaster, without knowing what they did, casual but steadfast, the glimmer they had which belonged to us all.   That was safe.   Our turbulent restlessness could not douse it.   When all was over, nothing much would be left for some of us, if we were there to hear the last shot. All we should find would be the lamp still alight in the dead hand of a friend; with that we might find our way towards something perhaps as good as symphonies and cathedrals. It was the only victory we should get, and our enemy would gladly share it with us. I looked at Jim to make sure of this, for what is of first and last importance to us is hardly seen but it is gone again, and Jim smiled at me in gentle irony. I knew that look of his. It was the best thing to be seen in France, and was almost as common there as the shells. I had seen a smile like it the day before. I had stooped over the body of a lad, left as offal on the vast midden of the Somme. In a hopeless attack over the mire, already without a date or a purpose, he had fallen. He was on his back, his arms out-stretched in surrender to our will, his eyes open but looking past me, and that little smile at his lips might have come there as I stooped over him, just as his hair stirred slightly in the wind. He had beaten us. The day was his. He could wait now.

"What are you thinking of?" asked Jim.

"Nothing. There you are, that's all."

THE moon had not risen. The lamps of Amiens were not lighted; the city kept itself dark and hidden at night, as well as it could. Jim was perplexed by an inconstant flickering, deep in the blackness of the street, as of a thin swarm of fireflies. It was a feature of war he did not know.

" What are those sparks ? " he asked.

" Widows," he was told. It was a familiar oddity to us, that faint glittering in the streets of Amiens, at that stage of our progress. " They're all widows."

He did not seem enlightened, but then approached us two shadows, which were damsels, and flashed on us, and then on their own faces, their hand torches. They spoke kindly. They said they were true Parisiennes.

Maynard was silent for a spell. He had been in hospital with a shrapnel wound, and now he was returning to the line after a course at a school for snipers. A strange man, he told me, was the officer in charge of that school. Hesketh Prichard. Did I know him ? Prichard imposed a monastic and searching ritual on the men who came to him to learn how to use their brains when blowing out their

460

enemy's. He made it as absorbing as chess. That fellow was a saint at heart, said Jim, forcing himself to beat the ingenuities of the devil, devotional at an alien task. But it would have given the insides of the best of the Knights of the Round Table a twisting to have adjusted a cylinder of poison gas to the true code of honour. Eh? The consequence to Prichard's mind was as bad as a bullet, if not so immediately conclusive. Had I met him? The success of his own school was killing him.

Yes, I knew Prichard. He went sick once, I remembered, for some weeks, because, with subtle cunning, he had put a bullet through the head of a German sniper who had been hitherto a secret, bold, and deadly nuisance.

"It gives the best fellows an awful twisting," admitted Jim. "The muck worries them. They can't wash it off. And they're the worst of the lot when it comes to killing; because they think everything is lost, I suppose, and that we had better all die. Not much good living if you are expected to be crazy and dirty."

I said nothing. The confidence of men, who visited us from the firing line, their voices quiet with astonishment that evil should be good, and good be evil, were frequent in our mess. They seemed to think that we, who were at the back of it, ought to be able to resolve the mystery. But we had nothing to say.

" I wonder sometimes," said Jim, " whether . . ."
he stopped.

" What ? "

" Whether it wouldn't be better to let go everything that keeps us from the untroubled beasts."

" Would it be easy ? "

" About as easy as stepping off your shadow. It's
your shadow that's the trouble. You can't get away
from it."

" When I was in hospital," he told me, " one of the
nurses about the place was that woman Charley Bolt
knew—Whittaker. She didn't know me. I noticed
she hadn't much shadow to worry her, and it was
lucky for some of the fellows she hadn't. It seemed
to me she gave herself out of her merry heart. The
fellows wanted her, and she was a giver. What about
that ? "

" What do you think ? "

" I'll let the proud virgins answer who think it
glorious for our friends to die."

We entered the hotel which was, just then, a
temporary home for the branch of the Intelligence
Department I was serving. Jim could feed and sleep
there that night, and go on to his battalion in the
morning. He sat on my bed, and noted the cheerful
name of the café opposite. " Tout va bien ! " He
repeated the name several times, quite happy with it.
He asked me what we were supposed to be doing
there ; but I explained, as well as I could, that to make

our position perfectly clear to him, as by full and unashamed daylight, would take some doing, and dinner would soon be ready. Have something to eat, I advised him, instead of an apologue. Had he been on leave at all?

"Almost forgotten it. Six months ago. I saw our friend Talbot, though. I think he is breaking up, poor old fellow."

"Why, what's wrong with him?" Talbot for me had receded into a past which the dust of events had dimmed.

"The years. He's getting on, you know. And our excitements have made him a lonely man."

"How does he take it?"

"He didn't say much about it. He asked me a question or two, but he didn't follow them up. I think he's shaken, all the same. The old boy had the child-like idea that a man who'd been in France must have met another man there. He asked me if I knew where a fellow named Earwicker was killed—my regiment. He was unaware that a regiment might have a dozen battalions—he seemed surprised. I asked him for some facts, but he only shook his head. 'It doesn't matter,' he said. But he did tell me that Earwicker was a parishioner, a youngster, married to a girl there a little while before. Old Talbot had just been round to her mother's place, and I suppose it was still on his mind. The girl had been ill with the flu, when the baby was near. Talbot told me that the

girl's mother was still fiddling with her grandchild's
first clothes, which wouldn't be used, when he called.
She folded them back into a drawer while she talked.
A telegram had come one day, it seems—Earwicker
had gone west. The mother told old Talbot that her
daughter had died crying. He couldn't forget it. He
repeated it, some time after, when we were talking of
something else. ' She died crying.' "

" That's not a story for the press, Jim."

" Not quite what you're looking for ? "

I tried to imagine the face of my own severe and
industrious little departmental colonel, with his
Sandhurst standards, if I offered him such an encouraging yarn of the campaign ; it was no good ; he
would never have seen the joke ; he would have
thought I had made an indifferent mistake.

" The old man," Jim went on, " seemed to get
another shock when I rose to go. He'd been so quiet
and absent-minded that I thought I didn't belong to
his room so much as once upon a time. I hadn't felt
altogether at ease. Perhaps it was my uniform.
You know how khaki flattens everything—men are
not names, only a dingy colour. All of us the same
colour, doing the same thing because we must.
Perhaps he had noticed it. ' Going ? ' he said,
and caught hold of me, and kept on looking
at me, to be sure I hadn't gone, I suppose.
Just as if we weren't going to see each other
again. He kept hold of me to the door, mumbling

something about his useless church, his useless church."

While listening to Jim, I had failed to notice that a staff servant was at attention behind me. The Tommy spoke with a suggestion of reproach. "The colonel has taken his place at table, sir."

We took our places. There had come, that day, word that the enemy showed, down on the Somme, definite signs of retirement. We were hopeful. We were, some of us, even a little exhilarated, though the soup was yet to come. The colonel was dry and hard in his speech, in spite of the good news, for he could never alter his demeanour, whatever the event. He gossiped of this small thing and that, sharply, breaking his bread abruptly, listening carefully to our answers as though his children were doing their best, but it was hardly good enough.

"There are some orders from the War Office which I shall have to read to you, later on," he told us.

One of our number was loudly, unnecessarily, and wickedly inquisitive. He had been celebrating what he assumed was a German retreat. "Tell us all about it, Colonel!"

"Oh, nothing, nothing. Merely orders, such as new regulations for the wearing of spurs."

"Spurs?"

"Yes, for officers of certain ranks. They must wear them now."

"Even if they don't ride horses?"

" That's nothing to do with it.   If an officer's rank
is affected, even if he works in the War Office itself,
he must wear them."

" But what for, Colonel ?   He couldn't use 'em—
could he ?—only stick 'em in the legs of the lift girl,
what, to get to the top floor quicker ? "

The colonel frowned and broke his bread impatiently.   He left the table early.   He could not stop
the bottles of celebrant champagne from coming to
the table, for a few of our men were not easily controlled.   An American correspondent especially was
gay.   His country was in it now.   He was in it, was
in it.   He got on a chair, with a foaming bottle in his
hand, gave himself a libation and spied through the
bottle.   He said he could see Berlin.

When Maynard and I retired, they were still at it.
They were getting noisier.   That hotel housed only
ourselves, and some officers of important rank.   It
was better to be behind one's own chamber door.

Jim was happy.   It was long since he had tasted
champagne.   He lay full length on the bed, in his
boots, and he began leisurely to relate a testimonial to
the excellent evening.   It was then that we heard the
signal bells going in the hotel.   Our floor !   The
floor above ; the floor below ; everywhere.   Im-
perative and loud !   An alarm ?

We looked out, down the corridor.   There stood
the American correspondent in his uniform, in his
steel helmet, with even his gas-mask prominent on his

chest. His deliberate finger experimented with the buttons of the electric sign-board, haughty and soldier-like.

A man in pyjamas, whom I recognised as a general, hurried down the corridor towards the cause of the electric storm in stern impatience. He stopped.

"What are you doing there, sir, what are you doing?"

"Who are you?"

"I am General Marbles, sir, and I ask what you are doing?"

"Go away. I don't want a general. I want a chamber-maid."

I slipped back, and quietly shut my door. Jim Maynard was on the carpet, resting on his elbow, in surrender to dissolute mirth.

MAYNARD's battalion was supposed to be in the line somewhere north of High Wood, the Bois des Fourreaux, near Flers. But nobody knew quite where the front line had wandered to in the Somme country. If you wanted to know, you had to go there, and find it. But Maynard knew he could not miss it, if he went towards it. It would be there. It would be there all right.

He did not believe that Jerry was retreating. He did not think much about it. The less you thought about it the better. The man in the line could write himself off. Maynard looked round him at the ruins of Albert-sur-Somme again, and he did not desire to see his lot clearly, to know it too well. He was afraid there would be nothing in it. He had dismissed the good cheer of the Amiens dinner-party, and its promising speculations. That was over. It did not concern him. He had come down again to his mud. Get as near to being plain animal as is possible—anyhow, don't think. Wangle through to the next day, if it can be managed.

That day was cold, neutral, and still. The light itself promised nothing, except one hour after another

468

by the wrist-watch. It was easy in Amiens to be hopeful, and to suppose that Jerry was on the run. But it was no good imagining release for yourself in a town like Albert, which was down to brick-dust and half walls, following Babylon, yet still had active life in it, for men lived furtively in the ruins; and so did the cats, which would not leave the old place, but slunk about the rubbish heaps, wild beasts again. Maynard surprised one of the tabbies, and tried to entice it to him, but it glowered at him and scuttled away to cover. That cat was no fool. Nothing could be trusted, no matter how friendly it seemed. Puss assumed all creation was the very devil, and dodged into the nearest hole when it heard a noise or saw anything move. It might live a bit longer, with that simple habit. All right for a cat. But was life worth having, at that surrender of everything but the first of the instincts? We were down to existence in the caves again; men were beasts who hunted each other. Puss was luckier than most of the men in the ruins. It had completely accepted a lapsed world. It had adjusted itself. A man did not always accept; he only submitted; and sometimes he had to go apart in the dusk—he couldn't help it—he had to go apart when he was shocked by the horror of Albert or Jerusalem. That was the only way to learn there was anything like a soul about you; sometimes you knew you had it because you felt it turn over stiff inside you, as though a cold iron claw had gripped your innards.

It gave you a twisting. Maynard grinned at a recollection he had of himself, groaning aloud once, when he was in a reverie.

" What's that, Jim ?   Got the tummy ache ? "

Strange, that the common spectacle of this world should cause grief in a man ! Why should anyone weep over Jerusalem ?   The people of Jerusalem did what they wanted to do, thought nothing of it, went to bed and slept, and would only have turned over and gone to sleep again had they been told that someone wept in Gethsemane. Crying is he ? What for ? Lost something ? Well, all right—let him get on with it.   Don't wake me up again over nothing.

Lots of men had had a taste of Gethsemane, this time. It was no sort of a blessed garden. But nobody cared, for nobody knew. A man went through that agony alone, and not another soul could share it. Sympathy be damned ! The world was gruesome with sympathy. It was worse than hate, for hate meant something, and sympathy nothing—no more than soft piety in self-comfort. Sympathisers who said they were sorry were liars, though they meant well.

Maynard spied, lonely in a corner of a field, a gathering of wooden crosses. All young men, all young men ! There must be something more important than life, thought Maynard, or else why are those boys there ?

There must be ? Well, there ought to be ; and if

there ought to be something more important . . . !

He was stopped, for a moment, by the appeal of that congregation of outstretched wooden arms. All young men, all reluctant, and all lost ! There must be something more important than life, or else the sun, moon and stars were nothing but an unintended joke, with nobody even to grin at it. The mystery of the universe was no mystery at all, if those young 'uns had been blown out, like candles, all wasted. The imposing universe meant nothing to men—there was no more mystery in it than there is in an empty room because its emptiness is dark. Well, if a man's sad consciousness of the futility of the material universe was the best thing it had produced, then an unimportant British soldier, about to enter the mud again, perhaps for the last time, could look up at the stars that night, and ridicule their silly useless wonders ; though for him to do that, Maynard felt, when he thought it over, was fairly comic.

For perhaps, if you only knew just a little bit more—that was the bit to reach, and nobody seemed able to get at it—you would see that those crosses, and the ruins, and a man's own inside twisted by the thought of the waste and cruelty of it, were of little ultimate consequence. All was resolved. A light was somewhere, if only it could be seen.

He looked round. It was a matter of faith, that light. No better than that. About those crosses still

GG

was craziness, war, and woe, and a bleak indefinite sky.
When would there be light ?

He trudged on to find the front line.   He had felt
too much of Jerry's weight to suppose that a speedy
lifting of it was in the least probable.   Jerry's weight
was like our own, and Maynard saw, listlessly, everywhere, the signs of the ponderous power of the
British arms.   This business might go on for years,
by the look of it.   It might last as long as coal and
cotton.   The wheels were well started, they could
grind on without much attention now, and there was
nothing to bring them to a halt, except failure in the
supply of raw material.   The seam of youngsters
would give out, at last.

He was going back to work, and, like the other
workmen passing, all in similar clay-coloured raiment,
he gave little attention to the signs of the success of the
industry of war.   The image of the Virgin with her
Child in her arms still hung over the chief highway
through Albert, about to fall, but Maynard did not
look up at it.   The drivers of the transport wagons
did not look up.   The big factory of the town,
collapsed by shell-fire, maintained one of its upper
floors aloft, undulating like an area of unsupported
cardboard, ready to shoot its load of hundreds of
rusting sewing-machines into the street.

Maynard had seen that wreck before.   He was not
interested.   He was watching the mud—he was
getting on, for the mud was getting worse.   The road

was full of transport; nodding mules with their legs
grey and shiny with mud, their loose wet ears flopping,
the mud hanging from the hair of their bellies like
bunches of earthly grapes. The men were masked in
mud, listless as himself, just getting on with it because
there was no way of getting out of it. He sniffed
the familiar smell of the Somme, the smell of smouldering wood and offal.

Flers was a long hike, if his bunch was there. A
battery of heavy guns by Pozières, their cocked barrels
the only clean and recognisable shapes in the boundless
quagmire and shapeless wreckage of the land, let fly
with a long blast of flame as he passed. The shock
jolted him, but he did not look at them. That was the
start of it. The work was still going on, and he was
joining it. Other blasts and roars came from nowhere
in particular, from pits hidden in the corruption of the
desert. He trudged on. There were filmy remnants
of copses topping low ridges on his right, and black
promiscuous spouts of earth from German shells,
yellow instantaneous clouds by the woods, and a bang
or two of shrapnel. He did not bother about them.
They were not near him. The mud was the worry.
If you tried to avoid it you were bogged. He turned
aside to go round a bad patch, and was stopped by a
horse which had foundered ahead of him; only its
sodden head and back showed above the ground.

Ground? There wasn't any. The very earth
itself was skinned. It had no hide. It would not

support. Its raw dark body was rotten, an expanse of wet entrails and decomposition. If you trod on it you sank into the soft pollution. Hard luck for a horse to sink into that, to be choked by that !

Maynard learned, at one headquarters, housed in a lean-to shed built of petrol tins and tarpaulins, that his battalion was beyond Flers. He had a longer journey than he had supposed. Jerry had shifted a bit, and nobody knew for certain where he had got to. They were trying to keep in touch with him.

Maynard understood that he was making for a place that had no features and no whereabouts, except that it was unpleasant and might be anywhere. He kept on, with a little headache. He toppled over a strand of wire, and his hand, put out to save him, sank to the elbow in the slubber. He stood and looked round to get his bearings. Beside him, sticking out of the slime, was a leg with its fat calf in blue hose, its boot in the air.

He came, wearily, to an area of disrupted trenches, a dissolving maze of stagnant ditches and mounds, and no place in it for foothold. The air had a sweetish sickly smell, for the slough was a compost of old wire, rags, clay, bones, flesh, and burst sandbags. A boy's alabaster face, all Maynard could see of him, hung backwards out of a heap of trash, what was left of his fair hair washed flat by rain, his eyes open to the indifferent sky, and his mouth gaping in astonishment and pain that belonged to the past. The offal was all human. Maynard, tired out by the show of established madness and its outrage on good things, was suddenly exasperated into blasphemy. He slipped into the filth again through weariness of mind. He got up and cursed and damned the people of the cities. Let them cheer this—it was their work— this was what they wanted! This was their bloody dream of Empire!

The winter front line had been here. Germans and British had faced each other here. Ahead was old German territory. Somewhere about here he would join up again. But join what? He could see only the Butte de Warlencourt lifting its pale back in the murk, an awful monster prone in solitude. All was over, all was dead. The flame of judgment had gone over the earth, and it was abandoned to melting rains. The sun would see it no more. The earth had ended. Maynard felt like the last man, left by an oversight, lost in the silence after the last day. The world was declining into livid slop, into nameless rubbish. What perhaps had been a deep road, long ago, was near. It was a ravine with a bottom of stagnant pools, the colour of blood, never to be stirred by the breath of life. That had fallen. What had been its roots and hedges were bones contorting out of grisly slopes of mud. The stump of a great tree stood above, a splintered column with rags of bark still hanging from its white body. Men floated below it, motionless in the pools. The life of earth

had finished ; all was over, all was dead, changed to a
ghastly apparition, trees, fields, streams, men.　Nothing moved.　They were mingling in dissolution.
The destroyed earth was pitted with wounds everywhere, ragged craters half-filled with green and red
liquid.　Earth's only shine came from those holes ; it
reflected the twilight from the serum of blind eye-
sockets.　The sky was pallid and sick with looking
down at it.　The land was dead, like its people.
There they were, as far as he could see, still dark forms
in the mud, merging with it, the dummies that used to
be his fellows.　A mound of them was near him, a
piled huddle of men.　In the last torment, the destroying blast had caught up a crowd of them in its vortex,
kneaded them together and dropped them.　Now
they rotted with their earth.　There was not a movement, and not a sound, except a rumbling far away, the
murmur of judgment departing.

He was alone in it ; then it could not matter what
happened to him.　He joined that.

THAT was a near one! A sniper, eh? So a Jerry
was living on there among the dead! Nearly joined
it at once. Maynard knew by that crack at his head
that he was not only not alone but not wanted. He
crouched, and slunk away into hollows to leeward,
and presently slithered into one at the other end of
which was a man in a blue shirt and khaki breeches.
The man turned to him a lathered face, for he was
shaving at a mirror stuck on the wall of mud. Maynard
had stumbled upon his own lot when he least expected
it—not a sign was above ground—and when he was
most desirous of something that was moving about
and was friendly.

" Hullo, Jim! Where've you come from? That's
the wrong way in."

" Why didn't you tell me before? "

" Next time you try it have your cold meat ticket
handy. Keep down. Come here. How's the happy
places far far away? "

His company headquarters was remarkable, even
to Maynard's experience of improvisations of shelter.
He waded to it, through one patch of glue, up to his
knees. Flattened petrol tins, beams, and decaying

tarpaulin were held together by mud, and mud was the ceiling and the floor. His grimace, as he went in, caused subdued mirth.

"What's the matter with that dug-out lower down?" he asked.

"Aha, what is it? Bogies live down there. You'd better keep out. There's a smelly old Boche officer sitting at a table there, for one thing. Also a bottle of beer on a shelf."

"Beer?"

"You bet, beer. Beer! Glorious beer! Jeffery here nearly took it. But Jeffery is still here, so far, as you see. He didn't. Up goes the donkey when you take that beer. That dug-out is mined."

But they didn't want to talk about it. He thought the gang looked fagged. They wanted him to talk of something different. Had he seen any shows? That was what they wanted to know. Were there cocktails at Charley's Bar? Did the Belle of Amiens smile at the desk of the "Tête d'Or?"

"I'd give my chance of a pension to pat her little hand. Did you pat it?" asked Jeffery.

Maynard learned that he had not come back a minute too soon. They were fed up. There was a new colonel—a new broom; they darkly and briefly murmured the unhappy fact. Bagpipes, their old Bagpipes—had he heard?

"What about him?" asked Maynard quickly.

One of them made a gesture. "Talking to me

one minute—there was a bump, and I went back. There was Bagpipes. We had a job. You wouldn't have known him."

Maynard could not imagine circumstances sufficiently drastic to change beyond recognition the salient image of their tall leader, who once, enthusiastic and simple-hearted man, marched him and a few others five miles, one hour's hard going, to enjoy the martial pipes of the Black Watch. Grand music, that, he told them. He was delighted, and thought they were. Old Bagpipes, silver-haired, daring, and patient, with his easy voice that carried like a trumpet when things looked like going to pieces.

They kept on chattering. Too much chatter. They brought absent Maynard round with news they thought he ought to hear. They were having a jammy time of it. Jerry was playing hide and seek, and their patrols never knew whether they'd run into the blighter, or find that he had gone. "You always hope he's gone, but you can't be sure of it till you see you're not dead." Jerry's rearguards, it seemed, were jolly good tricky beggars.

A message was brought to them from battalion headquarters; an officer and six men were to go out that night, and if possible were to enter the enemy's line. The chit was passed round, and then it was dropped on the central box, their table. They looked at Maynard, and nobody spoke.

"That's mine," said Maynard. "I know nothing

about it over there. Must learn it. Besides, I've got to report, anyway. We'll get the bright idea straight from headquarters. What is the colonel's name ? "

The new colonel was unfeignedly glad to meet Maynard. The poor little man was fussy. No doubt brigade was worrying him.

" We must keep in touch with the enemy," he told Maynard, fidgeting with his waistbelt. " Our orders are not to let him get away in his own time. If you can get a prisoner it would be of great assistance to us. You see . . ."

And Maynard saw. Between army command, which lived with an abstract war on dry land, and the enemy's wire in front of their battalion, they had, to interpret and fulfil for them the official delusions of distant generals, a leader who was afraid of what his signal wires would say to him. He would repeat brigade like a parrot. He had no blind eye to which he could put a telescope. He would let his men go to ruin when ordered in energetic ignorance by superior rank. It would not be wrong to him, in that case. Now, old Bagpipes, he was no more afraid of Haig than of Hindenburg. Maynard began to taste the meaning of absolute isolation. His company was unsupported now. Before long it would be wiped out by a useless task, and join the mud.

Maynard made what he could of the map, which was

sure to vary from reality. Sergeant Sturmey ran a grimy and knotty finger over it. The sergeant talked like a downy uncle. Maynard took another look at the sergeant. Well, here he had a solid man, worth a platoon of such colonels.

" Choose the men, sergeant—men who can keep quiet even if rats bite them. We shall have a long and sticky time." They agreed about a point, a course, and a return.

It was near nine that night when they crept out. There was a sprinkle of rain, but that made no difference ; it was a normal atmosphere. The men tailed behind Maynard—they became one body crawling over the paste on their buttons—and Sturmey was the wary old tail. The lines were quiet. There were no flares. There was no gunning. Jerry might have gone home, for all the signs he gave.

Maynard listened. No. Nothing. That noise was only from a lump of earth overbalancing to plop into the water of a crater. It was so dark that you could not see what was under your nose ; and plenty was there ; the uneven paste was stuck full of tosh, and the little hollows made a difference when you were crawling in the dark. The corporal behind—was he there still ? Maynard paused as his outstretched hand touched an old tin, and rolled it over. Damn that tin. It tinkled on a bit of iron . . . the corporal was still there—he signalled on Maynard's boot.

All right so far, as the man said when falling

from the tenth as he passed the sixth story.

Someone behind sneezed. The leader gave time for a flare to rise over them, but only the rain continued to fall. Perhaps Jerry had departed. The night was immovable. A flare, if it didn't make targets of them for hand-grenades, would be a bit of help.

Was he sure of where he was? Would he be able to steer these fellows back again? They depended on what he knew of it, and he knew nothing but the promptings of his instinct. His reason kept arguing with those promptings, and he didn't know which was right. His phosphorescent compass was playing the fool—or it seemed to be—but old metal was lying about thick everywhere. Was he right, or the compass? The corporal touched his boot. It was still all well behind him.

The ground stank, and you had to wallow in it. This bit was awful. What was this? An old bayonet! It was nearly into his face. Maynard, in spite of the cold rain, was sweating. He put down his right hand for support in his next heave forward; he laid it solid on a man's nose. Instantly he tried to withdraw it, but his quick weight was on it; his hand slid along and pushed the soft flesh off the bones of that face. Maynard fell helplessly over the body, and gulped in the stench of it. For a second he lay on it, his thoughts twittering; and then the body stirred under him. Maynard was electrified; he nearly cried out. He scrambled off the thing, shaking. Oh, God, rats were in it! He had nearly given the show away. He spat and spat. No good. It was his own hand he could smell.

The corporal touched him. All right, then. They were still there. Yet where were they? He was no good now; he'd forgotten everything. His brains were in a muck.

While he sweated, trying to think it out, one of the men behind him set empty tell-tale tins jangling. That put the lid on it. Now they'd know whether Jerry was at home or not.

The night was torn by the rush of a rocket, and then a pale glare hung over them. Napoo! A body on its face in front of Maynard, which he hadn't known was there, cast a black shadow. He was under the shadow of it. From his belly he peeped up, and a German sentry above him looked straight into his eyes. There they were, inside the German wire. He heard the movement of the German's rifle-bolt, and covered himself with his helmet, which he lowered as far as it would go. He had an impulse to jump for it, but subsided. That would only start his men running.

One! Maynard twitched at the report. How long would the flare last over them? Here ended the war for him. That beggar couldn't miss him again. Maynard had no feelings about it. He merely shrank his body to receive . . . Two! The bullet hit the

dead body, and shifted it.   He heard the bolt of the
rifle again, and there was a pause.   The fellow was
taking deliberate aim.   Three !

Got it . . . anyhow, it was in the ground under
his left shoulder.

The glare faded and Maynard heard the German
slipping another clip of cartridges into the magazine
of his rifle.   Maynard quietly heaved sideways into
a deep crater, and lowered himself into the water of
it till only his head and revolver hand were out.
Then another rocket glared above him.   He couldn't
hear his men, but in the blatant brilliance beyond the
inky rim of the crater he saw the crouching stealthy
form of the German sentry, uplifted and gigantic.
A bold fellow that ; he had come out to clear his
doubt.   The German peered down at him, and
Maynard moved his revolver to let him have it.
Maynard hesitated ;   no good firing, with his men
trapped inside the wrong wire.   They'd be smothered.

The German turned slowly away, and the light sank
into night.   Maynard remained quiet in the water
till his own shivering body agitated it.   Lumps of
the rim of the crater splashed by his shoulders.   He
heard the corporal whisper above, " You there, sir ? "
He groped for the man's warm hand, and grasped it,
to get some help out of that.   He was done.   Gently,
corporal, no noise !

His men were all there, and Sturmey silently nosed
out a way back through the wire for them.   Jerry

was behind them without a doubt. He had the wind up. He was dotting the mud with the red bursts of his grenades; the lucky mud helped to choke the exploding canisters. One of Gerry's machine guns began to traverse on their left. They waited once, while a stream of lead was loud over their backs. It was four in the morning when the little group stumbled into home.

"Maynard!" That was Jeffery's voice. "We thought they'd got you. All right? The colonel is in company headquarters. He's been waiting for hours."

And there the agitated little man was. Maynard's mates eyed the figure of their comrade, erect but loathsome, in surprise. They could smell him. It surprised them still more to hear the shivering object answer the sharp questioning of the colonel so clearly and slow, as though he were thinking it out in good shape. Maynard briefly indicated that he was a target at about ten yards from the enemy's trench. The colonel querulously nodded. "Why didn't you take the man prisoner?" he asked.

By order of my chief, I had to leave Amiens on a fair spring morning of that year, and journey to our chateau at Rollencourt. General Rawlinson was there to lunch, but I paid little attention to his exposition of the reasons that existed for a cheerful view of the war, because of a letter I found there from Annie Bolt. That young woman imagined, apparently, that any hapless man in France could be succoured, if he deserved it. She had lost track of her brothers for some weeks. Charley, she knew, had been gassed. How was he? Where was Jack's battalion now—was he still in the firing-line? It was wicked. Hadn't that child done enough for us? Did the brutes keep men in the line who were gassed and ought to be in hospital? And had I been to any trouble to see Maynard? If anything happened to those men, victory didn't matter to her. It was a stiff letter. She had to blame somebody, I suppose, and it is not always easy, though it may be essential for our pent emotions, to find an object to take the sharp edge of our angry dread.

"So I hear," I heard General Rawlinson say.

"Any truth in it?"

" Possibly. That's the word I get, we took Bapaume to-day."

" Not Berlin, General ?   You don't mean Berlin ? " questioned a hearty doubter. Bapaume, for years, had been no nearer, meant no more to us, than a mark in the moon.

The General laughed. " Give us time," he said. " Bapaume first."

If there were anything in the rumour, it was in that country that Maynard's battalion would be. Were the rivets which kept in place the age-long battle positions really beginning to work loose ? If so, it was useless to dwell upon the welfare of the Jacks and Charleys and Jims. They would, some day, emerge into daylight at the other end, should daylight be their luck ; and no power on earth, that I knew, could change for them their weird, could alter the celestial courses. I glanced at Rawlinson's jocular but truculent eye. No power on earth.

That Bapaume was ours I doubted, for only that week I had seen Loupart Wood on its high ridge, and knew it was full of German machine guns, while about it British artillery was raising a surge of smoke and lightnings. Bapaume was beyond that ridge, a remote city, invisible and inaccessible. How many tired and sweating Tommies, easing their accoutrements, had glanced at a famous sign-post surviving on their Via Dolorosa through the Battle of the Somme, and had noted with

HH

ribaldry its geographical fact ?   " Bapaume, 20 Ks. ! "
" Garn, twenty million bloody miles ! "

We dispersed from that quiet lunch.   Two officers
stood conferring together seriously in the room beyond, and they came over to me.   They had a
suggestion to make;   a suggestion I had guessed
before they spoke.   It was our duty, they thought,
to learn the truth of it by venturing at the walls of
Bapaume.   They spoke with reluctance, though with
sad conviction;   they might have been referring to
the necessity of Zion.   I pointed out the lateness of
the hour;   the sun was declining;   we were far from
Zion.

Well, so the sun was sinking, and the place was
far, and nobody knew what was there :   yet how was
conscience ?   What was to be done with conscience ?

As if one could help the boys with one's scraggy
conscience !   The Germans knew what they were
doing when they established their positions on the
heights of the Somme.   The war of attrition had been
grinding there for eight months and a bit.   Eight
months, and a million men, and tens of thousands of
incessant cannon which rocked the earth.   There was
no end to it.   The sensations of the melodrama of it,
" the epic splendour of this vast battle "—as one
London leader-writer described it in his early delirium
—had gone.   The public interest in the first of the
tanks, and in the heroism, so surprising to those who
knew the men, of bank-clerks and drapers' assistants

and dock-labourers, had faded, like the summer in which this battle began. It was long past a novelty. Nothing had happened. Yet, any day in the February of the following year, by Pozières, you could listen to the erratic but continuous hammering in the Somme's lowering foundry, pounding out the lives of men; and while you listened, there would come an inexplicable pause in it; the casual hammering would cease, as by a signal unknown. Then, in an instant, the light guns would begin concerted, a terrible throbbing of furious and multitudinous kettle-drums, with the heavy howitzers rolling the bass. The elemental urgency thundered round the horizon from demoniacal mid-air malevolent legions. The roll and drub returned in waves to beat above you an impetuous rataplan, and through it broke the convulsive shocks of the deeper explosions. The sky had opened in wrath.

But Fritz would not go. He had been blown off the Pozières ridge, and from the Thiepval plateau; even the Ancre valley had been pierced; and nobody at home ever knew what the actions of that winter were like on the hills of the Ancre before the village of Miraumont, when the earth was marble, and every shell scattered frozen marl which flew like splinters of masonry. Bapaume was still in the distance.

Just about sunset, the three of us crossed the old front line by La Boisselle. The rubble from the mine craters and old trenches in the chalk of the earlier days of the Somme glimmered phosphorescently in the twilight. We marched with our own thoughts. We went with our familiar ghosts. Gun flashes played like soundless summer lightning on the northern horizon, ten miles away; Bapaume was there.

The afterglow was as translucent and cold as cairngorm and amethyst. The battleground of the Somme, at long last, was curiously still and quiet. Day left us. The wilderness to the east, towards Longueval, Ginchy, and Sailly-Saillisel, fell into forgetfulness, into a gulf of night, with the raised rim of the bottomless pit just to be seen along the faint sky. Sparks floated far away and deep in that darkness, precarious and sundered. On the Pozières ridge, the pools in the craters of that tumbled ground were pale with a light reflected from nowhere—a little of the evening had soaked into them, very likely —or they were perforations in the earth, and we could see the faintest show of an antipodean day which might come up to us, some time or another, perhaps even in one's own lifetime. Was another beginning possible? Wrecked trees stood about, an assembly of gnomes, unlikely shapes so blurred that there was no need to believe them. A voice was whining and complaining. I don't know what it was; maybe it was the sundered limb of a gnome swinging by a shred of skin. But there was no wind. There was only that whining. The body of a careened tank loomed beside the skeleton trees, a dinosaur in Limbo. We were beyond men and time ; we need not look for an ordinary and next morning to light those shapes.

I fell over the legs of a stiff horse. I noticed in the gloom, as if for the first time, the tiny white crosses of the Somme. They were hardly noticeable by day. They seemed insistent, in that darkness, among the saurians and the misshapen lumber of what was past its importance. A wandering body of men went by, and they whistled the recollection of a gay air of the war ; the crosses knew it well enough. I could see nothing of those men, except the familiar shape of the steel helmet. They were, perhaps, the haunting victors of the famous but forgotten battles. We heard far halloas, distant gun fire, and blithe whistling. Low in the north was a film of rose in the night ; it might have been of an immense fire. One tiny isolated cloud was shaped by it, a patch of our invisible ceiling.

Our path curved. That flushed area of night mounted over it ; and what had been an indeterminate noise ahead of us became a stamping of hooves, a bumping of wheels, a jangling of chains. We saw then the lively helmets and shoulders of men dancing absurdly high with wagon tops and the heads of mules.

There was no doubt about the fires ahead of us now. We could count them. There were twelve of those northern and eastern villages burning. The land around us began to rise a little out of its night. We were walking directly into the vague glowing of Avernus. Once the whole eastern night went up in a great light; that was a mine, or an ammunition dump.

There is—there was—a village called Le Sars. It was one of the most foul of the dreadful heaps that had been a community in that land. It was invisible to us then, except as a mass dimly apprehended because of a flickering on its nameless protuberances. There was a track through it, and we lifted our feet—one foot after another, cautiously—over worse than mud. And by then I did not believe it was possible to get anywhere near Bapaume; it was six miles away. It was nearing midnight. The sound of the machine guns seemed not so far off.

"I think," said the Major, "there may be a battalion headquarters at Le Coupe Gueule. Let us push on to that, and ask again."

Beyond Le Sars we got a bearing from Loupart Wood. That wooded ridge beyond the German lines was startlingly near. Every tree on it, high in night, was rootless upon a florid and burnished sky. As the glow pulsed, the bony trees frolicked above us, an ecstatic and horrid company. We watched their spectral gambols, while sometimes we were almost sure we were on a path, and at other times were merely free to hope we might find a track again. Then the Major shouted that the road had gone. It had quite gone. A mine, blown by the Germans in their retreat, had left a crater, which, to the light of our hand torches, had no bottom. We worked round its margin, taking our feet out of loops of barbed wire between whiles, found the path again, and continued.

At Cut Throat Corner we discovered a post for the aid of men. In a deep cave in the earth, in a local air of iodoform, and to a tinkling of steel and glass, the desert which we had thought was abandoned to the flames disclosed subterranean surgeons under gloomy lamps who were too busy to give us information they had not got. They were bent over men who were past caring where we went. Cumbering the doorway, lying as bundles discarded against the walls of clay, collapsed on benches, were limp figures coated with mud; mud clotted the hair of some of them, mottled with blood. The muddy rags of an Australian soldier at my feet were drawn apart, showing a noble torso, and in the breast a tiny red mark around which gathered pink froth. He was asleep, with his eyes open. There was still a tincture of health on his cheeks.

Beyond that interlude the road was ominously perfect, except for the mine craters. The nervous brightness of the star-shells made a greenish fluctuating noon. We were alone there, and saw each other plainly at quick intervals. We met no more of our fellows. The close rattling of the machine guns shattered the order of the mind. Where were those guns ?

From the roadside a signpost was suddenly thrown at us by the glare of a rocket : " Bapaume, 2 Ks. ! "

As near as that ? But its nearness, with our fatigue, those wild lights, and the menacing and implacable sounds, made Bapaume a mere word with an indefinable sense of unreality. We stood by that post, considering it, in a common doubt, when a cluster of high explosives burst on the road ahead. The Major therefore considered the road was open for our use. They were German shells, so the enemy was not there. He led on.

Shrapnel broke over it, violent aerial fireworks with single instantaneous flashes. I fear shrapnel and its jolting crash more than any threat. We continued to tramp and stumble, wearied beyond care, and came to a mule of a transport cart, its head caught in a tangle of telegraph wires brought down by the crumps. The mule, the wires, and the littered road, gave us something to do for ten minutes.

It didn't matter. We should never get to Bapaume. Could we get back out of this ? The mule struggled in and out of conflicting lights made of changing red fires and the waxing and waning of pallid star-shells. The tearing rush of streams of machine gun bullets was as if the atmosphere were a harsh fabric being hideously torn; great lengths of it; torn to ribbons!

Those green stars, soaring to betray what was below and around, poising, expanding, and fading, without intermission, gave us an infernal day, inconstant and bewildering with solid black shapes which were immediately at hand, to retreat from us and then to shoot back at us again, though altered. We stood, I thought, in an avenue of poplar trees that were flickering smears on burnished nothing. The moving sky was crimson and lustrous; we saw heaven collapse through insurrectionary fires which had burned through its floor. The loud and frantic hammering of the automatic guns was the decrepitation of our world below.

We arrived at a barricade of trees on our road, worked through it, and a new glare showed us Bapaume. We were already in it. But that street of dark houses was vacant, except for the sounds of a hail of lead. We could be sure of nothing, except that this was the city at last.

The Major stopped. He cleared his throat. " Here we are," he said. " The boys must have done the trick."

The forms of trees and houses about us—we watched them for a little while, because we were afraid to return the way we had come—shook in dire lights. Bapaume, the name we had heard so often, was still only an apparition, the confusion of a nightmare,

where the fevered groan when they sleep.   The roof
of night was broken.   The boys had done the trick.
The sky was tumbling, and its airy rafters floated
incandescent to earth.   The earth and its cities were
falling asunder, to mingle with the loosened stars and
the downfall of the old seat of God.

" You shall see." At that headquarters of a French Staff, a French colleague promised us an excellent and transforming event. We listened carefully. We were anxious for words of good cheer, but had acquired a habit, because the currency was debased with nobody knew how many spurious words, of biting on them for their metal ; yet this elderly man, we knew, had duties in a corner where he would hear the grand resolves of the inner councils in Paris. The time had come, gentlemen! He gazed deeply into the future to the resolution of all our fears. All goes well! Something would happen very soon on the line of the Aisne. The war could end, quite comfortably, by the winter of 1917. General Nivelle, of Verdun fame, had replaced Papa Joffre. A new and decisive action was near.

Our French colleague, whose eyes dwelt in sombre brightness on us and on the fate of the Germans, with quiet but faultless logic demonstrated how and why this doom would descend on the enemy. He did this, and then sat up and combed back with the nervous fingers of both hands his grey hair, attractive in its abundant disorder. He then put his hands on

497

his knees. He nodded at me to reassure me, because my silence maybe hinted my Saxon sluggishness of understanding. He made the matter easier for a slow mind with dramatic action. " So, monsieur." He drew back one hand and shot it forth like an arrow. Thus ! Piercing the German vitals ! It would be complete, this German overthrow.

" But," doubted one of us, " if you name thus early and freely the Chemin des Dames, surely the Boche will know it also ? What then ? "

He pursed his lips and nodded, looking idly to a window. " The Boche knows ? So much the worse for the Boche."

And we, for our part, knew that Easter was near for the British. Spring was with us. The tiny blue eggs were again in the shrubbery, secrecy again was strictly enjoined upon us, and the British guns, moving to position for the vernal attack, rumbled in daylight undisguisable processions of terror along all the roads converging on Arras. The uproar would soon be acute and passionate. While the French attacked the heights of the Aisne, the British would assault the Vimy Ridge.

Our conversation began to falter. Whatever our doubts, this would come. Indeed, there was no more to be said. The end of trench warfare was at hand ; attrition had done its work. The little Frenchman rose, and took his nervous fingers to a piano ; and ah ! if only logic in the matter of warfare were as right as this Frenchman's grave understanding of Beethoven !

In the quietude of our own headquarters that night, I picked up, to pass the time, a recent American magazine. I think it was called " The Metropolitan." It announced, on its cover, " the greatest magazine story even written." But that was not its attraction for me. The cover of the magazine bore the portrait of a foreigner, a bearded rascal, with eyes, brows, and long dank hair so plainly the features of a laughable charlatan that I desired to learn his name. You never know when these energetic meddlers may fascinate us. What had this comic rogue to do with the tragedy of our wonderful days ? I turned to the pages of the magazine in curiosity. Nothing there, that I could find, related to the cover. Nothing of the contents was more sensational than is usual in popular magazines. I was disappointed. I looked up, petulant through failure.

An American of our chateau sat opposite, and I saw he had been finding amusement in my empty search. He came over. " You looking for that fellow in that thing ? "

" Of course."

" You won't find him. He is suppressed. Your Foreign Office got wind of it, and the story was cut out. That fellow is a Russian priest—I dunno— some bunk or other—got a name with a noise between a snarl and a caramel cream—Rasputin. You have

noticed his beauty? There's a court scandal at St.
Petersburg, through those eyes. But "The Metropolitan" had to disappoint you, though there was
no time to hide the cover. We mustn't upset the
Russian steam roller."

That explained it. No, it would be wrong to
allow the fair name of a loyal ally to be smirched.

I HAD then to cross the Channel to England. The little destroyers which escorted our transport—she plunged giddily in a heavy south-westerly gale—reassured us with their presence but occasionally, because most of the time they had either foundered or were hidden in the smother. It comforted us, if we could see no more than an escorting row of funnels show for a bare instant through a hurtling cloud of spume, for the enemy's submarines were many and very daring, just then. Yes, somehow those destroyers kept their stations. It was a bleak and threatening passage. In the saloon of the transport were army officers of high rank, whose complexion and lassitude may have indicated that they preferred not to be naval officers. Tommies going home on leave crowded the lower deck, and there they lay, sometimes in heaps, sliding hither and thither mixed helplessly with baggage, rifles, and wash, entirely careless as to what might happen to us the next minute. Three of them died of sickness that voyage, during their relief from the trenches ; a matter of no significance, for they might have expired in the trenches of other things. An infantry officer with me, who through all that

cold upheaval of the sea smoked his pipe, when he
could get it alight, confided to me that the tin box
he treasured under his arm did not contain official
documents of moment, as I might suppose, but the
eggs of rare birds, which he had collected in France,
that spring, and was conveying home to his boy.
" How old is he ? " I asked. " Too young to be in
time for this, thank God ! " he said.

It would not be easy, such chance details merely
indicate, to relate the full story of a war, even were
it known ; but it never is known. Like the Russian
court scandal, which our Foreign Office refused for
our delectation, what is insignificant is overlooked
until, maybe, it turns into a menace which is too big
to hide ; finally, in any case, the dross, the scandals,
the irrelevant torture of men, the cemeteries filled
with heroes wasted by the mistakes of haughty but
unteachable pride, all sink out of sight ; the irrelevant
is omitted by historians, whose science teaches them
what will make their records worthy and just ; and
in the end, nothing remains but the dusty rags of
revered regimental colours preserved in the holy calm
of our cathedrals, and some debts.

Why, I discovered in London, in surprise, that even
the battles of the Somme, a name I knew I should not
find it easy to forget, were already forgotten. But
they were hardly over, those battles—the slain sprawled
there yet ? No matter ; they were suppressed, like
the Russian scandal, perhaps in their case because

they happened to be a hope which could not come to fruition now. It is useless to look at hope when it has gone. It was felt that London's street lamps could not be re-lighted from Bapaume, though the boys had done the trick. The trick did not work the expected miracle. Still, there is no reason to doubt the possibility of miracles, even the miracle of the resurrection, for we know that though hope dies it rises again eternally. For that good reason the Quill Club, which had turned its face from the Somme, regarded now other regions of the war in warm assurance of good. A few of its members, better informed than the rest, knew, I learned, what was known to our colleagues at the French headquarters. Had I heard what was going to happen on the Aisne, at Arras, and elsewhere? For in war the idle winds of the world scatter important secrets as though they were thistledown.

The curtain rose on the play called the Spring Offensive. We watched, with an inkling of the official programme, the unfolding of events that should lead to a happy conclusion of the drama of Europe. Along the Messines Ridge, which had helped our enemy to dominate the Ypres Salient, nineteen British mines were exploded together as footlights to the stage of the year. That important ridge was put at once within the British lines, a first act as promising as the best things of April could be.

Easter Monday dawned. The Battle of Arras began

II

and the Vimy Ridge was stormed and captured, and
new names of dire import were added to the long list
which followed Mons ; Gavrelle, Oppy, the Railway
Triangle, Monchy-le-Preux, Bullecourt, Croisilles.
The French, in concert, attacked on the line of the
Aisne, and won the Chemin des Dames, but lost sixty
thousand men in twenty minutes. It proved to be
true that the Boche knew they were coming ; he
was ready for them. The poilus were shocked and
dismayed. They turned mutinous through the
squandering of comrades in an official confidence so
haughty but mistaken. They began to walk home.
They left behind them an unattended door, open to
Paris, for Ludendorff to pass through ; an unexpected
consequence of the triumph of his foes.

The play so soon began to go awry. There were
hurried changes, there was improvised adjusting of
scenery, and exits not by the book. The play was
playing itself, in a way not according to the words.
The actors were compelled, by a power unknown, to
perform a nameless drama they had not learned. As
in those legends when good men were thwarted, in
their righteous efforts, by unmerited calamity sent by
the gods who were unseen but jealous, so now it
was feared that inherencies mysterious but omnipotent
were using us for a celestial drama which transcended
our own, a great play which we could not read, but
must follow ; our stage was great, but theirs was
universal ; our need was vital, but theirs was in a

plan that was drawn at Genesis; our aim was righteous, yet righteousness is nothing to omnipotence, which is absolute. It had been granted to man to release great forces, by the devices of his cunning hands, and then he must needs let them obey a will not his, like the fisherman who released the Genie.

The British in July were compelled by circumstance to precipitate an action east of Ypres—the Battle of Passchendaele—to disengage the attention of the enemy from the dilemma of our ally protecting Paris. The greatest army the British ever had in the field was sent forward. It won ridges, woods, hills and forts of concrete. It attained the heights of Passchendaele. But rain came out of its due season. Flanders, in which gunfire had dispersed natural water-courses and pulverized the ground, was soon a bottomless quagmire which submerged fleets of advancing tanks, and drowned the troops. The Menin Gate of Ypres led out to a tornado of flame that swept men held helpless in a slough. The men marched through the Menin Gate to victory, but were lost.

It was a resounding and piteous drama, yet bewildering in its implications, which went contrary to all the actors said and did. Events just across the channel so stupendous yet mystifying lessened the shock of the news of a far-off Russian revolution; we gave but perfunctory attention to the end of the

Romanovs and their steam-roller. Yet we did hear freely of a man known as Rasputin ; his death, there was no doubt, had been delayed too long. This, however, was before the arrival of Lenin, of whom we had not heard. What is inherent and inevitable may choose the time of its coming. When it strikes its hour, then the devices of statecraft and the lawful science of the military academies are thrown out to join the empty sacks and the rats where last year's potatoes were stored.

CHAPTER XIV

OUTSIDE the railway station at London Bridge, in spite of the confusion in France, and the downfall in Russia, with whatever that might imply of German armies moving freely from Russia towards the English Channel, there stood, one morning, not without surprise to me, but to my relief, the accustomed fleet of motor-buses. Charing Cross! Strand! Oxford Street!

Yes, London stood in its immemorial place. I had not seen this station in daylight for a great while. In the meantime, the world had gravely altered, but the features of the courtyard of London Bridge Station were curious in their steadfastness. There they were, as in the old days.

And it was an ordinary London morning. It was not easy to discern that it was war-time. It was summer time. The sky was heavy with smoky and lustrous cumulus clouds, deep with gulfs, gleaming with rounded coasts. The city crowds streamed from the station, and went their various ways to work. Their work may have altered, for there were many odd uniforms in the multitude, some of which I had never seen before, especially those worn by the ladies; yet enough of the old sort mitigated the spectacle, the content of many women and men with commonplace raiment, ordinary people who were only hurried, intent, and dutiful.

This common daily round, I thought hopefully, will take a lot to stop it. I began to feel confident. I mounted a bus, and humped into a corner. The bus was empty. How often, I thought, as I waited in idleness for the bus to start, gazing out of its window, have I seen Charley Bolt hurrying along that pavement for the evening train he knew was the one for me! It was reassuring, that steadfastness of familiar things. When again should I meet Charley there? It was a natural expectation. I saw the same shops. In that one he used to turn for his tobacco. ("Hold on a minute.") There was the seed-merchant's, where we had examined curious saxifrages and Alpine plants. Wait, I promised myself, wait till all this is over. We will make up for it.

The bus started. I was still alone in it, and that was unusual. It dawdled down the slope. It kept its place in the slow procession of the crowded thoroughfare, and presently reached the foot of the bridge, and turned to the city. It began the ascent in crossing the river. Then it stopped.

I was reading my newspaper. After some minutes I lowered it; looked round. The conductor was swung outboard, gazing at the sky over the city. A stout brigadier stood on the footway beside the bus.

He, too, was engrossed astronomically. I saw that everybody had stopped. They were regarding the sky with fixed attention. London at its busy morning hour was suddenly so quiet that I heard the whistling of the wings of a flock of pigeons as they wheeled aloft in swift alarm.

Here, what was this! In France, so general a curiosity in the sky was never seen by the wary without an enquiry. I got out, and stared upwards with the rest. Under the cloud which was, I guessed, over the position of the Bank of England, was what appeared to be a high flight of rooks.

Surely not 'planes, in that number? Not there? They must be birds. Perhaps, I pondered, our airmen are practising; yet so many of them, over London, at that hour? It was an odd phenomenon, not easily interpreted by Londoners, with their secure habit of mind induced by the eternal sea and a war fleet which was dominant.

I suspected—yes—those little woolly balls at the tails of the further rooks were bursts of shrapnel. If those birds intended to fly over London Bridge the target was obvious.

I turned, and sought the steps for the street below, on the south side, and the cover of the railway arches. You cannot argue with a fleet of hostile 'planes and their consignment of bombs. A man darted past me when I was at the top of the steps. At that instant a warehouse came down by Billingsgate. The roar made the hurried man miss his footing; he fell to the bottom. I saw a stricken plane whirling to the river just as I reached cover.

London shook to its first daylight bombardment. The sheltering crowd looked upwards, in patient wonder, thinking the spasmodic dingy brickwork of the railway arches was about to fall on them. The explosions rattled the loose ironwork hysterically. A matron near me whimpered at each shock. " Never mind, mother," an elderly market porter called over to her. He sat, while waiting for the storm to blow over, on an upturned basket. " Don't you worry." He mopped his face with a red handkerchief. " Now I bet you the rotten shots miss all them tormaters I got t'shift before dark. No luck fer me." He flourished his handkerchief.

One near burst made me glance towards the opening to the street, and on the other side of the arch I saw someone I knew, waiting patiently, like the rest of us. Annie Bolt was clasping an attaché case, a neat and calm figure, ready to depart promptly on her way as soon as this shower passed.

I was not anxious to meet her. There was much to be said, yet nothing to say that was useful; and I remembered the reproach of an emotional letter from her, as though I were to blame for the war and its direction. She was a slight and acute little woman, and the refinement of her features, and her coolness, promised a frigid aloofness, from which irony might come sharp-edged, should my words seem insufficient. And they would seem insufficient.

Ah, well, she had seen me. Lord, that smile of hers was a queer reminiscence of Charley.

She was merely solicitous for my welfare. She did not mention her brothers. Nor did I, for nothing was ever gained by venturing on the names of men who were absent in France. She did not ask whether I knew anything of her brothers, but she touched my arm, and enquired, meekly, when last I saw Maynard, and, really, how was he?

Well, Jim was fine when I saw him. We had an evening together, not a great while back.

Strange, I thought, this self-interest of a woman. She mentions her lover, but not her brothers. She was not looking at me. She was contemplating in forgetfulness the street beyond—thinking of Jim, I suppose. Into that street the sheltering crowd was slowly venturing; there were no more bombs. She was still touching my arm. She had forgotten me.

She recollected herself. She met my eyes, and her own reminded me again of the tolerant understanding of her brother. " This has made me late," she said, " and we have said nothing yet. We can't talk here. Do come down and see Mother and Dad. Dad is not well—he would be glad. Any evening. He sees nobody now. He ought to see you. Please come."

CHAPTER XV

The suburbs of London, in those years, submerged themselves after dark, and did not desire even the moon to see them. They were chary of street lamps, and smeared the hoods of the few they lighted with purple, so they were of no help at all. They gave the gloom only dim local blobs where the ink happened to be translucent. People went home as soon as they could, and stayed within, trusting day would come without a warning from the maroons that the enemy was in the air; and occasionally it did. To venture into a suburb at night, to search for a house which had ceased to be familiar, was to go into a dark country that had lost its landmarks, where you might be kept till morning should the affairs of an attack from the clouds prove to be more unpleasant than usual. Though all was obscure, though little was to be seen in the darkness of those years, the tension of night was felt to be as much as it could bear. The unseen sky might roll up as a scroll, or the silent earth split open.

Searchlights wandered on the keels of clouds, disclosing them saliently, and then swept on, while I sought for the house of the Bolts. I met nobody

that I could ask. Only a dog passed me in that
street.

This might be it. I tried the outer gate. I felt
my way to the porch. It seemed to be the place, yet
all Victorian stucco is similar. In answer to the bell,
the shrouded fanlight dimly showed.

Right! Mrs. Bolt opened the door. She was
bent, and had aged greatly, or so I thought. It may
have been that Indian shawl over her shoulders, with
its air of a grandmotherly invalid. But there was no
mistaking the sincerity of her welcome. That was
as before.

Annie was not home yet. Her mother hoped no
raid would come before that poor girl got indoors.
Was there any news of one?

I did not know of any, but withheld my interest
in the searchlights.

Polly was married. Had I heard that? Her
husband, Mr. Drake, was in the Navy. Mrs. Bolt
nodded sagely at the comfortable cat. She said she
thought it was safer in the Navy. Let us hope so, she
added. I agreed with her, for one may always hope.

" It's so quiet here now. We are very dull, what
with Mr. Bolt keeping to his bed. I wish he would
pick up. I do wish he would. He has been there
a month past—sit you down—take that chair—that's
right. Let me see, yes, five weeks he's been in bed.
All five weeks. And never in his life before, the
hearty man. It does make him so irritable."

She considered that, and the cat, with her hands working in her lap.

" What is wrong with him ?   Too much to do, I suppose ? "

" Yes, too much of it.   They kept him at it, day and night.   I hardly ever saw him.   That and the margarine, the muck it is, he won't eat it."

" No good in that stuff, is there ? "

" Not a bit, the muck.   He won't touch it.   But I can't get butter for him, him that's been used to good food all his life.   He's such a big man."

She brooded again.   I began to wish Annie would come in.   Mrs. Bolt did not speak of the great events in the world which made all thoughtful people grieve. She was not curious for news of the fate of civilisation. This problem of the rarity of butter troubled her far more.   She was wearing that grey alpaca dress, and that large cairngorm brooch, which I remembered on other occasions, in that room. That all seemed long ago.

She lifted her head.   " I'm forgetting myself." She briskly assured me I must see Mr. Bolt.   He would never forgive her if I went without seeing him.   It was lonely for him, up there all day, and nothing to do, and nobody to see.

She rose to show me the way.   She turned, though, hesitatingly.   She looked at me, rubbing her mouth nervously with her hand.   Her hand was so frail that her wedding ring was loose on a bloodless finger.

" Before you go up," she whispered.   She repeated

that, and fumbled at a pocket in her dress. She brought out a carefully folded slip of paper, and handed it to me. Her hand shook.

" His father doesn't know," she said. " He doesn't know. He mustn't be told till he is better."

I could see my own hand shaking as I took that paper. I knew the colour of that official form. Which of the two boys was it ? " Deeply regret . . . Charles Bolt . . . killed in action . . ." A fortnight before !

" His father was so proud of that boy."

Proud of him ! My eyes roved to the china dogs on the mantelpiece. The portrait of Lord Beaconsfield stared down at us from over the mantelpiece. I wanted to be active, to blaspheme aloud ; to cry out something. But kept still.

" What shall we do now ? " his mother asked.

Yes, what should we do ! She sat down again, and pulled a handkerchief about quickly. She stooped, and touched the head of the cat with one finger. After a spell of silence she got up again.

" Mr. Bolt will be wondering who is here. Come you up to him. But he mustn't know. He might die if he knew, the state he's in."

" Hullo, mother," called the deep voice of the old shipwright, as we entered his room. " What's been keeping you ? "

He was up on his elbow, to see who was with her.

" What, you ? Where have you been all this time ?

What have you been talking about ?   Here, come and
sit here."   He touched, with a brown hand, that had
lost some of its substance, the edge of his bed.   He
lay back.

"Well, what's the best news ? "   He kept a hold
on me.

We gossiped of this and that, lightly.   He made
a show of his old vivacity, rebuking mother for her
food, starving him at his age, and me for the time I
had been away.   His eye was arrested by a needle of
light, as the shaft of a searchlight went by the parting
of his heavy window curtains.

"That girl in yet ? " he asked sharply.

"Not yet, Tom, it is hardly her time."

"What's this night like ? "   He turned to me.

"Oh, quiet now.   No wind.   But the glass has
dropped.   It looks as if we might get a south-
westerly blow."

"Huh !   Is that so ?   I hope we do.   We could do
with it.   But what are those searchlights up for ? "

"Practising, I should say.   I know of no warning."

"Well, then, that's all right," commented Mrs.
Bolt cheerfully.   "I'll see if Annie is coming along."
She went out of the room.

Old Tom Bolt plainly was glad I was there.   His
big body had collapsed, his eyes were hollow, but
something of his old fire was burning.   It could flash
up, with sardonic humour.   He touched on the great
affair, yet casually, as though he were wearied by it,

yet still must consider it, for there it still was. What did I think of it?

The time came when I guessed that I had better be off. This energetic talking might do him no good.

"Going? Not you, you've only just come. Sit down. You will wait till Annie comes in. Sit down."

He was quiet for a time, watching the passing and re-passing of the splinter of light. The night without was soundless. Then he got up on his elbow, and looked at the door.

"That door shut?"

The door was all right.

"Now I'll show you what puts me here. Over there!" He pointed peremptorily to a coat behind the door. "Go and feel in the pocket."

I could find nothing, except his tobacco pouch.

"No, no, not that one." He was testy. "Inside, inside!"

I drew out some papers, and letters. "Show me," ordered Mr. Bolt. "That one," he said. "Read it." He thrust it at me, and sank back.

It was from France. It said how sorry . . . Jack was a gallant fellow . . . wounded and missing . . . all were sorry. It was signed F. Gillow, Captain.

"Put it where it was, right to the bottom. Put that coat straight. As it was."

The minutes were interminable. I sat by him again, and waited, trying to form an answer. Then Mr. Bolt spoke.

" Now you know," he rumbled.   " But his mother doesn't.   She's not to know.   Can't tell her about her baby.   Luckily I took it in when she was out."

" She will have to know, though," he added. " Something will have to be done.   What is it? But it will kill the old girl.   It will kill her.   I know she couldn't stand it."

We both watched the flickering of the searchlights where the curtains barely met.   If there was anything to be said it was unknown to me.

" That's the door key," he muttered in relief. " There's Annie.   That child is home."

Then he turned to me, as if with the sudden thought of important news.   " I don't know what we should do without that girl."

She came up at once with her mother, and some light nonsense passed between her and her father.   It was not long before I felt the discomfort of an intruder, and took my leave.

From the outer gate, when I left the house, Annie walked with me a little down the street.   She paused under one of the blobs of purple.

" Did either of them tell you anything? "

" Both told me."

She gazed into the night with that expression I saw last in a trench somewhere near Ypres.

" What am I to do? " she pleaded.   " Each has told me, and I'm to keep it secret from the other.   How long? "

Iт was a matter that had to be taken to Talbot. As for Jim Maynard, where he was in that welter in France I did not attempt to discover. He could give us no help. He was out of it.

At the door of the Dockland vicarage—my first visit there for many years—I turned for a glance at the sanctuary opposite to which, once upon a time, a few of us resorted, where a bookseller sold a tobacco that was never put into packets by any of London's busy factories. Jones's old shop was changed, and even degraded ; it sold cabbages now.

Talbot's housekeeper could get no answer to her most respectful tap on the door of his study.

" I know he's in there," she whispered. " I took him a cup of tea not half an hour ago. You'd better go right in ! "

I went right in. At the shuffle of the door he lifted his head from a microscope to stare at the nature of this invasion. He got up from his instrument. His whitish eyelashes, directing the glance of dark eyes set widely apart under a placid brow wrinkled and shapely, and his firm mouth, gave me the impression that he stood in one existence, steadily scrutinising an object that was close, but elsewhere. He was in no hurry with his verdict.

" What's this ? " He came over with an out-stretched hand.   " I thought you had forgotten us."

" Why, one might remember well, in another sphere," I told him, " those good things of earlier days, and yet be unable to travel back to them through all the stars."

" You think we shall bear in mind the taste of old Jones's mixture when we are up above ? "

" We haven't forgotten it so far.   There's a bare chance.   And those antique jars in which he used to keep the stuff, cabalistic lettering and all !   I suspect that lettering—it was art magic ! "

Talbot sighed.   " Ah yes, those jars, those jars. Where are they ?   Do you think good tobacco jars have souls ?   I see them now.   Jolly good brown and gold and black they were—full round tummies—on slender feet . . ."

" And the smell of them ! "

" Yes—they could put heart into you with that. Better the memory of them than—well, much else."

We had a difficulty in venturing beyond those jars. We kept to what was safe, where words could put us in no danger.   Then the old man, after a pause, took the risk.

" And there was Maynard.   What about Jim—and the Bolts, and all ?   Tell me.   I hardly dare to ask these days—and I rarely hear anything—don't dare to ask when everything can change over night."

I told him then of the most recent change of which I knew.

He said nothing, but considered me. He removed his look to the window. He went over to it, and stayed there, as though he had noticed something in the street. He frowned out at that.

" There it is again," he said, as he returned to me. " That is the only view of this war which a man in my place gets, homes that are the same as usual outside, but hollow inside, all gone to dust. And what is there to do ? Is there anything but to leave it to time, and chance ? The last cord will snap for poor Mr. and Mrs. Bolt, and their daughter must wait for it. Still, I'll go over and see that girl."

He may have been meditating whether more was possible, for he continued to stand and inspect me, but then lifted his arms slightly, and dropped them.

He sat down, clasping his hands, studying his hearth rug. " Blaspheming life ! It's a foul desecration of the sanctities ! "

His eyes sought his microscope. " And our reasons for doing it ! We do it all for honour, even for God. God covers every abomination of it. You saw me at that thing when you came in. Don't be deceived. I had only run away like a coward from facts which bothered me to others that were neither good nor bad. I can't get the hang of these days. Instead of trying to, I keep to my atomies. There's that newspaper on the floor—to-day's—harping on it now—honour, our honour as a nation ! We go on, that paper says, to the last shilling, and the last man. Jack and Charley Bolt are not enough. Does Lord Northcliffe mean his own last shilling, and his own body ? He doesn't. Then whose ? "

I told him that I paid no attention to the ardent lies now. I could no longer respond to them.

" They're not lies. I wish it were as simple as that. It is genuine rapture. It works on the old original animal, and that's the very devil, for the beast is infernally energetic, and has grown to be so clever with his paws. No, we've restricted the use of beer and whisky, but we've forgotten to prohibit rhetoric—we get drunk on words, and then go and smash up the home. People can believe just whatever they want to, in that state, even that it is good to break the home up."

" Poor Bolt and his wife," Talbot went on. " There's honour for them ! What does that word mean ? What do Lord Grey and the rest of them mean by it ? I can't make it out. Yet they are all honourable men. But honour, when it is national, can work in a way which in your case or mine would be frightful. Such honour would make savages of us. It is all coming plain enough. Our honour as a nation, mixed up with Heaven knows what under-standings and agreements, can be the same as pollution.

These fine fellows, these statesmen, somehow get
changed by the sense of their responsibility. They
pursue figments which would disappear at the first
glance of good sense. They give us a ruined Earth—
honour demanded it. They are treacherous—it is a
national obligation. An agreement with one party
means they must betray another party. They
guarantee something, and that turns another guarantee
into a fraud. They have a concordance, and because
of it duty compels them to murder a population of
black people, and that they call pacification. Our
national responsibility may mean anything, any
brutality whatever, robbery, lies, massacre, any
rascality can be an obligation, when it is national.
The last shilling and the last man! It is lunacy.
And yet I'd dare swear Northcliffe does not intend
to give his own body as the last for a German bayonet.
The last shilling won't be his. So what does he
mean?"

I fidgeted. "Not altogether a matter of a country's
honour, Talbot, is it? That's not fair. They call it
that, but sometimes they call it our security."

"I know. That's what they call it. Security.
But it's the same thing. And behind security is fear.
Fear is at the back of it all; nothing but scatter-
brained funk. Yet to make war we must have a
moral purpose—a war must be righteous, my dear
man. That is always easy, though. Fear makes us
jumpy about our security, and logic does the rest.

The thought of our right turns to rapture at the call of honour, and there we are. We're in it to the last shilling and the last man. Men couldn't do this thing unless they persuaded themselves out of their minds. And now ask the women about here what they know of their security! There is Annie Bolt. What does security mean to her?" Talbot still considered his microscope. "Besides, wasn't security left out of the details at the creation? We were given bacilli, but no security. We can't get it. It doesn't exist. God either forgot it, or thought it was no good to us."

He was reasonable, but is there any comfort in making reasonably plain the cause of a fatal accident? Perhaps a lack of comfort was in my eye. "Well," I murmured, "what are we to do? That is what I want to know."

"Nothing," Talbot said. "It would be silly to resist it. We can do nothing, except attend to whatever comes our way. It is like one of its bombing raids. You can't stop it. You can only wait for it to pass, and give a hand, if something is upset."

"But even one raid night seems a deuce of a time to live through."

"Everlasting hours of it." Talbot looked over at me, with a smile which might have been ironical because my thoughts were stubbornly opposite to peace of the mind. He then turned to contemplate empty space. He quoted in a whisper. "' A thousand years in Thy sight are but as yesterday when it is past.' Though its evening is long to us," he admitted, "for our own time is so short, and we are always afraid it may be shortened. You can't expect to do much in an evening which is soon past."

" The thousand years are nothing to me."

"No, all gone, like yesterday's raid. We think they're no more than a dry relic or two of Osiris and Amen-Ra, don't we? What has the old Sun God to do with us? The camels walk over him, and don't know he is there. He's been there these five thousand years of evenings by the Nile. But I like to think now that God is not omnipotent. The camels walk over the beginning of his work. That gives me something to do. We mustn't let the feet of camels bury him. He gets no chance here unless we make it for him, and keep it. That kingdom of his—it's a far chance—but men were at it when they had no better idea of it than Ra. Off and on they've stuck to it. Many evenings have passed. Babylon has fallen ; over and over again it has fallen. We may get a city that is right, some time or other. We can't fix a date."

The light of that day was going. Not much more was to be made of the speaker than his quiet voice. "We can do little to hurry it. What has there been of civilisation yet?" he asked. "We've hardly started. Man is still a great baby. We'd better think of him as that. This original sin of ours is only original darkness. We may work through it. We know what light is. There the young people are—there's Jim Maynard and more like him; let us forget the rest. We'll remember them. If there is that better city, it is with them. The thought of them keeps me going. I sit here alone, and think of them, when the evening seems long. If there is a God, one that I can worship, he is in their fellowship."

It was evening again. I could hardly see the old fellow. His face showed brightly now and then, as he spoke, in the reflections of the columns of searchlights which marched by his window. We were going to have another night of it. It would seem the length of a thousand years. But old Talbot was not watching the searchlights. When I could see his face, he might have been peacefully regarding nothing.

At the door he drew me back. I was startled, for at that moment a searchlight made an impulsive stride near to us, and he had turned ghastly in his porch. But I was reassured. That reflection on his face was chance. He could see no danger that I did not. He gave no attention to that agitated column of light.

"My church is down," I heard him saying. "My God has been deposed again. They've got another god now, the State, the State Almighty. I tell you that god will be worse than Moloch. You had better keep that in mind. It has no vision; it has only expediency. It has no morality, only power. And it will have no arts, for it will punish the free spirit with death. It will allow no freedom, only uniformity. Its altar will be a ballot-box, and that will be a lie. Right before us is its pillar of fire. It has a heart of gun-metal and its belly is full of wheels. You will have to face the brute, you will have to face it. It is nothing but our worst, nothing but the worst of us, lifted up. The children are being fed to it."

It proved to be a night that was impenetrable and endless to the watchers. The only indifferent waiting heart, the only deathless heart, was that one of gun-metal. The central engine beat on. It drew its power, most likely, from an impulse which began in palæozoic ooze, and had been transmitted and enlarged through reptiles and mastodons, and now governed the earth with an automatic pulsation which drew from the same source as the tides. The night stretched on, past Christmas, and we found we were in March, 1918. Spring had come round again, but not morning. In the silence of the night, while waiting for the beginning of light, which everyone hoped was due, all we could hear, the only news we could get, were the regular and stealthy movements of those processes with their unseen wheels which revolved in place of human bowels.

Maynard's battalion was in the trenches of the support line. They had been warned to expect a great attack by the enemy. Though all the signs, for some months, had pointed to it, and the weight of it was estimated, and even the hour when the storm would break was well judged, it was hard to believe that it would come; desire was opposed to the facts.

In a partially ruined barn, Maynard drowsed in his accoutrements. He roused to a spurt of light—it was all right. The orderly was striking a match; lighting a candle. Maynard sat up. He could hear the distant trampling of gun-fire; he could hear running and shouting outside the barn. The orderly swore quietly at the reluctant candle. The man was agitated. He came over with a message. Man Battle Stations!

Maynard felt over his gear. Tightened it up. It was cold. He shivered. His fingers shook. " This damned buckle—all right, Meredith, all right." He scribbled some messages, and once or twice the pencil, nervous and hurried, shot uncontrolled across the paper.

He stopped to listen. Appalling! Great God, what gun-fire! It had come. To-day was the day. The earth burst open in light outside, and over he went with the blast. In the instant darkness tiles clattered on him. It was time he went. He hurried out and kicked over wreckage, soft wreckage. He flicked his torch on a face. Meredith! He kneeled and felt over the body, then went on.

It was not morning. It was darkness. It was fog, and an implacable uproar, and a veiled glimmering. He cocked his ear to pick out machine guns where none ought to be firing. What did that mean? They were cut off from brigade already, he heard.

That had one good point. Their colonel would not try to do half a dozen things, most of them impossible. They'd have to do the best they could with what they had. Their disposition was as good as possible ; the battalion machine was working. Now they'd hold off the beggars—do it somehow—get it over. It had come. The end had come.

Maynard tried not to speculate about the front line, but he could not help doing that ; waiting, waiting. Not a word from there. Nothing but the continuous and dreadful pounding of it—their job must come soon—the front line must be flat by now. Nothing could be there now. The earth rocked to the numbing shocks of the bombardment.

Rifle fire ? Where was that rifle fire ? Behind them ? This fog muddled everything. Nothing could be placed and nothing seen. When their turn came they'd know where they were. Something to do. He wanted to do something.

A man shouted. Our turn now, thought Maynard. His heart jumped, and he looked to his men. They were as still as dummies, watching their front. He warmed to those fellows. Good lads. Shapes came at them out of the fog. Now for it !

Hold on ! No, stragglers. They were our own men drifting back. Maynard wished they had been Bosches. The tension was gone, and he went limp. He was not sure that he could wind himself up again.

It was getting clearer. The sun was coming

through ; and there spying over them was a Boche plane. Now they could expect something to happen pretty soon. A heavy surge of rifle fire rolled out on their left ; too loud for him to notice much the shell-bursts behind his own parados. All right so far.

" There they are, sir ! " The Lewis gun beside him began its staccato exclamations. The trench went off full blast. Grey figures rose in regularity out of the earth, ran a little towards them steadily, staggered, and melted. Some of them ran back into a misty plantation. The Lewis gunners were grimly cheerful. That had done the trick.

" What's that, sergeant, what's that ? " shouted Maynard, turning, pleased with his show. But the sergeant was grim.

" Nothing on our left, sir. Boches are through. They're behind us. Firing from our rear."

*   *   *   *

Two days later Maynard found himself alone, while trying to get into touch with whatever stood fast in a land over which the enemy was flooding. Jerry was all round. The brightness of the sun was a mistake—the indifferent earth was cruel. He found his direction cut off by another storm of shells. As they bellowed closer, he sat down to wait. He saw the entrance of a dug-out near to him. His tongue felt too big for his mouth. Not a drink since he escaped from that

German escort.   When would this rot stop ?   Where were those reinforcements ?   Well, they would be too late to help his lot.   That was mopped up.   A geyser of earth rained clods over him.   Let it rain bayonets.   He was done.   He would get into that dug-out, and stay down there.   Never come out again.   Were they his hands ?   He noticed dry blood on them, as they hung limply over his knees.   Where had that blood come from ?   He had hardly the will to move towards that dug-out.

Another sound, a tiny trickling of music, took his attention.   His mind must be wandering.   He glanced up at the wreck of a tree, just above the dug-out, and saw what it was.   A morsel of life, an idiot bird, singing away as if it were in Surrey.   He watched it.   He could see its throat moving.   The silly little mite would be knocked out in a minute.   He and the bird would go together.   Maynard watched the singer curiously, and speculated on the time it would last.   Its song continued through the bellowing and clangs, in elfish meditative inconsequence.   That was a near one !   The bird stopped its song.   Then it began again, a frail soliloquy, persistent in chaos.   Poor little thing, thought Maynard.   You're no good here.

He rose, and went on.   In a near gulley, beyond the dug-out, he came upon a lost team of Lewis gunners. The youngsters were kneeling on the ground, trying to bury their heads in the dirt.   Maynard was amused.

Their behinds were in the air. He called to them.
They did not look up. He bent over them, and tried
to hearten them, and they answered into the earth.
They kept their mouths to the clods. They were not
going to raise their heads in that storm. Maynard
talked to them easily of things they knew. One of the
boys turned his face round to get a sight of this officer,
standing up there laughing, jollying them with one
hand in his pocket.

That boy scrambled to his feet. Then the others
got up. The team assembled. The boys stared dully
and open-mouthed at the shelling. The group of
fugitives, haggard and spent, moved off, following
this officer, doing what he did. He worked them out
of that. They met other stragglers, and several
bottles of wine and some loaves of bread appeared
from nowhere. The captain settled them all on a line
looking down a valley and a road. There they were
going to wait for the next thing. They faced east.
They were not going to do any more walking. It
didn't matter what happened now. If they had to die,
somebody would have to pay for it.

CHAPTER XVIII

THE tumult of that year, desperate and stupefying, lessened. We had leisure to breathe again. The Germans were expended. Ludendorff had gambled with his last reserves, and he had lost. The threatening colossus suggested by his name dissolved in vapour. His armies, wasted in spendthrift recklessness, stood dangerously upon an enlarged front. Behind them was a nation which had stoutly endured starvation within frontiers locked fast by the war fleets of its enemies while hope maintained it. Hope had gone. It saw starkly a reality which no device of words could hide. The victories of its heroes had brought it to this ; and the Americans, who could never cross the seas, were in fact in France, ready to begin a new war. Foch and Haig struck back rapidly alternating blows at the disheartened German front. Germany collapsed.

The guns would cease to fire on this November day, so we were told. It was true, maybe. We had been told many things. Now They, who ruled everything, even what we should read and know, even the number of potatoes we should eat, They who

534

had taken so much from us, for our good, that only ashes were left, They said the guns would cease to fire. We hoped so. But it was late.

It was a quiet winter morning. The perspective of the long trial was too deep. Nothing could be seen in it now, nothing but the wan sky over the Thames. We waited, lethargic, hardly believing. It was near the hour. London was still. Then a rocket burst over the river.

The end! That was the end of it!

A window was flung open. Someone was cheering across the street. Syrens began to hoot on the river. The whistles of locomotives kept up their whistling. There was shouting and singing below. I looked out. The city was erupting. An Australian soldier sat on the roof of a cab with a nurse on his lap. People were flooding from every door ; clouds of papers and official forms fell over the cheering crowds from the windows of offices ; the street already was a congested tumultuous torrent of released people.

When I turned to the room, my own office was deserted. It was oddly quiet. The staff had dropped everything, and had gone. Discipline had departed to sing and dance elsewhere. One had better join it, perhaps ?

But as I made for the door, there, only just visible in the shadow of a recess, was an old bowler hat on a peg. It was ancient with dust. It was ridiculously

LL

out of fashion. I stood and looked at it. That was Charley Bolt's old hat. He left it there, to go to war, four years ago. It seemed very much by itself. I got out a pipe; took a chair; I might just as well keep it company, on such a day.

CHAPTER XIX

WE looked out over the torrid silence of an uninhabited region of France. It was summer again. The tumbled expanse of the Somme's old battleground was hoary with thistle-tops and parched herbage. There stood distant Loupart Wood on its ridge. That road went over the hills to Bapaume.

Yet did it? I was not sure that I did not view it from another life, I was not sure that what I saw around us was there. Would that scene vanish, if it were tested? Would I? Did the names we remembered mean anything? Only a cricket answered in the sere weeds. The crown of a steel helmet just appeared in the dry stalks, like a smooth brown cranium. Jim Maynard parted the dusty stuff. The helmet topped a hidden cross.

Jim said he thought it must have been somewhere about there. That was about the very spot. I did not answer. The cricket answered. It maintained a dry whirring—the sound, possibly, of the ghost of a descending splinter of shell, which could not come to earth. In the distance was a small cloud of dust; it reminded us both, when we saw it first, of a belated shell-burst. It developed into a motor charabanc.

It approached us, and stopped. A large party of men and women descended from it, and grouped about a guide, who interpreted the dumb outlook for them. Those people wandered about. They were looking for souvenirs, I suppose. One man made a ball of paper, and struck it away idly with his stick, in the direction of Longueval. It was a holiday. They were touring. They called out to each other with light hearts. Two of the women knew of a matter which diverted them. Then their guide assembled them, and soon they were in the distance, only a trail of dust again.

I was disturbed. "You see, Jim? There's High Wood. There's the Butte. And you see what it all means to them. They allowed it to come, and they kept it going, and now the bitter end is a souvenir for them. It is not easy to forgive them."

Jim Maynard eyed the dust-cloud diminishing from this visit of democracy. He shook his head. "There is nothing to forgive. They never knew what they were doing. They don't know now. So how are they to know we see what they can't? How are they to understand what isn't there, for them? Our time is not theirs, old lad. We are not in their day. There he is," said Jim, displaying the lost helmet in the grass again. "There he is. Even he is in our day, though his name has gone. You can't read it now, but he belongs to our time, for he saw the sun of it, and they hav'n't seen it yet."

Jim fumbled in his pocket and brought out a book. He turned to the end of it, and handed the page to me. But I knew that book.   I knew well that last page.   I did not look at it.   I took his arm instead and we gazed in silence past the pale mound of Warlencourt, towards the hills of Bapaume.   " Only that day dawns to which we are awake.   There is more day to dawn. The sun is but a morning star."

THE END